COLLECTED NOVELS AND MEMOIRS OF WILLIAM GODWIN

Volume 7. *Cloudesley*

COLLECTED NOVELS AND MEMOIRS OF
WILLIAM GODWIN

GENERAL EDITOR: MARK PHILP

VOLUME
7

EDITED BY

MAURICE HINDLE

CLOUDESLEY

Routledge
Taylor & Francis Group

LONDON AND NEW YORK

First published 1992 by Pickering & Chatto (Publishers) Limited

2 Park Square, Milton Park, Abingdon, Oxon OX14 4RN
711 Third Avenue, New York, NY 10017, USA

*Routledge is an imprint of the Taylor & Francis Group,
an informa business*

First issued in paperback 2017

British Library Cataloguing in Publication Data

Godwin, William, *1756–1836*

The collected novels and memoirs of William Godwin

   I. Title   II. Philp, Mark   III. Clemit, Pamela

   IV. Hindle, Maurice, *1944–*

823.6 [F]

ISBN-13: 978-1-1387-5822-3 (hbk)
ISBN-13: 978-1-138-11742-6 (pbk)
ISBN-13: 978-1-85196-007-1 (Set)

INTRODUCTORY NOTE

Cloudesley: A Tale was first published in three volumes by London booksellers
Colburn and Bentley on 4 March, 1830. Within a short time it sold out and by
August a reprint was issued. There were no further English editions. As a result
of Godwin's request to his admirer and friend Washington Irving for help in
securing American publication, a two-volume edition from Harper and Bros.,
New York, appeared the same year. Also in 1830 a French translation by Jean
Cohen was published by H. Fournier in four volumes. The present text is based
on the 1830 London edition. A guide to the principles of textual treatment will
be found in volume 1.

The novel was received with high praise by most reviewers, a number of
whom – like Mary Shelley in *Blackwood's Edinburgh Magazine*[1] – were pleased
to note that old age had neither affected Godwin's skills as a storyteller nor as a
provoker of thought. Godwin's admirer and new acquaintance the novelist
Edward Bulwer was also impressed that *Cloudesley* read as the work of a
younger man, recommending it to his *New Monthly Magazine* readers as being
'full of a loveliness and an enthusiasm of sentiment, a bloom of mind, that
rarely outlives the keen autumn of experience'.[2] Both *The Court Journal*[3] and
The Examiner[4] cited Godwin's Preface for its argument in favour of 'fictitious
history' when 'executed with a masterly hand' (p. 6), over what he had once
called the 'study of mankind in a mass' in his unpublished essay 'Of History
and Romance' (written 1797, see *The Political and Philosophical Writings of
William Godwin*, vol. 5). *Fraser's Magazine*[5] not only felt that *Cloudesley* had a
'truer philosophy' than *Caleb Williams* but that there was more to be learned
from it than Godwin's previous novels. However, despite judging it his best
yet, the reviewer felt impelled to rehearse a familiar complaint that Godwin's
outlook was still cursed by a lack of faith. His old friend William Hazlitt was
also hinting at this perhaps by declaring the novel 'a dissertation on remorse' in
his essay on Godwin and his *oeuvre* in *The Edinburgh Review*. With characteristic acuteness Hazlitt thought that although *Cloudesley* was better written than
Caleb Williams – it was like 'a polished mirror without a wrinkle' – yet there
was little substance to it, the product of a mind imagining it could 'build a
palace of words on nothing.'[6]

As Godwin says in his Advertisement (p. 5, footnote), a key source for
Cloudesley had been the true story and celebrated legal case of James Annesley
(1715–60), an Englishman cheated out of his aristocratic title and inheritance

by the machinations of his uncle Richard Annesley. Both the account cited by Godwin, *Memoirs of an Unfortunate Young Nobleman* and the *Trial of James Annesley v. Richard Earl of Anglesey* (1744, 3 vols) were in his library, and his diary shows him consulting these during the novel's composition, as he did the 'Children of the Wood', the other source mentioned. A survey of the reading he recorded for this period (29.10.28 – 16.1.30.) establishes he spent a good deal of time researching in the British Museum library. Here he consulted a range of material for the novel: details on Prince Eugene, and for the duel between Lord Alton and Fabroni; Abraham De La Pryme's book on the Isle of Axholme;[7] and background information for the Italian episodes of volume three taken from books like Sismondi's *Histoire des républiques italiennes du moyen age* (1807–18).

Godwin drew on sources of information supplied as much by the people around him in 1828–9 as those he gleaned from books. These were principally supplied by Claire and Charles Clairmont, stepchildren by his second wife Mrs Clairmont, and Mary Shelley, though he also benefited from several meetings with Edward Trelawney, upon whom Cloudesley's friend Borromeo was modelled.[8] Charles, who had made his home in Vienna from 1818, working as a teacher of English, in mid-July of 1828 returned to England, and Godwin noted frequent meetings with him over the ensuing months. In October, Claire came home from Moscow, where she had been a governess, and she too met with Godwin a good deal. It seems certain their experiences of Austria and Russia found their way into the early chapters of volume 1.[9] For other elements of the text, Godwin undoubtedly drew on information supplied to him by Mary Shelley. The Greek patriots Colocotroni and Bozzaris were both described in a long letter that Trelawney, intimately involved in the Greek revolution against the Turks, wrote to her from the Isle of Hydra on 24 October, 1823.[10] Part of another letter Godwin used almost verbatim for his description of the waterfall of Terni (p. 226) is that of Percy Shelley to his friend Peacock, where the poet gives his rhapsodic impressions of the same waterfall.[11] Godwin's diary records his reading Mary Shelley's review article 'The English in Italy'[12] on 11 and 12 October, 1829, and it is this that seems to have given him the idea of incorporating an Italian improvisator into volume three. Although Godwin would undoubtedly have heard from Mary Shelley about Tommaso Sgricci, an Italian improvisator who had had a great impact upon the Shelleys during their stay in Italy, it seems much more likely he learned about the legendary Bernardino Perfetti from personal discussions with another friend of Mary Shelley, Gabriele Rossetti. Rossetti, whom Godwin records having visited on 1 September, 1829, had been a famous improvisator in Italy before he was forcd to leave after the failure of the Constitutionalist revolution of 1820.

Some days before reading Schiller's play *The Robbers* (1781) in late August 1829 as a stimulus for creating St Elmos's band of brigands, Godwin made two visits to the British Museum to research the semi-legendary figure of Robin Hood. In doing so, he was probably reminded of the old story of William of Cloudesley, whose skill in archery, according to Percy's *Reliques of Ancient English Poetry* (1765) (a copy of which he owned), had made him as famous in the north of England 'as Robin Hood and his fellows were in the midland counties'.[13] Godwin had settled on a title for his latest novel.

NOTES

1. *Blackwood's Edinburgh Magazine*, 27 (May 1830), 711–16.
2. *The New Monthly Magazine and Literary Journal*, 28 (April 1830), 365–6.
3. *The Court Journal*, 50 (April 1830), 236–7.
4. *The Examiner*, (25 April, 1830), 258–60.
5. *Fraser's Magazine for Town and Country*, 2 (November 1830), 381–96.
6. *The Edinburgh Review*, 51 (April 1830), 144–59.
7. For further bibliographical details see Godwin's note and notes b and c p. 39.
8. c.f. *The Journals of Claire Clairmont*, ed. Marion Kingston Stocking, (1968), p. 416.
9. c.f. *Journals*, ibid.
10. See *Shelley and Mary*, ed. Lady Jane Shelley (1882), IV 985 ff.
11. *The Letters of Percy Bysshe Shelley*, ed. Frederick L. Jones (1964), II 55–6.
12. *Westminster Review*, (October 1826), 325–41.
13. Thomas Percy, *Reliques of Ancient English Poetry*, ed. Henry B. Wheatley, (3 vols, New York 1886, repr. 1966), I 153.

Cloudesley:
A Tale

CLOUDESLEY:

A TALE.

BY

THE AUTHOR OF "CALEB WILLIAMS."

IN THREE VOLUMES.

VOL. I.

LONDON:

HENRY COLBURN AND RICHARD BENTLEY,
NEW BURLINGTON STREET.
1830.

ADVERTISEMENT

The following tale is built upon a fact that occurred about the middle of the last century. I have changed the personages, and endeavoured to clothe the story with the colours of the imagination*. /

When I wrote Caleb Williams, I considered it as in some measure a paraphrase on the story of Bluebeard by Charles Perrault.[a] The present publication may in the same sense be denominated a paraphrase on the old ballad of the Children in the Wood.[b]

January 30, 1830.

> Τῷ δ’ ἤδη δύο μὲν γενεαὶ μερόπων ἀνθρώπων
> ’Εφθίαθ’, οἵ οἱ πρόσθεν ἅμα τράφεν ἠδ’ ἐγένοντο
> ’Εν Πύλῳ ἠγαθέῃ’ ἔτι δὲ τριτάτοισι μετῆεν,
>   Ilias, Lib. I, ver. 250.[c] /

---

* It is but just that the reader should be informed, that a novel has been already written on this theme, and printed in the year 1743, under the title of 'Memoirs of an Unfortunate Young Nobleman, Returned from a Thirteen Years' Slavery in America'.[d]

[a] In Perrault's collection of fairy tales, *Histoires ou Contes du temps passé* (1697).

[b] Or, *Babes in the Wood*. The master of Wayland Hall, Norfolk, left a little son and daughter to the care of his wife's brother; both were to have money, but if the children died first the uncle was to inherit. After twelve months the uncle hired two ruffians to murder the babes; one of them relented and killed his partner, leaving the children in a wood. They died during the night, and 'Robin Redbreast' covered them over with leaves. Things now went badly for the uncle; his sons died, his barns were fired, his cattle died, and he finally perished in jail. After seven years the ruffian was taken up for highway robbery, and confessed the whole affair. The ballad appeared in Percy's *Reliques of Ancient English Poetry* (1765), and also in a crude melodrama printed in 1601 and attributed on the title-page to Rob. Yarington, called *Two Lamentable Tragedies; the one of the murder of Maister Beech, a chandler in Thames Streete, etc. The other of a young childe murthered in a wood by two ruffians, with the consent of his unkle.* It is uncertain which is earlier, the play or the ballad.

[c] Two generations of speech-gifted men had passed away, with whom he had dwelt in Pylos: he now lived among the third. (Mary Shelley's translation of lines she says Godwin was applying to himself 'as Homer made them applicable to Nestor': from her review of *Cloudesley* for *Blackwood's Edinburgh Magazine*, May 1830.)

[d] Published anonymously.

PREFACE

I feel inclined in the following eight or ten pages, to attempt to illustrate a proposition which has been stated before, but which has not yet perhaps received so full an explanation as might be given to it.

History – the history of masses of men – may be regarded under two points of view – as it relates to the vicissitudes of nations, their rise and fall, their progress in refinement and corruption, their literature, / their habits and customs, their philosophy and their religion, in a word, all that belongs to men in the aggregate – and as it relates to the conduct of those who occupy a considerable place in the scene. Of all and each of the former we may undoubtedly attain to some knowledge; but of the character of individuals almost nothing.

It is under the latter of these heads, that, however paradoxical it may seem, fictitious history is more true and to be depended upon, when it has the fortune to be executed by a masterly hand, than that which is to be drawn from state-papers, documents, and letters written by those who were actually engaged in the scene.

I do not say this to dissuade my fellowmen from the study of what we call real / human characters. We cannot, if we would, refrain from speculating on the motives, and endeavouring to penetrate into the inmost thoughts of Cromwel and Hampden, of Burleigh and Elizabeth, of Cicero and Cæsar.[a] And, since this will infallibly be done in some manner, it is certainly desirable that profound and ingenious persons should employ their leisure upon these problems, that what will be done well or otherwise, may be done in the way which shall be most skilful.

But, when all is ended, individual history and biography are merely guesses in the dark. The writer collects his information of what the great men on the theatre of the world are reported to have said and done, and then endeavours with his best sagacity to find out the explanation, to hit on that thread, woven

---

[a] Oliver Cromwell (1599–1658), leading puritan general of the parliamentary army during the English Civil War 1642–8 and Lord Protector of the Commonwealth 1653–58; John Hampden (1594–1643), English statesman prominent among the leaders of the parliamentary opposition to Charles I (1600–49), King of Great Britain from 1625; William Cecil Burleigh or Burghley, first Baron (1520–98), English statesman and chief adviser to Elizabeth I (1533–1603), Queen of England from 1558; Marcus Tullius Cicero (106–43 BC), Roman consul, orator, and writer; Gaius Julius Caesar (100–44 BC), Roman general, statesman and historian.

through the / whole contexture of the piece, which being discovered, we are told,

> no prodigies remain,
> Comets are regular, and Wharton plain.[a]

But man is a more complex machine, than is 'dreamed of in our philosophy':[b] and it is probable that the skill of no moral anatomist has yet been consummate enough fully to solve the obscurities of any one of the great worthies of ancient or modern times. A thousand incongruities are to be found in the characters which we seem best to understand; the same man often appears to be not the same, but different; and the explanations which are furnished by a Tacitus or a Machiavel,[c] will not fit all his actions. It may be affirmed without a paradox, that no man thoroughly understands himself: how then is it to be expected, that the historian, / who looks at him through a narrow aperture, and sees but a small part of his thoughts, his words and his actions, should arrive at a sounder result?

When I have studied a historical character with the most patient research, I can only make an approximation to the estimating it truly, and often not that. The most shewy virtues are frequently not those which would best abide the heat of temptation, or the severity of adverse fortune. Many men stand out to the eye of their fellows for better, and many for worse than they are. The folds of the human heart, the endless intermixture of motive with motive, and the difficulty of assigning which of these had the greatest effect in producing a given action, the desire each man has to stand well with his neighbours, and well with / himself, all render the attempt to pass a sound judgment upon the characters of men to a great degree impossible.

Analysis is in this respect a science more commensurate to human faculties than synthesis. When the creator of the world of imagination, the poet, or the writer of fiction, introduces his ideal personage to the public, he enters upon the task with a preconception of the qualities that belong to this being, the principle of his actions, and its necessary concomitants. He has thus two advantages: in the first place, his express office is to draw just conclusions from assigned premises, a task of no extraordinary difficulty: and secondly, while he endeavours to aid those conclusions by consulting the oracle in his bosom, the suggestions of his own heart, instructed as he is besides / by converse with the world, and a careful survey of the encounters that present themselves to his observation, he is much less liable to be cribbed and cabined in by those unlooked-for phenomena, which, in the history of an individual, seem to have a malicious pleasure in thrusting themselves forward to subvert our best digested

---

[a] Alexander Pope, *Epistle to Sir Richard Temple, Lord Cobham* (1733), 'Of the Knowledge and Characters of Men', 208–9.

[b] *Hamlet*, I. v. 166–7.

[c] Publius Cornelius Tacitus (56–?120 AD), Roman historian and orator; Niccolò Machiavelli (1469–1527), Florentine statesman and political philosopher.

theories. In this sense then it is infallibly true, that fictitious history, when it is the work of a competent hand, is more to be depended upon, and comprises more of the science of man, than whatever can be exhibited by the historian,

> long and dark,
> Drawn from the musty rolls of Noah's ark.[a]

In the drama it is a different thing. Whatever is offered there, must be expected to be sketches scarcely half made / up, and human passions and character distorted, to fit a plot, and chime in with an abrupt and violent catastrophe. But the writer of fictitious history has leisure to ripen his materials, and draw out his results one by one, even as they grow up and unfold themselves in the 'seven ages' of man.[b] He is not confined, like the dramatist, to put down the words that his characters shall utter. He accompanies the language made use of by them with his comments, and explains the inmost thoughts that pass in the bosom of the upright man and the perverse. This is his peculiar and enviable prerogative. – Among dramatists Shakespear is the exception. His conceptions are drawn from the profoundest abysses of thought; they seem to be supplied to him by the plastic principle to which the / universe is indebted for its harmonies; and he had therefore comparatively little need, like inferior artists, to proceed step by step in unfolding the seeds of character, and to watch with timid and cautious observation the modes in which they expand themselves, and the peculiarities by which they are divided.

Add to which, the characters of the drama, such as they are ordinarily found, are abstractions, or rather diagrams, and not pictures; the finishing and the reality are wanting. It is as if the shadows and first hints of men, drawn by a novice, walked out of their frames, before the substance and filling out of a man were added to give them reality; or as if the figures of Prometheus were made to act their parts on earth, without waiting till / the fire from heaven came to inform them with a living soul.[c]

> They mock our eyes with air.
> These are black vesper's pageants. With a thought
> The rack dislimns them, makes them indistinct
> As water is in water*.[d] /

* A few of our dramatists, contemporaries of Shakespear, are in a considerable degree to be exempted from this censure.

---

[a] Quotation unidentified.

[b] *As You Like It*, II. vii. 143.

[c] In Greek mythology Prometheus was a rebellious Titan who stole fire from Mount Olympus to succour mankind. In punishment he was chained to a rock, where an eagle tore at his liver until Hercules freed him. The later Roman elaboration of the Promethean legend has Prometheus as *plasticator*, a figure who creates and manipulates men into life, rather than saving them.

[d] *Antony and Cleopatra*, IV. xii. 1–11 (adapted).

CHAPTER I

The story which I now take up the pen to relate, derives no interest from myself. I was born in the middle, or I might rather say, the humbler walks of society, and should probably, as far as relates to my own rank and that of my parents, and to any intrinsic qualities I possess, have been born and die, like the herbage of the field, which to-day is, and to-morrow falls under the scythe of the great mower, who cuts down whole fields of the common growth of the soil at his pleasure. But, though insignificant in myself, and uncharacterised / by those vehement passions or that inordinate ambition, which places some men on the roll of the distinguished, and perpetuates their memory to honour or to shame, it has been my lot to be connected with persons whose story has a more substantial claim on the curiosity of mankind. It is their adventures, and not my own, that I am about to relate.

My father was the curate of Epworth in the isle of Axholme, where he reared a family of children with such advantages in point of education, as his small means enabled him to bestow.[a] His name was Meadows; and I was myself, who was called after my father William, his sole male progeny that reached years of maturity. He discovered in me a sound understanding and a tractable disposition, and therefore resolved to impart to me such rudiments of learning as he himself possessed. I read with him the works of Virgil, some odes of Horace, and a considerable portion / of the Greek Testament.[b] He could have wished that, after himself, I should have become a teacher of the gospel agreeably to the mode of the church of England; but to accomplish this far exceeded his powers. Even the slender advantages I might have derived from being intro-duced on the stage of the world under his protection I was deprived of, as he died when I was in the fifteenth year of my age.

I was always greatly devoted to the admiration of such wonders of nature and art as placed themselves before my sight; and even the obscure corner of the world where I was bred, was not destitute of such objects. Not far from Epworth existed the remains of a monastery of Carthusians, called the Priory in the Wood.[c] And, when I went sometimes farther from home to visit my

---

[a] Epworth, a village on the tract of land known as the Isle of Axholme, Lincolnshire.

[b] Celebrated Roman poets: Publius Vergilius Maro (70–19 BC); Quintus Horatius Flaccus (65–8 BC).

[c] The Carthusians, an austere Roman Catholic order founded by St Bruno in 1084 near Grenoble, France.

mother's relations at Barton, where is the noted horse-ferry to Hull, six miles over the Humber, I delighted to spend hours together / in wild reveries and romantic imaginations, as I saw and heard the dashing of the waters of this magnificent river.[a]

It was more than a century before, that the three sons of lord Sheffield of Butterwicke had been drowned in passing this river, at a ferry farther from the mouth at which it empties itself into the sea. [b] But the nearness of the geography of the scene counterbalanced with me the distance of time at which the event had occurred. They were all young men. The eldest was already married; and the son of that marriage afterwards succeeded to the family honours. There was something singularly melancholy and striking in so sweeping a catastrophe. I seldom resorted to the shore of the river without the event recurring to my memory. And, especially when the winds were high, the tempest rose, and black and threatening clouds were hurrying along the sky in a December evening, I seemed / to myself to see their faces indistinctly discovered from time to time in the atmosphere: they appeared even in the dawn of opening life, just as they had been in the hour that they perished. At other times I heard wailings and shrieks in the wind, which I interpreted as the voice of the genius of the stream, mourning for the dishonour that befel her in that fatal hour.

My father died when I was still young. My mother – the widow of a curate with myself and three daughters must necessarily be poor – could think of no better way of disposing of me than by sending me to sea, availing herself of her connections with persons engaged in the maritime profession. I was accordingly placed under a captain, bound for Archangel[c] in Russia.

The life of a sailor was ill-suited to all the previous habits of my mind. My father had given me some taste for classical studies. As I had always pursued such matters of learning as / he placed before me without any associate of my own age, my turn of thinking became contemplative and visionary. The communications of my father were essentially kind and affectionate; but the difference of our ages, and the authority at once of a parent and an instructor, did not operate to invite me to communicativeness in return. My thoughts were my own; they seemed to me a peculiar and darling possession; and I did not like to have them blown upon with the breath, and invaded and disordered with the comments, of another. I grew reserved, and, which is a part of the same feature of character, self-conceited and opinionated. As I had no habitual companion of my own age, I was in one respect so much the freer in my motions, my exercises, my rambles, and still more especially in my reveries.

---

[a] Barton-upon-Humber is now connected to the outskirts of Kingston-upon-Hull by a two-mile toll bridge over the River Humber.

[b] Lord Sheffield (1564–1646), created the Earl of Mulgrave by Charles I, had six sons in all. The three who were all 'unfortunately drown'd in the passage of Whitgist ferry, over the River Humber' (as recorded in a 1729 tract), were called John, Edmund and Philip.

[c] A port (in NW Soviet Union) on the Dvina River.

The contrast was great between the life I have just described, and that of a mariner. An essential / character of my new destination, was hard labour, and that of the coarsest and most ignoble sort. I had not a moment that I could call my own. I was placed incessantly under the commands of others, and those commands, so far as I was able to judge, frequently capricious and unmeaning. They were softened by no gentleness and conciliation. The captain, his mate, and their sailors, who, as their junior, perpetually assumed to control me, were as hard as the planks on which they trod.

The condition in which I was placed had a very painful effect upon me. I loved the green earth and the trees and the hills of my native country. I even called to mind the land-clouds of Axholme, so light, so airy, so undulating, – so different from those of the northern seas I was now destined to traverse. I hated the very sight of the barren ocean, and its eternal restlessness and unquiet. I pined in thought. I was / like what I have seen described of the Swiss, when far removed from their country; I felt that nothing but the sight and the tread of my natal soil could restore me to myself. I fell into a disease similar to that which sailors call a calenture.[a] In my paroxysm I imagined I saw on the surface of the ocean, meadows, enamelled with daises and flowers of a thousand hues, and trees that waved their mighty branches to the wind; and I could with difficulty restrain myself from plunging over the vessel's side, and desperately seeking those lovely, transporting objects, which I so vividly saw.

In a word, long before we reached the port to which we were bound, I became totally incapable of the employment to which I was destined, a mere incumbrance to the crew. The captain resolved to rid himself of me. He found a family in narrow circumstances at Archangel, who, in consideration of a sum of money he deposited / in their hands, were willing to watch over my recovery from the state of extreme debility into which I was plunged. The father of this family was an Englishman, who, like myself, had been discharged from a vessel on account of sickness; but who, being settled at Archangel, had married a Russian woman, and, through her connections, and various occupations he found in the place, seemed willing to pass the remainder of his life in that country.

There was certainly nothing very exhilarating in the situation in which I was now placed; a stranger, in an inhospitable climate, among a barbarous race, with no one I knew but my unlettered host and his wife, and with no prospect before me beyond the means of subsistence for a few weeks, which my captain had taken care to supply. Yet my dismission from the loathsome prison in which I had been confined, would have made any place of abode on land a paradise to / me. I took my leave of the captain and my fellow-sailors with the greatest pleasure. I stretched a point, though by no means in a condition to take

---

[a] Mild fever of tropical climates, similar in its symptoms to sunstroke.

such a freedom with myself, to repair to the pier, to see the vessel cleared out, and under weigh for England. And, from the moment of this glad event, my health continually improved.

For a short time, during my illness, my host generously confined his attention to whatever might renovate my vigour, and improve my health. He conducted himself towards me, as if there were no such thing as the future, and the small supply left in his hands for my use would last for ever. But, in proportion as I became more capable of conversation and reasoning, he examined me indirectly as to what I had learned, and what talent or skill I possessed that might be applied to my future subsistence. In this respect every thing appeared sufficiently gloomy. I was cast in a land of barbarians, / where all the arts of life were yet in their infancy. I had learned no trade, and had no skill in any of those crafts which are most in request in such a state of society. My landlord frankly confessed to me the anxiety he felt on my account.

One day he came home with an air of unusual cheerfulness. He said, something had suggested itself to him, which he thought might be turned to my advantage. Peter the Great at this time sat on the throne of Russia.[a] It is unnecessary to mention with what earnestness he applied all his thoughts to the improvement of his dominions. He laid the first foundations of the city of Petersburgh[b] in 1703. After the victory of Pultowa in 1709,[c] by means of which his great rival, Charles the Twelfth, was reduced to the condition of a fugitive, he became fixed in the idea of rendering this place the capital of his empire.[d] He founded in it a castle, a palace, / and a metropolitan church, which was destined to receive the remains of all the future sovereigns of Russia. He made a grand naval arsenal at Cronstadt.[e] And, lastly, he founded an academy for the improvement of science, and an university for the education of the more gifted or more fortunate youth of his dominions. As Russia was at this time plunged in a state of the profoundest ignorance, the emperor could discover no other means for its improvement in either science or literature, than the inviting such foreigners from all quarters as should be best able to assist him in his projects. My host had just learned that a commissioner had arrived at Archangel, for the purpose of discovering such persons as might be of use in the new institution.

My qualifications were of the simplest sort, and in no other country than Russia would have been held of the slightest value. I had read a / few of the Latin authors, and had mastered the first rudiments of Greek. I had never been at any school; and of consequence my acquaintance with the principles of these

---

[a] Peter I (1672–1725), Tsar of Russia from 1682, assumed sole power in 1689.

[b] Situated on the Gulf of Finland at the mouth of the Neva River. It remained capital of Russia until 1918.

[c] Peter conquered the Swedes on 28 June at Pultowa or Poltava, a region in E central Ukraine.

[d] Charles XII (1682–1718), King of Sweden from 1697–1718.

[e] i.e. Kronstadt, a port on Kotlin Island in the Gulf of Finland.

languages was slovenly and imperfect. But, such at it was, it was not without its estimation in the sixtieth degree of north latitude, and the thirtieth of longitude. In a word, I was introduced to the emissary of the czar. My origin, as a native of one of the more civilized countries of Europe, was of eminent service to me. The progress of my acquaintance with the humanities was ascertained; and I was immediately engaged as a sort of assistant to initiate youth in the study of these languages. I therefore set out, with the commissioner and two or three other persons, whom, in pursuance of his instructions, he had enlisted in his train, from Archangel to Petersburgh. /

CHAPTER II

I have met with few things in the course of my existence more striking, than my first approach to this new-created metropolis. It lies on the river Neva, which takes its rise from the lake Ladoga, and discharges itself from three mouths into the gulph of Finland, the eastern branch of the Baltic sea. The city stands on three or four islands, formed by these streams; and the suburbs extend into the provinces of Carelia on the north, and Ingria on the south. The area on / which it is placed was, a short time before, nothing but a vast morass, with no other buildings upon it than a few fishermen's huts. It was the mighty genius of the czar, that prompted him to remove his residence and the seat of empire from Moscow, which had been the abode of his ancestors for centuries, and was in the centre of his European dominions, and fix it on the western extremity, and on a spot so undesirable to all vulgar observation. But it is this act, that promises to place Russia among the foremost of European powers, and open to her a career among the nations of the civilised world, to which it is difficult for the boldest spirit of prediction to assign any limits.

When I reached the metropolis, it had been founded only ten or twelve years; but it had already made great progress, and wore the appearance of a city. Peter had built a formidable castle, well supplied with all the means of defence, / and a magnificent cathedral. He was wholly careless about his personal accommodations, and resided for a considerable time in a small wooden house, which many of his officers would have distained to occupy. At the same time, in the true spirit of a despot, he compelled his principal nobility to erect themselves houses in his capital; and, after a few years, having changed his plan, and determined that, not Petersburgh island, but Basil's island to the west, should be the site of the main buildings of the city, they were obliged once again to desert the stone edifices that had been erected, and begin afresh on the spot which had now been chosen.

I had scarcely arrived at Petersburgh, when this great man, the founder of this wonderful city, the creator of a mighty empire, died. He was in the vigour of life, not having yet completed the fifty-third year of his age: happy for himself, having known nothing of the ebb of / human life, or the infirmities of declining years; unhappy for his country, since every year of his existence added something to the civilization of Russia, and to his vast schemes for her future prosperity. He was indeed an extraordinary creature, aiming always at something vast, shrinking from no privations, deterred by no opposition of labour or difficulty. Meanwhile, conquering all outward difficulties, he was never able to conquer himself. The high priest of all civilization, he was himself a barbarian. He was subject to the most violent excesses of rage, which took from him all power of self-control. At these seasons his servants and his ministers underwent severe personal chastisements from his own hands; and the fit frequently terminated in a species of epilepsy, which for a time deprived him of sense. He was cruel and remorseless in the punishments he inflicted on those whom he regarded as delinquents, and / even occasionally made himself sport from being the executioner of his own sanguinary judgments.

I witnessed his funeral. Nothing could exceed the impression of this exhibition. He was buried in the midst of the city he had raised on the waves of the sea, and in the empire which he had first joined to the mighty confederacy of the civilized world. The solemnity was conducted under the direction of his widow, a woman whom for her talents he had raised from the lowest ranks of society, and made the partner of his throne; who adored his person, and shared in all his plans; and who by his own appointment became his successor, because in her he could best trust that, when he was dead, the immortal part of him would survive.[a] His principal minister was Menzikoff, whose appearance and physiognomy had first caught his attention, standing, as a boy, near the gate of the / imperial residence, selling pastry.[b] The minister did credit to the discernment of the master. He was a great general, and, like Peter, devoted to the cause of science and art. The year before his death, the czar caused his consort to be publicly crowned, an act which was understood as designating her to the succession in case of his decease. Subsequently there arose a misunderstanding; and it was conceived that the emperor had changed his design: but Menzikoff, whose mistress Catherine had been before she attracted the notice of Peter, embraced her cause, and secured her elevation.

Catherine had passed her early years in the utmost obscurity; and it is understood had never acquired the arts of reading and writing. But she possessed

---

[a] Catherine I (1684?–1727), second wife of Peter I, 'the Great', and his successor as Empress of Russia from 1725.

[b] Prince Alexander D. Menshikov (d. 1729), devoted chief minister and collaborator of Peter I.

the most valuable endowments, an unparalleled sweetness of temper, and great courage. It is well known, that by her presence of mind she saved Peter and his army / on the banks of the Pruth;[a] and the czar never ventured upon his most sanguinary executions, but when Catherine happened to be absent. During her short reign however the administration of government was almost entirely in the hands of Menzikoff. She early fell into a decline, and in little more than two years followed her husband to the tomb, being in the twenty-ninth year of her age. This event occurred in the year 1727.

Catherine had borne to the czar several children. The males died in their infancy; but she had two daughters, Anne and Elizabeth, whom she tenderly loved.[b] The eldest of these she designed for her successor. But the ascendancy of Menzikoff was too absolute; and he compelled her to give her voice for Peter the Second, grandson to the czar by a former marriage.[c] By an edict of the late emperor it was decreed, that the sovereign in possession should / in all cases have the power to name the successor. Menzikoff fixed on the young prince in preference, being a minor, only twelve years old at the death of Catherine. He believed himself so firmly seated at the head of affairs, as to enable him, under the name of the infant, to exercise all the powers of a sovereign.

The first step, taken by Menzikoff at the commencement of the new reign, was to dissolve the council of regency, and to lodge the czar within his own palace. By studied affronts he compelled the princess Anne, and her husband the duke of Holstein,[d] to withdraw out of Russia. Satisfied that the power of government was entirely in his hands, he paid little attention to conciliate the good will of the youthful sovereign. But his confidence proved his ruin.

Menzikoff was taken ill; and the Dolgoroukis,[e] one of them a counsellor of state, another engaged in the education, and attendant / on the person of the czar, took advantage of his absence, to deprive him of his authority. Alarmed at this intelligence, Menzikoff hastened to his post; but, when he arrived, he found that the Dolgoroukis had carried off the young prince to Peterhoff, a delightful retreat on the coast of Ingria, the summer-residence of the czars. He followed them, and was again disappointed; his prize had escaped. He then conceived that the best project he could adopt, was to make suitable arrangements for the solemn entrance of the czar into his capital; believing that, under cover of that solemnity, he should not fail again to get possession of his person; but, while he was engaged in these preparations, he was arrested, his property confiscated, and himself sent into exile, to one of the most northerly and inclement regions of Siberia.

---

[a] River Pruth, or Prut, rising on the NE side of the Carpathian Mountains, flowing east and south to join the Danube.
[b] Anne (1693–1740) and Elizabeth (1709–62). Elizabeth became Empress of Russia from 1741.
[c] Peter II (1715–30), Emperor of Russia from 1728.
[d] Duke of Holstein (1700–39).
[e] The Dolgorukys, an old and powerful noble family of Russia.

Here Menzikoff shewed that he was something more than the mere child of the caprice / of fortune. His wife, overcome with the sad reverse, did not live to reach the place of their exile. The government allotted to this proud man, who had for years lived in the possession of every possible magnificence and splendour, a pittance of about forty shillings *per diem* for his subsistence. Menzikoff however conformed himself to his circumstances, worked with his own hands, and founded a church with a portion of his income. His spirit was unsubdued; his serenity and self-respect seemingly unshaken: but the change was too great for his animal force; and he died in about two years from the commencement of his exile.

The Dolgoroukis were now apparently at the pinnacle of prosperity and power. The daughter of the younger Dolgorouki, sub-governor to the czar, was contracted by him in marriage to his master; and they directed all measures, and disposed of all offices at their pleasure. But finally / they experienced a reverse more stupendous than that of Menzikoff. The young czar was seized with the small pox, and died in the fifteenth year of his age, and in the beginning of the year 1730.[a]

The first thought of the elder Dolgorouki appears to have been, to place his own kinswoman, the contracted wife of the czar on the throne; and he was even accused of forging a will for him to this effect. He speedily found however, that his authority was by no means sufficient for this purpose. He therefore changed his plan, and looked round among the members of the royal family for a suitable successor. The duchess of Holstein had died just before the emperor, and had left a son, one year old. Dolgorouki however had fears from the character and popularity of his father, the duke, if he had been called to the succession. He accordingly fixed upon Anne, duchess dowager of Courland, daughter to the elder brother of Peter the Great.[b] He / believed he should be able to limit her prerogatives as he pleased. He assembled the council of which he was a member, and there digested a convention to be tendered to the duchess, which would in effect have stripped her of all authority, and have vested the government exclusively in the present ministers and the council. The elder Dolgorouki and two principal officers of state hastened to Mittau, the capital of Courland, to announce to the duchess her nomination, and obtain her signature to the conditions prescribed.

But all his schemes proved abortive. The Dolgoroukis had a majority in the council, which consisted of seven persons. But Golofkin, the chancellor, Osterman, the vice-chancellor, and Jagousinski, another member of the council, who had been an especial favourite with Peter the Great, entered into a conspiracy against them. They dispatched a secret messenger / to Mittau, who had the

---

[a] In fact the young Emperor was fourteen years old when he died on 18 January, 1730.

[b] Anne (1693–1740), second daughter of Ivan V and Empress of Russia from 1730; married Frederick William, Duke of Courland who died in 1711.

start of the deputies, to advise the duchess implicitly to subscribe to whatever was required, promising that in the sequel they would free her from the shackles that were imposed on her.

Anne complied with this advice, and set off for Moscow, where the court at present resided. In concert with her secret counsellors, she intrigued with the Russian nobility, painted to them in the strongest language the despotism of the Dolgoroukis, and incited them to demand the setting aside the convention. A public assembly of the grandees of Russia was then convoked, at which the empress was invited to appear. The nobility represented to her the unpopularity of the terms to which she had subscribed at Mittau. She commanded the chancellor to produce the document, and to demand the sentiments of the assembly respecting it, article by article. They were each of them condemned / in succession. The empress then took the document into her own hands, complained that she had been deceived respecting the wishes of her subjects when she set her hand to it, and tore it to pieces, declaring that she would henceforth rule alone, conformably to the ancient usages of Russia.

Anne was forty years of age at the period of her accession. She had been married to the duke of Courland in 1710, and in the following year became a widow.[a] The sovereignty of Courland was then conferred on her by the states of the country. She certainly experienced great kindness from her uncle, Peter the Great, her father having died when she was six years old. He had made this match for her; and, as she was well informed and highly accomplished, it is reasonable that we should impute these advantages in the same quarter. She had great courage, and was free from all affectation. She / must have been indebted for many of her good qualities to nature, as she derived others from education. She had a visible repugnance to stateliness and reserve, at the same time that the grace of her manner was such as to prevent those about her from forgetting her dignity. She had a voice peculiarly pleasing, and her smile was beautiful. Her temper was humane; she had great sensibility; and was often observed to shed tears, when a melancholy story was related to her.

She had had a favourite for years before she quitted Courland, John Ernest Biren, who afterwards became her principal minister, when she was seated on the throne of Russia.[b] He was of plebeian extraction, and, in point of abilities at least, did honour to the judiciousness of her selection. No scandal ever attached itself to this favouritism; his mistress brought about his marriage into one of the noble families of / Courland. The empress was governed by him in almost every thing, because she had full confidence in his judgment and integrity; and, though a thousand cabals were formed against him, they never had power to shake the steadiness of her predilection.

There was a glaring contrast between the manners of the empress and her

---

[a] See note b p. 16.
[b] Ernst Johann Biren or Bühren (1690–1772), chamberlain and virtual leader of Russia 1730–40.

favourite. She was herself refined, polished and humane. Biren on the contrary had a strong understanding and much sincerity; but he could never conquer the original ruggedness of his nature. He was devoured with ambition; and, the higher he rose in station and power, the less control did he exercise over the ferocity of his disposition. He was liable to extraordinary bursts of passion; and, where he entertained resentment or hate, he scrupled no means of gratifying his spleen. He is computed in the course of his administration to have sent no fewer than twenty thousand / victims to Siberia. Occasionally he seemed almost to delight in shedding blood under the forms of justice. The contentions between him and his mistress on this subject were said at times to afford a singular spectacle; she intreating, often with tears, that he would remit of his severity, in this case and another; and he insisting that the measures he adopted were indispensible, and protesting that he could no longer pretend to conduct the affairs of the empire, if justice was not permitted to take its course. Yet this same man was frank, easy and familiar with those to whom he conceived a partiality. He was a warm friend, but a remorseless enemy: add to which, he was somewhat dangerous in the former character, since he easily conceived offence where he thought himself unworthily treated, and then scrupled no means of punishing the man in whom he regarded himself as having been deceived. /

For two years after the accession of Anne to the throne of Russia, Biren seemed scrupulously to abstain from interfering in political matters, leaving state-affairs to the three ministers above-mentioned, who constituted what was called the cabinet. But in all this there was somewhat of delusion. Biren had a mind capable of comprehending the greatest things. During his residence in Courland he found nothing of a political nature that took hold of his spirit. Courland was but a mimic sovereignty; and her foreign connections the fit occupation for an intellectual dwarf. But, when his mistress succeeded to the extensive dominions of Russia, this was quite a different matter. He became aware that here was a theatre in which great good might be effected, and great glory acquired. He resolved to confine himself no more to the narrow field of a drawing-room, but to / become, what in his heart he felt himself capable of being, a great minister.

Having fixed his determination, he for the first two years exhibited no symptoms of what he designed. He rather strikingly kept aloof from politics, and appeared only the minister of his mistress's pleasures. But he devoted every hour that he could call his own to the study and contemplation of that, which to vulgar observation he most avoided. He studied history in secret; he surrounded himself with maps, charts, and elevations. He disdained no means of improvement; he called about him privately all persons who he believed could assist his researches. He read books of travels; he enquired into ancient and modern times; he examined the courts of princes, as far as this could be effected by reading or conversation, and made himself familiar with foreign nations, / their strength, their revenues, and their discipline. At the end of two years he came forth with the result of his labours; and, from this time forward, he may be considered as in effect the sole minister of the empress.

The result was, that the reign of Anne was glorious, and that she produced an impression on foreign states, hitherto unknown in the annals of Russia. The court of Vienna in particular felt her importance; and, in concert with that power, she placed a king of her own chusing on the throne of Poland.[a] No sooner was this effected, than she declared war against the Turks.[b] In this contention the success of her arms was memorable; and she was thought at one time to threaten Constantinople itself. At the same time that all this was doing, the Russian empire was improving in all other respects. The army, under the administration of Biren, assisted by the admirable talents of Count Munich, / was greatly improved in prowess and discipline.[c] Meanwhile the commerce of the country was increased, and all her internal institutions and establishments received their due share of encouragement.

While Biren thus watched over the interests of the Russian empire, he was not inattentive to his own. Immediately on the accession of Anne he was made great chamberlain, a count, and knight of St Andrew, the highest order of knighthood in the empire. In 1736 Ferdinand, uncle to the late duke of Courland the husband of Anne, to whom the succession of the duchy was conceived properly to belong, though the power of Russia turned it aside from its course, died. Anne seized this occasion to impart additional elevation to her favourite; and she, who had already given a king to Poland, did not doubt of her power to confer this principality. Accordingly Biren, at this occurrence, / was raised to the dignity of duke of Courland, and thus became enrolled in the catalogue of the sovereign princes of Europe. – To return from this seeming digression, to the narration of my own affairs. /

---

[a] Anne united with Austria in supporting Augustus of Saxony, son of the late King Augustus II, against the canditure of Stanislaws Leszczynski, who was seen as dependent on France and, indirectly, on Sweden and Turkey.

[b] In late 1735. The Austro-Russian forces lost to the Turks in 1739.

[c] Burchard-Christophe, Count of Munich (1683–1767).

CHAPTER III

Old as I am, for ladies' love unfit,
The power of beauty, I remember yet.
DRYDEN.[a]

In the university of Petersburgh my situation was humble. The professors were men in the meridian of life, and who had already acquired for themselves some reputation in France, Germany or Poland, the countries from which they came. I was the only Englishman, and, bringing with me a certificate from neither Oxford nor Cambridge, was looked down upon with / a sort of supercilious contempt. The office of instructing others had the effect of giving perspicuity to my own ideas, and arrangement to the principles with which I was acquainted. The attempt to explain things to my pupils, required of me in each instance that I should first explain them to myself. Being cast by the effect of hazard upon this species of occupation, I resolved to do my utmost to improve myself in those branches of learning which I was called on to teach. I applied to the professors in each of these departments, and intreated them to have the kindness to further my progress. But, in every application without exception, I met with a repulse. It was not their business to instruct those who pretended to be instructors themselves. They desired to keep up the line of distinction between a professor, and a raw and half-informed pedagogue. They had each of them countrymen or friends, whom they aimed / to place over my head, or by thrusting me out to get nominated in my stead. Every day, instead of advancing in my career, I seemed to myself to be losing ground. Though I was not ambitious, I grew dissatisfied under this conviction. I continued for years in my humble situation in the university, and every day became more disturbed with the wish that it was changed. Industry and application have been understood to lead to advancement; but here the order of nature seemed to be inverted to depress me. As the university increased in character and popularity, my situation in it became daily more insignificant.

By this time Biren was become all-powerful in the court of Russia. He looked into every thing; he examined every thing with his own eyes. Though not occupying any one of the great offices of state, he kept a *bureau de ministre*, just

---

[a] John Dryden, *Cymon and Iphigenia* (1700), I. 1–2.

as if he had been president of the finances, / or one of the imperial secretaries. He had a multitude of clerks, perpetually occupied in translating documents, and preparing memorials and instructions, under his own eye. About this time he conceived the idea, that he stood in need of a clerk familiarly acquainted with the English tongue. I was mentioned to him. He sent for me; and, being satisfied with my appearance, acquisitions, and intelligence, immediately took me into his pay.

I was highly gratified with this change. I had become heartily tired of the university, its cold, formal and imperious professors, and the monotony, which had occupied me for years, of initiating the dull and sluggish Russians in the rudiments of classical knowledge. My pupils had, most of them, the stature of men, without the apprehension of a southern school-boy. Their very aspect was spoiled with the accession of a load of superfluous and unanimated flesh, / which had never been subtilised and made flexible to the impulses of intellect.

In my new situation I had no unfrequent opportunities of communication with the favourite himself; and I looked upon him as belonging to a more gifted class of human beings. Whatever might be his defects in the eye of one who had observed the varied and wonderful scenes of active civilised life, I had never seen such a man. The versatility of his mind and the quickness of his comprehension were truly astonishing. He always communicated his directions with marvellous clearness and in the most concise terms, yet without obscurity. As has been already mentioned, the natural promptings of his mind were those of the utmost sincerity. Haughty and overbearing as he was to those whom he regarded as his enemies, and who appeared to stand in the way of his purposes and his will, to me, whose function it was to serve and oblige / him, he was always easy and familiar, and seemed scarcely to recollect the vast distance there was between us. There was no need that he should remind me of it; there was no fear that I should presume upon his kindness.

One thing that was gratifying to my inexperienced mind was, that we, clerks in office, were permitted to go to court on great public days, to swell the train of our superiors. I was as well acquainted with the countenances and carriage of the empress, the princess Elizabeth, daughter to Peter the Great, and afterwards empress, and the princess Anne, niece to the reigning sovereign, and who appeared destined to succeed her, as I was with those of my companions and equals.

Even my fellow-clerks in office and their connections constituted a species of society, that was as gratifying as it was new to me. We for the most part considered each other as equals, / and felt ourselves free and unrestrained in our mutual intercourse. We were animated with the gaiety of youth, and had to a certain degree that warmth of heart, which characterises uncorrupted man, not yet hardened and rendered suspicious by the practice of the world. This was a perfect contrast to the life I had led for several years in the university. There I saw only the professors, who regarded me as of an inferior order of the creation, and who found a cold and sullen gratification in making me feel all my littleness, or the raw youths I had to instruct, whom my occupation induced to consider as the enemy of their pleasures, and who shrunk from familiarity with me as sedulously on that score, as the professors did from supercilious insolence and contempt.

Among the young men I daily saw in the course of my present occupations, a particular attachment speedily grew up between me and a / clerk of the name of Alexis Scherbatoff. He was in some sense connected in the ties of kindred with the favourite himself. His mother was the half sister of Biren, being born of the same father by another wife. Madame Scherbatoff, as I shall now call her, had offended Biren by a marriage which he considered as degrading. He had therefore refused all intercourse with her for years, and had even done various ill offices underhand to her husband, crossing him in his views of life. After a marriage of some years however Scherbatoff died, leaving the partner of his days a widow, with two children, a son and a daughter. As he had been unsuccessful in all his views for an establishment, he left her in very narrow circumstances.

Biren, in the midst of all his sternness and disdain, was a man not altogether of an ungenerous disposition. Or, at least, the cause which / had produced his hostile feelings towards madame Scherbatoff being removed, his pride forbade his suffering her and her young ones to sink into destitution. He procured from the empress a small pension for the widow; and when the son became of an age to be useful, he placed him, as has already been said, at a desk in his *bureau.*

This however was in a very small degree advantageous to the young man. The kindness and courtesy of Biren were great; but, wherever he had conceived displeasure, it may be doubted whether in any instance he wholly dismissed the feeling of hostility from his bosom. Alexis Scherbatoff was destined deeply to feel this. There was not a young man in our office, that by his intelligence and industry was more fully entitled to encouragement. As being related to the favourite, he probably thought that in a twofold sense he had a right to expect this. / But he experienced the very contrary. Biren always regarded him with a severe and a frowning aspect. He seemed on all occasions to view him as the representative of his father, destined to remind this arrogant and ambitious man of the affront which in his opinion had been put upon him. He never accosted Alexis but with peculiar sternness. He appeared to take delight in withering the blossoms of his youth. He was perpetually putting upon him one slight or another. He was forward to shew a preference to any other member of our corps, rather than to him.

Alexis was a youth of high spirit, and could not patiently endure the treatment he experienced. Had he been no way related to the favourite, the case would have been different. It would have appeared only that he was discountenanced, because, for some capricious motive or other, he did not take the fancy of his employer. But, as / it was, the neglect that was dealt out to him had a peculiar sting, and made the light-hearted and unfeeling among his associates regard him as a person, that they also might consider as out of suits with fortune. He tried, by every means that could be practised by an ingenuous spirit, to mitigate the unkindness of Biren; but in vain. Failing in this, his next thought was to launch into some new scheme of life, where he should not be met, as now, with a determined and systematical discouragement at every turn. But no one dared help him in this. In Russia every one was servile to the prosperous and the great, and dared not thwart or dispute with their decrees. There, at that desk, Biren had placed his nephew; and, without an intimation from him, no one would venture to appear in an attempt to change his fate. The temper of Alexis was soured, and his very heart pressed down, with the consciousness that all his wishes were fruitless, / and that, the more he struggled, he was but the more sensibly to feel the chains that bound him. – I only pitied his fate, and became the more warmly attached to his society.

He had however one consolation; and, the more forlorn he felt himself, the more he hugged that to his bosom. His sister Isabella had a confidential friend and playmate from infancy, a girl of the same age as herself, Helena Ludolfski. They were in a manner inseparable; and when Helena was not at the house of madame Scherbatoff, Isabella was almost sure to be at the residence of her friend. Helena was of a tender and sympathetic disposition; and, when she saw the young and handsome Alexis, apparently labouring under severe depression, she exerted herself to the utmost of her power to console him. She gradually became the chosen confident of all his vexations and sorrows. Her father also liked the young man, and appeared / to think of him as the person he wished for his son-in-law. He was related to the favourite of the empress; that to the father of Helena was a great recommendation.

But Ludolfski was in an eminent degree a worldy-minded man. After a time he learned that Biren was far from being a friend to his nephew, but rather appeared upon all occasions desirous to keep him down. Those who favoured Alexis were sure to find sooner or later that that was not the way to win the favour of the man in power. Ludolfski was not slow to perceive this; and he was then as forward to discourage the pretensions of the young Scherbatoff, as he had before been to promote them. He forbade him his house, and enjoined his daughter henceforth to regard him as a stranger. At the earnest intreaty of Helena, backed with a solemn promise that she would not use this indulgence to bring about stolen interviews with / Alexis, he allowed her to persist in friendly communications with Isabella. Helena was a being of an ingenuous mind, and who had no conception of the art of promising one thing to her parent, that she might avail herself of his indulgence to do the very opposite to that which she promised. She therefore persisted in it, and kept her resolution, that she would not see Alexis clandestinely.

This was a thunderstroke to the young man, and he complained of it in the most pathetic terms to me and his sister. He said, that he had suffered the pangs of martyrdom from the severe and constant state of discountenance in which he was kept by his uncle, the empress's favourite. All that had remained to him, 'to make the nauseous draught of life go down,'[a] was love, the favour of the enchanting Helena, who, when the rest of the world frowned upon him, still kept him from despair by her fascinating / smiles, and by the ravishing tones of her heart-thrilling voice. This alone inspired him with courage. This made him feel that there was something still worth living for, and breathed into him a certain self-esteem, since the being who was in his apprehension the first and the purest of created natures, rejoiced in his joys, and fully sympathised in all his woes.

Meanwhile his sister was still admitted to visit and correspond with Helena; and through her he endeavoured to keep up his interest in the heart of her he loved. Helena was rigorous in keeping her faith to her father: she would neither see Alexis, nor correspond with him. But this, she protested to Isabella, was the limits of her filial obedience. Her father had at first encouraged their mutual attachment; it had grown up under his protection and encouragement; Ludolf-ski had now changed his mind; but she did not find herself capable of / a like instability; nor did she think her duty required so much at her hands. She solemnly assured Isabella, that her heart was wholly and unalterably vowed to Alexis; she desired patiently to wait the course of time and events; she trusted that, when Ludolfski saw that her attachment to her first love could never be altered, his fatherly affection would at length plead effectually in their favour; but she protested, let that be as it might, that she would never give her hand to another.

Ludolfski saw that, if Biren treated his nephew in a stern and unkind manner, I on the contrary was much favoured and distinguished by this illustrious minister. He would therefore most willingly, if it had been in his power, have transferred his daughter's affections from Alexis to me. Nothing meanwhile could be more alien to the whole tenour of my thoughts. I had been privy to their course of love, from first to last: / in the frequent occasions in which Alexis and I had wandered together on the banks of the Neva,[b] he could talk of nothing but the beauty and the admirable qualities of his Helena; and I, seeing that scarcely any thing else could have the power to sustain him under the sense of the perpetual injustice of his uncle, was forward to encourage him to expatiate on these to him so delightful topics. As I was free to visit his mistress whenever I pleased, and was even often invited by her father, I made use of all the opportunities which were thus given me, not to try my own fortune with her, but, whenever I could, to stimulate her attachment to my friend, and to carry tender messages from one to the other.

By this course of proceeding I recommended myself greatly both to Alexis

---

[a] Quotation unidentified.
[b] River in NW Russia, at the mouth of which is situated St Petersburg.

and his sister. About this time it happened that the young man was dispatched
by his uncle on a particular / mission to Moscow; and, being once there, was
detained by various accidents much beyond the time that was originally contemplated. During this absence I and Isabella were his principal correspon-
dents. From various causes it so fell out, that my letters were much more
frequent than those of his sister. I therefore conversed again and again with
Helena respecting his merits, the integrity of his disposition, and the sensibility
and tenderness of his heart. But I conversed much oftener with Isabella. I was
aware of the projects of Ludolfski for uniting me and his daughter; and I was
the more chary of my visits, that I might give no encouragement to a scheme
that might prove a fruitful source of disquiet to these virtuous lovers. I also felt
that Isabella would be a much more powerful pleader for her brother than I
could expect to be, and that Helena would open her heart in a more unreserved
tone to one of her own sex. /

CHAPTER IV

My own situation was peculiar; and it was not long before I experienced the
effects of it. The talk of Isabella and myself was all of love. We were both of us
most anxious to bring about the union of this enamoured youth and his
mistress. We spoke of the enviable delights which sprung from the sympathy of
two hearts devoted to each other, of the hopes, the fears, the anxieties, the
agonies, that grew out of an ardent attachment. The tones of our voice /
adapted themselves to the topics of which we discoursed; and, as we expatiated
on the enamoured feelings of the one party or the other, we unconsciously
adopted their language, and mimicked their gestures, and were for the moment
the very persons we so earnestly represented.

There was something more rarefied and refined in what passed in our
breasts, than would have been the case with Alexis and Helena, if they had sat
and walked together at the very time and on the spot where Isabella and I did.
Love is a disinterested passion, for the true lover would not fail to sacrifice his
gratification, and in extreme cases his life, rather than be the cause or the
witness of serious calamity inflicted on the object of his affections. Yet the
parties themselves are ordinarily pursuing their own interests, and seeking their
own enjoyments; and they cannot but know it. But our talk and our / thoughts
were detached from these narrow considerations. We were conscious that the
object we aimed at was the happiness, the consummation of the wishes of

another; and there was a nobleness, a conscious pride, in this situation, which could have held no part in the intercourse of Alexis and his Helena.

When I gazed on the countenance, and looked into the eyes of Isabella, I saw in her all that I had painted to myself of an angel, a celestial missionary watching over the fortunes of a mortal (her brother), void of any meaner feeling than that of fully discharging the office that belonged to his godlike nature. The lambent fire that played in those eyes had no alloy of any thing gross or of a frailer sort. It was wholly unearthly. I smiled as I observed the generous earnestness of her purposes; and, when she saw my smile, she smiled upon me graciously in return. /

It was then that I first observed so distinctly, how much, yet how sweet and chastised a fire there was in her look, when our eyes met each other. Her complexion was the most purely transparent, that in all the years of my life I ever beheld. Every grace, and every winning attraction played about her lips. She was somewhat above the middle stature. Her limbs were tapered by the hands of the God of love. Her bosom, when it heaved with the earnestness with which she expressed her deep interest for the peace of her brother, its quick and honest pants, that knew no thought of diffidence or shame, – it was irresistible. I was subdued in a moment. Oh, Isabella, how could I so long be insensible to your charms? Or, when we were separated from each other in the sequel, as separated we were, how could I have survived for a moment?

Unconsciously, and by insensible degrees, I / changed my topic of conversation. I expressed my wonder, that I, who was some years older than Alexis, had never yet become a victim to the charms of the sex. I observed, that I should be difficult and fastidious in my choice, as might naturally be expected, having outlived the heedlessness, 'the morn and liquid dew,'[a] of youth. I undertook to describe what sort of a person it must be to please me. I entered liberally and copiously into the subject. As was natural, in the eagerness with which I poured out my discourse, I sometimes ran myself out of breath, and was compelled to pause. I then looked in Isabella's eyes, and drew from thence vigour to proceed, and thoughts on which to expatiate.

As I went forward in the portrait of my imaginary mistress, it became more and more palpable that it was Isabella herself that sat for the picture. In proportion as I became aware of / this, I pleased myself slyly with describing little turns, minute gestures, and peculiar inflections of voice, that could be drawn from no other source. I described the individual temper of Isabella, the peculiar ways in which her ingenuousness displayed itself, and the very infirmities, which, tinged as they were with virtue, and the sensitiveness of an honour that had never known a cloud, rendered her in my eyes the more irresistible. In some instances I had seen an air of graveness come over her, as I unconsciously

---

[a] *Hamlet*, I. iii. 41.

expressed myself with less reserve than she approved. It was as if one veil of the thinnest gauze spread itself after another, the first wholly unperceived, till at length the entire visage, divine as it was, became darkened.

The offence was venial; and, when I had once detected myself, and forwardly confessed my error, the smile came back, and the prospect grew ravishingly bright. All this, point by / point, was comprehended in the portrait I made.

Isabella's remarks were intermixed with mine. She sometimes objected, that I was fastidious, that I demanded too much, and that my notions were particular and strange. I answered her, and defended myself. I grew warm; but it was not the warmth of contention, but of panegyric upon the supposed imaginary being I drew. My warmth however was not that of mere rapture and rhapsody; it expressed itself in a melting tone, which indicated a real object.

Isabella at length detected me. But it was late, and with a slowness of apprehension, that most feelingly disclosed the unaffected modesty of her nature. While I discoursed liberally and eloquently of beauty, of grace, and of excellence, she could scarcely bring herself to suspect that all this was meant of the fascinating creature that sat before me. As I went on, a / particular trait of which I spoke unveiled the whole. She blushed, the sudden crimson that overspread her cheeks unequivocally shewed that she had seized my meaning.

She answered me with averted eyes. Oh, Meadows, she said reproachfully, what is this you are doing? We were talking of the mishaps and adverse fortune of my brother. How came the subject to be changed? You have taken a most unfair advantage of the occasion that presented itself.

I asserted my innocence. When I had started the question of my particular tastes, and of what I regarded as perfections in a woman, I was actuated by no sinister purpose. I did not begin with the thought of her. It was in proportion as I became animated, and in the warmth of my soul wandered from one excellence to another, that I discovered the source from which my notions were drawn. I protested / that the discovery came upon me as a surprise, and was as new to me as it was to her, with this only difference, that it came to me a few minutes sooner.

In a word, I obtained my pardon, and made my peace. I observed that I could not be sorry for what had passed, since upon it I earnestly hoped might be built the happiness of all my future life. It was fortunate, that we had commenced with talking of loves not our own, inasmuch as by that circumstance we had been encouraged to express ourselves more freely, and had become better acquainted with each other's modes of thinking, feelings, and – might I add – each other's hearts, than we could have been by any other means. I protested, that I had never seen any thing so lovely in human shape as herself. In every conversation I had had with her since the departure of her brother, I had become more and more struck with the generosity / of her sentiments and the purity of her heart. I pressed my suit, and professed my everlasting attachment. I was not ungraciously received; and we made as much progress in mutual confidence and good understanding, as could be expected to arise in a first conversation upon so grave and momentous a question.

I withdrew from our conference in raptures. It was a beautiful summer-evening when we parted. The moon was just rising out of the peaceful bosom of the ocean. I paced along upon the banks of the Neva, light and elastic as if I had been floating on the breeze. I felt myself a new creature. Oh, Meadows, I said to myself, what a life hast thou hitherto passed! It has been all an incoherent and unsatisfactory dream. I had belonged to nobody. I had pleased myself with the image of friendship; I had attached myself to Alexis. But, oh, what a difference! It is only in woman, woman / lovely and affectionate, that the dawn and enthusiasm of opening life finds itself satisfied. I am no longer solitary. I am conscious that, under the roof I have just quitted, I have something laid up in store, dearer to me, a thousand times more valued, than my worthless self. Or rather I feel that I am not wholly worthless, since I am dear to, selected from all other candidates and rivals for her favour, by the most excellent of womankind. May no ill-fortune ever come between us! May the present kindness and distinction with which we regard each other, attend us uninterrupted through life, and follow us to a late and a peaceful grave!

I had no sooner reached my lodgings, than an urgent message was delivered from my employer, requiring to see me without a moment's delay. I hastened to the presence of Biren. He received me with a severe and a menacing countenance. /

Where do you come from? said he. Why did not you attend me sooner?

Meadows, he continued, I trust you are not now to learn my character, and the principles of my conduct. I cannot be a friend by halves. I give myself wholly either for good or for evil, to raise or to crush. But, in him I favour, I require obedience, and a spirit that shall even anticipate and outrun whatever I desire.

I took you up, sir, the outcast of a college, slighted there, and valued by nobody. I have preferred you to my own kindred. I have designed considerable things for you. I have not intended that you should stop where you are; but to raise you to a higher step, and yet a higher. But, as I am bounteous and liberal to those I love, so I shall be found destructive and withering as a pestilence to those who offend me.

Attend! I expect from those I favour, that they shall watch my looks, and copy out all I / think. If you purpose to belong to me, all my friends must be your friends, and all my foes your foes. I will not be thwarted. You must be true to me as my shadow.

You know the Scherbatoffs. In the vulgar sense of the world, they belong to me, and are said to partake of my blood. Blood is nothing. It is the mind, the adherence of the soul, that I require. Madame Scherbatoff gave herself away contrary to my liking, in defiance of my prohibition. The young Scherbatoffs are the offspring of that accursed union. They are the born, the predestined, objects of my hate. I have taken care that they should not perish with hunger; if I had not, I should have been reflected on by the spiritless world, by all those who are not endowed like me with souls of fire. But I hate them the more for this my extorted condescension.

I speak once; but I speak no more: that is / my nature. You have seen these Scherbatoffs. You made yourself familiar with the son. You have visited, repeatedly and lately visited, his mother and his sister. This must be put an end to, and instantly. Never again enter their doors, never hold the slightest communication by word or by letter with them. Do this at your peril. If you disobey, or but wish to disobey, you shall for ever curse the hour that brought you into existence.

Having said thus much, with an unaltered countenance, and disdaining to be replied to, he waved his hand for me to leave him.

What was the state of my mind, when I quitted the minister's cabinet! A more unfortunate contrast could not be imagined, than that between the new-springing sentiments of love in my hitherto untried soul, and the harsh and ferocious mandates that had been poured into my ears. /

My first feeling was to dash the favours of Biren to the earth, and bid him defiance. It was with difficulty I so far commanded myself as to withdraw from his presence in silence.

I was no sooner alone, than I presently felt that to defy the minister was to part with Isabella for ever. What could resist his omnipotence! In some countries perhaps such a thing might be attempted. But in Russia the knout,[a] the gallies, a perpetual dungeon, and the halter, waited but the motion of his finger. In any case, which I dreaded more than all the rest, I should never see Isabella again!

My soul was torn with conflicting emotions. Openly to have defied the minister would have been frenzy. But what should I do? The thing I dreaded most was to bring down evil on the idol of my soul. Comparatively I feared nothing for myself. But would the ferocity of this savage stop at me? /

At one time I resolved to return to his closet, and pour out my whole soul before him. Infamous as he was for his cruelty, there must be a corner in his bosom that was penetrable to human feelings. I would tell him how dear to me, beyond all power of words, was the passion that had newly sprung up within me. I would lay before him the sentiment of love in two young and inexperienced hearts, as the most innocent, the most blameless, the most beautiful thing, that the globe of earth had to boast. Whom could we injure? If the union which beyond all things I desired were displeasing to him, I would take Isabella from Russia, I would take her to my own country, I would retire with her to any part of the world he should dictate. I felt as if the God of love had touched my

---

[a] A stout whip used formerly in Russia as an instrument of punishment.

lips with his charmed rod, and I could pour out such strains as it could not be in mortal bosom to resist. I was mad – but my tide of madness / did not swell so high, as to carry me back to the closet of Biren.

I retired to my bed; but not to rest. The night was eternal: and more busy thoughts, more wild and distracting visions, seemed to be crowded into those few hours, than had occupied my life before. At length the morning dawned; and with it came the cruel necessity, that I should return to my desk in a sort of gallery annexed to Biren's palace. How I got through my task I cannot tell. I must have committed a thousand blunders; my pen moved mechanically over the blank that was placed before me; my thoughts refused all commerce with the implement that was between my fingers.

I no sooner left my office, than I resolved that at least I would not go to Isabella. By so doing I might draw down calamity upon her I loved best. I would do nothing rashly. If I / could prevail on her to be mine, I would plan the mode in which it was to be effected with the whole power of my understanding; and that which my soul elected should rise triumphant over the will of any other man.

I turned down a street the most opposite to the quarter in which she lived. I passed rapidly along; I could not stop myself; it seemed as if change of scene was essential to my existence. But what may appear most extraordinary, my steps however devious still brought me to the quarter I had most resolved to avoid. I passed through streets I had scarcely ever seen; I knew not whither they pointed; still the result was the same. At last, weary and tired, I entered the court in which the habitation of Isabella was situated.

She was shocked at the sight of me. I was as much altered, she told me, as if I had risen from a fit of sickness, which had lasted me for / months. My eyes rolled frightfully; I appeared like a man possessed.

What is the matter? she cried. What has happened to you? Have you just escaped from the dagger of an assassin?

Nothing has happened, I replied. Where am I?

Do you not know me? said Isabella. You were here yesterday. Do you know any thing ill of Alexis?

No, no, no. Let me depart! I did not intend to come here. I have something to say to you: but it must not be now. You shall hear of me soon, very soon. Do not be alarmed! Let me go! You do not deserve to be disturbed; least of all by me, from whom you have merited more than worlds can repay. Soon, very soon, you shall know all.

I left her abruptly, and in disorder. She never heard or me more. /

CHAPTER V

I again wandered the streets for hours. As I approached my lodgings, I found myself suddenly stopped by one, who seized me by the arm. I turned to see who it was, and perceived one of my fellow-clerks. I had given him a few lessons in the English tongue. He was homely, and in no way prepossessing in his appearance. He had no brightness of talent; but he had a sound heart. He was a person of simple integrity, of few words, never making any professions / of service, but upon all occasions conducting himself well in situations that challenged his aid. He had by no means taken my fancy; but I had taken his. And he wore well; the good opinion he acquired from others, he retained for ever. He had an honest desire to improve himself; I had lent myself to his wishes; and he was grateful.

Stephanoff (that was his name) said to me, You must not go home: there are men that lie in wait for you: come with me. He then told me that he had accidentally overheard Biren giving his orders to three or four officers of justice to apprehend me without fail, to repair to my lodgings, and, if I were not there, to wait, and by no means return without having done his bidding. Stephanoff added, that he knew not in what way I had incurred the displeasure of our employer, but he perceived by Biren's manner that he was greatly exasperated. / He observed, that I must have remarked as well as he, that the character of Biren was exceedingly altered. He was no longer the same man; whoever awakened his resentment was infallibly devoted to destruction; he delighted in cruelty and blood; all his talk in these moods was of the fiercest and most dreadful punishments; the mildest fate that could be hoped for by the object of his wrath, was to be consigned to a dungeon from which he should never come out, and should be heard of no more.

A few days only had elapsed since the execution of the Dolgoroukis. Biren had been made duke of Courland in June 1737. To many persons this elevation might appear not to be much: it was otherwise in his eyes. He had been for years the all-powerful minister of the vast dominions of Russia: the empress had been known to be once and again imploring at his feet. Still he was but a subject; he was in / strictness no more than an officer of the royal houshold. When his mistress had first raised him from plebeian rank to be a noble of Courland, the nobility of the duchy had refused to recognise him as a brother. Now he was past all contradiction the sovereign of an independent principality. He could make peace and war; he could raise taxes: he entered into treaties, offensive and defensive, with the kings of Europe. What his own duchy wanted in influence and weight, it mattered not: he could throw the empire of Muscovy in Europe and Asia into the scale at his pleasure.[a] Before, agreeably to the etiquette of courts, he stood in the presence of the empress, in token of inferiority. Now he and his duchess were entitled to sit with her as a symbol of equality.

To a truly good and uncorrupt nature elevation of rank gives additional grace. A subject in one stage of precedence, to a subject in another, / may think he has occasion to resort to artificial modes, to maintain his superiority, and to keep the insolence of pretenders at a becoming distance. But a sovereign prince is placed at his ease in that respect. He may be as free and familiar as he pleases without danger, provided there is nothing actually degrading, and that invites contempt in the manner of his familiarity. A sovereign should be always gentle and humane, still distributing courtesies and encouragement and protection and forgiveness.

It is a very old remark, that prosperity is emphatically the furnace that tries men's souls. Ordinary mortals at least are curbed and made tame by the laws, and a fear of the consequences that may follow on their ill actions. Why does this man not seize on the splendid prize that lies in his path, on a property adapted to his desires, and that with all his heart he covets? Why does another not waylay and stab the / enemy, against whom his malicious passions and his furious resentments rise up in arms? The poet has said, 'All men would be cowards, if they durst.'[b] It would be more true to say, that the majority of men, men of vulgar souls and undisciplined passions, would be freebooters and sanguinary bravoes, if they durst. It is the first step, that costs the most. When a man has surrounded himself with a certain number of bleeding carcasses, the victims of his rage, he finds himself so deep in blood, so fleshed with slaughter, that his very remorse can only be stilled by fresher murders.

An ill man in prosperity, is like the adder restored to life by the bright and cheering beams of the sun. Till that sun came, he lay in a torpid state; it was difficult to say that he lived. By and by he opens his eyes, and his scales are by degrees set in motion. Anon he rears his head, and shoots out his forked tongue, / and sends forth terrific hisses, and shines in his tremendous brilliancy of colours, and flies this way and that, and seems to be every where in a moment. No one is any longer safe from his venom. Even so it was with Biren.

The Dolgoroukis had been eight years in disgrace at the commencement of the year 1738. Some had been sent to Siberia; some imprisoned in Russian fortresses; some only exiled to their estates. The family was numerous and powerful; at its head were two brothers, field-marshal Dolgorouki, and Wasili, or Basil, one of the seven members of the council of state, which ruled Russia at

---

[a] Muscovy, archaic name for Russia and Moscow; also the name given to the Russian principality of which Moscow was the capital from the thirteenth to the sixteenth centuries.

[b] John Wilmot, Earl of Rochester (1647–80), *A Satire Against Mankind* (1679), l. 158.

the death of Peter the Second. It was Basil, that made his kinsman, Alexis Gregoriewitz, sub-governor to the minor emperor. This appointment introduced Iwan, the son of Alexis, into familiar intercourse with Peter; and the striking partiality and friendship which the young prince conceived for Iwan / formed the main link that supported the authority of the Dolgoroukis, which perhaps would never have been dissolved during the life-time of his master.

It happened toward the close of the year 1737, from some secret influence which I could never explain, that Sergius Dolgorouki, who had formerly served as ambassador to several of the northern courts, was called from the place of his exile to Petersburgh, with the declared intention of being sent by the empress as her representative to the court of London. He arrived at the capital; and the preparations for his mission were in the utmost activity.

This event raised all the fury of Biren. By one word from his lips he might no doubt have cancelled the appointment, and sent back Sergius to the obscurity in which he had so long languished. But this did not satisfy the new-made duke of Courland. He resolved to bring / about a signal catastrophe, which should make every man in the empire dread to move in any business that it was known he would dislike, and might operate as a warning to the empress herself.

He drew all the Dolgoroukis from the place of their exile, or of their imprisonment. He arrested those, who had been simply banished to their estates. He assembled all the males of the family, who had arrived at years of discretion, in the great state-prison of Petersburgh. He revived the accusation of a will that had been forged for the minor emperor. No one had seen this will. Dispassionate men did not believe that it ever existed. No matter: witnesses were produced; all the forms of law were gone through; and seven principal members of the Dolgorouki family were condemned to die. The field-marshal only escaped, though the head of his house, because he had never / dipped in any intrigues, and because he was of an unenterprising temper from which nothing was to be feared.

Prince Basil Dolgorouki, who had been the man to move that the present empress should be called to the throne, and who had gone to Mittau to announce to her her accession, and Iwan, the inseparable companion of the imperial stripling, and whose sister Peter had espoused, were broken on the wheel in the grand square of Petersburgh, in the sight of many thousands of spectators. They had lived, during the period of their prosperity, in the midst of every possible indulgence. Hundreds of men of the highest rank in Russia had attended their levees, watched every glance of their eye, hung upon every accent of their lips, and worshipped their very shadow. These men, one of them twenty-six years of age, the other near seventy, were brought out on a public / stage, stripped of their garments by the hands of the executioner, tied with strong cords to the fatal instrument, and died amidst the most excruciating and protracted torments. It is hardly possible for any one to have his bones broken, one by one, through every limb, and to be dumb. The cries of their agony pierced the air, and ran through the marrow of every spectator. At length they received the final stroke; and they suffered no more. All Russia, bony, and rigid, and unimpressible as for the most part were the majority of its inhabitants, trembled with horror. Those who were not eye-witnesses of the tragedy, could not believe that it had been acted. Death in this fearful and ignominious form is usually reserved for offenders of the basest class; and, when the noble and great are condemned to die, there is always some decorum that is observed in their concluding scene. – The other five of the Dolgoroukis / who had received sentence, suffered death, but not in this form.

I took the advice of Stephanoff, and resolved to return, if possible, to my native country. I know I shall be censured for my pusillanimity. Who, I shall be asked, that was truly in love, would matter being broken on the wheel?

I ruminated, but certainly not in cold blood, upon the situation in which I was placed. Biren seemed to me to be at present under a sanguinary paroxysm. When a man has bathed his hands in blood, he often appears to be impelled by an irresistible necessity to proceed. It is only by new and further atrocities, that he hopes to extinguish in himself the recollection of those he has perpetrated. The fence of modesty and moderation with which every man is at first surrounded, is broken down in him; his character for humanity is destroyed. What check therefore can you any longer rely upon, / against his indulging in the worst excesses? If I cannot be loved, such a man is apt to say to himself, at least I have one resource left, – I will be feared.

Biren must have received, either from some disciplined spy, or from some officious tale-bearer, the intelligence that, immediately after his denunciations to the contrary, I had repaired to the residence of the Scherbatoffs. He was now in no mood to be trifled with. If I defied him, he resolved that I should not defy him with impunity. It would be vain to attempt to appease him by any explanations. It was even certain that I should never again be admitted into his presence.

Stephanoff, who passionately interested himself in my safety, told me, that it had fortunately so happened, that he had spent the preceding evening with the mate of a vessel bound from Petersburgh to Amsterdam. It had been / a meeting between the mate, himself a Swede, and several of his friends, for the purpose of leave-taking on his quitting the Russian capital. The vessel was to sail immediately; the wind was fair; and he did not doubt to prevail on his friend to favour my passage. It was fortunate for me that I was an Englishman. If I had been a Russian, several formalities would have been necessary, and obstacles might have presented themselves. Stephanoff drew from his girdle a purse of fifty rix-dollars, which he pressed me to accept.[a] I had a considerably larger sum in my lodgings, and therefore made no hesitation. I gave him the key

---

[a] A rix-dollar was a small silver coin, current c. 1600–1850 in various European countries and used in their commerce with the East.

of my escritoire; and he undertook after having paid himself, to remit the remainder to me, on the first advice from me where I could be addressed. Every thing turned out auspiciously; we met with the officer; I was introduced by him to the captain; and we were under sail in a few hours. I arrived / without accident at Amsterdam; from thence I took my passage for London, and from London to Hull.

All clue to my disappearance was by this means cut off. It was if the earth had suddenly yawned under my feet, and taken me in. Stephanoff had immediately passed to my lodgings, and, with the key with which I had furnished him, had gone to my escritoire, and taken away my money, leaving every thing else as he had found it. The officers of justice who lay in wait for me, had an exact description of my person, and therefore suffered Stephanoff to pass without molestation. Their cue was to be silent, and create no alarm, till the moment came that they could at once pounce upon their prey. I was tall; he was short. I was fair; he was of a muddy and thick complexion. My eyes were quick, roving and alive; there was no fire in his; they were like those of a fish; he / was almost purblind. I lodged in a house divided into many apartments, and connected by a common staircase.

If I had been a great state-criminal, Biren would no doubt have made further inquisition respecting me. It is likely he might by some means have traced Stephanoff as the last visitor of my chambers. The torture is a mighty instrument in Russia for laying open secrets. It is true, that it often draws from the unhappy wretch upon whom its force is tried, gross falshoods and lying accusation. But it also has a chance of extorting facts. Stephanoff, my generous, my disinterested friend, would have fallen a victim to the tyrant. Biren also might have directed his inquiries against Isabella and her mother.

But I was not a state-criminal. Biren had suddenly been rendered my enemy, because my heedless vivacity had caused me to wound his / pride. In all other respects I was utterly insignificant. If he had caught me in his toils, exasperated as he was, he no doubt would have made me a memorable example of his vengeance. But I had suddenly disappeared from the soil of Russia, even as if a mighty chemical explosion had dispersed all the atoms of my frame, so that no where was there so much as a vestige left, to prove that I had ever existed. In this case the fury that had been awakened in the breast of Biren was in a short time calmed; and the perpetual demands of the great affairs of Russia upon his attention, speedily turned his thoughts into a different channel.

For myself, the recollection of Isabella had left a scar, a deep, trenched gash in my heart. Biren might forget; but I could not forget. Our acquaintance had not been long; the love-scene between us but one. But it was the single instance in which that deep vein of sensibility / had been opened in my heart. And to the latest hour of my existence it will live in my recollection. It made another man of me. Till then I had been totally ignorant of the deep and intense interest of which our human nature is susceptible on that side. I have but one pattern of female loveliness painted in the *camera obscura*[a] of my bosom. The most refined moments of my existence, the sequestered and consecrated privacy of my thoughts, are full of Isabella. I see her in the airy motions of her light figure; I see her in the lustre and transparency of her complexion, in the liquid sweetness of her eyes, in her maiden modesty, in the various expression of her lips, which told her thoughts ere her tongue had time to utter them, and in the unrivalled melody and sensibility of her voice. At such times she speaks to me, and I answer her; my soul melts away within me. Then comes the dreadful recollection, It is all over / now: I shall never, never see her again: it is to me as if she had passed to the regions of the dead. Happy in some respects it would have been for me, if it had been so. The dead are for ever sunk in one uninterrupted repose. They know no cares, nor sorrows. But Isabella is to me as a blooming and lovely infant, whom the mother has by some mischance irrecoverably lost. Where, cries the sorrowing parent, is he even now? What privations may he suffer? What injustice and cruelty may be exercised upon him? The whole world of imagination is open before her, to build up millions of scenes of despair to her soul at leisure. Oh, how much less tormenting would it have proved to see him dead at her feet!

How earnest was my desire, to go back to Russia, and dare all the fury of my omnipotent adversary! The thought was hopeless. For nearly three years, till the death of the empress / Anne and a short time after, Biren reigned in Russia without a rival; and, before the expiration of that period, circumstances had occurred, which made it impossible for me to gratify this, the first passion of my soul. /

CHAPTER VI

I had now been absent from my country sixteen years. I had gone out in the flush of youth, in the period most fitted for adventure. I had passed the whole of that period in deep obscurity, having gained nothing but experience, and a small portion of what is called knowledge of the world. When I had got together the whole of what I was worth, I found myself the possessor of one hundred pounds. I was in the situation of Adam, when he was expelled / out of paradise. I knew no one; I belonged to no one. The soil of England was before

---

[a] A darkened chamber or box into which light is admitted through a double convex lens, forming an image of external objects on paper or glass placed at the focus of the lens.

me, where to chuse my place of rest. I might wander as I pleased, uncontroled by any foe, unaided by any friend.

This is not exactly true. The forlornest creature that lives, especially if he returns, as I did, to the place of his birth, finds some one that knows him (though, God knows, with indifference enough), and can scarcely fail to find some one that is bound to him by the ties of kindred. My mother was dead; one, and one only, of my three sisters, was married. The others had removed to the market-town of Barton on the Humber, the birth-place of their mother, where they united their efforts in the conduct of a day-school for young children.

The husband of my married sister was a man of the name of Stirling, who maintained himself by the cultivation of a few acres of ground / about two miles out of Epworth, on the road to Glandford Bridge. He rented this little portion of land from earl Danvers of Axholme, whose residence was at Mil-wood Park in the parish of Owston. I was received kindly by my brother-in-law and my sister, and was invited by them to remain a short time under their roof, till I had determined on some plan to which to dedicate my future life. I accepted the overture.

I gladly devoted a few days to the revisiting the well known scenes of my childhood and youth. The ruins of the Priory in the Wood, the banks and the magnificent waters of the Humber, were inexpressibly interesting to me. I delighted to view the house in which my father had lived, and the meadows which had been the scene of my boyish sports. A new set of children now drove the flying hoop, and hurled the bounding ball. They were as eager / in their games, as ever I and my companions had been. Their voices sounded fresh in my ears; and their squabbles were as zealous and impatient, as those of any of the children which had gone before them in the same busy scene.

What a different creature had I returned to these rural haunts, from what I was when I left them! I had then been the most ignorant and inexperienced of mortals. I had scarcely seen a town larger that that in which I was born, or a scene more solemn and impressive than our parish-church on a Sunday. I had now visited ports and havens and cities and courts. I had seen the pomp of an imperial train, and been in almost daily intercourse with the statesman, the duke of Courland, who by his judgment and his *fiat*[a] ruled the vast area of Russia. My mind had been gradually unfolded by the scenes through which I had passed. My eyes had been familiar with objects of royal splendour, / and I had witnessed the baleful operation of tyranny, oppression and cruelty.

Farewel, I exclaimed to myself, to these scenes of ostentation and turbu-lence! I am contented to pass the rest of my life in the plainest manner and in the utmost obscurity, satisfied if I can eat the bread of peace, and spend my

---

[a] Authorized pronouncement.

days without crime. Without industry however it was impossible I could subsist; and I revolved in my mind a variety of plans, by which I could best hope to obtain that moderate competence that was all to which my wishes aspired.

Before I had determined however upon any mode of disposing of myself, to our great surprise a message was one day brought to the farm, that lord Danvers desired to see me at the manor-house. I should have observed before, that I had been in the practice of writing letters to my family two or three times a year: and, as these letters came from so remote a / country, described scenes scarcely ever heard of in Lincolnshire, and were composed with a certain degree of reflection and scholarship, they were regularly shewn to the steward, and in the last year past had in some way got to the notice of his lordship himself.

I had no sooner received this notice, than I became eager to enquire into the character and habits of the person from whom it came. He was little known in the neighbourhood, having only succeeded to the title in the preceding year upon the death of a distant relation. His father had been created an Irish peer by the title of lord Alton, of Alton in the county of Cork, being the younger son of an earl Danvers in the reign of Charles the Second; and the Altons had constantly resided since that period upon their estates in Ireland. The present lord had succeeded to the Irish title upon the death of his brother twenty years before; / but it was only one year, since, on the failure of the elder branch, he had taken the title of earl Danvers, and fixed himself at the seat of his ancestors in the isle of Axholme.[a] His family consisted only of himself and one son, he having buried his lady and several children before he succeeded to the English title.

With respect to his habits I was informed that he lived in an almost uninterrupted solitude. He kept up the establishment of a nobleman, and had many servants; but he associated as little as possible with his equals, and had even small intercourse with his tenants. His disposition was decidely of a melancholy cast; but he was understood to be a person of great humanity.

This was nearly all I could learn respecting the nobleman, who had sent to desire I would wait upon him; but I did not find in this any thing strong enough to induce me to decline his / summons. I therefore repaired to the Park the next morning. The mansion had been originally built by a baron Mowbray in the reign of Edward the First, but had since that time undergone the most extensive alterations and improvements.[b] It however still retained its ancient Gothic appearance. The park was well-stocked with deer; and a long avenue of

---

[a] Richard Annesley (1694–1761), upon whose situation and family background Godwin's Lord Alton is partly modelled, took his seat in the Irish House of Lords as Baron Altham in 1727 and was for a time governor of Wexford.

[b] Roger III Mowbray (1266–98), seventh Baron Mowbray; Edward I (1239–1307), King of England from 1272.

trees led up to the principal entrance. The windows in many parts resembled those of a cathedral; and the hall was spacious. An ample staircase of stone led to the upper apartments; and every thing was suitable to the residence of one of the ancient barons of England*.

I was addressed to Mr O'Reiley, the steward, whom his lordship had brought from Ireland, / and by him was introduced to his master. He reminded me beforehand, of lord Danvers's solitary and sequestered habits. He informed me, that his lordship, then captain Herbert, together / with lord Alton, his elder brother, had served under prince Eugene in his campaigns against the Turks, shortly after which lord Alton had lost his life in a duel in Germany, and the captain, who had succeeded to the Irish title by the death of his brother, had immediately returned home to his estates in that kingdom.[a] His character had at all times been grave, and his mind prone to sad and melancholy reflections. He had however endeavoured to conquer this infirmity. He had married: his wife was beautiful, accomplished, amiable and patient: his marriage had been blessed with a family of children. Still under all changes his melancholy pursued him. And, when he lost his lady, and one by one his children had died, save his only son, it had gone still harder with him.

While O'Reiley was engaged in relating to me these particulars, the library-bell rung, and / I was called for. I found lord Danvers seated at a table, which was covered with books and papers. He appeared to be about fifty years of age; and his hair was beginning to be grey. He had the air of a soldier, of a man who had been exposed to the influence of different climates, and had known the

---

* The peerage and honours of the family of Mowbray ceased in the year 1475. Since that time the property they possessed in the isle of Axholme passed through the hands of various proprietors. The mansion, which had long been in ruins, is thus described by Abraham De la Pryme, an indefatigable collector of topographical information.[b]

'It was a great and most stately building of many stories high, all of huge, squared stones, and wholly built upon vaults and arches, under which I passed a great way. All was huge stone staircases, huge pillars, long entries, with doors on each side leading into opposite rooms. I remember the dining-room also: it was at the end of one of the entries. In it were large oak tables. It was lighted with great church windows, much beautified by painted glass. The outside of the house was ornamented with semi-arches jetting from the walls, borne by channeled columns; and the top was covered with lead. The doors were huge and strong, and ascended up by a great number of steps; and places were made through the turrets to defend the house. The whole was compassed with a huge moat, still remaining. There were the fairest orchards and gardens I ever saw. But now none of these things are remaining; for, about ten years since, being in a ruinous state, the whole was pulled down, and a less house erected on its site.'[c]

---

[a] François Eugéne de Savoie Carignan (1663–1736), Austrian soldier who distinguished himself in the service of the Holy Roman Emperor Leopold I (1640–1705), against the Turks. The invasion of Austria by the Turks in 1683 was ended by the Treaty of Karlowitz in 1699 by the joint intervention of German, Polish and imperial forces. The Turks admitted the sovereign rights of the Habsburgs to most of Hungary.

[b] Abraham de la Pryme (1672–1704), antiquary and, from 1698 curate at the church of Holy Trinity in Hull, where he compiled a history of the borough.

[c] The full account can be read in *The Diary of Abraham de la Pryme, The Yorkshire Antiquary* (London and Edinburgh, 1870), pp. 173–4.

toils and hardships of war. His figure was graceful, and his person noble and imposing. He had an impressive countenance, in which the characters of care and anxiety were plainly discernible. His eye was quick, restless, watchful and suspicious. It was obvious to observe in him the tokens of a mind ill at ease within itself.

O'Reiley having introduced me, lord Danvers beckoned to him to withdraw. He made me sit down in his presence. He told me that he had read my letters from Russia, and from thence had been led to form a favourable opinion of / my understanding and dispositions. As I had very lately returned to England, he judged it likely that I had not yet engaged in any pursuit or plan of life.

I bowed assent to the suggestion.

Lord Danvers was pleased to say, that he found himself in want of a person of superior intelligence, whom he might employ in certain affairs, to which he felt that servants, even of the better class, were not entirely competent. Perhaps, he added, I had higher views. The affairs in which, if I were willing, he should be happy to employ me, the rewards he could bestow, and the prospects he could hold out to me, might be beneath my ambition. He conjured me to speak frankly to these points.

I assured his lordship that ambition formed no part of my character. My views had always been humble; my destination of the ordinary / class; and what I had seen of courts and ministers inspired me with no inclination to engage further in that career.

Lord Danvers proceeded. He told me that he had considerable estates in Ireland, beside those to which he had lately succeeded in England. He had brought over with him his Irish steward to whose personal services he had been accustomed; and there were consequently some matters in Ireland that would require a careful and enlightened attention. He would wish to send me over, but only for a short time. Having arranged them, I should return, and there were various concerns of one sort or another, that he should recommend to my care.

He then mentioned to me some particulars of his Irish estates, gave me a list of his tenants in that country, and of the various terms upon which they occupied his lands. He referred me to O'Reiley for a more minute detail, and / added that, when I had gone over the matter with the steward, he should speak with me of other circumstances on which he should give me his directions.

I was delighted with this commencement. I found in his lordship condescension with dignity. That he should thus immediately have conceived a favourable opinion of me, afforded me no common gratification. I was charmed with the idea of being settled in my own country to my heart's content. I had no relish for the perilous paths of life, but wished to pass through the world, unknowing and unknown, in moderate competence and entire obscurity.

Lord Danvers desired me to narrate to him the different scenes I had witnessed in Russia. He said, he also had passed some years in foreign countries, though in a very different climate. Encouraged by his courtesy, I entered more fully into circumstances than I should / otherwise have done. He questioned me particularly as to my feelings on each incident as it occurred, and the principles of my conduct. I could see that he was studying my character, for what occupations I was most qualified, and to what extent I was worthy of his confidence.

But, though his lordship interested himself in my narrative, occasionally started very trying questions, and was earnestly bent upon weighing my answers, I observed that he could not yield an unvarying attention to what I related. There was something passing in his own bosom, that would not be put off or eluded. A sudden cloud would spread itself over his countenance, his looks told of the desperation that seemed to dwell in his heart, his eyes rapidly changed from an expression of fixed attention to a wild and portentous stare, he rose from his chair, paced the apartment with tumultuous strides, and clasped his hands with an air of the deepest / affliction. I was overwhelmed with astonishment and pity. Yet it was incumbent on me not to appear to notice what I saw.

Several days passed between us in this sort of communication. I had my apartment assigned me, and soon understood the situation in which I was placed at Milwood Park, not being classed with the servants, but being always at his lordship's command. I sat at the same table with O'Reiley, the steward, and a respectable female, whose situation was that of housekeeper. I studied the particulars of his lordship's Irish estates, enquired of O'Reiley as to points which I did not immediately comprehend, and obtained from him the information I required.

A member of the family whom I saw occasionally every day, was the youth I have mentioned, lord Bardsley, earl Danvers's son and heir. He was about eleven years of age, finely / formed and agile, with sparkling eyes and flowing hair, an ungenuous disposition, and all the promise of a superior understanding. His voice was of a very striking quality, clear, penetrating, melodious, and under the guidance of a frankness and good nature well fitted to conciliate the kindness and sympathy of every one who heard it. It was easy to perceive that he was his father's doating-piece.[a] Lord Danvers seemed to live but for this child. When he came into his father's presence, then and then only, at that moment, I appeared to myself to see lord Danvers without a cloud, such a man, as his understanding, his station in society, and his many advantages led one to expect him to be. Yet, strange to say, this lighting up of his eyes at the approach of his son was but the sunshine of an instant. He embraced him with tenderness and fervour. Then a sort of convulsive sensation would come over the father. ·He would put his / son gently from him, would turn away his head, – a

---

[a] One who is doted on (rare usage).

shuddering seized his frame, and his eyes would fill with a passion of tears. It appeared indeed as if the lovely boy was not destined long to continue in this mortal existence. There was a hectic colour in his cheek,[a] that was of evil omen, and his frame seemed almost too frail and unearthly, to allow that we should expect him to reach to years of manhood. Was it from an anticipation of his shortness of life, or was it from some other and more secret cause, that I was to explain the painful sensations which always apparently came over lord Danvers, when the delight of their first meeting had subsided?

I had now been some weeks a resident at Milwood Park. Preparations were made for my journey to Ireland; and I expected every day to have my final instructions. One morning I attended his lordship in the library, / thinking perhaps that I should receive orders to set out the next day.

I do not intend, said lord Danvers, that you should travel westward, I rather propose that you should go to the continent.

I have known you, Meadows, now for more than a month. I have studied your character, and have determined to rely upon you. The question of sending you to Ireland, and the particulars connected with it, were necessary to enable me to get thus far.

I have a commission of the most trying nature to impart; and it was incumbent on me to find an individual adequate to the undertaking. I wanted a person in the full vigour and morning of life, a person that could encounter fatigue; and not be daunted with hardships; a person that had too much clearness of head to allow himself to be deceived, and that, having undertaken to sift a material business to the bottom, / might be depended upon, that he would not, while he had life, desert the enterprise. I have found that person in you.

Meadows, I now know you sufficiently to know that you are altogether free. You dare not return to Russia; and you have no connections in any other part of the world that have the power to shackle you. Are you willing to engage in the service upon which I am desirous to employ you?

I replied, that I had such confidence in his lordship's honour, as to be persuaded that he would not employ me in any business that was unfit for an honest man to undertake. And, with that restriction, I could promise that I would be deterred by no difficulties, but would discharge the task he should impose on me to the utmost of my power.

As to my honour, answered lord Danvers, we will say nothing about that. You see me / as I am. No man brings an accusation against me; and the individual whose character is unimpeached, is entitled to a certain degree of credit.

It is necessary however that we should be accurate in these preliminaries. I

---

[a] i.e. His cheeks were flushed, a symptom associated with consumptive or other wasting diseases.

expect that, when once you engage with me, you should not draw back. I am about to unfold to you the inmost secrets of my soul. I have a tale to relate, the particulars of which are wholly unknown to any man on English ground, and, so far as I am aware, to only one other person existing on earth. I will not confide in you by halves. If I do not disclose to you the whole of my story, my crimes, – I cannot expect that you will serve me to the extent I require to be served.

I listened to all that his lordship said with astonishment. I had some moments of hesitation. My curiosity was vehemently excited. I had no objection to travel or fatigue. I felt / flattered by the compliment which the commission about to be unfolded paid by implication to my understanding.

Lord Danvers will not require of me the perpetration of a crime?

I think not. All that I prescribe to you is of a passive sort. My wish is, that you should find a certain person whom I will describe to you. When you have found him, I require that you should not, in consequence of the discovery you shall have made, do any injury to me, nor shall you leave the person in question, at worst, in a less eligible situation than you find him.

Proceed, my lord. I am prepared to hear, and willing to subscribe to the conditions you have laid down.

I am afraid lord Danvers complimented me beyond my deserts, when he spoke of me as so peculiarly qualified for his purposes. But men / must work with such tools as they have. When we have a task of extreme difficulty, and that requires the most extraordinary qualifications, to impose, where are we to find the man? It is in this case, as in what may be called the most important affair of human life, marriage. If we are in love, we deceive ourselves; we ascribe to the favoured she the most unparalleled and super-human excellencies. But, if we enter into the engagement deliberately and in cool blood, we well know that it is a compromise. The creature that our exalted imagination has figured to us, does not exist on the face of the earth. Of those that do exist, only a small number are accessible to us, or are such as we have the smallest chance to win to favour our addresses. We contentedly give up some of the qualifications we should have desired in the partner of our life, and accept of such as are within our reach. /

It may also be supposed, that lord Danvers commended me beyond the merits he knew to exist in me, as well knowing the power of praise. Nothing more forcibly stimulates men to extraordinary performances, than that others should take for granted their undoubted competence.

The preliminaries having advanced thus far, lord Danvers came to a pause. He hesitated; the colour forsook his cheeks; the perspiration stood upon his brow; he struggled with himself; he worked himself up to the task he had resolved to perform. /

CHAPTER VII

I had a brother. That brother was killed in a duel in Germany, whither he had gone to serve against the Turks. He was one year older than myself.

I have been judged a handsome man, of a noble and prepossessing air. But, oh, what was I in comparison with my brother! His figure was moulded by the Graces.[a] His smooth and ample forehead was the abode in which majesty sat enthroned. His voice was music. In all things he eclipsed me. /

But for many aggravated circumstances which kindled the pernicious spark in my bosom, I believe I should not have been envious. My brother surpassed me in intellectual powers. He was of a clearer and quicker apprehension. He had an ardent thirst for knowledge. His temper was mild; and his courage was high. We were perpetual companions. He was born to an ample patrimony; I could expect nothing, but the slender pittance of a younger brother's fortune.

My father and mother directed all their attention to the welfare and advantage of their eldest son. I was seldom judged worthy to be made the subject of a smile, a caress, the smallest encouragement. I seemed only to stand in the way, to be a being that had intruded himself into a world where he was not wanted. Or, to speak more accurately, I was scarcely ever an object of notice; my parents never, / but when they could not avoid it, so much as recollected that there was such a being in existence.

Meanwhile my brother was a subject of perpetual solicitude. Every gratification that could be procured, was copiously showered upon him. If his little finger ached, the whole house was set in commotion. My parents scarcely ever condescended to ask how I did. My cheek might be blanched, my eyes glazed with indisposition; I was left to get well as I could. If any pleasure was in view, if any party of amusement was proposed, Arthur, the favourite Arthur, was sure to be included, and a reason was almost always found why I could not make one. Wherefore was all this? He was the heir.

In such cases I was left in the care of servants. They are almost sure to teach a child the worst lessons. Ah, master Richard, they would say, what a fine thing it is to be the / eldest! Your brother will have the whole estate; he will be called, my lord; this house and the house in Dublin will be his. But, I am sure, I do not

---

[a] In Greek mythology, the three sisters Aglaia, Euphrosyne and Thalia, bestowers of beauty and charm.

know what they will do with you. I suppose they will make a parson of you. You may be your brother's chaplain.

I withdrew into corners, and ruminated on these things. There were twelve months and a few days between the age of me and my brother. I studied the same lessons, I was taught the same accomplishments: my parents were not unjust to me in that. I made considerable proficiency. I was comparatively slow of apprehension; all that I learned cost me considerable labour; but I was indefatigable. To Arthur every thing seemed to be intuition. It was almost impossible to tell when and how he learned any thing. But his exhibitions, which cost him nothing, were lauded to the skies; he was pronounced a prodigy; while I / at best came off without blame, and our tutor, who took his tone from our parents, seemed almost sorry that I did so well.

I reflected much on this. Twelve months my elder! Oh, what virtue is there in twelve months! Arthur is destined for the whole term of his life to splendour; I to obscurity. It seemed as if we were born of different castes. He was to be the lord of palaces; I was to be launched in life at the expence of two or three thousand pounds, or to languish out my existence on an annuity of a few hundreds; and even that reluctantly torn from the vast heaps, which were carefully laid up for this exclusive favourite of my parents and of fortune.

It happened at the age of fourteen that my brother was seized with an alarming illness. Physicians poured in in plenty. The family, though in the hottest period of summer, was suddenly removed to Dublin, for the benefit of / better advice. In spite of every exertion that was made, Arthur grew worse. He appeared to be in extremity. He was given over. At length however, the strength of his constitution conquered the attack, and he recovered.

This event occasioned me many reflections. At first, when he was only pronounced to be in danger, and we prepared to set out for Dublin to take advantage of superior skill, my thoughts were of an antisocial order. I said to myself, Then perhaps, after all my sufferings and mortifications, I shall be the heir. I shall be My Lord, the master of thousands, possessor of this country-seat, and of the house in Dublin, a member of the Irish house of lords, and in no remote prospect to an English peerage. My bosom was lightened with the thought. I said to myself, I hope my brother will die!

But, when we came to Dublin, and Arthur lay at the extremity, I had far different thoughts. / Death is a thing, the sight and the approach of which sobers every man. I requested to be permitted to visit my brother's bed-side, and my request was granted. I had not seen him for nearly a week. Oh, how he was altered! His cheeks were colourless; his flesh was wasted away. Arthur, my dear Arthur! I said, how do you find yourself? Richard, he replied, is it you? Where have you been? I have not seen you so long. I think I am dying. But I shall always love you. We have never quarreled. God bless you! Give me your hand, my lad! – And he pressed it. His hand felt clammy and cold.

From this moment I was an altered being. I felt my heart relieved as of an atrocious crime. I retired into a corner, and prayed most fervently for my brother's recovery. My parents had been unkind to me; my tutor unjust; but Arthur never. Nature had moulded / him of the kindliest elements. He had never taken advantage of the undue partiality that had been shewn him. He had never, by any interference of his, brought down upon me a moment's mortification and sorrow. He had made me the equal partaker of all his little possessions.

At a proper age we were sent together to Trinity·College, Dublin. We were inseparable companions. The injustice I had suffered in my early years passed away. It is a commoner and an easier thing to put down and discountenance a child or a school-boy, than it is to persist in the same treatment towards a young person verging on manhood. I was no longer left to be the associate of footmen, and to imbibe their pernicious lessons. We were each of us remarked as graceful and prepossessing. We grew more alike. I had been the shorter of the two; but, as I advanced in my teens, I / shot up, and Arthur had scarcely in any thing the advantage of me. Our parents, though late, grew proud of their sons. Add to which, when we left the paternal roof, I was less subject to the caprices of the individuals from whom I derived my existence. Still however I did not at all times forget, that Arthur was the heir, that he was destined to be the rich man and I the poor; and I then bitterly repined at the partiality of fortune.

Arthur's tastes were military. He not only imbibed this passion from his classical studies, Achilles, and Alexander, and Caesar;[a] but his ambition was stimulated by the modern examples of Condé and Turenne and Villars and Luxembourg,[b] but above all by that of our fellow-subject, the duke of Marlborough.[c] Arthur was of a generous strain; and it has often been observed that a bounteous and liberal spirit has a kind of instinctive congeniality with military / heroism. I was less enamoured of camps and fields of battle than he was; but I wished not to separate my destiny from that of my brother, and I felt that, if I succeeded in this career, nothing could more obviously supply to me my want of the goods of fortune. If I were not born to a title, the honours of the field, and the character of a distinguished soldier would place me fully upon an equality with the men who bore a coronet. My father favoured our wishes; and

---

[a] Achilles, the foremost of the Greek warriors at the siege of Troy; Alexander III 'the Great' (356–323 BC), King of Macedon from 336.

[b] Louis II de Bourbon, Duc d'Enghien, Prince de Condé, and called the Great Condé (1621–86), French marshall in the Frondes 1648–52; Henri de la Tour d'Auvergne (1611–75), Vicomte de Turenne, French marshal in the Thirty Years War 1618–48 and the Frondes; Claude Louis Hector de Villars (1653–1734), French marshal distinguished for his command in the War of the Spanish Succession 1701–14; Francois Henri de Montmorency-Bonteville, Duc de Luxembourg (1628–95), distinguished French soldier who successfully invaded the Netherlands (1672).

[c] John Churchill, first Duke of Marlborough (1650–1722), English general, commander of the British army in the War of the Spanish Succession.

at a proper time Arthur became a lieutenant, and I a cornet[a] in the same regiment.

But the bare idea of wearing a red coat, and figuring at a review, was by no means the gratification to which my brother's ambition aspired. A war was now on the point of breaking out between the Austrians and the Turks;[b] and the period had not yet passed away, when a campaign against the infidels was looked upon in somewhat of the same light, as that in which / our ancestors in the middle ages regarded a crusade for the delivery of the Holy Sepulchre.[c] Prince Eugene, the brother in arms of our own Marlborough, was appointed by the emperor to the command of an army of one hundred and twenty-five thousand men; and we were desirous of placing ourselves as volunteers under his standard.

The proper authorities were easily obtained, enabling us to quit the army of Ireland, and enter upon this enterprise. A short time before we set out, my father died; my mother had deceased in the preceding year. These events however did not detain us long. Some steps it was proper my brother should take in person on his accession to the title and estate; but he left the details in the hands of a confidential agent. /

CHAPTER VIII.

Eugene set out from Vienna to take the command of the imperial army on the first of July 1716. He won an important victory over the Turks at Peterwaradin;[d] and marched from the field of battle against Temeswaer,[e] which fortress he reduced on the twelfth of October. The ensuing winter was passed by him at Vienna; and here in the following spring he was joined by a crowd of distinguished volunteers, French, German and Italian, and among others by lord / Alton, as I shall henceforth call him, and myself.

The battle of Belgrade in 1717 was more obstinately contended, and the Turkish army was commanded by a more gallant leader, than had been

---

[a] Fifth commissioned officer in a troop of cavalry, who carried the colours.

[b] It lasted from 1716–18, when the Treaty of Passarowitz was concluded. See note c p. 48.

[c] The tomb in which the body of Jesus Christ was laid after the Crucifixion, according to the New Testament.

[d] Peterwardein, where in August 1716 Eugéne defeated an army of 110,000 Turks led by Darnad Ali Pasha.

[e] Temesvar (Timişoara), the last Turkish stronghold in Hungary, held by the Grand Vizier Ali Kumurji.

encountered by the imperialists in the preceeding year.[a] My brother achieved wonders both of valour and conduct in the events of the campaign, and was proportionably honoured in the applauses and favour of our illustrious chief. The town of Belgrade capitulated the day after the battle, on the seventeenth of August.[b]

Never, in modern Europe, had two campaigns been crowned with a more splendid success, than these of prince Eugene against the Turks. The war seemed at an end. The negociations for peace commenced early in the following year, and ended in a treaty, which was signed in July, by which the emperor acquired / Belgrade and Temeswaer, and extended the bounds of his dominions.[c]

But this splendour lies in a great degree on the surface of things. The rainy season came on immediately after the reduction of Belgrade. The infectious odour of unburied bodies, the confinement of such multitudes within the narrow limits of a camp, and the unwholesome weather, spread diseases on every side, and turned the camp almost into a hospital. The victor-forces, who with such elation of heart had humbled the insolence of the crescent,[d] now crawled about, emaciated and dejected, and seemed scarcely able to bear up under the weight of their existence. Eugene withdrew his army over the Save, and encamped under the walls of Semlin.[e]

Here the same train of disasters pursued him. The weather became exceedingly tempestuous. / The winds roared; and the incessant rains poured down in torrents. The bridges which had been constructed for the accommodation of the army were broken down; and the bridge of boats across the Danube[f] was utterly annihilated. The prince, who had before moved his camp to the northern bank of the Save, now found it necessary to break it up entirely, and disperse his army into winter-quarters.

The Turks, immediately after the battle of Belgrade, seemed entirely to have disappeared. The foot had in great part been cut off in the battle. The main body of the horse had crossed the Morava, and retired towards Moldavia and the banks of the Pruth.[g] The prince, expecting to find the province of

---

[a] The Turkish commander at the Battle of Belgrade (16 August, 1717) was the Grand Vizier Khalil Pasha.

[b] 21 August, according to modern accounts.

[c] By the Treaty of Passarowitz 21 July, 1718 the Emperor also gained Wallachia as far as the River Aluta (Romania) and a portion of Serbia, though yielding the Peloponnese to the Turks.

[d] The emblem of Islam or Turkey.

[e] River Sava in N Yugoslavia flowing east to the Danube at Belgrade; Semlin (Zamun), a town on the River Danube near Belgrade.

[f] The River Danube rises in the Black Forest in Germany and flows through central and SE Europe to the Black Sea.

[g] River Morava, flowing north from the Danube at Bratislava in SW Czechoslovakia; Moldavia, a region in NE Romania.

Bosnia[a] in a manner deserted in this general reverse, first sent thither a detachment of sixteen hundred horse. The commander of the detachment speedily advertised / him that he found the Turks gathering a force in the vicinity of Zvornich.[b] The prince therefore dispatched three thousand foot with cannon and mortars to cooperate with the horse, and shortly after made up the detachment ten thousand men. They formed the siege of Zvornich.[c]

Hassan, the bashaw of Bosnia,[d] however, far from giving way, under this general calamity, determined to make the imperialists repent of their temerity. He assembled his forces with the utmost expedition. He was informed of a body of Turkish cavalry, to the amount of no fewer than fifteen thousand, which had broken away from the rest, and had marched upon Croatia. He immediately advanced towards, and joined them. The forces which had been quartered for the defence of the Austrian part of Croatia, not expecting to be molested, amounted to no more than two thousand. The Croats / however, who are all of them warlike, finding the danger of a merciless enemy immediately impending over them, assembled as volunteers, to the assistance of the small bands of regulars, to the number of seven thousand, and promised in the course of a week to produce as many more.

Hassan, who well understood the nature of the foe he had to contend with, felt that on his side every thing depended on dispatch. He marched upon the imperialists, and by his manœuvres compelled them to an instant engagement. He killed three thousand in the battle, and made as many more prisoners. The two Austrian generals escaped with difficulty. The army he encountered was utterly annihilated.

All this was the affair of a few days. The people of Croatia had been delighting themselves with the success of the imperial arms and the prowess of their illustrious commander. At / the news of the fall of Belgrade they gave themselves up to all the extravagance of joy. They considered the formidable despot of Constantinople as disarmed for ever. The felt the same sort of security, as if a wall of impenetrable brass had shut out the unhallowed footsteps of an invader. They ploughed their fields in entire confidence. They sat, each man under his vine, surrounded with his infant progeny. The dance, and the sound of the tabor and fife, exhilarated all hearts.[e]

Hassan was a fierce and atrabilarious[f] devotee of the ascendancy of the

---

[a] Region in central Yugoslavia.

[b] i.e. Zvornik, on the River Drina, which enters the River Sava about a hundred miles above Belgrade.

[c] Under the command of General Petras. See note c p. 50.

[d] Not further identified.

[e] Tabor, or tabour, a small drum used chiefly as an accompaniment to the fife, a small high-pitched flute, in military bands.

[f] Irritable (from Latin, *atra bilis*, black bile).

crescent and of the religion of Mahomet. He had always dwelt with transport upon the victories of the descendants of Ali. He delighted to recollect the days when the provinces of Africa bowed before the standard of Mahomet, when his followers crossed into Spain, and fought in the battle of Tours for the dominion of France.[a] He hated the / Christian dogs, the followers of the prophet of Nazareth, who conjured the devil into a herd of swine.[b] He had therefore meditated on the events of the present and the preceding campaign with sentiments of frenzy and rage.

The victory he had just gained, put it in his power to avenge on the Christians the disgraces of Belgrade. He was, as we find in many warriors of Asiatic origin, alike brave in the hour of conflict, and merciless in the moment of triumph. He poured with his victorious troops upon the fertile plains of Croatia. He laid waste all the produce of the year. He spread fire and sword on every side. He consumed with flames the cottages, the granaries, the farm-houses, the villages and the towns. He spirited on his soldiers to every kind of licentious ferocity. He drove along the inhabitants amidst a whirlwind of cavalry, to be sold for slaves in the more distant provinces of Turkey. / Never was a scene of desolation more perfect, never a more unbroken solitude, than that which he left behind.

The prince of Brunswick Bevern,[c] who commanded at the siege of Zvornich, was induced by the accounts that reached him of the calamities of Croatia, to detach several troops from the besieging force to endeavour to put a check upon the enormities of Hassan, and to protect what remained of the country. Lord Alton commanded one of these troops, and I went with him. Hassan had withdrawn himself previously to our arrival. Having defeated and annihilated the army of raw recruits in Croatia, he hastened to complete his work by raising the siege of Zvornich. Here he was not less successful than in the first object of his expedition. By the celerity of his movements he took the besiegers completely by surprise. He fell upon them in their intrenchments; he dispersed them / like chaff before the wind; he took their camp and baggage, and speedily delivered his government of Bosnia from the annoyance of an enemy.[d] This was, locally speaking, a complete reversing of the face of the campaign: but the Turk did not attempt to cross the Save or the Danube, and therefore the fortunes of the war continued the same as if Hassan had made no efforts, or his efforts had terminated in disappointment.

But, though Hassan had quitted Croatia previously to our arrival, he had left behind some detached portions of his force, for the purpose of preventing the

---

[a] Muslims engaged the Franks in more or less constant warfare 712–32; at the battle of Tours, or Poitiers, October 732, the Frankish army gained a great victory over the Muslim Berbers and Moors, and thus stemmed the tide of Moslem expansion into Europe.

[b] Alluding to Matt. 8: 28–34.

[c] Ernest Ferdinand, Duke of Brunswick Bevern (1682–1746).

[d] The siege was raised by the Bosnian Vizier Nunman Pasha Tshuprilitsh in 1718.

Croats, who were essentially of a warlike character, from assembling a new army, and reversing that helpless state of things and that desolation which he had created. These troops, no longer under the eye of their chief, were, if possible, more brutal and inhuman than they had shewn themselves immediately / after their victory. They doled out that violence and murder piecemeal, which Hassan had perpetrated on a grander scale. Lord Alton and the captains who had been dispatched on the same errand, concerted together, and skilfully arranged certain *points d'appui*,[a] by way of shelter for the defenceless peasantry, and for the purpose of holding in awe the petty bands of the infidels, who had before straggled from their quarters, with views of depredation, or the design of satiating their most brutal passions upon such as had none to help them.

During the whole of this melancholy scene, a scene which exhibited all the sad results of war without any of those glaring and dramatic effects which cloak its deformity from the eyes of the unthinking, my brother displayed in himself the very soul of humanity. He was every where; he appeared never to sleep. He was all ear for the complaints of the miserable; he / penetrated into their wants before they had time to express them; he contrived remedies, where the sufferers had persuaded themselves that remedy was impossible. He brought out to the light of day children for parents that had pronounced themselves childless, and parents for children, who but for his activity must have perished by the way-side for lack of sustenance. With the unerring eye of divine compassion he always flew to the spot where his assistance was principally needed, and in the critical moment effected miracles of beneficence. His very look and the character of his countenance were changed. His eye swam in the liquid dew of love; his voice melted with the all the softest tones of sympathetic kindness; his strength was preternatural; his activity was ever fresh and new; he was like a messenger from heaven commissioned for the relief of unutterable woes. /

CHAPTER IX

One evening, that we were returning from one of these godlike expeditions, and approached the banks of the Unna,[b] there started before us from the neighbouring forest the figure of a beautiful woman, pursued by two persons attired in the Turkish uniform. They were on horseback, and had nearly

---

[a] The base or area upon which a battle line was centred.
[b] River Una, flowing into the River Sava.

overtaken her. Sure of their prey, one of them wheeled round, with the intention to take her in front. They would otherwise have been in danger of throwing her / to the earth with the weight of their steeds; but by this manœuvre the nimble rider counted to make her their prisoner without injury to her person. We approached the spot in an oblique direction, and were not at first observed by her pursuers. As soon as we were, they turned their horses (for we were to the amount of twenty or thirty), and were presently out of sight. The lady whom it had been their purpose to seize, as long as they were engaged in the chace was mute, and concentrated all her powers in the rapidity of flight. But she no sooner saw that deliverance was at hand, than she uttered a scream, with a mixed expression between agony and joy, and fell to the ground.

In a moment we reached the spot where she lay, and Arthur and two or three more, alighting from their horses, flew to her assistance. It was long before she could be recovered. When she opened her eyes, she looked / wildly about her with every expression of the bitterest anguish, and immediately again became insensible. Three times did the paroxysm return; and we began to apprehend that the shock she had experienced was too great for her strength to endure. Her complexion was white, like that of a corpse. Her features were sometimes convulsed, but oftener collapsed into the semblance of death. She knew not what, nor where she was.

Yet it was easy to see under all these disadvantages, that a more beautiful creature never existed under the sun. I cannot speak fully of this as she appeared at that moment. But this encounter was the commencement of a familiar intercourse; and I may therefore reasonably describe her, as she was seen by us when this paroxysm of agony had passed away. – She stood before us in the lustre of that beauty, which is seen in the frailer and more delicate / moiety[a] of the human species, when born beneath a glowing sun. She could not be more than nineteen years of age. – The first thing that struck the beholder was the extreme regularity of her features, so that the eye wandered over the whole countenance without meeting with a single harshness which might disturb its inchanted gaze. Her forehead was low and broad, yet arched, and, being for that reason in a considerable degree concealed with the hair, a double interest was given to the eyes, which thus became in a certain sense the sole interpreters of the mind. These were full and round, the dark balls dilating with innumerable rays, and fixed in a liquid heaven of the deepest, purest blue. The sweeping arch of the upper lid gave a peculiar look of nobleness and openness to the countenance. There seemed, so to speak, full room for the thoughts to come forth, /and display themselves. Her nose was broad at the root, and, descending straight from the forehead, terminated in due season in a rounded point. Her smile was tender and full; and, while it possessed extraordinary

---

[a] Half.

powers of expression, disturbed less the shape of the lips than the smile of an European, which most frequently widens in lines into the cheek. Her chin, which was round and turned up, formed as it were a base to the entire countenance. Her cheeks were not full and prominent, but on the contrary seemed to withdraw, and thus to place the features strikingly in relief. Her complexion was brown and glowing, and, on any sudden emotion, her eyes and lips and cheeks simultaneously partook of the same suffusion, each with a hue peculiar to itself, yet blending into one delicious whole. Her figure was smaller both in size and fulness than that of the beauties / of the North usually are, while it was at the same time more defined in muscular appearance, more airy in effect, and compact in the entire whole*.

More than an hour elapsed, before the blood, which had rushed back to the heart, resumed its ordinary functions, and gave to her limbs the power of voluntary motion. At the same time her faculties of recollection returned to her.

My father! Where is my father? she exclaimed. I must see my father!

She was about to fly from us with the speed of lightning. But her strength was not equal to her desires. After a few steps she fell. My brother raised her from the earth, and soothed her with those accents, which I had heard so often, and which had a power over the human heart that no other man ever equalled. He / offered himself as her assistant; he intreated her to point out the way. We came to a cavern in the rock.

What a spectacle then presented itself before us! At the mouth of the cavern lay an old man with his face upward; a deep wound was in his breast; the blood was still flowing; but the man was dead. A middle-aged woman in a state of insensibility was groveling on his corpse. That man and woman were the father and mother of the female we had saved. Those renegades had murdered the old man, and were pursuing the daughter, at the time that we interposed, and drove them into flight. /

* This description of the person of the Greek lady was obligingly supplied to me, by one who had the happiness to be intimately acquainted with her.

CHAPTER X

The father and mother of the damsel we had saved were Greeks. The name of the father was Colocotroni, that of his daughter Irene. He was of the race of the Mainotes, the descendants of the ancient Spartans.[a] He was of the noblest class of this people, and had been the proprietor of considerable wealth. In his youth he had devoted himself to the contemplation of the heroic deeds of his ancestors, who in ancient times had repelled the Persian invasion; / and he indulged in dreams of being himself an instrument to shake off the yoke of the more barbarous Turk. He had fondly dwelt upon the contrast of character between the ignorant and presumptuous conqueror, and the ingenious and inventive enslaved. The latter were tenfold more numerous than the former. The victor left to the Greeks the various pursuits of arts, manufactures and commerce, while he proudly flattered himself that he was born only for conquest and indulgence, and the others sent into the world to supply his wants, and anticipate his wishes. The Turk was unquestionably brave, and well trained in all the discipline of the followers of Mahomet. His was the strength of thews[b] and sinews, while the ingenuity, the subtlety and active invention of the Greeks were in his opinion only calculated to make them more serviceable slaves. The creed of Colocotroni was of a diametrically opposite / character. He held, that mind was destined by nature to be the master of the universe, and that, where intellectual faculties existed, they could not fail by perseverance to bring all other things into subjection and obedience.

Colocotroni had been in his youth a fervent patriot. He had passed from the volumes of the ancients, and the meditations which those volumes suggested, into the world. He had studied his countrymen, with an ardent desire to find in them all that his fond wishes suggested, but with a feeling that, if they rose in arms to shake off the Turkish yoke, it was a deep stake that they played for. He knew that, if they failed in the attempt, there was no inhumanity that their barbarous masters, in revenge of their audacity, and in contempt of the Christian

---

[a] Colocotroni, italianised form of the name of the Greek patriot Theodorus Kolokotrones (1770–1843), an illiterate warlord who controlled the Peloponnese during the struggle to liberate Greece from the Turks in the 1820s; the Mainates, remarkable for their acts of piracy, frankness and love of independence; the Spartans, inhabitants of the ancient Greek city of Sparta famous for their military prowess and austere way of life.

[b] Especially strong or well-developed muscles.

dogs that dared to rise up against them, would not inflict. He had weighed his countrymen in the balance, and found them wanting. They / were sufficiently inflammable; but they had an instability, the utter foe of arduous undertakings. They were easily excited, and easily daunted. If the whole business could have been effected by one bold exertion, then the Greeks would not fail. But they were not prepared to encounter reverses, to sustain the most trying sufferings and privations, and against hope to believe in hope. In addition to all other disadvantages, they were totally deficient in subordination and concert. Every one abounded in his own sense, judged that his plan was the one that should be followed, and that he himself should be the leader. In the deep recesses of his soul Colocotroni resolved that he would not be the person to urge his country-men to enterprises, in which, alone and unsustained, he became convinced they would not succeed.

Having looked on all sides for the succour of which the Greeks of the Morea[a] stood in / need, he at length persuaded himself that he had found it in the republic of Venice. The Venetians had lost the island of Candia to the Turks in the year 1669. But they had previously sustained a siege of twenty-eight months; and Morosini, the governor, had surrendered it in the last extremity, with the reputation of the most consummate commander both by sea and land, that Italy had produced for more than a century.[b] The fame of this man perpetually increased; and his ascendancy in his native state was such as no efforts of those who desired to destroy it could succeed to undermine. Colocotroni saw in the government of Venice a race of profound politicians, while its armies were led by a general from whose prowess every beneficial result might be expected. The Venetians were Christians, cultivated by every art, and excelling in various literature. How much more beneficial must it be for the Greeks of the / Morea to be placed under the protection of Venice, than to be scourged, as now, by the despotism and contempt of the barbarous Turk! Colocotroni could earnestly have wished that his countrymen might have been valiant and resolute enough to be their own deliverers. But, satisfied that that was not the case, he believed that he had found in this expedient the only practicable mode of arriving at the good he desired.

The Venetians, the Austrians and the Poles, the hereditary and inexpiable adversaries of the power whose flag now waved from the minarets of Constan-tinople, having had some years' respite from the toils and the calamities of war, took in the winter of 1683–4 counsel together, how they might in the most effectual way expel the hordes of the Asiatics from the shores of Europe. Colocotroni, authorised by the most considerable of his countrymen, resorted to this / conference, laid before them a plan for reducing the peninsula under the sovereignty of Venice, and promised the unanimous concurrence of the

---

[a] Traditional name for the Peloponnese.
[b] Francesco Morosini (1618–94), famous Venetian soldier and Doge of Venice from 1687.

Moreotes to carry it into effect. Morosini accordingly sailed with a fleet for the execution of this purpose, and in a series of uninterrupted successes reduced St Maura, Modon, Coron, Navarino, Lepanto and Patras, and annexed the entire dominion of the Morea to the government of the Venetians. Corinth and Napoli di Romania were the last trophies of his success.[a] The expedition took place in the year 1687.

Nothing could be more complete than the success of the plan which had thus been suggested. But the result was similar to that of Aesop's fable of the horse and the stag.[b] The Greeks got rid of the enemy, whose tyranny they had deemed insupportable. But they found no advantage in the exchange. The arbitrary / power of the Turk they had felt from time to time in all its severity. The oppression of the Venetian satraps[c] was yet more systematical, invariable and insupportable. The Venetians did not seem to consider the Greeks as in any way entitled to their indulgence. They despised them as an effeminate and unorganised people, and of consequence worthy only to be trampled on. Their determined purpose was to draw as large supplies from them as possible, to fill the coffer of the paramount state. Nor was this all. The provincial governors, finding that such was the policy of the senate that deputed them, determined to imitate their masters, and proceeded to fleece the subject people, not only for the benefit of their masters, but also for their private advantage.

Colocotroni, thus painfully disappointed in the result of his endeavours, resolved henceforth to withdraw himself from public affairs, / and concentre the activity of his spirit in his studies and the circle of his private friends. The dominion of the Venetians lasted nearly thirty years. During this period the effervescence of his youthful thoughts had greatly subsided. He married somewhat late in life; and his bride, according to the mode of the warmer climates in these cases, had been considerably younger than himself. They had only one daughter, that survived the period of infancy. The wife had been beautiful. Beauty in these climates in eminently a fragile flower; but, as the beauty of the mother subsided, that of the daughter continually developed itself in greater splendour and fascination.

It was in the year that preceded the campaigns of Eugene against the north-

---

[a] St Maura, Modon, Corone, Navanno, Patras and Corinth became Venetian fortified centres on the S. peninsula of Greece to give Venice control of the Straits of Otranto. Lepanto and Corinth; towns in S. Greece. Lepanto was seized by Spain from the Turks in 1571 and subsequently fell to Venice.

[b] Aesop (6th century BC), to whom is attributed authorship of a large number of animal fables; Aesop's fable of the horse and the stag which tells of how there was once a horse so annoyed by a stag's invasion of the choicest eating places of the meadow he has thus far had to himself that he seeks the help of a man to turn out the unwelcome visitor. 'Yes, by all means,' says the man, but on condition the horse allows himself to be ridden with a bridle in his mouth. The horse agrees, and soon the two of them have turned the stag out of the luscious pasture. Only now does the horse realize he has traded a temporary irritant for a permanent master.

[c] Subordinate rulers (especially despotic ones).

west frontier of the Turks, that the armies of the Ottomans had fallen with so great a force, both by sea and land, upon the Morea, and the invasion / was so totally unexpected by the now supine and heartless Venetians, that all the fortresses built for the defence of the peninsula against an enemy were reduced at a blow.[a] The Greeks looked on at this entire transfer of dominion with a perfect neutrality. Their very hearts were filled with aversion against their Italian lords. They believed that the former success of Morosini was mainly owing to their cooperation; and they saw how all their services and good-will had been requited. The vigilance of their Venetian governors, so far as applied to the oppression of the natives, had never relaxed for a moment; and they found the methodised extortion of their new masters, infinitely more vexatious than the crude and skill-less impositions of the Turk.

Colocotroni had taken no part in this event. He had the most cogent reason to be dissatisfied with the Venetians, whom, thirty years / before, he had invited into the country; and he believed that he should have no personal cause to regret the resumed dominion of the Turk. What was his astonishment therefore to find, that one of the first acts of the Ottoman government was to drag him from his peaceful home, and cast him into a dungeon!

This proceeding was the fruit of a cabal. One of the most esteemed friends of the early years of Colocotroni, was a brother Mainote and a neighbour, of the name of Bozzari.[b] Their youthful studies had been similar; they had meditated, and had communed together, respecting the sentiments and the virtues of the ancient Greeks. They had set out in life as patriots; but they had each come to the same conclusion, that their contemporaries, who had grown up under the Turkish dominion, were not made of such elements, as should afford a rational hope that they would be able of themselves / to vindicate their independence. Colocotroni and Bozzari therefore, with others of their countrymen, had concurred in the project of calling in the aid of the Venetians.

Bozzari had died in the prime of life; but he had left a son, the sole heir of his property. He had married earlier than his friend; and his son was ten years older than the daughter of Colocotroni. But this did not interfere with the attachment which the young man cherished for the fair Irene, whom he had been accustomed to see every day. He had been the protector and friend of her infancy. He had been her instructor. It will be found in many ways advantageous, that the preceptor should, as little as may be, exceed in years the years of the pupil. Irene felt herself particularly charmed with the lessons of the young Bozzari. There is a natural caressing and accommodation of manner in a boy

---

[a] The Ottomans regained the Morea in the Peloponnese with a land-sea expedition in the summer of 1715.

[b] Almost certainly named after Marco Bozzaris, a leader of the Suliotes, a group of Albanian migrants who with other bands of Greek patriots fought the Turks in the struggle to liberate Greece in the 1820s. Known as the 'Leonidas of Modern Greece', he led 1200 men in an attack that put to rout 4000 Turko-Albanians at Keripenisi (1823), but was killed; see note b p. 67.

just growing up into manhood / towards a being, ten years his junior, especially if that being is a female, that renders his communications delightful. Irene had the profoundest reverence for her father, almost amounting to adoration; and yet there was certainly a variety of things that she more eagerly learned from the son of her father's friend. The stripling had in him the seeds of a violent and ungovernable character; but this native of the forest curbed his temper, and sheathed his fangs, whenever it was his cue to address himself to the beautiful child. – The scene I describe was not in accordance with the manners of these countries; but the close intimacy of the fathers sanctioned the innovation. And, as these things occurred when Irene was no more than five or six years of age, the unripe age of the pupil banished any scruple which might otherwise have arisen.

Such for the most part the younger Bozzari / had appeared during the life-time of his father. When he was nearly twenty years of age, the father died, and left his son under the guardianship of his friend. This was the signal for the young man to break loose from all restraint. For some time before the death of his parent, he had secretly connected himself with a band of licentious rioters, though the awe of fatherly authority had kept him within bounds, and his wanderings had been carefully concealed. In fact the junior Bozzari had for a considerable time only carried himself speciously in the presence of his father, and the house of his father's friend, while all those of inferior station knew him for what he was, tyrannical, cruel, and a profligate.

At the death of his father he at once threw off the mask. In the precepts of a parent he recognised the voice of nature; but he considered the directions of a guardian as flowing / from a factitious and an usurped authority. He grew every day more rebellious and stubborn, and at length totally broke off from all intercourse with Colocotroni. He became the slave of habits of debauchery, and for a time forgot all the haunts of his youth. It was during this period that he contrived to dissipate his inheritance. He had been reduced to the most desperate straits; and, in proportion as his difficulties increased, his morals became more relaxed. All sober and creditable persons now shunned his society; and he associated only with men of villainous principles and desperate character. Such had been the style in which he proceeded for a period of seven years.

Meanwhile the season at length arrived, when like certain other prodigals, he appeared to have grown tired of a career of dissipation, and to have adopted the plan of a reformed life. / He sought once more the protection of Colocotroni. He regarded the friend of his father, the instant he professed the purpose of an altered course, as obliged to become his patron. He reminded the venerable Greek, of the devoted attachment he had felt for his fair daughter even in infancy, and added that the sure way to reclaim him for ever, was to give him her hand, and establish him in a system of domestic life. Colocotroni felt the truest devotion to the memory of the deceased; he would not have been deterred from acceding to the proposition that was made him, by the poverty of the suitor; but he thought his daughter's happiness far too precious a stake to be embarked in so uncertain a venture. He therefore set before the young man a picture at large of his prodigality, his debauched courses, and the disgrace into which he had plunged himself, and rejected his suit. He offered to do every thing in his power to / restore his ward to his former station in society, but refused to assist in the mode now suggested. He was even careful not to give to the professed penitent encouragement to hope, that at a future time he might be found more favourable to his suit.

The young Bozzari was radically of an unforgiving spirit. He had not anticipated this repulse. He swore in the inmost recesses of his soul, that Colocotroni should rue to his latest hour the affront which was thus put upon him. He returned to his former associates, his mind rankling with revenge. It was at this time that a correspondence was entered into with the Turk by some of the Moreotes of the looser sort for the expulsion of the Venetians. Bozzari believed that he could make this revolution in some way subservient to his animosity against Colocotroni, and engaged in the conspiracy. The event was the entire restoration / of the authority of the Porte[a] over this beautiful country.

The Austrians immediately declared their discontent with the revolution that had taken place, and loudly complained of the invasion to the Ottoman government, as an infraction of the peace of Carlowitz.[b] Prince Eugene of Savoy had a genuine passion for military enterprise; and, partly from his instigation, war was declared by the emperor against the Turk. Achmet, the officer who had been commissioned by the divan to effect the reduction of the Morea, found himself placed in a very arduous predicament.[c] He cast into prison a certain number of the most considerable Greeks; and, as he was himself unacquainted with the tempers and views of the inhabitants, he was directed in the choice of his victims by the unworthy natives who had invited the expedition. Colocotroni was one of the imprisoned. /

But the revenge of Bozzari did not stop at this point. He represented his guardian to the Turkish commander, as engaged in a secret correspondence with the court of Vienna, and industriously urging them to throw down the gauntlet against the Ottomans. This at the present moment was a most dangerous accusation; and the Turks were accustomed to be in a high degree summary in the administration of what they called justice. The life of Colocotroni was in the most imminent peril; and the reputation of his great wealth increased the danger. Bozzari was instigated to accomplish his destruction by the joint

---

[a] Short for Sublime Porte, the court or government of the Ottoman Empire.

[b] The Treaty of Karlowitz (1699), by which the Ottomans lost substantial territories to the European powers allied against them.

[c] Grand Vizier Damad Ali conquered the Morea in the summer of 1715, ordering Sari Achmet Pasha to enforce the siege of Corinth, which fell on 2 August.

impulses of hatred and of love. He resolved never to forgive his guardian for the
affront he had put upon him; and he believed that, when Colocotroni was
removed, he should easily be enabled, particularly in the present convulsed state
of the Morea, to dispose of his orphan daughter / as he pleased. Already in his
villainous imagination he had taken away the life of the father, and gratifying at
once his hatred and his love, made the daughter the victim of his lust. There even
seemed to be nothing that could prevent him in his crimes. Colocotroni was
greatly loved and honoured by his countrymen; but at the present crisis it was not
believed that a single Greek would be listened to by the Turkish commander,
except those who had been active in reducing the Morea once again under the
dominion of the crescent. /

CHAPTER XI

It is impossible to depict the agony of mind to which the wife and daughter of
Colocotroni were reduced on this dreadful occasion. The wife felt for her husband
the most tender and undivided attachment. Being many years his junior, she
regarded him as her father, her protector, the only person who could conduct her
in safety and honour through the perilous paths of life: at the same time that, in the
intimacy and reciprocity of the connubial state, / she felt for him that ardent spirit
of affection, which appeared to her to exceed all she could have known towards
the author of her existence. There was yet another link that bound him to her
heart-strings. Irene, the fruit of her womb, for whose safety she felt inexpressible
misgivings, must be deserted, must, as she believed, inevitably be lost, in the
present wild state of the newly conquered Morea, without a father's protection.

Irene was herself in a state of mind considerably different from that of her
mother. She loved her father with the most perfect devotion; and she was not
insensible of the forlorn condition in which she and her mother would be left, if
Colocotroni became the victim of Turkish policy. But now first there burst out
within her bosom emphatically the seeds which had been sown by the education of her father. She did not abandon herself to despair. She felt / that she
had resources within her. She had derived benefits inestimable from the lessons
of Colocotroni; and she believed that the time was now come for her in part to
repay those benefits. She could not believe that she was nothing, a mere gaudy
flower in the parterre[a] of nature, or, like the beauties of a Turkish harem,

---

[a] A formally patterned flower garden.

existing only for the gratification of the senses of imperious man; and she determined to make experiment of what was in her power. If there was hazard in the trial, the danger, should she remain nerveless and supine, would be nearly equal; and she could not expose herself to the tempest of the public scene in a more glorious cause.

She consulted an intimate friend of her father, a most honourable man, a Greek, of the name of Adrasti. He assisted her by his advice; but the suggestion of what she had resolved to undertake, was purely her own. Whatever were / the difficulties and discouragements that attended it, she determined to encounter them. The circumstances proved in reality more favourable, than could have been expected. She requested Adrasti to make himself acquainted with the personal dispositions of the Turkish commander. Adrasti found that Achmet was of a character of which all men stood in fear. He was fierce, severe and repulsive. His temper was ferocious; his orders often inhuman; mercy seemed altogether a stranger to his breast; and he even appeared to delight in blood. But, with all this, he was a fervent lover of justice, according to his own conceptions of that virtue. He did not indeed, in the execution of his military designs, feel greatly prompted to stop and discriminate. When a people were to be driven into exile, or sold to slavery, he gave himself no trouble to distinguish the innocent from the guilty. He took / it for granted, when the honour of the crescent demanded a sacrifice of this kind, that all were of equal demerit. But, when an individual case came before him, in which flagrant injustice was supposed to be committed, he rose like a lion in vindication of his favourite virtue. Here he appeared to be in his element; he was impartial and equal in his judgment of the merits of the case; and he was exemplary in his vengeance upon those who sought to impose upon him. He had also another quality, which in some respects was not unfavourable to the enterprise of Irene. He exhibited in his own person that rare phenomenon in the Turkish nation, a man indifferent to the allurements of the fair sex. Though his philosophy was altogether of the barbarous sort, yet, such as it was, it engrossed the devotion of his soul. He thought woman beneath his attention. He believed the individual who bowed at the shrine / of beauty, unworthy the name of a man. His austerity was proof against all assaults. While he was young, he had never been a boy; he had never engaged in childish sports, or been amused with trifles. His rigid features had never relaxed into a smile. His heart was unimpressible as the nether milstone.[a] If this character was in one respect unfavourable to the generous purpose of Irene, in another it was propitious. There was no danger that Achmet should form any project hostile to her chastity.

Achmet at present administered his government at Corinth; and Corinth was the prison of the unhappy Colocotroni. Hither therefore Irene repaired.

---

[a] i.e. The bottom millstone, often used figuratively to denote hardness.

Corinth was the see of a Christian archbishop; and this dignitary was at present from motives of policy treated with some degree of consideration by the Turkish conquerors.[a] The archbishop entertained a due esteem for the virtues of Colocotroni; and / Irene first addressed herself to him. Most gladly would she have obtained an interview with her father; but that was impossible. Indulgence obtained no quarter from the temper of Achmet. Colocotroni was shut up in rigorous solitude in the dungeons of the citadel; and no mortal but the jailer and his servants was permitted to approach. All that the archbishop could obtain for the fair Greek, was that she should be allowed access to Achmet, and to tender her petition to him in person. Aware of the temper of the governor, he had not even mentioned to him the name of the suitor. His request had been, that Achmet would permit a distressed Grecian female to lay her sorrows at his feet.

Irene ascended the hill, anciently called the Acrocorinthus, upon which the citadel is built, and Adrasti was suffered to attend her. The citadel, and the hill on which it stands, command / the finest prospect in the world, the gulphs of Lepanto and Egina, the sacred woods of the ancient Delphi, and a country upon which from every side nature has lavished her most exceeding bounties.[a] Irene pursued the path which had of old been constructed, leading up to the seat of government; she resolved to break through the restraints of Turkish manners, but her person was covered with a thick veil; she saw nothing to her right or her left, before her or behind her; her mind was engrossed with those sentiments of filial piety which had prompted her undertaking.

Achmet was engaged, at the very moment in which she entered the chamber, with one of the officers of the prison, who was calling over to him the list of the prisoners in durance[b] for offences against the state. He ordered variously, some to be sent into banishment at the foot of mount Caucasus,[c] some to be imprisoned for a / term of years, while he deferred his decision on the case of others. The name of Colocotroni was enunciated. Let him die, said Achmet, in the public place of Corinth, at the hour of noon.

Irene at this moment had reached the spot where the general stood. Her senses were arrested; she heard the name of her father; she heard the award of the Turk. Struck to the heart in an instant, she fell suddenly to the earth. She lay, with her brow at the foot of Achmet. Unmoved by the incident, with unaltered features he motioned to the attendants to raise her up.

What woman is this? he demanded.

---

[a] Lepanto, also known as the Gulf of Corinth; Delphi, ancient Greek city on the southern slopes of Mount Parnassus and site of the most famous oracle of Apollo. See note to p. 56.

[b] Imprisonment.

[c] Probably referring to Mount Elbruz, highest peak of the Great Caucasus mountain range, which stretches from the Black Sea to the Caspian Sea, and in which Prometheus was said to be chained to a rock by Jupiter; see above, note to p. 8.

It is the person whom, at the suit of the Greek primate, you consented to hear.

Explain yourself, said the general. What is it you would have me do for you? – She threw back her veil. /

I am the daughter of Colocotroni.

Bear her hence. I have pronounced his sentence.

Will Achmet be unjust? Oh, my lord! my father is guiltless. Stain not the sword of righteousness you bear, with the blood of the innocent!

Woman, I have decided on the most unerring grounds. You rather brought in the Venetian thirty years since, and perpetrated the deepest offence against the Porte. He has grown grey in rebellion and treason. He stirred up the Venetian then; he had stirred up the Austrian now. But he shall offend no more. He dies. Would I had known in what suit the primate solicited me! Remove this woman. Officer, I have given my final orders.

Irene struggled with the men who were engaged in thrusting her from the presence of the general. She loosened herself from their hold; / she was once more at the feet of Achmet. With imploring hands and tearless eyes she claimed his attention.

Yet, yet, she cried, the blow is not struck. I do not plead for the guilty. If my father has done any thing worthy of death, let him die! But hear him! Achmet will not refuse a hearing to the man who is able to vindicate himself. Bring him and his accuser front to front, and then judge between them! My life upon his innocence!

There was something in the manner of Irene, that shook the confidence of the Turk. It was not pity that moved him; it was not the power of beauty. In these directions he was inaccessible. It was the voice of truth; it was the tone of deep-felt and entire conviction. It was impossible not to feel that the suppliant infallibly knew the truth of what she uttered; it was / impossible not to imagine, that the oracle of heaven expressed itself by her organs.

Colocotroni finished what Irene had begun. Achmet yielded to the suggestions of his suppliant. He commanded that the father should immediately be brought into his presence: he directed that Bozzari should be summoned. Irene was removed. The business was to place the veracity and assertions of the accuser and the accused in equal balance. And, though Achmet did not doubt the inflexibility of his judgment, he resolved that the single object before him should be the parties themselves.

Both were taken by surprise. But the effect was different upon the one and the other. Bozzari was disturbed at the presence of his victim. He had felt from childhood that Colocotroni was a being of another order from himself. He knew that he had endeavoured to / crush him under the weight of a false accusation; and he had counted upon his death as instantaneous and certain. He was summoned to the presence of Achmet. To see there the man he had injured, alive, and able to speak for himself, appalled him no less than the apparition of a departed spirit would have done.

Colocotroni was brought from his dungeon. He knew not whither they were leading him; probably, as he conceived, to the place of execution. Instead of that, he found himself in the presence-chamber in the Acrocorinthus. The good man is never unprepared, to stand in any presence, to repel any accusation, to face the monarchs of the earth, and to justify his own integrity. He saw Bozzari placed together with him, front to front, before the Turk. The whole truth was revealed to him in a moment.

Bozzari was called on for his indictment. He hesitated and grew pale. He related a / story of conspiracy among the Greeks, of intelligence conveyed, and incentives administered, to the cabinet of Vienna. He told of the result, of troops assembled by the emperor, and prince Eugene actually appointed to the command.

Colocotroni felt what it was incumbent on him to do. He cared little for his own life; but his wife and his child had no other protector; and he trembled to think what might happen to them in a newly conquered and disturbed country, when he himself should have been cut off by the executioner as a criminal against the state. He felt that he was called upon for a bold and unshrinking defence, that should overwhelm his accuser with the contempt he merited.

I will tell to your highness at once, said Colocotroni, the entire truth without colouring and disguise. I am a Greek, and the lover of / Greece; I aspired to emulate the heroes who in ancient times fought against and baffled the innumerable armies of the despot of Persia. I saw in the state of Venice men who worshipped the same God, and believed in the same Saviour, as we did. I persuaded myself that the Venetian senate would prove our protectors and our brothers. I invited them into Greece; I assisted them with all my might; I resolved that, if any exertion of mine could effect it, the Turk should not possess a foot of land in the Morea. I succeeded. If the question is to punish an offence against the divan of Constantinople[a] committed in the year 1687, – here I am; use me at your pleasure.

But I soon found the mistake I had committed; I found the Venetians our unrelenting oppressors. I resented this the more, because they came among us under the pretence of being our deliverers. I felt less aversion to the / Turks, because they were at least honest enemies, and did not attempt to deceive us. But I resolved henceforth to retire into myself, to converse only with my studies and my private friends. I became convinced that I could render no important service to my country as a country. It is not in my disposition to be any thing by halves; whatever I undertake, I undertake with my whole soul, and keep for myself no loop-hole, no retreating place behind. the private course of life I have chosen, I have preserved inviolate for more than twenty-five years.

My accuser pursues me from personal motives. I was appointed his guardian

---

[a] Muslim Privy Council.

by his deceased father. I endeavoured with sincerity to do him all the good that I could. He rejected my advice, and became a prodigal. His associates have uniformly been chosen from among the most abandoned of the Greeks. At / length, when he had squandered his fortune, and blasted his character, he pretended to turn repentant. He asked of me the hand of my only child, the staff of my age, in marriage. I refused him. Hence his present hostilities. He has resolved by false accusations to destroy the father, that the daughter may fall defenceless into his hands.

In speaking thus to your excellency, I lay before you without disguise the true account of my imprisonment, and of this man's accusation. But it is not just, that you should found your judgment either on his story or mine. He alleges that I have corresponded with, and endeavoured to stir up against you, the court of Vienna. Let him produce his proofs. If I have written letters hostile to your government, or to that of Constantinople, with the contents of which he is acquainted, he must have intercepted some of them. Let him shew those / letters; or let him bring forward witnesses that have seen them. I on the other hand am ready to produce witnesses of the inoffensiveness of my life, and that I have held no society with persons of doubtful character, or who can be suspected of engaging in political conspiracies.

Bozzari was unprepared for this severe examination of evidence. He sought however to bring himself out of the affair as he could. He owned he had no letters. But her undertook to present witnesses to Achmet, who had seen the letters, and could attest the truth of his information. The witnesses were called for. They were persons of the lowest description, and apparently dependent upon the accuser. Achmet insisted upon examining them separately. Thus tried, they could not agree in one sentence of these imaginary letters. Achmet demanded the letters themselves. If they had been intercepted in the manner pretended, and fixed on as the / ground of a criminal accusation, it could never be imagined that they would have been destroyed.

In conclusion, Achmet became satisfied of the falshood of the charge, and drove Bozzari with scorn from his presence. It is thus, said he, that in state-affairs the officer who would serve his prince, is reduced to contaminate himself with the intercourse of the worst of men. I well know that no honour-able Greek will prevail upon himself to be the friend of the Turk. Our religion, our manners are different. It is the principle of the Mahometan faith to reduce all unbelievers into subjection. Every virtuous Greek will desire the independ-ence of his country. You may become good subjects, submitting with patience to the yoke you cannot relieve yourselves from. But you cannot be our confed-erates. All this I knew; and I take shame to myself for being governed, in a matter / of plain justice, and where the life of an individual is at stake, by the assertions of a renegade. It is a poor apology to say, that, in the midst of a people newly reduced to the obedience of my master, one has not leisure for every thing, and that in such a situation it is unavoidable to distrust all who appear to have the power to disturb the government. In fine, judging as I do of Bozzari and yourself, I am reduced to the necessity of employing the one, and discountenancing the other.

If I were a private man, I should desire the friendship of such an one as Colocotroni, his religion only excepted. As a public officer, I am compelled to act otherwise. The policy of the divan of Constantinople requires that you should be removed out of this our newly recovered province. You were principally instrumental in the year 1687, in expelling the Turks out of the Morea. You are well known to be hostile / to the subjugation of your country-men. These are not offences against general justice: but they are offences against the master I serve, and the standard I bear. In atonement for the flagrant injustice you have suffered, I will make the doom of your banishment as light as I am able. I will give you reasonable time to dispose of your property in the Morea to such advantage as you can; and I will suffer you to carry out of the country whatever is capable of being transported into another. I allow you one moon,[a] before you shall be required to resign your fields, and take leave of your abode. /

CHAPTER XII

The meeting of Colocotroni on the one side, and his wife and daughter on the other, was full of congratulation and joy. They had not expected to meet again in this world. They knew the summary style of Turkish justice; they knew what was to be expected in the convulsed state of the country; and they had heard of the ferocious and sanguinary character of Achmet. They met however; and, which is more, they met in freedom. They were permitted / to carry with them out of the dominions which were now subjected to the Turk, whatever was capable of being transported. But, which was still more gratifying to them, they met with acquittal, with honour and virtue. This sudden change of fortune which had taken place, was wholly owing to the heroic qualities of both father and daughter. Irene, a young girl of nineteen years of age, had had the courage to present herself, urged by the insuppressible passion to save her father's life, alone, before the Turkish conqueror, surrounded with his officers; and the result had been such as her courage and devotion merited. Colocotroni had finished what his daughter began. He stood before the barbarian in all the

---

[a] i.e. Month.

magnanimity of a son of Leonidas.[a] He had told his story with the frankness
and simplicity, with the subdued manner and the unconquerable soul, which
adorned it with a thousand nameless / graces, and which had taken captive one
of the fiercest and the most formidable spirits, that the school of Mahomet ever
bred.

Colocotroni had always been of an infirm constitution. Rescued from the
danger of a violent death, and discharged from prison, he and his family had at
first entertained no other feeling than that of joy at his deliverance. When
however the tumult of congratulation had passed away, they began to reflect
with terror upon the exile to which they had been sentenced. To quit the
delightful plains of Arcadia and Pylos was to them a grievous thought.[b]
Whither were they to go? They had all the feeling of their remoter ancestors,
and regarded the whole human race as divided into Greeks and barbarians.
The fields of Italy itself were not exempted from this prejudice. But Gaul and
Germany and Poland and Hungary they viewed in much the same light as we /
should regard an exile among the savages of North America. Add to which,
Colocotroni's infirm health had suffered much from his brief, but severe
imprisonment in the dungeons of the Acrocorinthus. He had been shut out
from light and air in a solitary cell; no literature, his constant resource, to
amuse him; no indulgences to cherish, no kindness to cheer him; his days and
nights passed in monotonous uniformity, and no other prospect before him,
but that of perishing, he knew not how soon, by a Turkish sabre. Death in any
form is a bitter draught; but death from the hands of a barbarian, against whom
he had done nothing, whose vengeance he had not even had the satisfaction to
provoke by a generous, but hopeless, opposition to their aggressions, was
doubly revolting and intolerable. Then his poor wife, his sole, his beautiful, his
spotless Irene, to be exposed to the despotic tyranny, and, still worse, / the
brutal lusts of the conqueror, – when he thought of this, he tore his hair, and
threw himself on the earth, his flesh quivered, his limbs were convulsed, and he
felt all the agonies of the last despair.

Colocotroni came forth from this undescribable trial and anguish. He was in
urgent need of tranquillity and repose, to soothe his soul to peace. Instead of
this, he was called upon to sell his lands, to collect the wreck of his property, to
pack up and drive away all that could be removed, to take leave for ever of his
pleasant and long-endeared abode, and to set out on a weary pilgrimage
through the deserts and wilderness of an unknown world. And for all this he
had the allowance of one little month. A thousand times he sunk under his task,

---

[a] King of Sparta from 490?–480 BC who died along with his 300 Spartans while heroically
defending the pass of Thermopylae against the Persian army of King Xerxes.

[b] Arcadia, a department of Greece in the central Peloponnese which classical and renaissance
bucolic poetry represented (sometimes calling it Arcady) as an idealized rural setting; Pylos, a port
in the SW Peloponnese, scene of a defeat of the Spartans by the Athenians (425 BC) during the
Peloponnesian War, and of the Battle of Navarino (1827) during the War of Greek Independence.

and threw up his labour in despair. How much better, he thought, it was, to deposit his aged bones at once under the turf of his beloved Laconia! / But then the recollection of his Irene and her mother flashed upon his mind; and he felt that he had more than mortal strength, and could undergo unheard-of labours, that so he might place these beloved pledges in a land possessed by Christians, and where, with all his prejudices, he could not but acknowledge they would be protected by the laws of a civilised community. At length, with the assistance of Adrasti and a few other attached friends, every thing was prepared, and they set out.

Their journey was by land. They passed by Salona and Yanina and Elbasson and Scutari; they traversed the Arnauts and Monte Negro.[a] Every where their way lay through savage tribes, and a people that lived by pillage. But proper precautions had been taken; and they were protected by the rescript[b] of the Turkish governor of the Morea. Again and again their quarters had been approached; and the alarm / had been given by the wild and almost lawless Albanians. At length however, wearied and almost destroyed by the anxieties and inconveniences of their march, they reached the banks of the Unna. They could no more; and Colocotroni gladly took up his rest in the first Christian district, protected by the banner of the emperor king of Hungary, on which he had placed the sole of his foot.

War had by this time been declared by the Austrians against the Turks; and the subsequent successes of prince Eugene at Peterwaradin and Belgrade seemed to render the north-western bank of the Unna as safe from the inroads of the Turks, as Paris or London would have been. It proved otherwise. Colocotroni had just fixed himself in a quiet and simple abode not far from this beautiful stream, and had begun to reconcile himself to his exile, when Hassan, the bashaw of Bosnia, and the / fifteen thousand horse which had escaped from the battle of Belgrade, suddenly burst forth upon the defenceless and unapprehensive inhabitants of Croatia. They desolated every field, and set fire to every village.

To render the mischief more terrible, as far as related to our unhappy exiles, Bozzari was among them. He was an officer in one of the brigades of Turkish cavalry, which had broken away from the battle of Belgrade to fall upon the Hungarian Croats. Soon after his arrival, he accidently met with the intelligence, that Colocotroni, the man against whom he entertained so many feelings of alienation and rage, was in his immediate vicinity. He remembered that Colocotroni had refused him the hand of his daughter; he remembered that he

---

[a] Salona, town in west central Greece; Ioánnia, city in NW Greece; Elbasan, in central Albania; Scutari, Italian name for Shkodër, a market town on Lake Shkodër in NW Albania; the Arnauts, unidentified but possibly another name for the Picssiov Mountains lying between Montenegro and Hercegovina; Montenegro, province bordering the Adriatic Sea.

[b] Official announcement or edict.

had himself sought the life of Colocotroni; and he remembered that the vigorous defence made by the man he accused, had caused him to be / driven with scorn from the presence of the Turkish governor of the Morea. He knew that the lawless condition of all that now surrounded him, afforded himself every facility for perpetrating whatever revenge and lust might prompt him to execute.

He had hastened on the wings of all the baser passions to the dwelling of Colocotroni. He had found it deserted and tenantless. He eagerly seized the gratification of setting it on fire; and, as he saw the flames ascend, he thought he felt his heart lightened of his part of its burthen. Stimulated by the savage feelings that fermented in his bosom, he obtained a clue that led him to the hiding-place of the virtuous and unhappy Greek. He thrust his spear into his heart. Irene happened at that moment to be absent. He turned his head, and saw the beautiful Greek, who had withdrawn herself for a short time to see whether by any means relief might / be obtained for her parents, and was now returning from her brief excursion.

What an instant was this for the wretched Irene! She saw her father in the agonies of death. She saw Bozzari, the man on earth she had most cause to fear and to abhor, standing over him armed, his spear yet dripping with blood. There was nothing doubtful in the scene and the attitude. She would have given worlds to have been able to succour her father, to try if it were yet possible to save his life. But, the moment the figure of Bozzari presented itself to her sight, nature itself wrought within her; she felt an instinctive horror; and, though he was within the cave, and she only approaching, her imagination represented to her herself within his hold, and his hand, smeared and red with the blood of her father, already grasping her arm. She fled with the rapidity of lightning. Bozzari at the same moment caught a glimpse / of her person, dropped his weapon, and pursued. He had not proceeded far, when he saw our party, twenty or thirty imperialists, advancing directly in his path; and, turning his horse, he was out of sight in an instant.

As long as the pursuit lasted, Irene was silent, concentrating all her powers in the rapidity of her flight. But she no sooner saw her deliverers advancing to her rescue, than she uttered a piercing shriek, and fell to the ground. Arthur, myself and another, alighted from our horses, and flew to her assistance. From the joint effect of the scene she had witnessed, the evil she feared, and the suddenness of her rescue, she fainted. Never had there existed a situation or more complicated horror. It was with much difficulty, and after many fruitless efforts, that we recovered her. At first she gazed wildly on one of us and another, bereft of recollection and judgment. Her complexion / was white, like that of a corpse. Her features expressed no definite thought or conception. She knew not what, nor where she was. Presently her countenance became con-vulsed with more than mortal agony; she screamed out, My father! and fell again lifeless to the earth.

It was with more difficulty, that she recovered the second time, than the first. She started up, and endeavoured to move her feet, but was unable. Help me, she cried; for God's sake, for pity's sake, assist me!

Which way shall we lead you? said my brother.

It is not far. But to yonder point.

We obeyed, not knowing whither we went. We approached the fatal cave. We saw an old man with his face upward, and a middle-aged woman in a state of insensibility, who appeared to have thrown herself forward upon his corpse. The old man was evidently dead. We removed / the woman, and caused some of our followers to lead her to the air. Irene gazed on the face of the dead man, next took hold of his hand, and then laid her own hand on his heart.

Is he dead? she cried impatiently. Are you sure of it?

We answered in the affirmative.

Exhausted, as she had already been with fatique and horror, and feeling that there was nothing to be done, she sunk insensible into our arms. We dragged her out of the cave. The garments of both the females were stained with the blood of the murdered. Arthur continued with them. I returned into the cave; and, my followers being inured to such offices, I caused them to compose the limbs and features of the deceased, foreseeing that the first impulse of the women, when they had recollected their senses, would be to require that they might see the body of their husband and father. / It happened, as I expected. My brother detained them for a time; be besought them to have courage; he bade them fear nothing, and promised to do every thing for their safety and relief. They listened for a time in desperate grief. Sometimes they uttered the most mournful wailings, or pierced the air with their shrieks. At length I shewed myself, and gave Arthur to understand that we had, as well as we could, restored order to the cave. He yielded to their impatience. His followers, who had till then ranged themselves before the entrance, opened their ranks. Arthur led the way.

Irene, younger and more active than her mother, flew to the couch upon which the body was laid. She gazed for a time in agonised silence, and then exclaimed:

My father! my father! best of parents! most excellent of men! is it possible? shall I never see those eyes again? shall I never hear that / voice? Oh, he was the first of created beings. All that was left of Greece, dwelt in that bosom. He lived but for others. In his youth he led the levies of his countrymen, and drove out the Turks. In his age he was the adviser of all, the friend of all. What treasures of wisdom and learning dwelt in that head; while all the virtues were congregated in that heart! His voice fell upon the ears of mankind, like the music of an angelic host. All that was kind and lovely, combined with the most penetrating sagacity, beamed in his eye. I have sat from morning to night under the instruction of his speech, and never was wearied. He never said to me an unkind word. I lived but in him, and was all his care. And now, oh God, I implore thee, let me die with him!

And can he be thus cut off? cut off by the hands of a villain, who sought to destroy him by false accusations, who drove him into exile, / and whose malice was never satisfied till with his weapon he had pierced his heart. It is too much! Too much of sorrow was heaped on that aged head. But lately he was compelled to seek refuge in a strange land. Thither he was pursued by infuriated savages, his property laid waste, his house burned to the ground. And now, the most abandoned of men, the author of all his adversities, has found, and has murdered him. God of heaven, hast thou seen, and dost thou suffer all this? /

CHAPTER XIII

My brother devoted himself at once to the women, and begged me to supply his place with the troop. It is difficult to conceive a case more distressing, than that of this mother and daughter. They had had in Colocotroni a protector, in whom they confided for every thing. But a few days before that in which we found them thus desolate, they had had a convenient abode; they had had servants. All was now gone. Their dwelling was burned to the ground; / their property consumed; their servants dispersed no one knew whither. They were alone, surrounded with military bands, not a face among them that they had ever seen before. Arthur supplied every thing to them. He led them to a neighbouring village, and provided them with a decent apartment. No enemy was now to be found in the Austrian province. By dint of enquiry my brother traced two of their servants, a male and a female, and thus gave them attendants to whose assistance they were accustomed. Their means were irretrievably dissipated; but Arthur took care that they should feel no want.

The campaign was now concluded. Eugene had dispersed his forces into winter-quarters: Hassan was satisfied with having raised the siege of Zvornich, and delivered his province of Bosnia from the annoyance of an enemy. Our troops were drawn off to their winter-quarters / in Hungary. A carriage was provided for Irene and her mother; and they proceeded in the rear of the detachment.

My brother had a confidential servant, by name Cloudesley. The character of this man was sufficiently extraordinary, to make it proper for me to mention the history of his early years. Arthur had met with him in a visit he paid in England to the then earl Danvers, the head of the elder branch of our family. He had set up, when young, in a small way of trade at Hull in Yorkshire, being at no great distance from the seat of the Danverses. He was the son of one of lord Danvers's tenants. At his outset he was distinguished for sobriety, integrity,

and the most indefatigable attention to business. His character was unblemished. Her had great frankness of disposition, and was exceedingly remarked for his good-nature, and invariable kindness and tenderness of heart.
In Hull, at / his hours of relaxation in an evening, he got acquainted with a man
somewhat older than himself, of great shrewdness of understanding, adventurous, bold, and intent upon making a fortune. He appeared to consider the
acquaintance of young Cloudesley as of some importance to him. He had a
sister, upon whom the beginning tradesman cast an eye of affection; and
Norton, that was the name of the adventurer, encouraged the attachment.
Norton was always engaged in speculations, which, if successful, promised to
lead on to fortune, but which, not seldom, were attended with considerable
risk. In one instance, he proposed to Cloudesley to become his security for a
sum which to the sober tradesman was very considerable, two hundred
pounds. The latter hesitated; but the specious representations of Norton, his
own exceeding good-nature, and the affection he entertained for Norton's
sister, overcame his / scruples. Norton's speculations miscarried; and Cloudesley
was ruined. Norton absconded; and the severe creditor to whom Cloudesley had
given security, threw the young man into jail.

Arthur had known something of Cloudesley in his visits to England. Arthur
was fond of rural sports; and Cloudesley, as the son of one of the nearest
tenants, had frequently been of use to him in scenes of this nature. There was a
propriety, a good sense, and a sagacity in the rustic, which had strongly
prepossessed my brother in his favour. In a subsequent excursion he had
missed his favourite ally, had enquired for him, and heard all his misfortunes.
The intelligence had so strong an effect upon Arthur, that he could not rest;
and he prevailed upon his cousin, the English earl, to concur with him in
rescuing the young man from a state of unmerited calamity.

Cloudesley came out of prison a totally altered / man. He had before been
friendly and confiding. Conscious of no ill in his own bosom, he had suspected
none in others. He was never asked for an act of charity, that he did not feel
prompted to perform. He never saw a scene of distress, that he did not wish to
relieve. He was a person of great sagacity: otherwise the goodness of his heart
would have induced him to credit tales the most monstrous. And, as it was, he
had often been deluded by figments, that even a child, with a spice of the devil
in him, would have rejected.

But, in proportion to the original integrity of his nature, was the bitterness of
his soul, when he became so flagrantly the victim of unmerited calamity. As,
before, he had loved all men, so it seemed now that it was sufficient to present
any thing in human shape, to excite his antipathy. Before, the whole world was
illuminated to him with sunshine, and decorated with the / most brilliant
colours of the rainbow; now all was dinginess, darkness and eclipse. He saw on
all sides a disposition to cheat, to overreach, and to oppress. He saw all men
armed against all men, restrained by no principles of justice, or feelings of

humanity, but merely by the law of the land, and a fear of the ill construction that might be put upon their actions. He that could sin in secret, and reap the advantage, would infallibly be guilty. He had lived for months in a jail; and here, as it appeared to him, he had first seen the true character of his species. He had studied it with the earnestness of the discoverer of an unknown country. He discarded all the antiquated prejudices of his youth, and formed to himself a new code, suitable to the sort of creatures with whom he was henceforth to associate.

The history of this man affords a striking example of the disadvantages arising from a / defective and neglected education. Recollecting the excellent qualities with which he had been originally endowed, we may safely pronounce that, if his mind had been unfolded in the climate of even a slight degree of literature, the treachery of a friend, or even a six months' initiation in the mysteries of a jail, could not in so great a degree have changed his principles, and made him consider the species whom he had hitherto regarded as his brothers, as worthy only of his hatred, and engaged in a general conspiracy against him. But, accurately speaking, he had never had principles: his good impulses were merely the creatures of feeling, and arose from his ascribing to others the uncorrupt sentiments he found in his own breast; and, when experience, as he construed it, had shewn him his mistake, he no longer found any thing within him to control his misanthropy. He and his fellow-creatures, as he judged, were in a / state of war; and the laws of war, not the laws of peace and benevolence, were to be henceforth the regulators of his conduct.

When Arthur had taken him out of prison, and set him even with the world, it struck him that he had done little for Cloudesley, if he did not proceed to launch him in a different sphere, and enable him to engage in a course of life, which, if it were not his own fault, might be productive of tranquillity and content. Cloudesley, such as my brother had known him, was not placed above other men, except by the goodness of his heart, and the soundness of his judgment in the common affairs of life. The education that had been bestowed upon him, was ordinary and narrow. The slender capital with which he had set out in the world, was now gone. Arthur therefore thought he was doing him sufficient justice, in offering to take him for his personal and confidential servant. / We had already formed the plan of embarking in the wars of Hungary. And Cloudesley, who had small reason to be pleased with his first voyage on the ocean of life, received with pleasure the suggestion of proceeding in his next, to untried scenes and 'pastures new.'[a]

From this epoch there was a perpetual struggle in Cloudesley's mind, between what I may call the old man and the new. The rules of conduct which he had framed to himself during his residence in the castle at Hull, were of an

---

[a] John Milton, *Lycidas* (1638), l. 193.

anti-social cast. He had formed the resolution that he would fight his own way in the world, regardless of the wishes, the prejudices, the joys, and the sorrows of others. Nay, in his gloomiest moods, he anticipated a gratification from avenging on his future associates the injustice he had suffered from those that had gone before. This was the new man.

But the better propensities of his early years, / in spite of himself, would be perpetually pressing into action. He was a knave by principle. But he was often much better, from the remains of what was honest and more truly human within him. He could not help being grateful for what Arthur had done to make him a man again. My brother's qualities were such as won the regard of his fellow creatures in proportion as they were more intimately acquainted with him. Cloudesley admired him in a superlative degree. Arthur treated him with invariable kindness, humanity and consideration. Cloudesley would at any time have laid down his life for Alton. – It is also right to mention, that Cloudesley's early habits were always uppermost. The creed he had learned, was concealed in his own breast. It lay there like a hidden treasure; or rather, like an oracle, which he was accustomed to resort to and consult, when the eyes of all other mortals were closed in sleep. / In the day-time, he was apparently the same mild, agreeable, friendly creature he had ever been. His physiognomy had contracted the peculiarities of his better years. His voice had still the same prepossessing character. He appeared the most simple-hearted and guileless creature in the world. Without perhaps exactly designing it, he had realised to a considerable degree the poet's suggestion: 'Look like the innocent flower; but be the serpent under it.'[a] – Such was the man to whose special protection my brother now consigned Irene and her mother.

The bier which contained the remains of Colocotroni, was inclosed in the midst of our troop, partly that they might not for ever impress his survivors with melancholy; and we desposited them, as we passed, with military honours in the church of Novigrad.[b]

The situation of these ladies was singularly / forlorn; and, conscious of this, and moved with the truest sentiments of pity and sympathy, Arthur did every thing in his power to alleviate their distress. He rode up to their carriage repeatedly during the route, to see that they were safe, and to enquire if there was any thing necessary or agreeable to them that it might be in his power to supply. Wherever the detachment halted, he was attentive to their accommodation in the minutest particular. At first, they begged that they might dispense with his personal attendance, partly as apprehending that it must be a burthen to one whose professional duties demanded his incessant attention, and partly because, overwhelmed as they were with the mighty loss they had sustained, they felt whatever called upon them for the observances of society, as unacceptable and

---

[a] *Macbeth*, I. v. 66–7.
[b] Novigrad Dalmatinski, village in western Croatia on the Dalmatian coast.

distressing. Arthur was at first therefore brief in his visits, referring them to the attendance of / their ordinary servants, and to the mechanical and unobtrusive interference of Cloudesley. His kindness however by degrees won upon their partiality. There was something so unaffected in all he did, so fully in accord with the truest sympathy, that, when he was mute, they were in no way embarrassed with his presence, and when he spoke, silence

> Was took ere she was ware, and wished she might
> Deny her nature, and be never more,
> Still to be so displaced.[a]

On the other hand, so far as Arthur was concerned, he felt himself transported into a scene to which he had been hitherto a stranger. He was not unacquainted with the fascinations of a court, and his humane and kindly dispositions had in multiplied instances made him familiar with scenes of distress. But he was persuaded that he had never beheld any thing so fascinating as the countenance, the manners, / and every gesture of this beautiful Grecian girl – every tear she dropped was in his eyes a gem of unrivalled lustre, and the plaintive tones of her grief might have subdued the hardest hearts, and breathed a soul into rocks and stones. /

CHAPTER XIV

We arrived at Vienna, where it was proposed we should take up our winter-residence, in expectation of another campaign to commence in the spring of 1718. We had no succeeding campaign. The war was substantially at an end. The scenes we had anticipated never occurred. But on the other hand how great a variety of events, which we had never in slightest degree foreseen, did we encounter! / The next eighteen months constituted the most critical and momentous period of my life.

The first care of my brother on our arrival was to provide a suitable retreat for the widow and daughter of Colocotroni. He fixed on a romantic spot, about eight miles south of the metropolis, and nearly in the road to Italy, called the Briel. This is a narrow defile, bounded by high rocks on each side, and with a mountain-stream at the bottom, which is skirted by a foot-path on one side, and a road on the other, along the banks of the stream. The rocks are every

---

[a] John Milton, *A Masque presented at Ludlow Castle, 1634* (1637), or *Comus,* ll. 557–9.

where interspersed with shrubs, dwarf-firs, and patches of green sward;[a] and the scene is not altogether unlike the walk at the foot of the rocks along the banks of the Avon, beyond the Hot Wells at Bristol.[b] After you have proceeded about a mile, the rocks disappear, and you find yourself in a broad valley of rich pasturage, with grassy hills on the right, / and steep woody mountains on the left. The valley, as it proceeds, winds deeper and deeper into the mountains, and the scenery becomes every moment more magnificent and romantic, discovering, when you ascend the acclivities, a prospect of Vienna, and the immeasurable plains stretching to Moravia beyond, the whole being bounded, to the south-east by the Carpathian ridge, and to the south and the south-west by the mountains of Hungary. In this valley lie scattered various dwelling-houses of the farmers and others; and in one of the most remote and sequestered nooks stood the cottage, which Arthur destined as a residence for the Greek ladies whom he had taken under his protection.

It presently became apparent that the health of the mother was in the most precarious state. Her constitution, naturally delicate, suffered a severe shock, first from the sentence of banishment which had been awarded against them, / and next from the dreadful scene that had recently occurred in Croatia, where the whole country, houses, granaries, and the fields themselves, had been consumed with flames. The death of Colocotroni, murdered almost in her arms by the inhuman Bozzari, filled up the measure of her sufferings. From this moment she scarcely lifted up her head. She spoke not; she slept not; and, when she arrived at the close of her journey, she was more dead than alive. Her daughter had had to sustain her, and to watch over every thing that could afford her relief, during the entire route. At first, repose, and the beautiful scenery with which she was surrounded, seemed somewhat to revive her: but this was only like a lightning before death. In a few days, the balmy air, the refreshing fields, the foliage, the mountains, and the streams appeared to lose their effect. She sunk into a quiet, but rapid decline. She / scarcely tasted of nourishment; and the powers of digestion were altogether suspended in her frame. Her greatest exertions, immediately after her arrival at the Briel, were to proceed to the door of the cottage, to partake of the cheerful light of the day, and the balmy air; and, once or twice, to reach a seat in the garden, from whence the view was at once rich in the fore-ground, and romantic in the distance. But she became every day weaker. She was confined to her bed; and in a few weeks, the powers of nature being altogether exhausted in her, she sunk away, and, without a struggle or a groan, calmly expired. Her remains were deposited in the cemetery of the parochial church of Meidling, in which parish the cottage of the Briel was situated.

Thus was the young, and not long before blooming Irene, left in a situation

---

[a] Turf or grass.
[b] Wells producing naturally-heated water from hot springs.

singularly desolate. She had lost father, mother and / country, and was robbed of the last remains of that opulence which had belonged to her ancestors for centuries. The goods of fortune however occupied no part of her attention. She thought only of her parents, and principally of Colocotroni, the learned, the refined, the accomplished, the true patriot, the friend of man, the individual from whom she had derived every thing – not merely life – that, considered by itself, was a gift of small price – but all that she knew, her tastes, her sentiments, her virtues, her elevated tone of thinking, all that made her a model of whatever was to be admired and esteemed in woman. Colocotroni was, to the thoughts of his daughter, all the world. She had never known any thing in human form that could enter into competition with him; and, now that he was gone, the whole world appeared to her one unvaried blank. Then she recollected in addition to / this, that she was torn from her country. She saw no face, her two domestics excepted, that she had ever seen in her past life. Fatherless, an orphan, she was cast upon tribes and nations, with whom she had no fellowship. She was one solitary and unconnected individual, among an immense crowd of beings, whose thoughts, whose pursuits, whose customs, and whose language were wholly strangers to her. What was there left to her, that was worth the living for? What was there, for the sake of which the burthen of existence could be endured? It seemed in the eyes of Irene a sort of profanation, that she should dream of outliving the existence of Colocotroni, that she should entertain the idea of joining in the commerce and the interests of another race of men, wholly different from and inferior to those among whom she was born. It was as if one, by descent a princess, should suddenly be made a / slave, and should be so desenterated[a] of spirit, as to become a companion for slaves, to join in their amusements, to enter into their squabbles, and having once had 'a kingdom for a stage, sovereigns to act, and monarchs to behold the swelling scene,' should now quarrel for sugar-plums and nuts.[b] No: there was nothing that Irene so earnestly desired, and impatiently longed for, as to die, and go to her father.

The despondency and indifference with which she regarded every thing around her, rapidly increased. She would sit alone in her apartment, and appear to be talking to Colocotroni. If any one intruded on her when she was thus occupied, she manifested great displeasure. At some times indeed she seemed wholly abstracted. She was engrossed with what stood before her mind; and whatever of reality passed under her eye, whatever speeches were addressed to her, she shewed like a person that was deaf and / blind. If however she was roused by something that it was impossible to resist, she became fretful and indignant. And it appeared as if a greater degree of injury was done to her animal constitution and the frame of her spirit by such interruptions, than could have resulted from the allowing her diseased imagination to take its course.

---

[a] Deprived.
[b] cf. *Henry V*, Prologue, ll. 3–4 (adapted).

She sometimes strolled beyond the precincts of her little dwelling, and wandered among the rocks which shut in the defile of the Briel. This was usually in the dead of the night. Once and again, when she returned, or was brought back by the vigilance of her attendants from these roamings, she dropped words which intimated that, in the depths of the cliffs, she had seen Colocotroni. He had looked out from a fissure of the rock with a wan and deathlike countenance, and had by his gestures invited her to join him, or chidden her delay. /

During this period my bother was her only visitor. At first she took no notice of him, and seemed absorbed in her sorrows. it was something that was gained, so long as she endured his visits, and did not protest against them as a molestation, or refuse to admit them. It was impossible, that so fine a young man, so eminent in his endowments, should persist in shewing himself daily solicitous for her consolation and relief, and that this should not awaken in her some degree of admiration and gratitude.

His first visits were silent. He spoke to Cloudesley, and to the attendants of Irene, but did not attempt to interrupt the sacredness of her sorrow. By degrees he addressed her. He took her hand, and led her forth from the cottage. He seated her on a bench, and placed himself near to her, but unseen. He advanced nearer, and seated himself. He told her of his exceeding desire to serve her. He dwelt with / fervour on the merits of Colocotroni. He had heard of his eloquent defence before the bashaw of the Morea. He had read certain papers drawn up by this admirable man, which testified alike his taste and his virtue. He lamented that it had not been his own good fortune, to have improved his mind under the instructions of Colocotroni.

Irene was gratified to her very heart, to hear the praises of her father from the lips of a stranger. She was astonished to find my brother so fully informed on these topics. They shed tears together to his memory.

It was apparent that Irene was silently wasting away under the afflictions that had befallen her. Her aberrations of mind, when she left her midnight-bed, and when amidst the mountains she held imaginary communion with the ghost of Colocotroni, acted like a worm that unseen consumed within her the very springs of / life. But, when she met with sympathy, when she saw a person beside her, who seemed to give words and articulate voice to all she had felt in the secrecy of her grief, this produced a favourable revolution in her case.

The visits of my brother were for some time unmingled with any retrospect to himself. They were dictated merely by compassion for the unhappy situation of Irene, mingled with admiration of the qualities of her mind. It was not likely that his thoughts should go further than this. He had not yet listened to the idea of settling himself in the way of marriage. When he did, it was to be supposed, as a native of the British isles, that he would look among the high-born damsels of the English court for a suitable consort. His accomplishments were such as were likely to secure him against being refused in any quarter in which he might think proper to apply. He had not only a plentiful / estate in Ireland, but was in no distant prospect to succeed to the title of earl Danvers, and a still larger property, in England. He was not destitute of the anticipation and the wish, so usual among prosperous men, of leaving a still more splendid succession to his children and his children's children.

But this adventure in Croatia eventually operated to interrupt all these ambitious projects. There are no two passions that are more insensible in the gradation by which they melt the one into the other, than pity and love. "Twas but a kindred sound to move.'[a] Beauty never appears so beautiful, as when it is under the dominion of sorrow. Beauty, in its hour of exultation and pride, has a tendency to arm the spectator against its inroad and usurpation. We feel the impulse to resist aroused within us, and resolve to shew, while it comes on fifty-thousand strong, that we will not be made the / dust under its feel. But beauty in sorrow is the adversary that has thrown down its arms, and no longer defies us to conquer its prowess. It is the weak and tender flower, illustrious in its lowliness, that asks for a friendly hand to raise its drooping head. The colour had faded in Irene's cheek; but the paleness that succeeded was only the more interesting. Her dark eyes did not flash with Grecian fire; but they were melting, the twin-born messengers of sympathy. You saw that sleep had fled from her pillow. But the languor that followed, was more powerful and resistless than the bloom of health. Her face was stained with tears; and what heart, young, generous and affectionate like my brother's, was not impelled to fly to succour and relieve her?

When Arthur talked of the virtues and high qualities of Colocotroni, it was impossible that Irene should not take her share in the discourse, / bring forward endowments of which my brother had scarcely been aware, and supply incidents and illustrations which were stored in her memory, more than in that of any one that lived. She was taken before she was aware, and compelled to speak at a time when the faculty of speech seemed to have abandoned her. She was raised as from death to life. Her eyes, which had before been constantly declined, were now occasionally lifted up, as she spoke of some illustrious deed which had distinguished the career of her father. A blush of generous pride would suffuse her cheek, when she suddenly called to mind and related the noble achievements, which had rendered him the idol of his contemporaries and countrymen. But the part of Irene in these conversations was not all elevation and joy. When she eulogised this memorable Greek, he appeared sometimes to stand out to her mind in all the vigour of manhood, / or all the venerableness of experienced wisdom. The moment before she repeated some of his acute and well considered remarks, she seemed to herself to hear them, enriched with the tones of his well-known voice. But then it suddenly recurred

---

[a] Dryden, 'Alexander's Feast' (1697), l. 95.

to her, that the tongue was now for ever silent, and that voice sunk in the oblivion of the tomb, and her whole frame became convulsed with unutterable anguish.

The fair Greek was cast pennyless and portionless upon the wide theatre of the world. It was some sacrifice for the pride and ambition of my brother, to think of marrying an alien and an exile, without possessions or connections in any part of the globe: and he had not been without an internal struggle on the subject. The public however, and the fashionable part of the public, do not refuse to make allowances for high birth and noble blood, though denied the advantages of wealth, especially if the person / so highly born is first introduced to them, already raised from the destitution into which she had fallen, by a partner, who had had the generosity to discover her excellencies in the midst of her unfortunate destitution. Irene also had accomplishments that would have adorned a throne; and her beauty was such as all eyes admired, and all hearts bowed down to. In reality however Arthur made no sacrifice. Irene had already made him her conquest, before he thought of, and before he had time to ask himself the question I have spoken of.

While we continued at Vienna, my brother received a commission from the court of London, empowering him to enter into communication with the imperial cabinet respecting the provisions of a treaty, since known by the name of the Quadruple Alliance.[a] We had been presented to king George the First previously to our embarking for the continent, my brother / on his accession to the title, the presenter being Robert earl Danvers our kinsman:[b] and Arthur was at that time much taken notice of at court for the nobleness of his air, and the pregnancy of his replies. The Quadruple Alliance was the favourite project of lord Stanhope, at that time secretary of state; and he, who had more than once invited lord Alton to his table at London, now selected him as peculiarly well qualified to smooth certain difficulties which were presented by the emperor's ministers to the completion of the treaty. This affair detained us in Vienna considerably longer than we should otherwise have remained in that city.

Where the intercourse between two young persons of different sexes is so frequent as was that of my brother and Irene, love, the audacious intruder, is apt to come in, before any one has had notice of his approach. The fair Greek, having now been roused from the death-like / silence of despair, and in some degree restored to the offices of existence, could not but observe the graces and elegance of lord Alton, and could not but be gratified by the attentions of a

---

[a] The Quadruple Alliance 1718–19 developed out of the Triple Alliance, in which England, France and Holland joined together against Spain, whose king, Philip V, had aspired to regain Spain's former possessions in Italy and the Mediterranean and also to succeed to the French throne. After a Spanish expeditionary army attacked the Austrian forces in Sardinia and Sicily, Austria joined the anti-Spanish coalition, thus converting it into the Quadruple Alliance.

[b] James Stanhope, first Earl Stanhope (1673–1721), eminent soldier and statesman.

person of such acknowledged distinction. When the topics which related to the memory of Colocotroni were somewhat exhausted, these young persons necessarily reverted to other themes. Irene was no longer dead to the beauties of nature, though she shrank from the thought of scenes of promiscuous intercourse, and from public places. As the spring advanced therefore, my brother prevailed on her to suffer him to accompany her in visits to spots the most worthy of her observation in the beautiful environs of Vienna. She felt that she had no pleasure but in the society of Alton. And he on the other hand, whenever he could escape from the duties which his own government now imposed upon him, was sure to fly to the presence of / Irene. Speaking now only at intervals of the virtues of Colocotroni, topics of general literature would sometimes intrude themselves. They spoke of poetry and the arts. Irene descanted with enthusiasm upon the remains of Phidias and of the ancient Grecian architecture.[a] She was perfectly conversant with the rhapsodies of Homer, and would point out beautiful passages, that Arthur till then had too cursorily considered.[b] The verses of the prince of poets, when articulated by the lips of beauty, and with that exquisite taste and that depth of feeling which Irene so powerfully possessed, had charms and an ascendancy over the soul, that was irresistible. It was like the power of music, that drank up the spirits. It was the harp of Orpheus.[c] On the other hand, Arthur had a much more extensive acquaintance with the Italian poets than Irene. And he endeavoured to repay her with passages from the bards of Ferara / and Vaucluse for the divine inspirations of Homer.[d]

Arthur particularly admired the story of Bireno and Olimpia in the Orlando Furioso.[e] At first sight this tale might seem little appropriate to his suit to Irene. But the effect of contrast is often not less powerful than that of resemblance. Bireno arrived a stranger and an adventurer in the land where he first beheld the forlorn and orphan Olimpia. Bireno, after many perils and hard fortunes, proposed to carry Olimpia by sea into a country in which they might both be settled in everlasting content. But, proving himself the falsest and most worthless of his sex, he, instead of conducting his mistress in safety to the place of their destination, touched at the shore of a desert island, and there, while she slept in confidence and security, left her alone to be devoured by wild beasts, or to fall into the hands of savage freebooters more to be feared than they. /

While Arthur recited to Irene the particulars of this tragic tale, it could not

---

[a] Phidias (5th century BC), famed Greek sculptor.

[b] Homer (1050–850 BC), Greek epic poet to whom are attributed the *Iliad* and the *Odyssey*.

[c] In Greek mythology Orpheus was said to be so skilful a player on the lyre that he could move trees and rocks by his music.

[d] Ludovico Ariosto (1474–1535), Italian poet, who wrote, lived and was buried at Ferrara, N. Italy; Francesco Petrarch (1304–74), Italian lyric poet and scholar who lived at his country house in Vaucluse in SE France until 1353.

[e] Told in Ariosto, *Orlando Furioso*, IX. 22–X. 32.

but occur to both, that my brother, like Bireno, had arrived a stranger and an adventurer in the land in which he first saw the fair Greek. Irene, like Olimpia, had been bereaved by cruel fate of her parents, of all she loved and all she possessed. Arthur would also, no doubt, if his suit were accepted, propose to carry away his mistress into a far country, that they might settle there in tranquillity and happiness.

But here the parallel ended. Bireno was false-hearted and treacherous, the most deceitful of mankind. Alton carried in his face the full exposition of the nobleness of his nature. Never did falshood harbour under so glorious an outside. No one could look at him, and not be conscious of his virtue. That voice, that tone, could never be the vehicle of any thing but the sentiments of his heart. All his motions were free and graceful and unrestrained; you / could not find the slightest, the most indifferent impulse, that was not utterly incompatible with an artificial character. There was something in the liquid lustre of his eye, that conveyed I know not what of tenderness and soft humanity. The lines of his countenance were marked with the expression of nature, and varied with every gradation and variety of sentiment. His face was the transparent glass through which you saw all that passed in his soul. There was no knot in the surface, nothing that interrupted the view, or for a moment clouded the apprehension of the person with whom he communicated. There was an impetuosity in his manner totally incompatible with duplicity and trick; and yet that impetuosity was attuned to the gentlest nature that ever inhabited a human bosom. The purity of his soul might indeed be called his ruling principle. It is not my interest to speak thus of my brother; I would suppress it, if I / could; but the irresistibleness of truth constrains me. The consequence of all this was, that the tale of Bireno served but the more to bring out to view the excellencies of Alton. That he should deceive, that he should act in a manner unworthy of the trust reposed in him, was of all things in nature the most impossible. Irene felt this, and gave him her heart.

The marriage of lord Alton and the fair Irene was solemnised privately in the English ambassador's chapel at Vienna in the spring of 1718, six months after the death of her mother. The mutual attachment which had grown up between my brother and the lovely mourner, served to reconcile her to life. But her spirits were still tender; the sensitiveness of her nature was greatly increased by the complicated and dreadful evils she had encountered. She shrank from all society; and lord Alton, proud as he was of her beauty and accomplishments, / and, thinking as he did, that justice to her required that he should shew he was proud, made it a law to himself to conform to her inclinations in this article.

My brother had never been so happy, and his spirits so buoyant, as they became through this change of his condition. Though he delighted above all things in the society of his bride, and they were never tired of each other's company, yet the duties of his station required that he should not lead a life altogether sequestered; and Irene was far too considerate to desire that he should sacrifice every other object of existence to her gratifications and her tastes. In conversation with a few intimate friends he would repeatedly boast of the alliance he had contracted, as a league between two nations, and a grand experiment on human happiness. In the lightness of his heart, and the elevation of his spirits, he would good-humouredly observe, / that Greece was the most eminent and highly endowed nation of ancient times, and England of modern; and that the happiest consequences might be executed to result, from thus bringing them together in the compass of one family. It was too much the practice of mankind for different races to sequester themselves in a sort of sullen disunion from each other; but benevolence prescribed, and improvement required, that this supine monotony should be abolished, that the prejudices of different tribes should be brought into collision, and their various accomplishments made to encounter and combine, for the common advantage. If human creatures were thus made without distinction the members of one universal family, the whole species would be raised to an excellence, of which we could now with difficulty conceive an idea.

The affair of the negociation in which lord / Alton had been employed by the court of London was finished in the autumn of the present year; and he once more became in the strictest sense a private individual. By this time however his consort was advanced in her pregnancy; and for that and other reasons he resolved not to set out on his return to the British dominions till the spring. Nothing material occurred, which it is necessary to particularise in their history, till the month of January following. /

CHAPTER XV

But what is the happiness, and what are the prospects of man! This mighty edifice, at the thought of which my brother had felt such elation of heart, and which he had deemed secure against all the storms of life, was swept away in a moment. It was in vain that this accomplished pair found themselves supremely happy in each other; their happiness was destined to be of transient duration.

They had now been united for the greater portion of a year, when the unfortunate event / happened that put an end to their felicity on earth. It was at the time of the carnival, a period of festivity, which begins on the sixth of January, and continues till the beginning of Lent. During this period, assemblies, or ridottos as they are called, take place at the public rooms in Vienna two or three times a week, to which every one is admitted on paying a stipulated sum at the door. The entertainments consist of dancing, a masquerade, refreshments, and supper. The majority of the females who partake of the amusement are masked; but the men are, for the most part, unmasked. On principal days, especially on the last day of the carnival, the emperor and the court attend, and make the promenade of the rooms for a short time. This is early in the evening; and, when the royal family is withdrawn, everyone enters gaily into the pleasures of the place, within the limits of a certain decorum. /

Lord Alton had more than once participated in the amusements of this scene, in company with some volunteers, and the officers who had served in the war against the Turks. It was on the eighteenth of January that he encountered here a certain signor Fabroni, a young Venetian of high rank, and nearly related to some of the first families of his native city. Annexed to the principal saloon at the ridotto, are several smaller rooms with tables for supper, several of these tables being large enough to accommodate fifteen or sixteen persons, and where of consequence it not unfrequently happens that individuals are seated next to each other, having no previous knowledge of each other's names or condition. Fabroni and lord Alton were in this way brought into contact.

The conversation happened to turn upon the late war, which had been terminated by the peace of Passarowitz in the preceding July.[a] / Fabroni, though at this time he happened to be present at the Austrian festival, was full of ill blood and indignation against the measures of the imperial cabinet. Nor was he altogether without reason for this. The primal cause of the war had been the aggression of the Turks in seizing the Morea when hostilities were least apprehended, and expelling the Venetians, who had been in quiet possession of the province for nearly thirty years. The emperor laid hold of this occasion for taking up arms against the aggressor; and yet, when he had won two great battles, and his inroads had been crowned with the most splendid success, he made a peace by which Belgrade and Temeswaer were annexed to his hereditary dominions, but in the articles of which not the smallest attention was paid to the interests of the Venetian republic. From this time forward the Morea has been considered / as an integral part of the dominions of the grand signior.

Fabroni was not destitute of many brilliant qualities. He had a fine figure and an expressive countenance; and the elegance and ease of his manners were such, as upon ordinary occasions conciliated him many friends. But he had all his country's pride and haughtiness of soul. And he was as yet too young, to have learned the useful lesson of making a due allowance to the prejudices and opinions of others. Along with this he was a 'most profane and liberal censurer,'[b] when any thing awakened his displeasure, and by no means scrupulous in the choice of epithets by which to express his dislike. He had too much

------

[a] See note c p. 48.
[b] cf. *Othello*, II. i. 163–4 (adapted).

judgment however to attack the Austrian government in the metropolis of its dominions; and therefore, though this government was the real object of his resentment, he / gave vent to his displeasure by falling foul of the Greeks.

Fabroni and one or two Italians were seated at one of the tables that have been mentioned, when lord Alton and two friends, myself being one, took their places immediately opposite. The topic of conversation with Fabroni was the late war, with the caution I have spoken of, not directly to inveigh against the imperial government. He described the Greeks as a set of the most contemptible wretches that ever disgraced the human form. He lauded in the highest terms the followers of Leonidas and Miltiades in ancient times, and the glorious specimens of intellectual greatness handed down to us from Homer and Plato and Demosthenes, for the sake of placing in an invidious contrast the worthlessness of their present descendants.[a] He asserted, that the minds of these were wholly immersed in commerce and gain, that all their / actions were tricks, and all their words were lies, and that they were the most spiritless, fawning and perfidious race of men that ever deformed the face of the earth. He finished with the common-place maxim, that men who do not effectually assert their own independence deserve to be slaves; and, thank God, the Greeks had now got their deserts, in being again subjected to a worse than Egyptian bondage to the infidel.[b]

Alton interposed, in the mild and ingenuous manner in which he was accustomed to speak, in behalf of this much injured race. He said, it was a mistake to imagine, that the Greeks were not Greeks still, and did not retain many features of their illustrious ancestors. They were ingenious, sharp-witted, and animated with spritely and brilliant thoughts. They had not a particle of dulness about them; and all the dreadful oppression they had suffered / for centuries, had not yet made them slavish in mind, or patient beneath the yoke. It was not just, he added, to compel men to be miserable, and then condemn them for the vices which misery engenders. He gave it as his opinion, that the day would yet come, when the Greeks would redeem their lost honours, and shew themselves worthy of the name which antiquity had consecrated.

He combated the vulgar maxim, that all men who did not energetically vindicate their freedom, deserved to be slaves. A thousand circumstances must concur to enable a race of men to recover the advantages which their fathers had lost. The most eager and generous aspirations after freedom might exist in bosoms, where from many causes it became impossible to give scope to those aspirations. Fate often shuts them in with adamantine bars, which it is impracticable for them to burst. Nor should / we make the mistake to suppose that

---

[a] Miltiades (540?–489? BC), Athenian general, who defeated the Persians at Marathon 490 BC; Plato (427–347 BC), Greek philosopher; Demosthenes (384–322 BC), Athenian statesman, orator, and lifelong opponent of the power of Macedonia over Greece.

[b] Alluding to the Israelites' bondage in Egypt, which, according to Exodus, lasted 430 years.

courage is every thing, or that other treasures of the highest value may not be found in the magazine of mind. A man of constitutional timidity might yet be a most estimable man. It was not a disgrace to us, that we should calculate consequences, and not enter on a perilous action till we had some sort of assurance of success. The men who plunge into danger headlong and without reflection, were not the only men worthy of our commendation and esteem. Courage in public affairs, was like a confident temper in the affairs of private life. The man who comes forward warily and with diffidence, the tongue that hesitates, the cheeks that blush, and the eye that looks but half-assured, are not always harbingers of the least splendid and honourable success. -- While Alton uttered these words, in the secret chambers of his soul he thought of Colocotroni.

Fabroni, who had listened to all this detail / with marks of the greatest impatience, answered as if to the thoughts of his opponent. There was Colocotroni, he said. (He thought of the illustrious Morosini, his kinsman, who, cooperated with by Colocotroni and others, had wrested the Morea from the Turks in 1687.) – There was Colocotroni. He pretended to restore the ancient discipline of the Greeks. He devoted himself to the study of their authors. He boasted to be a patriot upon the purest model. He was impatient of the yoke of the infidel, and called in my countrymen with Morosini at their head. We rescued the Greeks from subjection to the Turk. What then did Colocotroni? He pretended to be dissatisfied with his deliverers. He became of the sect of the whimsicals, whose approbation no government can obtain. He withdrew himself into the obscurity of repining and discontent. And, when, three years ago, the Turk attacked the Morea with a / fleet and an army, he with his countrymen stood aloof, did not move a finger to help us in our hour of trial, and pretended by his actions to say that the dominion of the Venetian republic was no way to be preferred to that of the Scythian barbarians.

But, curse him! he had met with his deserts. The Turk himself would not endure so pernicious and perfidious an inmate, and had driven him, the hoary traitor! out of their dominions. The judgment of God had pursued him in his exile in Croatia. His house had been burned and his property spoiled by the Ottomans, whom he had allowed to resume their tyranny in Greece; and, last of all, his life had become a sacrifice, as he well deserved, to the knife of one of his own countrymen. He would become a beacon and a warning to all future traitors, and his memory would stink to the latest generations. /

In reality it was the virtues and high attainments of Colocotroni, that rendered him the butt of Fabroni's abuse. Colocotroni had done nothing more than the great majority of his countrymen on the occasion of the Turkish invasion: but his illustrious character and his spotless excellence had caused Fabroni to single him out as the individual upon whom to spend all the fury of his bile.

Alton listened with the utmost impatience to this tempest of invective. His soul was on fire. Irene and her father were to his idea amalgamated, were one single object of boundless affection. His love was never so vast and overflowing as at this moment. He had lived with Irene as his spotless wife for now eight months. Every day his attachment grew: every day he had found in her mind and soul some new vein of excellence unexplored before. Her misfortunes had rendered her a thousand times dearer / to him. That she was a solitary slip, torn off from the vast plantation of human kind, and that but for him would have been thrown away neglected among whatever is least the object of man's protection and care, awakened his most sacred sympathies. She had lost her father, her mother, her property, and her country. But for these losses she would have been to him the object of a less intense and uncontrolable love. And whatever touched her father, that glorious image shrined in her inmost soul, he considered as touching her in the most sensitive point, the very core of her existence. Colocotroni was the theme of his most ardent devotion; Colocotroni was the disembodied and etherialized counterpart of his beloved.

Alton sat with the most burning impatience, a witness to the copious invective of Fabroni. Once and again he rose from his seat, unable to retain his posture. Once and again he endeavoured / to interrupt the speaker, and turn him into another course. It was in vain. At length Alton, the mildest and most polished of men, bursting with indignation, struck the Venetian.

The bystanders had in no degree anticipated this excess. Every one, the friends of Fabroni and of Alton, started from his seat. The public rooms at Vienna are within the verge of the palace; and all personal violence committed there is an offence against the emperor. Fabroni was worked up in a moment into inextinguishable rage; and it was with difficulty that the friends of each prevented the violence from proceeding farther. Fabroni and Alton were forced by their partisans to leave the assembly by different doors. /

CHAPTER XVI

In the different governments of the continent a blow, given by one gentleman to another, is an affront that can only be extinguished in blood. The first business however, was to remove Alton to some hiding-place where the myrmidons of the police should not reach him.[a] The government of Austria probably connived at this, unwilling to proceed against a British nobleman, and

---

[a] Myrmidons, a warlike race of people inhabiting Thessaly, who followed Achilles to the siege of Troy; also used in derogatory sense, as here.

who had lately been a minister from the court of London, with extreme severity. / The next business was for the friends of each party to adjust the preliminaries between them. Fabroni was fervent in his demand of expiation; and Alton knew sufficiently the established laws of honour, to feel that the demand could not be controverted. It was settled between the parties, that they must immediately leave the Austrian dominions; and the neighbourhood of Saltzburg in Bavaria was fixed on as the place where the difference was to be decided.

In a case of this sort the rule is that the combatants must fight with swords, and that the duel can no otherwise be terminated than by the death of one of the parties. My brother was overwhelmed with the thought of the terrible predicament in which he stood. He had a presentiment that he should be the victim of the strife. His courage was of the highest order. But there is a great difference between / danger incurred in the tented field, where every thing is conducted on a magnificent scale, where, as in the battles of prince Eugene, a hundred thousand combatants are drawn out on each side, and the whole is accompanied with the clangour of trumpets, with shouts which rend the skies, and all the pomp and circumstance of glorious war; and the narrow encounter of two individuals, brought together in a manner in cool blood, and where the law of the encounter is, that one of them is of necessity to die by the sword of the other. This is unquestionably a sober and a solemn transaction; it is a mournful, almost a funereal meeting, fit to be solemnised and darkened with congregated clouds and blackening skies. Add to which, lord Alton felt an unconquerable impression, that he came there to be the victim, and this was the last day of his life. All that remained for him was, to meet his fate with / constancy, to stand forth undismayed to the last, and to die with the same pure and unblemished honour which had attended him through life. Thus in a moment was the face of all things changed to the most generous of men. In the commencement of this very evening, he had had every prospect before him of a long life of love, of prosperity and happiness. Now, he laid his head on his pillow in a condition parallel to that of the condemned criminal on the morning of his execution, who at one instant stands before us in the undiminished possession of all his energies of body and mind, and the next is seen a powerless and unanimated corpse.

But the ruling idea in the mind of lord Alton was Irene. She had been stripped of all, had been without a friend in the world. Alton had then become every thing to her; she had received him in lieu of father, mother and inheritance, irrecoverably lost. What was to be her / condition, when he was taken away! His feelings were also modified in this crisis by the thought of the fruit of her womb, his unborn child.

Alton went to the Briel, that he might have one parting interview with the idol of his soul. His manner was inevitably sad. He told her, that he was obliged to go to Saltzburg upon unexpected business, but that that business would soon be dispatched. He affectionately exhorted her to be cheerful; occasional separation was one of the laws of human existence. Poor Irene had not the slightest apprehension of the thought at work in the mind of her lord. She asked him, for what reason he appeared so unusually solemn? Alton replied, It was his first separation from her, in whom his very heart was bound up. – He was unaccustomed to practise this concealment, this suppression of what was uppermost in his mind. / It was working in his features, and seemed ready to burst from his lips. He tore himself away.

I accompanied my brother in this fatal expedition. We took with us his valet and my own. Irene was left in the care of Cloudesley. We were thirty-six hours on the road. Fabroni arrived almost at the same hour that we did. We reached the place of our destination, an Austrian village a few miles north of the Saltzburg road, about eight in the evening on the twenty-first of January. We chose this place as being in the confines of Austria, and at the same time affording the opportunity of expeditiously retiring into Bavaria, so that, whatever might be the event of the conflict, we should be exposed to the animadversion of the government of neither country, the act not being committed in Bavaria, and the offender having immediately withdrawn himself out of the territories / of Austria. The seconds fixed on the precise spot for the meeting the next morning; and the encounter was appointed for the hour of noon.

Fabroni and lord Alton were both skilful swordsmen. The spot we had chosen was a little valley between two hills, at some distance to the left of the high road, and apparently remote from observation. The combatants threw off their coats and waistcoats. They were both tall; and each of them in his mode, a pattern from which for a sculptor to copy. They were both serious, collected, quick of eye, agile of limb, and with countenances strikingly expressive of firmness and self-command. There was no delay on either part to proceed to immediate decision. Each appeared to scan and measure the other, as they stood for an instant with their swords unsheathed. Both advanced a few paces. Several passes were made and parried / on each side without effect. At length lord Alton made a desperate thrust at his antagonist, which, but for a sudden turn in Fabroni, would have gone through his body. A slight wound was inflicted, and blood followed. The smart excited in some degree the temper of the Venetian, and the exchange of passes grew quicker and more determined. One thrust of Fabroni finished the contest. It took place; and the sword pierced the body of my brother deeply on the right side. He instantly fell.

The fatal event had scarcely occurred, when a party was seen on the hills, apparently sportsmen, with guns and hounds, led thither by the pursuit of their game. They beheld two persons engaged with drawn swords, and observed one of the combatants fall, as desperately wounded. They immediately made towards the valley in which we were posted. Fabroni and his second, perceiving this, and convinced that we should / want no necessary aid, took to their horses, and made, as had been previously concerted, for the Bavarian border.

Meanwhile the sportsmen approached. The principal person in the groupe was a baron Stahlhoffen, whose seat was at a small distance. One of his companions was a person not unskilled in surgery. He bound up the wound as well as he could; and, a sort of litter being prepared, lord Alton was, by the express order of the baron, conveyed to that nobleman's seat.

It was apparent that my brother had a very short time to live. The effusion of blood had been great on the spot; and, on the way to the mansion of the charitable baron, though every possible care was exerted in the removal, the wound broke out afresh. After a short repose however, lord Alton desired to be left alone with me, and spoke as follows.

My dear Richard, I am dying; and my / death occurs under circumstances which render death bitter. There is no person on earth to whom my life was of so much moment as to the unhappy Irene. She will now be indeed alone. Oh, how faulty, how unpardonable my conduct has been! A Briton, a noble, and a soldier, to have had his passions no more under control! I have paid the forfeit of my violence, and I well deserve it. But why should the most virtuous and excellent of her sex be destroyed by my folly!

I have one consolation. Richard, we are brothers, the sole remains of our father's house. We have always lived together, and lived in harmony. I trust I have never done any thing to merit from you unkindness or resentment. This therefore is my consolation; I leave all that is dear to me in your hands. I have no other friend in this country. Watch over my beloved, I intreat you. Be tender of her, as / the apple of your eye. Think of her as all that remains of your poor Arthur, and exercise towards her in its full extent all a younger brother's love! Think that in her your Arthur still lives!

She is pregnant. I have not strength, nor is it in the least required, that I should remind you of all the vigilance, the care and the love, which this sad situation will demand from you. I rely upon you, even as I should upon my own heart. Farewel, my dear, my ever dear Richard!

Lord Alton was exhausted by the length at which he spoke, and still more by the earnestness, and deep and solemn feeling which accompanied his words. He wrung my hand. In a moment after he sank back in the bed, and fainted. It was a considerable time before he recovered. He lived the remainder of the day, and part of the night. But he spoke little / coherently, after having thus imparted to me his last injunctions. He expired at four o'clock in the morning.

Of all the sorrows with which the death of a human creature ever afflicted me, I know nothing that I ever felt comparable to this. Arthur said to me, 'We have always lived together, and lived in harmony. I trust I have never done any thing to merit from you unkindness or resentment.' But in saying this he did not say a thousandth part of the truth. There never was such a brother. Father, mother, and the persons who were about me in early youth, had done many things that inflicted on me exquisite pain; and Arthur had often been the subject to which these things related. But he, – oh, never, never! The kindest heart that ever existed in a human bosom was his. In all the various relations of existence he was exemplary. In no moment of his life did he forfeit / this praise. The idlest, the most unconsidered of all his actions, did not detract from the most excellent and heroic. A pillar of spotless marble erected over his grave would have been the suitable emblem of his character and his course.

The remains of my brother were transported to England, and for that purpose were embalmed. They were conveyed in the first place to Saltzburg, where every requisite accommodation was to be found to that end.

What a dreadful practice is this of duelling, which seems to be so deeply rooted in the habits of modern Europe! The best and the most generous of our race are more exposed to its tragical consequences, than the ignoble and the base. It is said to be indispensible to the keeping up the courtesies of polished society. In that case those courtesies are bought at a high price. It is held that no man without the deepest disgrace can abstain in certain cases / from the receiving, or even the giving a challenge. What can be more barbarous than that two men should go in cold blood to stand out as a mark, or even to press forward as to a mark against the life of a fellow-creature, for some unintelligible point of imaginary honour! We all confess this; and yet the evil is not remedied! Surely the wit of man ought strenuously and unintermittingly to be applied to find out the cure for so tremendous an evil.

The death of such a man as my brother, in the flower of youth, and for so frivolous an occasion, so generous, so accomplished, so noble and perfect in heart, was a loss to the age in which he lived, and perhaps to all future ages. He was a man that could not have been spared from the general cause and weal of his species. For myself, all that gave me serenity and the sunshine of the soul, was buried in his grave; and from the moment of his death my heart has / never known an instant of peace. Oh, what would I not give that he had not thus perished! – Lord Danvers was for some time to that degree agitated with this thought, as to render him unable to continue his narrative. /

CLOUDESLEY:

A TALE.

BY

THE AUTHOR OF "CALEB WILLIAMS."

IN THREE VOLUMES.

VOL. II.

LONDON:

HENRY COLBURN AND RICHARD BENTLEY,
NEW BURLINGTON STREET.

1830.

CHAPTER I

Lord Danvers proceeded:

Up to this period I deemed all the evil propensities of my puerile years mortified and exterminated from within me. This was the achievement of Arthur, my brother. No mortal perverseness could resist the genial climate of his virtues. He conquered me, and dragged me a willing captive at his chariot-wheels, drawn by the silken chains of love. I had not a wish but what was his. There was nothing I desired / but his gratification, his honour and happiness. Self was annihilated within me.

I now saw the form of him I so truly loved laid forth unanimated and insensible. I was in a new world. The load-star which had guided me in the voyage of life, was blotted from my hemisphere.[a] I had no longer an oracle to consult at every turn in my path of existence. I had no longer a judge to approve or condemn, whose approbation was the end of all I did. A total eclipse had obscured the luminary of my days.

Henceforward I was to shape my own course, and to pass through the various currents and difficulties of life by the guidance of my own judgment and my own will. I was like a flower that folds up its glories at the setting of the sun. I was to live in a more contracted circle and a narrower sphere. I did not disguise this from myself. I said, I will accommodate myself to / this my new mode of existence, and proceed accordingly.

The first thing I thought of was, what there was that was left, now that this dearest object of my affections was gone. Lord Alton had left a widow, his beloved Irene. Irene was pregnant. This was all that was nearest to me.

The salutary influence of the character of lord Alton, which had in a manner new created me, being removed, I in a certain degree fell back into what I had been before that influence was exerted upon me. The old notions I had entertained respecting title, and rank, and opulence revived. I was the second son of a branch of the Irish nobility, and in no distant prospect to an English earldom. Title and rank and opulence resumed their attractions in my mind. I valued them, not as they would be estimated by a philosophical and enlightened judgment, not even as they appear to the gross and undiscerning / thoughts of the majority of men, but with fearful

---

[a] i.e. Lodestar, star (especially the North Star) used in navigation or astronomy as a point of reference.

exaggeration, and a devouring earnestness to grasp what those words represented to my mind.

It was a singular position in which I stood. My brother had died without
issue. My father and mother had left no other progeny but him and myself. I
was obviously prompted to call myself lord Alton. In a certain sense I was so.
How long was this to continue? That was a secret I had no power to discover?
Irene might die, and never be a mother. Her child might be still-born. It might
be a son. It might be a daughter. If it were the latter, I felt that I should cherish
and affect[a] it, beyond all things that lived on the earth.

On this little thread depended all that I was, and was to be, in the mighty
muster-roll of mankind. It was not only an empty title; it was a question of high
station and ample wealth. / Hitherto I had been a younger brother, with a
younger brother's slender provision. If Irene gave birth to a son, I should
become so again.

It may well be supposed that strange thoughts arose in my mind upon such
an occasion. If Irene gave birth to a son, and the mother lived, she would
doubtless be able to assert his rights. If Irene gave birth to a son, and the
mother died, – what then?

I spent two nights and two days in anxious care respecting my brother's
remains. The situation was absolutely new to me. The direction and the
deciding upon every thing devolved on me. Baron Stahlhoffen conducted
himself towards me with the utmost delicacy. He begged that I would use his
house and his servants with entire freedom, just as if they were my own. He had
learned from our servants the rank and title of the dying man whom he had
received under his roof. Some hours after / the decease of my brother, the first
necessary offices having been already performed to his remains, I desired to see
the baron. He came. We met in the antechamber of the apartment in which
lord Alton expired.

I was overwhelmed with grief. The baron repeated his professions of a desire
to serve me, and requested me to inform him in what way he might be useful to
me. I mentioned that it would be by all means my wish that the remains should
be transported to England, to be deposited with our ancestors of the house of
Danvers. A messenger therefore was dispatched to Saltzburg, to procure
proper assistance for that purpose.

I wrote, the first thing, to Cloudesley, informing him of the melancholy close
of our expedition, and enjoining him to use every imaginable precaution, that
no fatal effect might be produced on my sister in her present critical / condition. I sent the letter by my brother's valet, charging him to keep out of sight, to
communicate to no one what he had witnessed, and to place himself entirely
under the direction of Cloudesley. In these cares I consumed two nights and

---

[a] Like, love.

two days. Early on the morning of the third day it was directed, that the remains of my brother should be removed from the seat of baron Stahlhoffen, and set out, with suitable attendants, for Saltzburg.

The night before this removal, was the first time that I was left at leisure to converse with my own thoughts. The previous interval was all a period of action and agitation. I had seated myself in a chair, or thrown myself upon a bed, and caught a few hours of oblivion as I could. At length I seemed to myself to be wholly exhausted, and was desirous of closing the doors, drawing round me the curtains of my bed, and being alone. /

I thought I should now find a period of necessary repose. Oh, how much was I mistaken! This was the first of those miserable nights, which have since been so familiar to me. I had no sooner shut out the world, than all the demons of guilt and guilty contrivance assembled round me. The tempter had already whispered in my ear his pernicious suggestions; but I had turned to some indispensible occupation, and he withdrew. Now, alone, and in midnight solitude, my thoughts were all tumult, confusion and alarm. Plain dealing and all the crookedness of art contended for the empire of my soul.

> The genius, and the mortal instruments,
> Were then in council; and my freighted bosom,
> Like to a little kingdom, suffered
> The nature of an insurrection.[a]

During the whole night I slept not. I could not continue for more than a minute in one / posture. I paced my chamber with perturbed steps. With my clenched fist I struck on my forehead. I said, Oh, integrity, come, dwell within me, and be my guide! What do I not owe to lord Alton! What do I not owe to Irene! and to the offspring, if a son it should happen to be, of their mutual love! I said this: but the innermost whisperings of my soul were of another nature.

I accompanied the remains of my brother to Saltzburg, and saw them deposited in a suitable retreat, till the time should come for their final removal.

The mind of Irene had dwelt with insupressible anxiety on the behaviour of my brother, when he set out on his journey to fulfil the appointment he had made with Fabroni. The sadness of his countenance in parting, incessantly occurred to her. She recollected the mysteriousness of his manner, which had seemed / to intimate that there was something that remained untold. These things had not struck her so much at first; but in the uninterrupted uniformity of solitude they occurred to her with superadded force.

She was left under the protection of Cloudesley; and it was a compact between her and her lord, that during the short period of his own absence and mine, she was to refer every thing to Cloudesley, to address her enquiries to him, and to him to issue all her commands. She anxiously enquired of him

---

[a] *Julius Caesar*, II. i. 66–9 (adapted).

when lord Alton would return. My brother had already mentioned that his absence would not exceed a period of four or five days; and Cloudesley repeated to her the same information. As long as that interval lasted, she sat in silent resignation; she considered the evil as unavoidable, and tasked her resolution to encounter it. It was not the length of the separation that affected / her: this she could have borne with firmness: but it was the sad look and the melancholy carriage of my brother in the act of parting.

On the fourth day and the fifth, she reminded Cloudesley that the period of separation was expiring, and asked him if he had heard any thing. He had not. She made several little preparations for the welcome reception of her lord. This agreeably beguiled her hours. She smiled, and grew doubly assiduous, in the anticipation of his near approach; but it was a wintry smile, and accompanied with strange doubts and misgivings of the soul.

On the evening of the sixth day, two days after that on which lord Alton expired, my brother's valet reached the Briel, bearing the letter which announced the fatal event. In the course of that day the anxiety of my sister greatly augmented. She looked wistfully at / Cloudesley every time he entered the apartment. It was strange, she said. Four days, five days had gone by; this was the sixth. Cloudesley told her that this period of expectation would soon be at an end; we should see my lord, or at any rate hear from him, in a few hours. He exhorted Irene to compose herself; the indulging too much to her apprehensiveness would be painful to his lord, and might be dangerous in her situation. The admonitions of Cloudesley were thrown away; the distress of her mind was uncontrolable.

Every evening Cloudesley mounted his horse, and took the road to Vienna. He anticipated news, and wished to meet it at a distance from his mistress, that he might have time to take his measures accordingly. If lord Alton were victorious in the duel, and it was at the same time attended with a fatal result, Cloudesley knew that it was his purpose to take refuge for / a time in Bavaria.[a] This evening he met lord Alton's valet at a small distance from the Briel. He received my letter, read it, and immediately resolved to proceed to Vienna, and not return till the next day. Cloudesley was overwhelmed with the fatal intelligence. He was passionately attached to his master.

Cloudesley had been in the habit of sleeping every night at the cottage at the Briel; and his absence was a new source of alarm to Irene. He was deeply distressed at the news of lord Alton's death. He had lost the most generous of patrons and of friends. He felt most deeply for the effect this intelligence would produce upon his mistress. He saw himself in a new world. The protector he had so passionately loved was taken from him for ever; and for the colour of his future life he would perhaps be dependent on me.

---

[a] Duels were illegal.

After having passed the night at Vienna, he / arrived the next morning at the Briel. He was unable to form any plan for his conduct; it seemed impossible for him to conceal the event from Irene; all that remained was, to break it to her by degrees and in the gentlest terms. But every plan that he could form, was disconcerted by the impetuosity of his mistress. The moment she heard of his arrival, she ordered him to be called to her.

Well! she said. Cloudesley, where is your master? – She looked in his face, and saw that he had some fearful intelligence to impart.

I see it, I see it all; she exclaimed. Your master, my lord, my husband, all by which I was yet held to earth is, – dead!

Cloudesley was confounded, speechless. He stammered, and was apparently in the greatest distress. Willingly would he have suppressed a part of the fact; willingly would he have qualified whatever was most overwhelming in the / story. There was that in Irene which rendered such a proceeding impossible. She would know all; she would know the worst. Her earnestness was fearful, was irresistible. You might as well have thought of encountering the force of universal nature, when all its elements were in a state of the wildest uproar, when the winds were loudest, and the waves were in convulsion, and like mountains.

The circumstances of the tale were more envenomed and terrible, than the tale itself. A duel! A life, such a life, thrown away upon a point of imaginary honour! The subject of the duel, the character of Greece, and the good name of Colocotroni!

Till Irene was thoroughly mistress of every circumstance, her importunity was unappeasable. Every articulation of her body was in motion, every feature of her face convulsed with agony. She was no sooner assured that she / had nothing further to learn, than all this was reversed. She withdrew to her own room. Her limbs were motionless, her eyes were fixed. Every muscle was rigid; and she was as cold and as white as marble.

Cloudesley saw the urgency of the case, and ventured to follow her. He caused her own female attendant to be called. He informed her in a few words of what had happened, and directed her on no account to leave her mistress for a moment.

Irene remained in a state seemingly stupified, for hours. When she recovered from this, she looked wildly about her; she· clasped her hands, and pressed them to her forehead. She did not shed a tear. It was not till the midnight-bell had tolled, that she could be prevailed on to take a particle of nourishment. Her female attendant, to whom she had been accustomed from her youth, conjured her by the memory / of her father and her husband to support herself. It had been at all times their principle not to sink under inevitable events, to gather together the fragments of the storm, and to consider what yet remained to be done. She would shew herself unworthy of them, if she gave way to despair. This faithful creature reminded her of the fruit of her womb, and that to her was intrusted all that might yet remain to the world of Colocotroni and of Alton.

This thought supported Irene, and she determined to live. When I arrived at Vienna, she was in a state of the deepest dejection; she seemed as if she had received a mortal blow; but her fortitude was still apparent. Great apprehension however was entertained of the approaching crisis.

I saw her; and the sight of me produced upon her a very striking effect. Till now, the fact that her beloved lord was no more, was represented to her by words only. But, when I / entered the apartment in which she had shut herself up, the truth seemed for the first time to be set palpably before her senses. She uttered a piercing shriek, and presently sunk into an alarming syncope,[a] from which she was brought back with great difficulty, and after a considerable lapse of time. It seemed to my guilty conscience, that she had seen into the secrets of my soul, and that the sight had withered her. I fled from her presence, and left her to the care of her attendants.

My journey from Saltzburg to Vienna was a memorable period in my life. I saw none of the objects that presented themselves on the road; whether I went forward or stopped, whether I were waking or asleep, to me all was the same. What passed before my bodily sense was nothing; my mind was occupied only in its own imaginings. Function

> Was smothered in surmise; and nothing was,
> But what was not.[b] /

I called up all the images of my boyish years. I recollected the slights and contempt which had been put upon me by my parents; how my brother had been their idol, while I seemed only to stand in the way, to be a being that had intruded himself into a world where he was not wanted. I recollected the senseless and pernicious speeches of the servants: 'Ah, master Richard, what a fine thing it is to be the eldest! Your brother will have the whole estate; he will be called My lord; the house here in county Cork, and the house in Dublin, will be his. But, I am sure, I do not know what they will do with you. I suppose they will make a parson of you. You may be your brother's chaplain.'

All this was now on the point of being reversed. The whole was suspended on an invisible thread. Every thing was at the disposal of that most capricious of umpires and autocrats, / Chance. Would the child with which my sister was pregnant, be a male, or a female? Would it live or die? Would she, who was now in so alarming and perilous a state, bring it alive into the world?

Then all that depended on this chance passed in full review before me. I saw the house in county Cork, and the house in Dublin. I saw the pillars of marble, and the apartments of state. I saw the numerous train of tenants and dependents.

---

[a] Technical word for a faint.
[b] *Macbeth*, I. iii. 140–2 (adapted).

Were all these to call me master in the proper sense of the word? Or, was I to administer them only as the functionary of another, to take care of them, that they might be properly managed, and delivered in perfect condition to the brat of Irene, and then to be cast out as a loathsome weed, unworthy to grow in the garden of the peerage, either English or Irish? /

CHAPTER II

I made it a point to seek out Cloudesley immediately after my arrival. I had been led, as it should seem by accident merely, into an attentive observation of his character. I had remarked his devoted attachment to his master. At the same time I had heard, principally from my own servant, his blunt and unmeasured professions of misanthropy. His motto was something like the declaration of Ancient Pistol in the play,

> Why then, the world's mine oyster,
> Which I with sword will open:[a] /

with this variation, that Cloudesley did not profess the design, to be one of 'Diana's foresters, gentlemen of the shade, minions of the moon,' and to carve his way among men by dint of plain violence; but rather to employ the superiority of his wit, and so to render others tools to his purposes.[b] Having remarked these things in the man, I judged him peculiarly well qualified to enter into my schemes.

Cloudesley had also thought much respecting me on the present occasion, and had ruminated how he was to shape his course under the direction of a new commander. His attachment to lord Alton had been personal, the result of the unspeakable obligations my brother had laid upon him. Lord Alton being removed, he looked upon the rest of the world as entirely indifferent to him. He was to take care of his own affairs, and to consider, in the circle of society upon which it was his lot to be cast, how / that was to be done in the most masterly manner. He had no check upon this selfish and unfeeling principle of action, but in the remains of his original character, the tenderness of his heart, and the invariable good-nature which accompanied his actions.

When we met, I can scarcely tell which of us first entered on the subject, that was uppermost in the minds of both, but that scarcely either of us could

---

[a] *The Merry Wives of Windsor*, II. ii. 2–3.
[b] *King Henry IV, Part I*, I. ii. 29–30.

venture to express in words. We were both forward in the commendation of his late lord, and in grief for his untimely end. In these things we spoke with the most perfect sincerity. The new situation in which we were placed, seemed to impose upon me the necessity to enter into a greater familiarity in my communications with Cloudesley, than under any other circumstances I should have thought of adopting.

I enquired of him very minutely respecting / Irene's health, and in what manner she had received the intelligence of the melancholy catastrophe.

In return Cloudesley gave it as his opinion that every thing was to be feared from the dreadful impression the event seemed to have made upon her, in the very critical condition in which she stood.

He looked at me intently. He said, in what a perilous situation stand at this moment the Irish estates, and the title of Alton!

I replied, that I had already written circumstantially all that had happened, to earl Danvers.

We stood in each other's presence, mutually daunted, fearful in reality that each might find in the other some relic of virtue, some ancient offset of principle, not to be reconciled to the thought that was now uppermost. I may say of myself, like king John in the play, /

> How oft the sight of means to do ill deeds
> Makes ill deeds done! Had not he been by,
> A fellow by the hand of nature marked,
> Quoted and signed, to do a deed of shame,–
> Had he but shook his head, or made a pause,
> When I spake darkly what I purposed;
> Or turned an eye of doubt upon my face,
> Or bid me tell my tale in express words;–
> Deep shame had struck me dumb, made be break off.[a]

In a word, Cloudesley and myself insensibly got into unreserved communication, and began to consult how the business was to be conducted under all the variety of circumstances that might arise.

He, as I have said, now that his patron, almost his saint, was removed, looked upon the rest of the world as indifferent to him. he was to take care of his own affairs, and to consider how his fortune might most effectually be promoted. He had no check in this matter, but from the mildness of his temper, and the milkiness of his heart.

Regarding the subject in this way, he saw a / great personal advantage to himself, that would result from his being trusted by me with a dangerous secret. He would be paid well in the first instance. He would take care to be provided for. And, if at any time I did not so conduct myself that he should be satisfied,

---

[a] *The Life and Death of King John*, IV. ii. 219–22 and 231–5 (both adapted).

he would always have me in his power, would be able at will to inspire me with nameless terrors, would hold me effectually in chains, and treat me as his slave.

For the moment I was entirely blinded to this. I thought only of the advantage to accrue to myself. I thought of the contrasted prospects that were placed before me, to be a king, or to be a beggar. I was drunk with ambition. Few men have been placed in so critical a situation as that in which I stood, where it depended upon the minutest variation in the balance of accidents, whether I was hereafter to be regarded as a person eminent in the scale of / civilised society, or as a zero, an individual that almost every one was entitled to despise. My whole soul was in tumults. Surely this, if any thing, was the furnace of temptation, the fire adapted to try a man's heart to the inmost core. And then, how easily, with what a noiseless tenour of action in all probability, might this be accomplished. Far from our native home, in a foreign and a remote country, the father dead, the mother dying! Both 'time and place did now adhere,'[a] and every thing invited me to embrace the opportunity, and seize the succession that my brother's death had left vacant. Was it to be endured, that, in defiance, as it seemed, to the order of human events, Alton and Irene should die, and yet that there should be a posthumous successor, a phoenix arising out of their ashes to baffle me? – It was thus that I reasoned; and I shaped my plan of conduct accordingly.

Both Cloudesley and myself were impatient / to join issue on this question, lest the golden opportunity might escape us. He saw with sufficient clearness, that, if Irene survived the danger of child-bearing, the whole matter would be at an end with us. Irene would be powerful enough to assert her son's rights, if it were a son she bore, and it would be hopeless for me to attempt to resist. If on the other hand it were a daughter, my road would be clear; I should have no scheme to form, and should need no ally to assist me. Cloudesley therefore was desirous, while these questions were still at issue, to enter into a confederacy with me, that, by the consciousness on my part that he possessed certain secrets, would in every event secure him an ascendancy. He would by that means become my bosom's counsellor, and a familiarity would take place between us, which, once established, would probably go on and continue, as a matter of course. /

I on the other hand was no less impatient; since, if the event that I feared, should occur, and a son was born that promised to live, it was necessary that timely precautions should be used, and every thing carefully prepared, 'to leave no rubs, nor botches in the work.'[b]

Cloudesley, though the misfortunes he had experienced previously to entering into my brother's service had changed him into a resolved misanthrope, was not by those events materially altered in his feelings towards the female sex. It

---

[a] *Macbeth*, I. vii. 51–2 (adapted).
[b] *Macbeth*, III. i. 134.

had been partly by the inflammableness of his disposition in that respect, that Norton had drawn him on to his ruin. It was by the charms of the sister that he had been urged to become the dupe of the brother. The disappearance of Norton, who left Cloudesley to encounter all the consequences of the ill-judged confidence he had reposed in him, and the subsequent / events, had of course put an end to that amour. He had therefore brought with him a heart disengaged as to the sex, when he entered into my brother's service. Thus disposed, the charms of Eudocia,[a] Irene's female attendant, had lighted up a passion in his bosom. Eudocia had the advantages, so generally to be found, though in different degrees, in the Grecian females, – a dark eye, a clear olive complexion, and an animated and expressive countenance. Her figure was graceful; her step was airy; and she had an inexhaustible fund of vivacity and chastised and half-retiring playfulness. The intimacy between her and Cloudesley increased every day; and he resolved to make her a party to the plots in which we were engaged.

On the third day from my arrival, Irene was taken in the pains of labour. After no very protracted period of suffering, she was delivered of / a male child, beautiful in limb and feature, and with every promise of health and a sound constitution. But those operations of nature in the mother, which should follow after the birth, were never perfected. It was soon apparent that her case was one of extreme danger. One of the most skilful of the practitioners of Vienna, relative to child-bed cases, was called in; but in vain. After three days of suffering she expired. The cause of this event, no doubt, is to be found in the previous circumstances, in the distress of mind and debility of frame, which grew out of the disastrous fate of her lord. She saw and noticed her son only once. In an interval when she seemed to have the greatest degree of self-possession, she caused me to be called to her bed-side. She thought she had something of high importance, respecting which to address me. But, after various efforts, and ever and anon a period of bewilderment, she / was obliged to give it up, and could only say with tokens of distress, 'I have lost it!'

Such was the fate of lord Alton, his wife and child. Two short weeks had produced this memorable change. Only half the period of the age of the planet of night had elapsed, since this lovely and accomplished pair had stood forth in the full promise of life and health, well qualified and exemplarily disposed to be the ornaments of the civilised world, and the benefactors of all that came within the sphere of their influence. Now their eyes were closed in death, and their mortal remains were of no more worth than the clods of the valley. The eye that saw them, would see them no more; and the tongue that blessed them, would have no fresh occasion to pour out the accents of gratitude. The place they occupied would be filled up, such is the law of human society; the chasm they

---

[a] Possibly named after the wife of Peter the Great, the provincial noblewoman Eudoxia Lopukhina, from whom he eventually secured a divorce.

left behind, would be closed; in a / short time they would seldom be remembered; and the affairs of the world would go on, for the most part, as if they had never existed.

Far different was the fortune of their single offspring. But for the calamitous events which, by a short time, had preceded his birth, he would have grown up in glory and honour, the care and the pride of his gifted and illustrious parents. They would have watched over his health and the opening blossoms of his mind. Their smiles would have awakened his first sentiments, and have softened and humanised his spirit. They would have defended him against all the world, and have caused him to be recognised in the station that was due to his birth. Now he was an orphan both by father and mother, with not one faithful and entire friend on the face of the earth.

But these were not the reflections that first occurred to my mind in this crisis of my fortune / and my character. I had worked myself up almost to frenzy by this question, Was I to be lord Alton, or was I not? There was no stop, no precious moment for pause or hesitation, in the career I had begun to run. Cloudesley was at my elbow. The least false step would irretrievably ruin the project we had concerted.

In fact however I felt no compunctious visitings of soul. I had considered every thing, and had nerved my spirit to the decisive act. I said to myself, Here is the subject concerning which my proceedings are to be exercised, a new-born child! There is no essential difference between the son of a king and a peasant. Their joints and members are the same. The account of the muscles which an anatomist may reckon up, is equal in the frame of one and the other. The accident of birth alone makes all the difference. Why is this man born to the throne of all the Indies, while that springs into life the son of a / negro slave? He can find no cause. It is time and chance that happeneth to all. The great master of the workshop of nature, 'maketh of the same clay one vessel to honour and another to dishonour.'[a]

> He that is robbed, not wanting what is stolen;
> Let him not know it, he is not robbed at all.[b]

This child, bred as the son of a peasant, may in all probability be happier, than if he were lord of thousands, and the hereditary member of the parliaments of two mighty realms. He shall not stand between me and the light of fortune and of honour. But he shall be happy. I will watch for his welfare. In the vale of obscurity he shall know no anxieties; and I will take tenfold more care of him than if he were sprung from my loins.

The plan that was concerted between me and Cloudesley required the instant removal of the infant. We resolved that Irene and her child, / apparently

---

[a] Rom. 9: 21.
[b] *Othello*, III. iii. 343–4 (adapted).

deceased a few hours after the birth, should be inclosed in the same coffin, and interred in the same grave. This, by the joint contrivance of Cloudesley and Eudocia, was without difficulty accomplished. Irene had lived in the utmost obscurity at the Briel. She associated with nobody. I broke up her little establishment, as soon as decency would admit. Cloudesley and Eudocia, with the infant foundling, removed to Neustadt, an Austrian town thirty miles from Vienna on the road to Italy, and speedily became man and wife. This was one particular of the original project.

It was requisite that due precautions should be taken to authenticate the death of my brother's child. This was accomplished without difficulty. Cloudesley, who was singularly adroit in matters of circumstantial detail, found means to procure from a woman of the town in Vienna, a still-born child. The body of this / child was laid out in due form, by the side of the body of Irene. The inspector, whose office it is to take account of the dead, drew up a report of the bodies of Irene, baroness Alton of the kingdom of Ireland, and her still-born son. I applied to the foreign commissariat in the police-office of the capital, who sent out his precept to the burgomaster of Meidling, the town in whose limits the Briel is situated, to certify these particulars. I next had recourse to M. St Saphorine, the English resident, whose business it was to set his seal of office to this certificate, of which I transmitted duplicates, one to earl Danvers in England, and another to the solicitor who was intrusted with the law-concerns of our Irish estates.

There being no Protestant place of interment within the Austrian dominions, I obtained permission to deposit the bodies of Irene and / her child in a vault under the great church of Vienna, it being stipulated that they were to remain there, till some ulterior resolution was taken as to their final destination.

It was my determination to return with all practicable speed to the British dominions. I loathed the country which had been the scene of these recent events. They had succeeded each other with such rapidity, as to confound my powers of apprehension. I felt as if I had a load of guilt on my soul, almost too vast and overpowering for mortal ability to endure. My feelings were those of a murderer! And yet I had committed no murder. Could I not with safe conscience assure myself, that I had in no way been a party to the destruction of Arthur or of Irene? Their child was not dead. But he was, by my sole means, civilly dead to his property, his rank and his country. / I had determined that he should be an outcast, belonging to no one, an uncertain and solitary wanderer on the face of nature.

Oh, how I detested myself in the recollection of the base and hypocritical scene that I had caused to be played in the presence of the corpse of Irene! I had laid by her chaste and spotless side the corpse of a child, the offspring of disgrace and infamy. I have often read that the blood of a murdered man would flow anew from his veins, the instant his body was touched by the finger of his murderer. Well might I have expected, that the hapless Irene should start again into life, with indignation at the lie I imposed upon her, the contamination with which I approached her. She was certainly dead! If the smallest particle of perception had remained in any portion of her frame, it would have shrunk and shuddered on this dreadful occasion. I had tried the question to the utmost. I had never / seen death till now. Never was such a penetrating trial, such a demonstrative ordeal of its reality, devised by mortal man. Her features were calm; there was a sweet and complacent serenity on her countenance. She was turned to earth.

I called to mind the dying injunctions of my brother. 'I have one consolation. Richard, we are brothers, the sole remains of our father's house. We have always lived together, and lived in harmony. I trust I have never done any thing to merit from you unkindness or resentment. This then is my consolation; I leave all that is dear to me in your hands. I have no other friend in this country. Irene is pregnant. I have not strength to remind you of all the vigilance, the care, and the love, which this sad situation will demand from you. I rely upon you, even as I should upon my own heart. Farewel, my dear, my ever dear Richard!' / These were the last coherent words he ever spoke!

All other guilt shews contemptible in comparison with that which I perpetrated. In defiance of my brother's latest wish, I had robbed his offspring of every thing he was born to inherit. I had robbed a helpless infant, the poor and the fatherless, that had none to help him. The curse of God was upon me. – My deed was foul. My act shewed horrible and grim. My heart was turned to stone; 'I struck it, and it hurt my hand.'[a]

But my crime was completed. There was no retreating. 'There remained no room for repentance; but a certain fearful looking for of judgment.'[b] I could not recal the child I had sent away with Cloudesley. I could not acknowledge that I had imposed the body of a spurious infant upon the constituted authorities, that I had obtained the certificate of the police / of Austria, and the seal of the English ambassador, to a lie! My soul was doomed, and I was recorded a villain in the chancery of heaven to all eternity. Like Cain in the Bible, God had set a mark upon me, that all men might shun, and abhor me.

As lord Danvers said this, he paused. Large drops of sweat stood on his forehead; and he seemed for a brief interval deprived of the powers of speech. – He resumed. /

---

[a] *Othello*, IV. i. 190–2 (adapted).
[b] Hebrews 10: 26–7 (adapted).

CHAPTER III

I have already said that, from the moment of my brother's death, my heart has never known an instant of peace. In my journey from Vienna to London I was beset with a thousand demons. The purpose of my return home was to assume my rank, and take possession of my estate. But this thought was an insufficient preservative against the inroads of remorse. As long as I was engaged in the forbidden acts necessary to the accomplishment of my purpose, / the cabals with Cloudesley, the secret sending away of my brother's child, and the possessing myself of the lying attestations of his death and interment, ambition possessed me alone. I had no leisure for any other thought; one step seemed indissolubly linked to another in my career. My whole soul was inebriated, or rather was wrought up to a sustained and continuous frenzy.

But these things being completed, I was now, alone. I had lost by brother, my sister-in-law, and my nephew. I had no longer any one near me, to whom I was bound by natural ties, or the still more sacred bonds of affection. I had lost even my partner in guilt, with whom to talk over the crimes I had perpetrated, and to measure and ascertain the advantages I had gained. The good man can be contented and serene in solitude: but such a one as I, needed a thousand diversions to beguile the time, and / enable him to forget the substantial realities of life.

I was alone in my carriage, as I traversed Germany from Vienna to Ostend, or worse than alone with my valet in the same vehicle, to speak when he was spoken to, and do as he was directed. I traversed in my route many extensive forests, and many sandy and dismal plains. My journey was made in the bleakest and most naked season of the year. Dark clouds were perpetually hurried along the horizon; and the air was nipping and severe. I seldom slept in my carriage, but was left to the uncomfortable communion of my own thoughts. I slept not, but was lost in long and vague reveries, unconscious how the time passed, but feeling that it was insupportably monotonous and tedious. My mind was in that state in which a man has an undefined feeling that he exists, but in which his sensations rarely shape themselves / into any thing that deserves the name of thoughts.

In this situation, particularly when the shades of evening began to prevail, and in the twilight, my senses were bewildered, and I seemed to see a multitude of half-formed visions. Once especially, as I passed through a wood by moonlight, I suddenly saw my brother's face, looking out from among the trees as I passed.

I saw the features as distinctly as if the meridian sun had beamed upon them. The countenance was as white as death; and the expression was past speaking pitiful. It was by degrees that the features shewed themselves thus, out of what had been a formless shadow. I gazed upon it intently. Presently it faded away by as insensible degrees as those by which it had become thus agonisingly clear. After a short time it returned. I saw also Irene and the child, living, and dead, and then living again. No tongue / can tell what I endured on these occasions. It was a delirium and confusion and agitation that continued for hours. The fits were not periodical. If I had a visitation of this kind at night, that afforded no security that it would not return again in the morning, and again at noon. My appetite deserted me; my eyes became fiery and blood-shot. /

CHAPTER IV

Immediately after my arrival in England, I repaired to this place, at that time the residence of Robert earl Danvers, my cousin, who died here somewhat less than a year ago. He was about fifteen years my senior. As being the representative of the elder branch of the family, it seemed due to him that I should in person give him some account of recent events, previously to my passing over to Ireland, to take investiture of my honours, and possession of the / estates, in that country. He was gratified with this mark of attention.

I found my cousin a man of a singularly grave turn of mind, yet of great urbanity and a conciliatory and prepossessing manner. In all his motions it was easy for me to see that he recollected that he was an English earl, while I on the other hand was only a baron of an inferior and dependent kingdom. He was however a widower without children, and felt that, unless he married again, to which at present he had little inclination, I was destined to be his successor.

I related to him many events with which he was not previously acquainted, of my brother's and my own share in the campaigns of prince Eugene against the Turks. I related our adventures in Croatia, and how we had met with Irene and her mother. I did justice to the beauty and accomplishments of Irene, and / spoke of the fearful misfortunes to which she had been exposed. In fine, I related the unhappy affair of Fabroni, and spoke with rapture – no man could do otherwise – of the admirable qualities of the late lord Alton. His body was already deposited in the tomb of his ancestors at Owston.[a]

---

[a] Now known as Owston Ferry, on the West bank of the River Trent, near Epworth.

Thus fair it was well. I could speak with a free bosom and an ungalled heart, of all that pertained to my brother to the period of his decease. I tasked my nerves to relate with plausibility and composure the rest of the story. I spoke of my return to Vienna, and my visit to the sequestered retreat of my sister. I related the unhappy effect which the fate of lord Alton had produced on her, and the consequent perishing of both mother and child. I laid before lord Danvers, as in duty I was bound to do, the evidence of these unhappy events.

The whole passed off clearly, and without exciting / the slightest suspicion. My voice did not falter, my brain did not split, while I told the lying tale, and exhibited the counterfeit certificates. Oh, what a piece of work is man![a] How little correspondence is there between the outer seeming and the inner substance, especially where no previous suspicion exists in the spectator and hearer! Could lord Danvers have drawn back the curtain and looked at what was passing within me, how indescribable would have been his astonishment! My disguise was but skin-deep; but it served me instead of walls of brass and towers of adamant.[b]

I passed clear and unsuspected through the scene. But for the wealth of India I would not have gone through it a second time. All the racks and tortures that ingenious cruelty ever invented, seem to me to be as nothing, in comparison with this torture of the mind. I set my teeth, and strung my eye-balls, that nothing sinister / or injurious might escape me. Or, when I did not do so, I played freedom of heart and an easy manner, a thing a thousand times more trying. I felt astonished that lord Danvers, a man of experience and the world, did not detect me.

From England I passed over to Ireland. I caused my succession to the barony to be enrolled in the office of arms at Dublin. Here I met with no difficultly. I exhibited the same documents to the proper office there, which I had previously laid before lord Danvers.

Thus then I attained to the summit of my ambition. It had been a subject of the most poignant discontent to me in early youth, that I was a younger brother. I was no longer a younger brother. I had repined that I was born twelve months too late. That subject of uneasiness was now removed. The house in county Cork, and the house in Dublin, were / mine. I had rank, title and equipage. I had the estate to which that title was annexed.

But was I happy? No. The worm within gnawed at my heart. I was a lord; but I was also a villain – so my conscience whispered me. I was a foul usurper. That I should become what I was had been effected by lying, forgery and fraud. The son of Alton and Irene, the heir of all their admirable qualities and all their virtues, was an exile in foreign lands. It was necessary to my purpose,

---

[a] *Hamlet*, II. ii. 23 (adapted).

[b] Adamant, an alleged rock or mineral of contradictory and fabulous properties, used rhetorically to denote impregnable hardness.

that he should be for ever unknown. What had his parents done to merit this at my hands? I was his natural protector. The tragical end of his father and mother, by means of which he had come into the world deprived of guardian, cherisher, instructor, of those who should have defended him against the injuries of the base, rendered this a thousand times more incumbent on me. What I had done was to the last degree dastardly and / contemptible, and substantially struck me off for ever from the roll of all that was worthy of the name of man. But I was a lord.

I looked round me, and began to consider how I was to be occupied, and in what manner my days were to be diversified, and my life rendered tolerable. I had received a liberal education, and felt a suitable value for the accumulated treasures of mind laid up for successive ages. The history of the world in its various climates, the advances of mankind from barbarism to civilisation, the inroads of despotism, the struggles for liberty, the profligacy and servility of some, and the generous elevation of others, with all the varieties of human propensities and human character, presented to me an immense storehouse of observation and wisdom. The depths of science, and the magnificence of poetry, with all that bards and romancers have feigned of chivalrous and heroic, all the wonders / of created nature, and all the sublimity of devotion, were at my command. An ample collection under these different heads was to be found in the library at Dunmaine.[a]

But what was all this to me? I could not endure to be alone. I carried that about me, that rendered solitude the most dreadful of evils. Whatever of the remains of the excellent of the earth I placed around me, I brought into the midst of them an essence of contamination, that withered all their laurels, and turned the wholesome hue of the soul into pestilence and death.

Sensible how slender were my resources from this quarter, I sought by plunging into dissipation to quiet the reproaches of conscience. I repaired to Ross, to Kinsale, and even to Cork.[b] I associated with the gentry and the *bons-vivants* of my own neighbourhood. They all eagerly accepted my overtures. I joined them in the sports of the field. But in vain. By what I / had seen in my campaigns, and in my winter abodes in Vienna, I was unfitted for their society. And, though in their midnight orgies I found enough of noise and apparent hilarity, yet in the riots of the bottle I discovered no medicine for my inward grief.

I then changed the scene for Dublin, and the metropolis of England. I became a member of the clubs. Here certainly I observed a considerable superiority of refinement and of intellect. But my nights were sleepless. And

---

[a] Possibly adapted from Dunmanway, situated mid-way between Bantry and Cork in the SW corner of County Cork, Eire.

[b] Ross, now known as Ross Carbery, on the coast about ten miles east from Dunmanway; Kinsale, on the coast, about fifteen miles south of Cork city.

often when conviviality was at its height, the recollection of the means by which
I had climbed to my present eminence, would rush on my thoughts, and
convulse my very soul. In the midst of crowds, I was alone. The evil genius that
haunted me perpetually, self-contempt and conscious degradation, were my
sole property; no one participated them with me; no one so much as suspected
what was passing in my / bosom. My life became a burthen to me. I felt an
ardent, but a fruitless wish, to exchange my miserable condition, with all its
external splendour, for that of the meanest rustic, whose joy it is,

> To see the sun to bed, and to arise,–
> To view the leaves, thin dancers upon air,
> Go eddying round, and small birds how they fare,
> To view the graceful deer come tripping by,
> Then stop and gaze, then turn they know not why,
> To mark the structure of a plant or tree,
> And all fair things of earth how fair they be;*–

and this with a heart at ease and an unstained conscience. But such could never
be my envied lot. My health declined; my flesh wasted away; I was reduced
almost to a skeleton. /

CHAPTER V

At length I bethought me of what I believed would be a more effectual remedy.
My cardinal calamity was that I was alone. Of all the persons in contact with
me, none in truth came near me. They cared not for me; I cared not for them. I
saw a pictured world, a multitude of faces that flitted by me, but nothing of
reality, nothing that gave impulse and motion to my soul. I resolved that this
state of things should cease. I knew that, of all things that bind a / man to the
earth on which we dwell, and give him a genuine interest in his kind, there is
nothing so sovereign, as the ties of a domestic circle. This thought brought me
once again into intercourse with my species. I frequented the assemblies where
persons of both sexes meet and communicate with each other. I enquired out
the families of such as lived in the best reputation, and were applauded for
vivacity, elegance and mutual good-will. The very thought had a salutary effect
upon me. I had an object to pursue; and hope sprung up in my bosom.

---

* John Woodville: a Tragedy.[a]

[a] Charles Lamb, *John Woodvil: A Tragedy* (1802), I. ii.

In conclusion I met with a family of the name of Fortescue, which particularly fixed my attention. It consisted of a father, and five daughters; they had lost their mother. They eldest daughter especially interested me. She had an expressive countenance, a look of singular gentleness, and a complexion uncommonly / pale. Their late mother had been a most exemplary parent; and the girls had been in a high degree benefited by her care and instruction. The father was rude and illiterate; he had been bred in the navy; and his system for governing his daughters, was the same that with sufficient success he had practised on board a man of war. His great aim was to marry the young ladies, and launch them respectably in the world as mistresses of families.

Selina, the eldest, had an admirer, a young man of fashion and fortune. He was eminently coxcombical, and endowed in a high degree with the grace of assurance. He was a member of all the clubs; his conversation consisted entirely in slang and cant phrases; he was a black leg and a jockey,[a] and was always foremost in scenes of debauchery and riot. He was importunate in his suit to Selina. She regarded him with dislike and terror; but he was strenuously / patronised in his views by captain Fortescue. It was the main object of this gentleman to marry his daughters; and he judged it necessary for his purpose, that the eldest should be led first to the hymeneal altar.[b]

Selina was labouring under the combined persecution of her father and her lover, when I first met with her. I instantly conceived a strong partiality for her, and in no long time made her understand the feelings with which I was animated. The success of my suit was no doubt greatly owing to the character of my rival. I had not passed through so many scenes in Hungary and Vienna, without having eminently imbibed the manners of polished life. My carriage had been insensibly formed upon that of my brother, the late lord Alton. I had seen much of military life and a court, and had the power of detailing what I knew, in a manner which contributed much to the entertainment of / my hearers. A lover is perhaps always prone to adopt the character of a relator and an historian. In a word, my conversation appeared with eminent advantage to Selina, in contrast with that of the empty and impudent coxcomb that had by a short time preceded me.

> She loved me for the dangers I had passed,
> And I loved her, that she did pity them.[c]

Even the depression under which I laboured, and the apparent melancholy of my disposition, served to complete the contrast between me and my presumptuous

---

[a] Coxcombical, foolish, conceited, showy; black leg, underworld slang for a swindler at the horse races; jockey, a horse thief. (Jockie was also the vulgar name for a penis.)
[b] Marriage altar.
[c] *Othello*, I. iii. 167–8.

rival, and to make my addresses the more acceptable. I asked Selina whether she thought she could always endure as a husband, a man so deficient in cheerfulness and gaiety; and I received the most encouraging answers. Selina said, she was of a tender disposition and a quiet temper; and she thought anything was better, than the ranting and obstreperous character of her former suitor. I / should find, if it was our lot to be united, that she would know how to soothe my sorrows, and study in what manner she could heal my wounded peace.

With respect to her father, his sole object was to dispose of his daughters for life. In that point he was not inclined to relax. But I was in every way as good a match as the lover he had patronised: and therefore, as far as that went, he was willing that Selina should indulge her own preferences. The negociation was not long in hand; and we were married.

The event fulfilled my warmest expectations. Till the day of my brother's unfortunate duel with Fabroni, I had had scarcely a solitary gratification or desire. My attachment to him had been complete and without reservation. My true character, up to the time of that fatal event, had been that of a self-lover in the narrowest sense of the word reformed. The death of lord / Alton, had removed the dam which shut up my evil propensities as with doors, and the stream returned once more to its old course with increased violence.

But to love one's self exclusively, supplies too narrow a field for the natural propensities of the human mind. It became necessary for me to love another as the instrument of my own happiness. Not that this was altogether the case in the union of myself and Selina. I admired her for her inherent qualities. I felt a rational and an earnest approbation of the mildness of her temper, and her steadiness of purpose. I should certainly have entertained the same sentiment, although her virtues should have had no application to my own interests, although she had been the wife of another. The more I knew her, the more I loved her. All this had an extremely favourable effection [on] my own tranquillity.[a] /

My situation was a new one. I had not anticipated the pleasures of a married life. Selina therefore to an extraordinary degree engrossed my thoughts. We arranged together our modes of life, our plans of society, and the disposition of our time. I did not find in her a single fault. To read in the countenance of an agreeable woman her approbation of my suggestions, and to consult it that I might learn from it her wishes and desires, was a situation in which I was wholly inexperienced; and it had all the charm of novelty to me. I began to entertain a comparative value for myself, because I was valuable to her. We talked; we read; we made little excursions and sought amusement together. I could now go into company with a new zest, because it was agreeable to her. When I talked to others, I stole from them a furtive glance, to see whether she

---

[a] Effection, effect.

was at her ease, and was happy. At public places her being pleased / was the main source of pleasure to me. For a time I even forgot the wound of my heart.

This however was a good fortune that I could not long enjoy uninterrupted. Sometimes I was alone: sometimes in society or public places, though I was present in body, I was absent in mind. A sudden fit of anguish would overcome me. I recollected that the whole part I was playing was a falshood. I was not the genuine lord Alton. The rank I bore was a forgery; the income I spent was the property of another. And I was involving the most amiable and deserving of women in an unconscious participation of my guilt. Then, where was my brother's child? I had placed a thousand miles distance between us; I had left him with no other protector than the partner of my crime. What misery, what degradation might hereafter be his! And I, I was the author of this, his nearest relative, the person to whom / his father and mother, so untimely removed from the scene of existence, had looked, and looked with such ample reason, to shield him from every evil. Then, if I considered only myself, what reliance had I that the lying part I was playing on the theatre of the world, would be permanent! I was at the mercy of the confederate of my guilt, a villain, who had sold every sacred principle, and the strictest ties that can bind a man to a just proceeding, for gain!

My condition however was inexpressibly different from what it had been before my marriage. Then I might grieve as much as I thought proper, un-restrained. No one had a motive to restore me to my self-possession. No one dared to throw himself in the way as an obstacle to the career of my misery; and I was left to pursue and exhaust it to the utmost extent that the powers of my nature would / sustain. But now I had a friendly eye at hand, ever ready to watch for my tranquillity. What words can tell the magic that there was in that eye! It was the serenest blue of the most exhilarating and life-giving sky, that ever the great author of nature spread out for the comfort and consolation of his creatures. Nothing more was necessary at almost any time, than for my eye to meet that of Selina, to restore me at once to peace and contentment. There was in the glance of that eye so much benevolence, such an anxious watchful-ness for my good, such a godlike pity, such an earnest and unrivalled sympathy. Could I refuse to be happy, when so excellent and lovely a companion shewed that it was the first wish of her soul to make me happy? Could I fail to set some value on myself, and to be proud, when Selina manifested to me, that it was the incessant theme of her care that I should be composed / and enjoy myself? No, I was no longer alone!

That which beyond all things constituted the merit of my wife's conduct, was, that it was free from all inquisitiveness, and the desire to know more than she was told. She saw that I had a secret sorrow. She feared to probe my wound; lest, however kind might be her intention, she might inflict injury where she purposed benefit. She did not believe that there was any perfect analogy between the wounds of the body and the mind. In the former it is perhaps necessary to search to the bottom, to remove the diseased flesh, to use the caustic[a] and the knife, with an unsparing, but a judicious severity. The way to restore the general health and soundness of the machine, is for the man of skill to apply himself to reinstate the functions of the diseased member or part of the frame. No so in mind. To set the mind at ease, it / is often most judicious not to approach the seat of the distemper: it is better to call of the attention from the source of the misery, than to direct the thoughts of the patient to the cause of his affliction. Once give occupation to the spirit, fill the soul with lively and stirring thoughts, wake up the secret chords of pleasure, give a companion to the solitary, present new pursuits and objects of attention, – and the clouds that oppressed the man with heartbreaking gloom will insensibly disperse, and a general and complete health will take possession of the machine.

The merit of Selina in her treatment of me consisted in the entirely divesting herself of all self-retrospect, and the cleansing her spirit from the whisperings and inspirations of pride. She saw that I had a secret sorrow; and she loved me the more. Pity mingled with, and added fuel to, the flame of her affection. She was / willing to be the nurse of my mental disease. She did not think there was any thing in the case, of which she had a right to complain. My behaviour towards her was mild, respectful, even in some sort deferential. My infirmity was of an older date than that of our acquaintance. She loved me the more, because she was of use to me, and because it seemed as if I could not do without her. She had made up her account from the hour of our first inter-course, that, if we became man and wife, it would be necessary for her to watch over me, to observer my symptoms, and to endeavour to reconcile me to life and myself; and she felt a deep complacency in the discharge of her duties in these particulars. Thus to employ herself, was to her real happiness.

But, though the exemplary conduct of Selina was an incalculable advantage to me, it must not be supposed that I was perfectly happy. / The recollection of my precarious situation and my crimes, would occasionally spread itself like a dark cloud over my horizon; and I became convulsed with agony. At these times I grew unreasonable, impatient and ferocious; the mildest treatment would not make me tame; and I revenged on the innocent and kindly bystander the shooting and bitter pangs that had their source in my own bosom. All this Selina bore with unaltered patience; pity for my sufferings never failed to remove every shade of resentment from her thoughts. And I, when I saw the angelic sentiments speaking in her eye, was brought back as by magic to a sense of justice and humanity. My ferocity departed from me; and I became all compliance, tenderness and gratitude.

Thus passed the first period of our married life, till it became evident that Selina was pregnant. I then proposed, and she consented that / we should pass

---

[a] Burning chemical, especially alkali.

over to Ireland, and take up our residence at the seat bequeathed by my late father in that country. There we had few neighbours, and those of no great refinement; but Selina made herself respected by all. For my part, I was never so happy, as when I had no society but hers. The interruption of occasional visits only served to give additional zest to the periods when we were alone. I likewise sometimes joined myself to the neighbouring gentlemen in the sports of the field. The sisters of my wife also favoured us with visits from England.

The condition of Selina gave new interest to our retirement. I already anticipated the period when I should be a father; and this added mutually to the kindness we felt for each other. The scheme of life into which I had entered was dissimilar from all my former experience; and it now promised to become complicated with new ties. To be a happy husband and the / father of a beautiful and promising offspring was a thought that was balm to my soul; and, if the recollection of those witnesses of my crime which still were in existence somewhere in the south-eastern division of the European world sometimes occurred to my mind, the dearer objects that were perpetually subjected to my senses, proved of more powerful effect, and brought me back to speedy and substantial enjoyments.

In process of time Selina made me the father of four children, two sons and two daughters. She proved no less exemplary as a mother, than she had before done as a wife; and under her able and judicious management our happy progeny daily expanded in new loveliness and virtues. Their alternate frolics and caresses rendered my rural retreat a very paradise to me. I remembered the error into which my own father and mother had fallen, and its pernicious / consequences; and I resolved that not the smallest difference of treatment should be allowed to introduce itself between my sons, the elder and the younger. They lived therefore in uninterrupted harmony and love.

Never was man more fortunate in his experiment of the connubial state, than I had been. I seemed to possess every ingredient that might have constituted the most unalloyed happiness. What occasional spectator would not have envied a lot, which falls to the share of so few among mortal men! But it was all unsubstantial and hollow. The consequences of my misdeed pursued me. Heaven, though sometimes slow in executing the retribution laid up for us, is still in vain to be expected to forget the vindication of its justice. And I have finally been made a fearful example of what may reasonably be expected to be the concluding scene of the perpetrator of audacious guilt. /

CHAPTER VI

The establishment of Irene at the Briel was broken up after her death with all practicable expedition; and the persons who had had any connection with it were dispersed in different directions. I and my suite repaired in the first instance to England. Cloudesley and Eudocia, with the infant foundling whose fortunes they had undertaken to conduct, set out, even sooner than I had done, for Neustadt, an Austrian town, on the road to Italy, and there took up their residence. /

I have already explained the mixed character of Cloudesley, compounded as it was of the original gentleness and affectionateness of his nature, and the bitter and severe misanthropy which his misfortunes had instilled into his soul. It was the latter part of his complicated disposition which prevailed, and dictated his proceeding, in the compact which had been entered into between him and me, to enable me to take possession of the title and estates of his deceased master. He resolved, in pure and exclusive selfishness, and in contempt of all other interests than his own, to take advantage of the situation in which he was placed. He would no longer be the shuttlecock of chance, to be the servant of Irene or myself as long as either of us might think proper; and, when we pleased, that we

> Should whistle him off, and let him down the wind,
> To prey at fortune.[a] /

His determination therefore was taken, in a bold and unflinching spirit, to make his price of me; and his terms were no less than a firm and clear engagement on my part to pay him an annuity of five hundred pounds as long as he lived. He undertook in return, in consideration of this provision, to take charge of my brother's infant son, to preserve my secret inviolate, and that I should never be disturbed, whether Cloudesley lived or died, by any claims to be set up on the part of this child. An engagement of this kind could not have the sanction of a legal instrument. But we both of us seemed to have no contemptible security for the performance of the bond. He could expect the payment of his annuity no longer than he adhered to the conditions on which it was granted; and I on the other hand, if I failed in punctuality, must make

---

[a] *Othello*, III. iii. 262–3 (adapted).

account that I should rouse a sleeping lion. He / had therefore a deep interest in preserving the life of the child; while nevertheless he knew enough of my disposition, to feel tolerably certain that, even if the child were dead, I should think five hundred pounds a year a cheap purchase, to preserve my reputation untainted, and to prevent so infamous a story from being published to the world. It is true, that men would not give implicit credence to a tale promulgated by a confessed accomplice: but it was not in my nature to suffer the tenour of my life to be canvassed *pro* and *con* by the discussion of so horrible a story, if it were possible for me at any price to prevent it. I could – it is sufficiently evident – work myself up to the perpetration of a crime: but there were no mortal sufferings that I would not have endured, rather than be exposed to the imputation of it.

When Cloudesley took the infant in his arms, under the engagement that no obstacle should / arise from this quarter to my assuming the title and possessing myself of the estates of my deceased brother, he had not yet determined in what way to proceed to accomplish his undertaking. The first thought that occurred to him was that he would remove the child for ever from my sight and his own, by disposing of it to some poor person, in consideration of a comparatively trifling sum to be paid for its future support. This plan had many obvious recommendations. If he adopted it, it would have the advantage of banishing everlastingly an object, the sight of which would at no time fail to remind him of the guilt he had contracted. Attached as he had been to his late master, and indebted for the most essential benefits, he felt that he was acting a most base part in conspiring against his helpless and orphan child. But, for the moment, the idea of insuring to himself a handsome, almost a gentlemanly, provision / as long as he existed, was too strong for these recollections. He would of course have left the party that received the child in perpetual ignorance, as to the parentage of the unfortunate outcast. By this conduct therefore he would seem to have secured the reward he had so dishonourably earned, and at the same time be enabled still further from day to day to erase from his memory the recollection of his baseness.

The project however which Cloudesley had thus formed, was overturned in a moment. When he took the infant in his arms, with the determination at all events that it should be deprived of the rights of its birth, there were many contending sentiments at war in his mind, and the expression of these sentiments in his countenance must necessarily have been such as a mature person would have found it painful to contemplate. His complexion was pale, his / hair dishevelled and staring, and his eye was haggard. But (as if it had been under the direction of an all-ruling Providence) the child of my brother, void of all experience, and therefore of all terror, saw nothing of this. He turned on the gaze of this wicked and fearful visage, and smiled. Nothing can be more dissimilar than the simple and unadulterated smile of an infant, from the smile of a creature already acquainted with conjecture and doubt, and apprehension

119

and hope. It resembles the serenity of ether,[a] and the purity of the blessed in heaven.

In addition to the instantaneous effect which this smile produced upon Cloudesley, he saw also, upon a more attentive perusal of the child's features, several lineaments strongly reminding of the countenance of his late master. For this he had not been prepared. By a violent effort he had endeavoured to separate in his mind the sentiment of fidelity to my late brother, from / the injustice he had consented to practise towards his offspring. The subtle and artificial reasoning he had employed to quiet his conscience, was now swept away in an instant. The soul of my confederate was totally changed. He vowed that the orphan boy should never lose the advantage of his watchful care, or be removed from his sight.

By the operation of this circumstance the mind of Cloudesley was brought back to its original character. He was by nature mild, friendly and affectionate. Adversity had in a considerable degree hardened his heart; and the temptation which had been presented by the death of my brother and my inordinate ambition, had been too much for his integrity to resist. But the idea that now presented itself of taking care of the child, making it his own, and omitting no means to secure its improvement / and substantial advantage, took a weight from his mind, which, though he had resolved to endure, was not the less depressing and afflictive to him. It was a return to his former self, and a comparative jubilee to his soul. He had felt too bitterly the apostasy into which he had been tempted from the right onward path. Integrity and kindness were his natural element. And he swore that this should be the last deviation into which he would be betrayed.

When he announced to his wife his new resolution, she felt the truest delight in the intelligence. She had yielded to the masculine and resolute determination of her husband in the first instance; but she had yielded with reluctance. Her consent had been wrung from her by the imbecility of her nature; and she secretly repined, even when she most seemed to subscribe to the will of her lord. She now received / the child from the arms of Cloudesley with the sincerest joy, and promised to be in all points a mother to it.

Cloudesley, with his wife and infant ward, as has been before mentioned, took up his residence at Neustadt. Though not populous, its streets are handsome, and it contains several squares. Its fortifications render it tenable against an enemy; it boasts of an imperial palace, and is the see of a bishop. The wall of the town is washed by the stream of the river Leitha.[b] Here, that Cloudesley might not be without occupation, he engaged in the cultivation of a small tract of land, and surrounded himself with a little collection or horses, cows, and

---

[a] In ancient cosmology a 'fifth element' conceived of as a purer form of fire or air.

[b] The River Leitha once formed a part of the old historic boundary between Austria and Hungary.

other animals, such as are seen in the neighbourhood of the dwelling of a rustic in the middle condition of life. He kept servants and dogs, and occasionally amused himself with fishing, and shooting such animals as are not / protected as game by the nobility and great lords of the soil. As the income I paid him was fully adequate to all his wishes, he regarded the pursuits I have mentioned, both the more constant and the occasional, merely as they might contribute to his diversion and his health both corporeal and intellectual, and did not make himself their slave.

Eudocia, his wife, whose character I have already described, had all the advantages that usually fall to the lot of a Grecian female, of a lively and cheerful disposition, and not without some pretensions to beauty. She was not troubled with any very strict notions of moral principle, as may easily be inferred from the passiveness with which she yielded to the conspiracy of Cloudesley and myself, respecting the future destination of the offspring of Irene. Her offence in this sort against religion and morality sat but lightly upon her thoughts. But / she was in other respects of a kindly and obliging temper and an affectionate disposition. Cloudesley and she were a handsome couple; and, though they did not at first come together from the impulse of a very romantic love, they daily became more pleasing and attached to each other. The husband had greatly the advantage in strength of understanding; and the schemes of life they pursued were deliberated and determined on by him.

They had no children; and therefore the infant they had undertaken to bring up in ignorance of his origin, was emphatically an object of attention to both. Many of the particulars I have to relate respecting their mode of proceeding are drawn from a journal kept by Cloudesley, which a few years ago fell into my hands; and in which he has put down with more ingenuousness and clearness of perception that I could have expected, whatever has reference / to their sentiments and conduct at this period. The child was beautiful in limb and feature, with every promise of health and a sound constitution. His disposition was in no small degree docile and affectionate; and all his infant ways were winning.

Cloudesley and his wife, though imperfect characters, and capable of being misled from the paths of rectitude and honour, were both of them in different ways endowed with a tender and affectionate disposition. They were at their ease, possessing abundantly the means of every luxury which their moderate habits demanded. Exclusively of their little list of domestic and rural attendants, they had but one human creature under their roof, to give variety to their existence, and agreeably to occupy their attention, if at any time they should feel an excess of each other's society. This was my brother's son. They named him Julian. He passed for / their own son, and therefore bore the surname of his supposed father. Their feelings towards him were of a mingled character, but were all of them conducive to the advantage of the child. They viewed him as the source of the income they derived from me, and were therefore prompted to cherish and make much of him. They viewed him as a helpless being, whom they had concurred to injure, had concurred to cut off from the high expectations to which he was born, and reduced to the condition of having no friend in the world but themselves. They felt therefore a melting tenderness towards him; they resolved to bestow upon him all the honour which it lay within their limited power to confer, to strew his path with roses, and to give him reason to consider existence and the lot which had fallen to him as a blessing.

These good resolutions might by possibility have remained ineffective and barren: but there / was that in the child which perpetually gave them new vigour and substance. He had received from his birth the invaluable inheritance of much sweetness of temper. There was that in his smile, which irresistibly insured the kindness of those about him; it had in it the essence of confidence and love. He was all animation and life; his new-born limbs seemed to seek for a sphere in which to expand themselves. No cloud ever appeared on his brow; he never betrayed the slightest symptom of sullenness and stubbornness. Cloudesley and Eudocia were all he had of father and mother; and abundantly he paid them all the love they could have looked for from the offspring of their bowels. He stretched out his little hands to meet Eudocia, and to be received by her husband. His laugh was of genuine high spirits, expressive of and exciting gaiety; and he crowed with a voice of health and a bounding soul. /

But the season of jubilee to those by whom a child is truly loved, is when he begins to talk. Words of love and endearment are among the first he utters. How delightful is it to them, that his tongue should assure them of what they had before learned only from dumb signs and uncertain gestures! It is like the first declaration between a lover and his mistress. No; there was nothing doubtful before; but articulated sounds are as the seal to the bond, and make assurance doubly sure. It was now that Julian began to be caressing, that he would stoke down the hair upon Cloudesley's brow, and, when he saw him returning from the daily circuit of his fields, would run to meet him, and proudly lead him in to his refreshment and his rest. Cloudesley would present him with a flower, a fruit, or a cake. The lispings, the imperfect efforts which the child would make to tell his supposed father of what had happened / in his absence, were all of them acceptable, and would smooth the brow of toil. In proportion to the want of power was the eagerness of the child to tell, till at length his mouth was stopped with kisses.

It is very early that a boy begins to display invention and ingenuity, and a sort of childish industry, all of which is exquisitely entertaining to seniors whose time is at their command. He imitates every thing he sees; and plays visits and entertainments with a seriousness of face, and an earnestness of attention, which is irresistibly comic. He gives his whole soul to it, and performs his part with a mixture of affected demureness and simplicity, which might put professional practitioners to the blush. The ingenuity of Julian was truly extraordinary.

He made houses, and collected the little implements of furniture about him, which are usually supplied to children; and, when all of a sudden / he observed Cloudesley or Eudocia laughing at the gravity of his demeanour, he would join in the laugh, and sweep away his little apparatus, with a sort of consciousness of its worthlessness: at the same time that, as soon as the laugh was over, and the attention of his critics withdrawn to other objects, he would return to his contrivance, and grow immersed in it, as if nothing had happened to tarnish its glory.

Every day that passed over his head inspired Cloudesley with a more affectionate interest in the destination, the character, and the happiness of his ward. He felt towards him in many respects more than the sentiments of a father; but with these sentiments were mingled a mysterious sense of his dignity of birth, and a recollection that the name he had an hereditary right to bear, removed him far from the sphere of the plebeian herd. The blood that flowed in his veins was noble; and its pulses had for / ages beat with high aspirations, and the meditations of chivalrous enterprise. He was surrounded in the imagination of Cloudesley with a sort of atmosphere of prerogative, which no vulgarity and rudeness must dare to approach. Yet the yeoman saw him daily, almost perpetually; and from this familiar intercourse the language and thoughts of equality in love inevitably flowed. Julian listened to Cloudesley with all the docility of a son, and obeyed him with implicit deference and a ready submission. /

CHAPTER VII

The child was scarcely yet three years old, when the feelings of Cloudesley prompted him to transport him to a different scene. All that related to the future destination of Julian was yet in obscurity; he might by some unexpected event, without the concurrence, and even in defiance of the efforts of those by whom he had been made an outcast and an exile, be restored to his proper station. Cloudesley resolved, that he should be so educated, and brought up / in such habits, as should prevent him from being a disgrace to any condition in which he might be called to move. His present pretended father had the means amply in his power to do him justice in that respect. Situated as he was, at a distance from his native soil, and with his activities necessarily contracted into a narrow circle, Cloudesley gradually came to consider the education, the improvement and well being of his ward as the great business of his thoughts.

At three years of age he determined to removed him to Lombardy, and fixed upon the city of Verona as the place of their abode. Cloudesley had travelled in his mind southward to Carinthia, the Tyrol, and the foot of the Alps.[a] He went to Vienna to procure the best statistical accounts of these countries, and he enquired of all persons who were likely to afford him the fullest information. He was deeply / impressed with the conception of the severe climate, the avalanches, and mountains of ice, that were to be found north of the Alps, even to the foot of the mountains, and the divine and paradisaical climate that presented itself the moment you had passed over them to the south, and had placed them as a mighty and almost insurmountable screen against all the harsher influences of the Arctic heavens. Cloudesley was of opinion that inestimable advantages of education and society might be obtained by this removal; but most especially his imagination reposed upon the refreshing breezes and the abundant fertility of Lombardy, and its varied and magnificent scenery. He persuaded himself that, for a child, especially between the third and the tenth year of his age, such a climate would be of incalculable advantage. His blood would flow cheerily, and his spirits would be for ever airy and gay. Cloudesley aimed in / the first instance at the happiness of his ward in each succeeding day as it passed. He wished that nature should smile upon Julian, that so Julian might be prompted to smile in return. He wished that the child might have for ever before him the magnificent foliage, the health-inspiring fruits, the rivers and the lakes, the brilliant skies and the peace-breathing sounds, the flocks and the herds, the beautiful cattle and the everlasting gaiety, in which no country on earth can compare with Lombardy. Thus would Julian be led to the idea, that existence itself was joy. No dark clouds would intervene to disturb his happiness. His mind would be a stranger to all evil passions, all animosity and hatred, and the very temptations to stray from the paths of ingenuousness and truth. By this process two great ends would be attained, the present peace and felicity of his ward, and the foundation gradually laid of a temper full of / philanthropical propensities, happy itself, and disposed to make all others happy.

One of the earliest acts of Cloudesley, subsequently to his arrival at Verona, was to reconcile himself to the church of Rome. His first object was the education and welfare of Julian; and he knew that it would be many ways disadvantageous to his ward, to be held the son of a Protestant father. Cloudesley could not give him the appearance of nobility and high station; but for that very reason he was the more anxious to move out of his way any disqualifications and obstacles to a hospitable and encouraging reception in the province where he dwelt. Eudocia had paid small attention to the peculiarities of religious creeds, and was scarcely aware of the difference between the Greek and the Roman church: there arose therefore no difficulty on her part to the

---

[a] Carinthia, S Austrian province; Tyrol, W Austrian province noted for its Alpine beauty.

plan which her husband had formed in this respect. They / took every necessary step on this point, which might smooth their admission into good society.

Cloudesley gave himself out for the son of an English yeoman, a member of that class of his countrymen, whose occupation it is to cultivate the land, or cause it to be cultivated, for their own personal benefit. He affirmed that his father had left him in such circumstances, as might enable him to set himself down with a competent income, in whatever part of the world he pleased. He avoided naming the province of England from which he came, that so, whatever report he thought proper to make of himself, his story might run the less risk, through any unforeseen accident, of being contradicted. His own station had been so far limited and obscure, as to afford small chance of his being identified as having been formerly a shopkeeper in a country-town. He also said nothing of the / Hungarian campaigns or of Vienna.[a] Silence in this respect was made incumbent upon him by the stipulations that had been entered into between him and me. He gave out that he had fixed himself in Verona, principally for the advantages that might there be procured for the education of his only son.

A circumstance which contributed to Cloudesley's choice of Verona as his place of residence was the accident of his and Eudocia's engaging a girl, a native of that place, as a nurse for the child. She was brought from Italy by a Venetian nobleman, who had been appointed resident from his native republic to the court of Vienna. The countess Morelli, his lady, had a child of two years, a boy, to whom Camilla, the Veronese girl, had officiated as nurse from the hour of his birth. The child had sickened on the route; the parents had felt impelled to suspend their journey on that account at Neustadt; / and, after two days' illness, the child died. Camilla had been deeply attached to the infant: but, that tie being removed, she requested her master and mistress to excuse her from proceeding further. She was accordingly left behind. She found an aunt of hers married and settled at Neustadt; and it was agreed that she should remain with her aunt, till she was otherwise disposed of.

Julian was a few months older than the child who had died. He was of singular beauty. Joyous, well-tempered, and unsuspicious of harm, he rarely failed to meet the caresses of those who noticed and courted him, with the caresses of confidence and innocence in return. One fine summer's day, when Eudocia was walking in the fields near Neustadt, with the child holding by her hand, they fell in with Camilla. The girl, who had just lost her little darling, a beauty of the first water in her apprehension, / was struck by the living beauty of Julian. The Grecian wife and the Italian maid resembled each other in the frankness of their manner. The Italian attempted to tell the little story of her woes; and, though Eudocia understood her very imperfectly, she felt much

---

[a] See above, pp. 47–51.

interest in a tale by which the relater was deeply affected. The Italians tell much of their story in dumb show; Julian listened very attentively, even when the two females scarcely thought of him. He attempted to bid Camilla not to cry and distress herself; the artless sympathy of a child can hardly fail to make his prayer successful. She hastily dried up her sorrow, smiled on him through her tears, and almost devoured him with kisses. When they were to part, Julian refused to let her go. They proceeded together towards his home. The bargain was soon made. Cloudesley and Eudocia were both of them delighted with the girl; / and from this time she became Julian's nurse. Camilla had a decided partially to the young and helpless beings, who for so long a time need the most watchful care of the adult; and thus the fortunate Julian added a third friend to the two exemplary protectors, whose good will he had enjoyed from the hour in which he could first distinguish a friend from a foe.

The child had therefore been singularly circumstanced at the period when his organs were first formed to the imitation of articulate sounds. Cloudesley spoke to him in English; Eudocia, with the pliability so characteristic of female love, learned a good deal of English from her husband; but she could not refrain, especially in moments when the heart most pours itself out without constraint, from mingling words of endearment borrowed from her native tongue; the German servants, and particularly the girl whom Camilla had succeeded in the care of the / child, addressed him in German. Cloudesley was desirous of putting an end to this eternal jargon, and resolved, that, as soon as possible, the language of his ward should be Italian only.

When Cloudesley arrived at Verona, he soon fixed his residence in a *podere*, or little farm just without the walls of the city, and surrounded himself with Italian servants, as at Neustadt he had been surrounded with Germans. He further entered into an engagement with a student of the university, to reside in his house, for the purpose of instructing Eudocia and himself in the Italian language. He had it also in contemplation, that, as time rolled on, this young man might be rendered additionally useful as an instructor to his ward. The university of Verona consists merely of a suite of apartments under a single roof, destined to the purpose of lectures, a library, a museum, and the different / halls for experiments and operations, while the students and even the professors provide themselves with lodgings as they can, within the city and suburbs. The young man therefore, with whom Cloudesley entered into this engagement, and who was destined to the profession of the church, but whose parents were in narrow circumstances, deemed himself happy in the opportunity of exchanging his instructions, and such other service as he could afford consistently with his attendance on the university, for a residence and diet under the roof of the English yeoman. Possessed of these advantages, Cloudesley made a rapid improvement in his acquisition of the Italian language. He read with his youthful instructor the writings of Bandello, Boccalini, and Boccaccio's

Genealogy of the Heathen Gods, and advanced himself in the business of conversing and expressing his ideas in Italian, by his colloquies, not only with the / young student, his inmate, but also with the servants and labourers that were employed by him in the affairs of his establishment.[a] His progress was the greater, on account of the express object that had brought him into Italy, the advantage of the concealed son of his late master. This gave him an impulse, and accelerated the career in which he had resolutely engaged.

Having to a considerable degree effected this purpose, Cloudesley resolved in the next place to frequent the coffee-houses of Verona. He judged that it would be necessary for the benefit of his ward, that he should not be shut out from the usual intercourses of society, but that on the contrary he should be brought into contact with young persons of the best condition in Verona. Cloudesley, who had now an income amply sufficient for his purposes which was regularly remitted to him, in no long time / acquired the confidence and demeanour which characterise an independent station. He forgot his inferior origin, his bankruptcy, his imprisonment in a jail, and that he had so lately been the servant of the father of Julian. He was a handsome man, with a form approaching to the athletic. His natural gifts were not contemptible, and he had seen somewhat of the varieties of human life. Add to this a well-stored wardrobe, and a carriage easy, well assured, and conscious of the new and more elevated sphere of life into which he had entered; and certain it is that the advances of the English yeoman were not slighted by the best heads of families in the city of Verona.

Among the many distinguished residents at this time at Verona, was count Orsini. He had been a traveller, and had visited England. He found in Cloudesley a sagacious observer of men and things; and there was a variety of / topics upon which these two delighted to compare their remarks. Orsini studied agriculture as a science, and was desirous of reducing into practice such improvements as had suggested themselves to him in his travels. Cloudesley had yielded an enlightened attention to this subject in his youth; and now, having resolved to apply a portion of his leisure to the cultivation of the fruits of the earth, he also called to his recollection whatever he had seen at home, or observed in foreign countries, that he might use the land he had taken under his direction for the most advantageous purposes. Orsini, in addition to his palace, as it was termed, in the city of Verona, had a *podere*, or *ferme ornée*,[b] at a very small distance from the residence of Cloudesley.

---

[a] Matteo Bandello (c. 1480–1562), Bishop of Agen in SW France and writer whose 214 stories and novellas 1554–73 gave themes to Shakespeare, Massinger and others, and which are invaluable as a source for the social history of the period; Traiana Boccalini (1556–1613), satirical Venetian author; Giovanni Boccaccio (1313–75), Italian writer, disciple and close friend of Petrarch. *Genealoia deorum gentilium* (begun c. 1350, first published 1472) was translated as 'On the Genealogy of the Gods of the Gentiles'.
[b] Agricultural smallholding.

This circumstance gradually brought about an intercourse, not only between the Englishman and the Italian, but also between their respective / families. The countess had a numerous offspring, male and female; and, unlike the generality of Italian mothers, she devoted a great deal of her attention to the improvement and education of her children. It had happened early, that, in the walks for health and recreation in which the countess accompanied them, she had encountered Camilla and the little Julian. She admired the English child, who was remarkable for symmetry and beauty, and had a fairness of complexion seldom seen on that side of the Alps, and entered into conversation with his attendant, as to what he was, and who he belonged to. The conversations occurred again and again. The countess addressed herself to Julian. He seemed delighted to be noticed by so fine a lady, smiled upon her with uncommon sweetness, and answered her, when he could, in his broken Italian. The countess called upon Eudocia. In the frequent meetings / that took place, an intercourse also arose between the younger members of the party. There was something novel and alluring to Orsini's children in the appearance and air of the little foreigner. Julian on his part was not backward to meet their advances; and his animation, his good temper and his frankness made his acquaintance an advantage not to be despised by his juvenile neighbours. He was inventive and frolicsome: his inventions amused his little companions; and his frolics were an inexhaustible source of hilarity and laughter. /

CHAPTER VIII

Cloudesley and his family had lived nearly three years in Italy, when Julian was seized with the small-pox. For a day or two before the disease manifested itself, he appeared exceedingly indisposed, was in a high fever, and slept but little, and that uneasily, and with restless and convulsive startings. The little fellow laboured under great depression of spirits, and expressed a presentiment that he should die. Cloudesley and Eudocia were alarmed with his / situation, and treated him with the utmost tenderness, overwhelmed as they were with the apprehension in what way the symptoms they observed would terminate. They had no children of their own; the behaviour of Julian had been at all times kind, affectionate and amiable; he had never, till now, given them a moment's pain; and their lives seemed bound up in the life of the child.

On the evening of the second day, about sun-set, he became more tranquil and serene. He felt exceedingly weak, but was able to collect his little thoughts. Eudocia was in tears; and Cloudesley had hold of the child's hand, and gazed on his countenance with disturbed thoughts and anxious observation. Julian looked first at the one, and then at the other. 'My dear mother!' said he, 'my dear father! do not afflict yourselves for me. I think I shall die; and I can bear that very well. If I die, I / shall be happy. Our Saviour loved little children, and said, Of such is the kingdom of heaven. But I cannot bear to see you uneasy. Of what consequence am I? If I had lived, it should have been my study to recompense the great trouble you have taken about me. I have nothing to recollect in all my life, but your perpetual goodness and kindness to me. Cheer up, my dear parents! Do not make death bitter to me, by the sight of your sorrow! God will bless you, because you are good. Lay me in the cold ground; put the sod over me; and return, and be happy in each other! Oh, how you deserve to be happy!'

The words of the child were intended for comfort and consolation. But they were so affectionate and so resigned, that they produced something of a contrary effect. At intervals both Cloudesley and Eudocia betrayed their feelings in sobbing. But they endeavoured to / restrain themselves. And, when he had ended his kind expostulations, they dried their eyes, kissed him, and smiled upon him as they smoothed his pillow. He had a sweet and composed sleep. Towards morning, the poison that lurked within him, broke out, and shewed itself upon his body, his limbs, and his face. From that hour he grew better. The distemper was of a favourable sort; every thing turned out well; and finally not one mark remained in his face, of this critical visitation.

When the child was lying, as they thought, in the most alarming situation, and which would probably terminate in death, the conscience of Cloudesley did not fail bitterly to accuse him of his misconduct towards the little victim. 'Here he is,' said he, 'like a lamb brought out to the sacrifice. I am his murderer; and he thinks me his friend, and calls me his father. I ought to have stood by him, when every one deserted / him. Was not my late lord my great benefactor, who took me from a jail among felons, and made me his companion and friend? He confided in me, and felt sure that I would suffer no harm to happen to him or his, which it might be in my power to prevent. I had a right, it may be, to think ill of the human species, and to regard war as declared between me and my kind. But this should only have bound me a thousand times the more to my generous master, who assuredly never did me any thing but good. And what have I done in return? Why, when this child was deprived of every friend, and lay at my mercy, while in his infant form was centred every claim to my humanity and my gratitude, I conspired with his enemies to destroy him. Who can doubt, that, if I had stood up in his favour with a firm and manly mind, the conspiracy would have been quashed, or rather would never have existed? He would have / been acknowledged, as he was born, an Irish peer, and in near prospect to an English earldom. An ample provision would have been awarded him by the laws of his country, out of the estates to which he was born to succeed. But I have sold him, as Judas sold his Saviour, for a miserable pittance of dirty pelf.[a] He would have had guardians appointed him, and have been taken care of as a British nobleman. All this was in my power; and what glory should I have acquired, by dissipating even in embryo, every plot that was hatching against him? I could have placed him under the protection of prince Eugene, and the English ambassador, and the imperial court of Vienna. He would then never have contracted this fatal disease, in a corner so remote from his true country, here to perish unacknowledged and unknown. He would have lived, and not thus have been cut off in the morning of his days. He would have entered in due time upon the career of honour; / and his name would perhaps have been consecrated to the latest posterity in the page of history. Can I ever forgive myself? Am I not the most consummate of criminals, blasted with ingratitude towards the noblest of masters, and at the same time guilty of the murder of the sweetest and most promising child that was ever born to breathe the vital air?'

It was about twelve months after this, that Cloudesley himself was taken ill. He had been engaged in a hunting party; the chace was long; and he had come home exceedingly heated, and quite worn out with fatigue. He had retired early to bed; but, before morning, all the symptoms of a virulent fever shewed themselves in him. He was delirious for several days; and it was only by the care of a very skilful physician that he was at length restored. Julian was, to the extent of his power, his indefatigable attendant. Not Eudocia herself was more careful; and the patient, when insensible / to every thing else, always shewed tokens of being particularly soothed by the kindness of the boy. Julian watched all his symptoms with unwearied care; when they appeared most threatening, he would for a few moments leave the room, that he might indulge in a passion of tears; and, when they were favourable, his eye would glisten, his cheek was suffused with a glow of intense pleasure, and he would give vent to his feelings by running to embrace his pretended mother. When Cloudesley was recovering, the convalescent a thousand times called up to his recollection those beautiful verses of Shakespear,

> He with his hand at midnight held my head;
> And, like the watchful minutes to the hour,
> Still and anon cheered up the heavy time,
> Saying, What lack you? and, Where lies your grief?
> Or what good love may I perform for you?
> Many a poor man's son would have lain still,
> And ne'er have spoke a loving word to him –
> But I, at my sick service, had a prince.[b] /

'I am in truth the serpent that stung him, the conspirator that stripped him of

---

[a] Contemptuous term for money or wealth, especially if dishonestly acquired.
[b] *King John*, IV. i. 45–52.

all his rights. And this innocent, unsuspicious, affectionate boy, in return for all this evil, watches over my infirmity, and is perhaps the saviour of my life. I, who, if I were known for what I am, and if I were innocent, am scarcely worthy to perform for him the most menial offices, have a young cherub, rich with noble blood and kingly virtues, to watch at my pillow. Had I been void of fraud and of crime, he perhaps, in the thoughtless pride of his lofty heart, would have disdained me: and now, because I am unworthy to live, and deserve to be held up a warning and an execration to mankind, he calls me father, and performs towards me more than the duties of a son.'

Soon after his recovery I received a letter from Cloudesley, which you shall read. (It was as follows.) /

I write from the overflowings of a contrite heart. May what I have to say be read with feelings like mine, which it well deserves to excite in the bosom of him to whom it is addressed!

It would be in vain for me to attempt to describe to you the beauty and the admirable qualities of the child under my care. His rosy hue is like the first blush of a glorious morning in an Italian sky. The motion of his limbs is like that of the gazelle in the hills and the forests of Arabia. His eyes send out sparkles of fire, yet softened by the feelings of the tenderest heart that ever beat in a human bosom. His lips are red, pulpy, and varied with every expression that can charm and subdue the beholder. His voice is soft and clear, and has in it the model and extract of the divinest music. He is all affection and sweetness. To me and to his reputed mother he never gave a moment's / pain. He is all compliance, all love, and the very soul of sympathy.

His understanding is of a very extraordinary nature. He comprehends every thing, and retains every thing. What would be a severe trial and a task to others, is sport to him. He has an unquenchable desire to know, and whatever is presented to him that is new, instantly rouses all his faculties. He learns, because learning is a passion in him, and for the sake of giving pleasure to the gentleman who teaches him, and to those whom he believes to be his parents. He is delighted with tales of adventure; and it is not to be told, with what intenseness he listens to and anticipates the fortunes of the persons to whom the tale relates, and with what generous sentiment he enters into the heroism and the virtues which the relater undertakes to describe. He bursts into tears of uncontrolable sympathy with the feelings / that occur, and can no longer retain his posture and his station, when the story approaches to a crisis. He threatens the evil-doer, and strains as it were to his heart the imaged figures of those who merit his regard. He clenches his fists with the earnestness of his emotions, while involuntary ejaculations ever and anon burst from his lips.

He is exceedingly ingenious. His soul is stirred up within him, when he contemplates the trumpet and clangour of war. The enterprises related in the poems of Ariosto and Bojardo rouse up his whole spirit.[a] He amuses himself in the field adjoining to the house with cutting mimic trenches, and carrying on imaginary sieges. All that he hears of an exciting and glorious character he imitates. He shews in every motion, that he belongs to another sphere, and that the spring and soaring of his nature cannot be subdued. He is born for high / things; and his soul claims the place to which the rights of his birth had destined him.

Had it been otherwise, I could have been contented. I would have endeavoured to make him happy, and to have reconciled him to a humble lot. But, no! he is out of his place. I cannot look at him, without seeing the exalted and high-born nature which betrays itself in him at every instant. I must not be the obstacle to press down this aspiring plant, and bend its vigorous branches to the earth, which in their own nature are destined to 'dally with the wind, and scorn the sun.'[b]

In your case and mine, virtue is its own regard, and vice its own punishment. I boldly appeal to your own heart; have you ever known a serene and a tranquil hour, since you robbed your brother's son of his birth-right? 'The soul's calm sunshine, and the heart-felt joy,' are the indispensible conditions of pleasure /to man.[c] When our hearts are furrowed with care, and we have the thorns of conscience to prick and sting us within, in vain are all the dainties that would solicit our appetite, and the generous wines that would elevate our spirit. All the wealth in the world will not in that case make us truly rich; all the water in the ocean will not wash us clean. We carry that for ever about with us, that poisons every enjoyment, that fades the fairest colours, that clouds the brightest sky, that turns the most exuberant field into a barren heath, and makes life itself wearisome and insupportable. I appeal to yourself, whether you have ever forgotten for twenty four hours the act, by which you profaned you brother's ashes, and made a mock of the most sacred tie that could in any case bind the spirit of man.

Even I have one consolation that you have not. I have this blessed child for ever under / my eye. I can exert myself at every moment to drive away the shadow of evil from his sacred head; I can apply all my power to procure him good. I can do him some justice, and purvey for his intellectual improvement. I can see that he is happy; I can administer to his enjoyments. Yet all this comes tainted to me by the thought, that I am his jailer, his robber, his worst enemy presenting myself to him with treacherous smiles under the guise of a friend.

But you, – you cared not what became of him. All you thought of was, that

---

^a i.e. Matteo Maria Boiardo, Count of Scandiano (1434–94), Italian poet whose *Orlando Innamorato* (1486), a recasting of the Charlemagne romances into narrative poetic form, was eclipsed by the *Orlando Furioso* (1516) in which Ariosto adopted Boiardo's characters and brought his narrative to a close.

^b *Richard III*, I. iii. 264.

^c Pope, *An Essay on Man* (1734), Epistle IV, 167.

you would take to yourself what was his. You cared not to whom you intrusted him; even I was for a moment his enemy. You cast him out to perish; the sooner the better, you thought, provided you were not charged with his murder. You cast him out to what was worse than murder – the chance of many years of destitution and misery, or, as it might be, of many years / of all that disgrace and crime, to which destitution and misery are usually the prologue.

I most earnestly adjure you to turn round. It is never too late to do an act of justice. What a load of remorse and self-accusation will you take off from your mind! How will you 'cleanse your overcharged bosom of the perilous stuff that weighs upon the heart!'[a] You are the natural guardian of the child; every rule of equity will allow you some compensation in that character. You are not without a younger brother's provision, as the son of the first lord Alton. But what are wealth and luxury in comparison of an honest mind! How happy is the man, confined to the barest necessaries, whose heart brings against him no accusation! Give to this child his proper title, and his true name. Clear to him the space assigned, that he may run the career of honour. Let him know what he is destined to, that he may prepare / his weapons in time, and gird himself for the combat.

Meanwhile, act as you will, my part is determined. I will no longer be a sharer in this complicated villainy. I will tell the boy what he is: he is already capable of apprehending the difference between a prince and a peasant. I will bring him to England; I will present him to lord Danvers; I will lay his true story before the king and the peers of England. The tale I shall tell, and the proofs I shall bring, will carry conviction to every honourable mind. I only wait your answer, to commence the proceeding, which I have no doubt will procure justice to my much-injured ward. /

CHAPTER IX

This expostulation, and these menaces, resumed lord Danvers, I resisted. The most exemplary of women had already borne me a son and a daughter. Could I break up this little establishment? could I overturn the prospects of creatures tied to me by the most sacred and heart-felt bonds, and record myself, the husband of the one, the father of the others, as the most pernicious of villains? No. I had put my hand to the plough, and could not draw / back. I had

---

[a] *Macbeth*, III. iv. 43–4 (adapted).

engaged in a voyage, that could never be terminated as long as I lived, and they lived; and I must proceed.

No words can describe the agonies this letter inflicted upon me. Cloudesley threatened in it, that he would come to England, that he would bring with him my brother's son, that he would lay his appeal before the king and the house of peers, and would present to the English nation the tale he had to unfold. He said he would wait for my answer, before he proceeded. What security had I for that? But I sent my answer. I could not trifle with so formidable an adversary.

Hitherto the story had slept in the profoundest obscurity. The infernal legend had never found access to mortal ear; I stood to all that knew me an honourable man, a well educated and universally received peer of Ireland, against whom no word of censure had ever been / breathed, whose character no one presumed to question. Henceforth I knew not, any morning that I rose, that the fatal blow would not be struck, or that the evening sun would not witness my eternal disgrace. It was not a question of fortune and station merely. The same blast that took them from me, would also tear away the cloak that covered me, and the mask behind which my true features were hid, and shew me to all the world an unheard-of monster, from the sight of whom every human creature would instinctively shrink.

For six months from the time at which my letter must be supposed to reach the depositary of my secret, I looked upon it as unquestionably certain that this was to be the issue. It might be a little sooner, or a little later: an adverse wind might defer for weeks the arrival of the vessel, that had in its cargo the fatal box freighted with destruction to the fortune and character / of me and every thing that was mine. But it would not the less certainly arrive at last.

Yet on one thing I determined: I would not be a party in any way to effect the ruin that by rapid and unceasing strides was coming upon me. It might never come. That was possible. I would cling to the last fragment of the vessel in which I had embarked my peace. My destruction was suspended by a hair; and every hour, every moment, this miserable security might break, and I should be overwhelmed.

it is astonishing that, amidst these terrors, these mortal thrills, these shudderings of the frame, the well known forerunners of death, I continued to live. I slept not; or, if I forgot myself for a moment, that was the signal for all undescribable and unendurable visions to crowd on my soul. I had no appetite. Whatever was called by the name of pleasure was decreed never to come within my grasp, within my / sight, within my hope. I was wasted to a shadow.

How different was my state of mind now, from that in which I had left Vienna, and come to England, after my brother's death, seven years ago! I had then been divorced from my innocence and my honour; a foul mass of loathsomeness and moral putrefaction had been fastened on my heart, which no operation, and no incision-knife, though guided by the most skilful hand, could ever extirpate. From the hour of the death of Arthur by the sword of Fabroni, I had never known an instant's peace.

But that was a question of sentiment only. When I retired into my closet, when, by the reaction of my human spirit, I withdrew from the world, and communed with my own soul, I felt that there was one companion that went with me into my solitude, and that no doors and no bolts could ever shut out: and that was / the image and representation of my guilt, my worthlessness, my unparalleled, my complicated, my cold-hearted and remorseless crime.

Still, whatever it were that my conscience secretly whispered to me, I held up my head in the face of the world, and challenged any man to cast an imputation on my integrity. Richard lord Alton, returned from the campaigns in Hungary against the Turks, was every where greeted with welcome, was embraced as the successor of his virtuous ancestors, as the gallant Englishman who had served with honour under the imperial standard, and had the attestation of the immortal Eugene to his achievements performed, and his courage displayed on the most trying occasions. Even the exploits of my brother swelled my honours, and were entwined in the laurels that crowned me. Fathers pointed me out to their sons as the pattern after which they should copy; and female beauty, in its / most brilliant constellations, sought to distinguish me with its smiles, as what was unquestionably my due.

I had guilt in my heart. But I sheltered it under the panoply of honour, so that not the slightest glimpse ever betrayed it to the most penetrating eye. The scheme of my usurpation was so perfectly arranged, that nothing could ever assail it. I had the most authentic attestations to my brother's death, and to the interment of his consort and his child. My pernicious secret was confided to only one human bosom, beside my own. For the fidelity of that confident I had every security that the most prosperous criminal could desire. Cloudesley received from me a regularly remitted income of five hundred pounds *per annum*; and I could imagine no motive that could prompt him to betray so gainful a trust. If I could learn the art to tranquillise the vivacious, the never sleeping / monitor in my own bosom (it was thus I reasoned),

> I had then been perfect,
> Whole as the marble, founded as the rock,
> As broad and general as the casing air.[a]

In how different a position did the repentance of my confederate place me? I had thought myself miserable before. But that I had to myself. The curious and well constructed fabric, that before had hid me from mortal observation, was now shivered into dust. I was to be like Cacus, when Hercules demolished the

---

[a] *Macbeth*, III. iv. 20–3 (adapted).

den in which he had dwelt secure, and laid all his secret plunder open to the observation of the triumphant and insulting multitude.[a] /

CHAPTER X

Cloudesley had no sooner dispatched his letter, than he began again, and with redoubled earnestness, to ruminate on the conduct he should pursue. He of course entertained a very uncertain hope that his expostulation, however fervent, would have the effect, to recal me to the path of duty, and to induce me to tread back again the devious steps in which I had involved myself. He had also threatened me. He had not felt sure, even while he wrote, / that he would launch into the hostile proceeding he had menaced. But he had judged it right to strengthen with this additional force the considerations with which he assailed me.

The purpose that was uppermost in his thoughts, was to promote the real interests of the little Julian. He had taken the blooming child for the centre of all his designs. He had made an idol of him; if it can be called idolatry, resolutely to pursue that which his understanding pointed out to him as most eligible. Julian was not of an age to judge for himself: Cloudesley therefore felt that he had the double task, to fix on what was best, and to take on himself the awful responsibility of proceeding, where the result of that proceeding would be virtually to affect the future respectability and happiness of a child.

There was nothing that Cloudesley so devoutly desired, as to see his ward recognised as / the undoubted son and heir of his late master, as to see him admitted to the family honours, and acknowledged as the unquestioned proprietor of the Alton estates. This he regarded as the consummation to be wished for.

But there were two sides to this question. Was it certain that the exertions of Cloudesley would be effectual to secure to him this just and merited triumph? If there were much to be gained, there was also something to lose. Up to the present moment the little Julian knew nothing of titles and honours and luxuries and splendour. He was happy, and might be for every happy in his ignorance. It was in the power of Cloudesley to supply him with a humble competence. He was now an inhabitant of the delicious climate of Italy; he was

---

[a] In Roman mythology Cacus, son of Vulcan, hid cattle stolen from Hercules in his cave. When Hercules passed by with his herd, the captured cows bellowed, upon which Hercules discovered them, and Cacus, whom he killed.

now, and might be for ever, happy in moderate pursuits and humble pleasures. No one with whom he would need to be in intercourse, would look / down upon and despise him. He would have the most valuable of all inheritances, independence. He would have no cares, no vain pursuits, no contentious vexations. The sun would for ever shine upon, or the shade for ever protect, his unambitious brow.

This however was not his proper place. No one felt more keenly than his present generous protector, that this would be a fit situation for the real son of Cloudesley, but not for the heir of the proud family of Herbert. What Julian had at present, and in prospect not to be disputed, was something, and was not to be thrown away, without mature deliberation.

The exertions of Cloudesley might be ineffectual to secure him a just and merited triumph. Supposing this to be the event, then what would happen? Julian would be the most contemptible of all spectacles, a pretender, a needy and disappointed adventurer. A perpetual blight / would follow him; he would feel himself an outcast. The more equitable were his claims, the more acute would be his sense of the wretched figure he made in his own eyes. He would hate the world; he would be dissatisfied with himself; he would fly into the most impenetrable retreat, that so he might be concealed from the scorn of the multitude. No, said Cloudesley to himself with unalterable firmness: my beloved Julian shall never be an adventurer.

But what reason had Cloudesley to anticipate an unsuccessful issue? He knew that he had a tale to tell, full of truth, full of power, capable, it may be, of carrying conviction to every unprejudiced mind. But it is not thus, that the graver affairs of this world, as they are called, are settled. Cloudesley knew that world. He had perhaps no proofs to adduce, that, in a court of law, could put down the formal attestations with which I was furnished. Then, in a / court of law, money is every thing. It is no trifling undertaking, to thrust from his place a nobleman, whose title is already authentically recorded, and who had been admitted to the possession of the estates and the income annexed to that title. What a delightful resource is to be found in the procrastination of the law, where the steps to be multiplied in behalf of the rich man are eternal, and every step requires all but the purse of a monarch, before it can be surmounted!

Cloudesley had talked of going to the earl Danvers, and there in person laying before that nobleman, in his princely mansion of Milwood Park, the true case of the youthful Julian, and the cogent reasons with which it was supported. Lord Danvers was already advanced beyond the middle period of human life, full of ideas of his personal consequence, and of the unstained honour of his race. I had been beforehand / with lord Danvers; and this question of a pretender he had never heard of before, would have appeared the question of an upstart. I had laid before him my certificates and attestations; his lordship had examined them with all due solemnity; and he had in the sequel admitted me to his bosom, and which was more, to the honour of his protection and countenance. No; lord Danvers was not a man that would ever submit to the disgrace of retractation, and the recording himself (such would be his version of the proceeding) a dolt and a driveller in the face of the world. He had made my case his own; and now no argument and no evidence would ever prevail upon him to separate himself from me.

Another consideration, calculated to make Cloudesley's application to lord Danvers desperate, was his lordship's impression as to the unstained honour of his race. His family had / been in possession of the peerage for centuries; they traced the distinctions of their house in regular progression from father to son, from the time of William the Conqueror. Some of them had acquired laurels in the Holy Land; some of them had taken a distinguished part in the conquest of France by Edward the Third;[a] they had contended before monarchs in the listed field; they had immortalised themselves by deeds of chivalry, had protected innocence, and put down the oppressor of female honour by the dint of the sword. Lord Danvers looked through the long table of his family genealogy, without encountering the name of an individual for whose actions he felt he had reason to blush. When he was gathered to his fathers, which in the course of nature must occur in no long time, he would be succeeded by Richard lord Alton, who had fought with honour in the wars against the Turks, and whose elder brother had died / abroad, being a volunteer in those wars. Richard lord Alton again had one son, and would probably have more, to perpetuate the honours of the family.

What was the purpose of Cloudesley, if he came into the presence of lord Danvers, and gained a hearing from him? To tell him that here was one base villain, whose name was inscribed in the roll of his genealogy, a man who had perpetrated the most ignominious of crimes, had taken advantage of the premature deaths of his brother and his brother's wife, had stripped the helpless orphan, and turned him out nameless to the world, and had usurped the estates his only claim to which was founded upon the perpetration of this crime. The act which was charged upon him, stamped him at once, if proved, a man without courage, feeling, honour, or principle.

In what temper of mind would lord Danvers / listen to the tale? He would have said to the late lord Alton's menial, who had come over to England to prefer such a charge, Who are you, that I should give credence to your story? If you persist in it, go before the king, before the assembled lords, and the courts of law; but come not to me. But no; you are conscious that it is all an imposture, and think that with a specious narrative you can impose on my declining age. But I have still the strength of mind to resist your intrigue, and the firmness of temper to drive you from my house. Have not I the certificates

---

[a] Edward III (1312–77), King of England from 1327. He inflicted a terrible defeat on the French at Crécy in 1346, but failed in his attempts to annexe the kingdoms.

of lord Alton's death, and of the interment of his wife and child, and what can you bring that in point of cogency can compete with these? Thank God, my name is still undishonoured; and this base conspiracy against it shall be detected, as all other base conspiracies are, by the all-seeing eye and the righteous judgment of my God! /

In fine, the decision of Cloudesley was, that, unless he could strike my heart with compunction, things should remain as they were. He resolved, that his beloved ward should never become that most pitiful of all things, a defeated adventurer, an animal crawling on the earth, claiming things that should never be conceded to him, and exhibiting to every one he met, his barren hopes, his secret repinings, the brand of defeat and discontent for ever conspicuous on his brow. Cloudesley was able to bring him up obscurely, but with tranquillity and cheerfulness. The worm of disappointment should never prey on his soul. Meanwhile, he would secure to him every advantage of education that Italy could afford, and render him the admiration and envy of all his contemporaries, as by his natural gifts he was so well qualified to be. Cloudesley in reality still retained in his heart the sanguine persuasion, that the day would / come, when the friendless Julian should be restored to all his honours, and when, adorned with every accomplishment, and instinct with the sublimest virtues, he should be acknowledged for the honourable representative and successor to an illustrious race. He purposed to expect the fulness of times that should bring all this to bear.

It was long however, before I became acquainted with the alteration that had taken place in the mind of Cloudesley. For six months I expected every day when the storm would burst upon me. By degrees the intenseness of my anticipation subsided. But it left behind it an entirely new tone in the feelings of my mind. I was like a man laying in prison for a long time under sentence of death. The execution was deferred year after year; but the warrant was drawn, and only waited for the executive magistrate to affix his signature. The world in / reality was nothing to me. Pleasure was not pleasure; and amusement ceased to be amusement. I lived under the oppression of an obscure and opake atmosphere, which took away all spring and content from my soul. I could not rise, I could not be moved, to joy. Life was a burthen.

And, if I were wretched from conscious guilt even at the best, there were seasons in which I suffered an anxiety and excitement of soul that baffles description. I anticipated the fatal blow that would fall upon me before the setting sun. On these occasions society was insupportable to me, and exertions of every kind not to be endured. I shut myself up in solitude. Every whispering wind seemed to bring with it the intelligence of my ruin. If the floor but creaked, it was converted into the creaking of chariot-wheels, that brought with them the intruder who was to drive me in nakedness and execration / from the roof that sheltered me. When the door of my apartment opened, it shook every limb in my frame. I shivered, like a man overtaken with mortal agonies. Cold drops of sweat stood on my brow. And, when at length, after the long and endless hours of the day were passed, the darkness of night shewed itself, I was lost in astonishment that the luminary of the world went down, no otherwise marked than the suns of all the preceding days had been already.

It is further necessary to observe, that I could not reason on lord Danvers as Cloudesley did. His premises were true: the earl was decidedly my friend; and he was as sensitively alive to the honour of his family, as the cherisher of Julian supposed. But could I look forward to the issue of an appeal made to his understanding and justice with heart unmoved? Lord Danvers was a man of penetration and judgment. / Cloudesley had a tale to relate, the very kernel of which was truth. He was capable of doing justice to it; and his deep feelings of compunction for the crime to which he had been accessory, would give to his narrative irresistible energy. With what feelings could I enter upon the trial, a trial for what was to me much dearer than life, my good name in the face of the world? I should be called upon to hear Cloudesley's relation, to encounter his eye, to face his earnest appeal addressed to myself for the truth of what he said. I should have to confront, to answer, to overturn as I could his various allegations. What would be the issue of our mortal contention?

If it had been a trial in a court of justice, the case would be different. I should have to instruct a hired advocate; and he would varnish over the circumstances with all the speciousness and effrontery that belong to his trade. He / would shrink at nothing; he would feel no trembling, no secret misgivings; he would be disgraced for ever in his profession, if he did. I need not utter a sound; I need not even be present at the awful crisis. He would have to produce the precise documents the law requires; and he would have them in readiness and full. He would have to disarm the circuitous and indirect circumstances which were brought against him. The judge and the jury would be called upon to decide, not according to the instinctive feelings by which an ingenuous mind is led to the touchstone of truth, but by rules of evidence, by acts of parliament, and all those musty precedents by which truth is ever and anon overwhelmed with discomfiture and confusion.

But, in reality, it was not the issue of the trial, be it which way it would, that I regarded with the greatest terror. That the disgraceful / tale should be gravely and publicly canvassed, was the thing that, more than death, I was desirous to avoid. If the story were divulged, every man in every street would make his judgment of it as he pleased. My character and good name would be torn into a thousand fragments. Nothing could satisfy me and give peace to my soul, but the assurance that the story should be for ever suppressed, and that my dishonour, my fabrication and cold-blooded plot to circumvent the child of my dying brother, should never be whispered in the ear of the meanest individual, dwelling in the obscurest corner of the earth. This was what my welfare demanded; what chance had I to obtain it?

In a certain sense I had perhaps a right to consider the letter of Cloudesley, as having dissolved our contract on his part, and giving me a right to depart from it on mine. I might withhold from him the income, which had hitherto / regularly been paid. He was in a country at a formidable distance both from England and Ireland; and under these circumstances might I not defy him to do his worst? If his supplies were ever so suddenly cut off, I might perhaps conclude that he would have wherewithal to defray the expences of his journey home with his wife and the child under his care. But these expences might probably make a fearful reduction of his means; and he had in all likelihood no resource from which to supply himself in future. He would come home poor, and would every day grow poorer. A poor suitor always labours under great disadvantages. Might I not rely upon my power to prevent his making a friend of lord Danvers? And without ample means he would have small hopes of obtaining success to his plea in the courts of law.

But I could not reason thus. To think of his arriving in England on any terms was no / less an evil than death to me. He had my secret in his keeping. What he would do respecting that secret, if provoked, and what success would attend his hostility, were problems I could not bear to reflect on. No: the only part that I conceived was left me, was to soothe him to the utmost of my power. He was like a wild beast, which I could not shut up, and which therefore by blandishment and temporising I must endeavour to disarm of its ferocity. I accordingly resolved that I would neither subtract from nor delay the instalments of the income I had engaged he should receive; and I took care to signify to him that such should be my conduct, as long as he did not throw away the scabbard, and proceed to the last extremeties against me.

I was besides not dead to some remains of sympathy for my brother's son. The wonderful accounts of him that Cloudesley transmitted to / me, were not without their effect on my choice. I wished him no further evil. I had already done him mischief enough. I quieted my conscience with the reflection, that the distinction of ranks was artificial and ideal. To me it was much, for I had been brought up in the lap of aristocracy. But to him, if he were educated as the son of Cloudesley, I persuaded myself that his chances for happiness would be fully as great, as if the expectation of inheriting the fortunes and rank of his fathers had been instilled into his infant mind. I would not for worlds, that he should, by any proceeding on my part, be reduced to poverty and destitution, and all the evils and temptations that too often fall to the lot of an unprotected vagabond. /

CHAPTER XI

From this time forward Cloudesley applied his principal attention to the education of his ward. It was his resolution that Julian should not be the son of disappointment; and he therefore determined that he should be bred in profound ignorance of his real parentage. He was to be brought up as the son of an English yeoman, who, with means sufficient for content and abundance, had fixed his residence in Italy; and he was never to know any other father / than Cloudesley, unless a new and truer career in the vicissitudes of human life should be opened to him under the most auspicious circumstances. There did not exist in Italy, any other person acquainted with his real origin, except Cloudesley and Eudocia; and she was accustomed in all matters of primary importance to conform implicitly to the will of her husband. It was therefore entirely in the power of his protector, to save Julian from that ambiguous character and fortune, which his affectionate guardian justly regarded with indescribable horror.

Cloudesley was anxious in the first place for the robustness and sound health of the corporeal frame of his pupil. He knew, that without health the enjoyments of a human being must be greatly curtailed, and that moral courage, that first of intellectual qualities, is intimately connected with animal strength and / dexterity. The life of Julian's protector, like the lives of all human beings, was of an uncertain tenure; and Cloudesley wished that his ward should be able to make his own way in the world. It is the destiny of man, like that of the animals inferior and brute, to grow up for a certain time under the parental wing, and then to be launched in the world, and enter upon his independence in turn, the only difference being that the brute undergoes this change a little earlier, and man a little later.

Cloudesley took the child with him in the fields, as soon as in the fine climate of Lombardy he was capable of this discipline; and he kept him, as much as possible in the open air. He taught him to run and to vault, inciting him to the first by the view of some object to be overtaken and seized; and to the last he found the pleasure annexed to the development and play of the limbs to be motive enough. / One of the first exercises he taught to his pupil, different from those which were as constantly resorted to as the day came round, was swimming. There are days, when the Benacus, or Lago di Garda,[a] though frequently

---

[a] Largest lake in Italy, situated between Lombardo and Veneto in N Italy.

subject to storms scarcely inferior to those of the Adriatic, is as serene and smooth as glass; and on those days Cloudesley unhesitatingly committed the child to the beautiful element under his own protection and care. After this, and when Julian was seven and eight years of age, he suggested to him shooting with the bow, wrestling, and horsemanship. Cloudesley was curious in the breeding and management of horses; and under his tuition Julian became expert in equestrian exercises, at an earlier age than is usual even with boys who possess the greatest advantages for that purpose.

Cloudesley wished him to associate with other boys, and from the trials of animal strength, the / collision of the passions of that age, and the competition and characteristic dexterity of childish wit, practically to prepare himself for the more serious intercourses and rivalship of mature age. He found the peasant children of Lombardy admirably adapted to his wish in that respect. They were animated and well tempered. They had warm hearts and frolic dispositions. Their eyes flashed with a dark fire, which however seldom failed to be tempered with benignity. They were for the most part sympathetic and generous. Yet they had an earnestness in their pursuits, and a quickness in their desires, which gave to their sports all the advantages of emulation, at the same time that they seldom degenerated into anger and the fierceness of muscular contention.

While Cloudesley was attentive to the advancement of his ward in corporal strength and dexterity, the improvement of his mind was not / neglected. The protector of Julian had been fortunate in his selection of the young man from the university, whom he had received as an inmate under his roof. It was little that Giuseppe, such was his ordinary appellation, soon became partial to the boy; for nature had been so bountiful in her provisions for the infant Julian, that, wherever he commenced even the slightest intercourse, he scarcely ever failed to make an entire friend. But, in addition to this it fortunately happened, that Giuseppe was very young. He was only seventeen years of age, when he became the inmate of the family, at which time Julian was little more than three. To the recollection of the child therefore it seemed as if he had always been a member of the establishment. He appeared to Julian more in the character of an elder brother, than any thing else. Giuseppe would be his playfellow, tossing him in his arms, bearing him on his / shoulder, and assisting him in his games, with no other conspicuous advantage over the child than what consisted in greater judgment to chuse their sports, and greater strength to execute what was consulted on between them.

Even almost from the first, when Giuseppe was giving Cloudesley lessons in Italian, the child would often plant himself near them unperceived; and, as he was endowed with surprising quickness of memory, he would con over a stanza or two of Ariosto or Bojardo in a subdued voice, and then would surprise them with a high-toned and somewhat theatrical recitation of the passage, partly caught by his ear from the animated manner of Giuseppe, and partly suggested by his anticipated feeling of the poet.[a] Sometimes he would trip from a sudden defect of memory, or perhaps because the syllables of the verse were too complicated for his childish organs; but this even added a / grace at his time of life, and excited his hearers to break in on his rehearsal with a thousand kisses.

Cloudesley in his more serious discourse, when they two were alone, applied himself to stimulate Giuseppe to do the greatest justice he could to the quick apprehension and superior intellectual faculties of his pupil. He remarked, that the boy was born to no station, that he should be able to provide for him slender and moderate means only, and that Julian must look therefore for the figure he should make in future life to his personal resources and acquisitions. It was too early to determine, to what pursuit or engagement in life he should hereafter be devoted, but there were many things that would be useful and ornamental in all.

Giuseppe did not need to be excited. He sincerely loved the boy, and was therefore anxious to impart to him every benefit in his / power. The studies of Julian could scarcely be said to cost the child labour or pains; at the same time that the preceptor endeavoured in every practicable case to make him feel the *cui bono*, the satisfaction and advantage he would reap from his acquisitions. The instructor and the pupil played the game into each other's hands: they were both enthusiastic, both earnest; and therefore what they did had seldom the formality of a lesson; but each, almost unconsciously and unintentionally, strung his nerves for the task, and strove which of the two should most amply perform the part which the nature of things assigned him. In a school, the preceptor cannot apply himself to the peculiarities of each boy in his class, but must to a great degree make a common rule for all, bringing forward, as nearly as may be, the dull and the ingenious, the mercurial and the reflecting, to the same point. But, where the instructor has / only a single pupil to attend to, the case is widely different. Giuseppe watched the variations of Julian, even as an experienced navigator watches the variations of the needle. When excursion and sport was the order of the day, Giuseppe appeared to think of nothing but excursion and sport. And yet even in the wildest of their sallies, an apt quotation from the poets, a hint for science, or an observation on nature and the general system of things, would come in, and, instead of throwing a damp on their gaiety, would give to the feast of gaiety a zest unknown before.

Italian was to the boy in a manner his native language; and therefore at a comparatively early age his tutor began to initiate him in the rudiments of the Latin tongue. But all this was without formality. The inflections of nouns and verbs were treated as a sort of game. When Julian had laughed sufficiently at the / sing-song of declensions and conjugations, they were laid aside for something else. The next day Giuseppe would propose that the boy should try

---

[a] See note a p. 132.

how much he could recollect of the exercise of the day before; and, when he did well, his instructor would commend him, and perhaps turn the whole into an agreeable recollection by a toy, a tool, an amusement, a promenade, happily interposed, so as to produce unconsciously a pleasing combination of ideas between the lesson and the gratuity. The meaning of sentences in Latin was acquired, by Julian's first learning by heart a distich or stanza for its musical cadence, at which he had a marvellous facility: and then his inquisitive mind instinctively prompted him to enquire after the sense, which, by means of the lively and prepossessing manner of Giuseppe in expounding, he was well contented to learn word by word, till he had mastered the whole. Thus they entered / together upon the first steps of an acquisition, which, as the boy grew up, was to be pursued with a graver method, and a more defined conception on the part of the learner, of the value of his studies.

In this manner the years of the child for the most part rolled on in uninterrupted happiness. One incident however is perhaps worth relating, consisting as it did of a dissention of a more weighty nature between Giuseppe and Julian. It occurred when the latter was about eight or nine years of age. Cloudesley had gone, which was somewhat rare with him, on a journey for some urgent purpose to Venice, and had left the household consisting of Eudocia, Giuseppe, Julian, and the servants. One day Julian was missing. He had gone out early in the morning before breakfast, and did not return either to dinner, or at the usual hour of evening refreshment. This was a circumstance wholly unprecedented, / and produced considerable alarm. Eudocia, who loved the boy as entirely as if he had been her own, was overwhelmed with agitation, and her uneasiness rendered the incident additionally impressive to Giuseppe. He considered also the deep responsibility in which he held himself bound to Cloudesley for the safety of his pupil. He had just returned from his classes at the university, and set out immediately in quest of the vagrant. The sun had already gone down, and every thing was considerably darkening in the shades of evening, when Giuseppe met him returning homeward from the banks of the Menzo, a quiet stream which discharges itself into the Adige two miles below Verona, in company with some peasant boys. Giuseppe immediately separated him from his associates with an air of much seriousness, and conducted him towards the *podere*.

As they passed along, the student questioned / his pupil where he had been all day. Julian answered with unsuspecting simplicity, that he had gone out in the public road to amuse himself for a few minutes only, that there he had met with these boys, who had proposed to him a ramble to a copse at no great distance, where he would find plenty of nuts. In the amusement of nutting hour after hour had crept on unperceived, and, when they were tired of this pursuit, they had wandered to the banks of the Menzo, where they stripped, and refreshed themselves with bathing and swimming.

Giuseppe represented to his pupil, how improper it was that he should absent himself for so long a time, without the smallest intimation to his mother or any one else, and described the exceeding anxiety and uneasiness he had occasioned to Eudocia. Julian was struck with this account, and immediately acknowledged the fault he had committed, and promised it should / not happen again. But the tutor aggravated the matter, by enlarging on the impropriety of his associating with these village-boys in their sports, who were very unfit company for a young gentleman like him. From this remonstrance Julian dissented, and told Giuseppe in plain terms, that his father (Cloudesley) had sanctioned the acquaintance.

This struck the preceptor as an untruth; and he immediately reproved the boy for endeavouring to cover a fault by a falshood. Julian defended himself, and persisted in his assertion. Giuseppe was offended with the child for his obstinacy in reiterating a tale, that he supposed had first been uttered without consideration. The most scrupulous care had always been taken about the boy's morals; and indeed, indulgently as he had been brought up, and happily as his days had passed, he could scarcely have any / temptation to say the thing that was not. Accordingly, truth and Julian had never for a moment been divorced; and whatever he asserted was always sure to be believed. – This however appeared to Giuseppe not to be reasonable in the present instance; and he lectured the child emphatically upon the disgrace he would incur if he persisted in such a practice, and the pernicious consequences that would follow. He told him that sincerity and plain dealing were the characteristics of an honourable mind, and added that he hoped he should never again have occasion to apply to him a reprimand, which should be addressed only to the worthless.

Julian could scarcely believe his senses, that such language should be used to him, and by a person for whom he had always felt both respect and love. This was the first time in his life that the thought of dishonour had ever approached / him. He replied to Giuseppe somewhat indignantly, and with an air not unmingled with scorn, I have told you the truth.

A person of greater discernment would at least have been made doubtful of the judgment he had passed, by the firm and unhesitating manner in which the boy repelled it. But the student had been bred to the vocation of a priest; and, though not yet in orders, something of the spirit of the vocation had already taken possession of him. He was offended that the child should presume to say he was in error. He had addressed to Julian a brief discourse of a religious character; and his penitent, instead of listening submissively, and improving by the lesson, had stood erect, and scornfully rejected the charge that was brought against him.

As soon as they got home, Giuseppe with much gravity led him to his chamber, and ordered him to bed. He left him with a dry / Good Night, and added, I shall talk to you further in the morning. The boy took all this grievously to heart. It was the first time injustice had ever been committed towards him. Giuseppe and he had lived together, not like tutor and pupil, but as brothers. Add to which, he felt with poignancy the meanness that was imputed to him, and the dishonour with which he was branded. The longer he reflected on it, the less he could endure it. He became choaked with a sense of the unworthy treatment he had received, and was almost in convulsions. He then burst into an agony of tears. Eudocia came to his bedside, and soothed him in the best manner she could. She sat by him, till he was asleep. But his slumbers were disturbed. He called out in the night, I cannot bear it. I did go with you; my father bid me; I swear it; bear witness for me! Did I ever think I should be treated so? At another time he rose from his / bed; he passed into the sitting-room, and thence in the garden.

Cloudesley arrived early in the forenoon of the following day, and immediately vindicated the veracity of Julian. He said he had been struck with uncommon good qualities of the peasant family with which Julian had rambled, and had observed to him, Though they are dressed in homely clothes, I have found them full of address and right-mindedness, and you will meet with no companions with whom I should be more happy to trust you.

Cloudesley, as has already appeared, was in the highest degree attached to his ward, and made him in some sort his idol. He passed him for his son; but he secretly regarded him as belonging to another order of beings, and was therefore full of indignation that Giuseppe should have treated him with such severity, and / especially on an occasion in which the boy had really told nothing but the truth. Julian inherited the noble blood of all his ancestors; and Cloudesley deemed it little less than sacrilege, that base and plebeian vices should be imputed to him, of which he scarcely ought to have known so much as the name.

The generous yeoman expressed his wrath against Giuseppe in his absence, the student having already gone to his classes at the university when Cloudesley arrived. The impressions of Julian were at first of a mixed nature. He felt the relief of which he stood greatly in need, when he found his father acquitting him, and vouching for the truth of his statement. But Cloudesley proceeded to censure in unmeasured terms the folly and insolence of the upstart probationer, who had dared unmeritedly to tax Julian with a lie. He declared that there / should be an end of all intercourse between them, and the fellow should never have an opportunity of so much rashness a second time.

At this harsh decision the feelings of the boy suddenly changed. He recollected all the causes he had to love the youthful student, his kindness, their mutual frolics, the way in which Giuseppe had a thousand times condescended to his little freaks and fancies, the good humour of his lessons, the patience of his explanations. He was at an age now to understand all this much better than he had done at the time, and to feel the intrinsic superiority of Giuseppe, when he had most put himself upon a level with his pupil.

Julian burst into a flood of tears. He intreated Cloudesley not to be angry with the student, who had done all with the best intention. He intreated him not to take his friendly monitor from him. He protested that he could / never be easy without him, and could never follow his little lessons and tasks with any body else.

The wrath of Cloudesley was appeased by the passion of the boy. He drew Julian to him, kissed his forehead, and told him it should be as he desired. He was delighted with the strong marks of a forgiving spirit and an affectionate disposition, which this incident brought out to view. /

CHAPTER XII

But he could never in reality pardon Giuseppe. In exact proportion as he has been delighted with the early experiment of his kind method of instructing, and the tenderness he had put into his communications with Julian, Cloudesley was struck with the different character of what had lately passed. Every time that he saw the student, the thing occurred fresh to his mind. The stripling has turned himself into the pedagogue! said Cloudesley internally. The revolution / that this brought about in the tone of the yeoman's feelings, called up to his mind a plan that he had various times contemplated, of removing himself and his charge to a new scene, and thus separating them from Verona and Giuseppe together.

The scene he fixed on was Tuscany. The residence of Lombardy, in the outskirts of the beautiful region of Italy, had done well enough for the immature years of his ward. But now nothing would content him, except the state that had given birth to Dante, Petrarca, Boccaccio and Michael Angelo, and where the delicious Italian language was universally acknowledged to subsist in its utmost purity.[a] Florence was the depository of many of the finest works of art in the world; the Florentine gallery was their superb centre; and the generous patronage of the Medici had given peculiar advantages in that respect to this happy city. / If Cloudesley did not profoundly understand this, it had been reported to him by the most competent witnesses; and he resolved that, as far as depended on him, Julian should have the best opportunity for improving himself in language, for cultivating his mind, and frequenting all those great monuments of excellence which are supposed to contribute the most to refine the taste of him that beholds them.

---

[a] Dante Alighieri (1265–1321), Italian poet; Michelangelo, properly Michelagniolo di Lodovico Buonarroti (1475–1564), Italian sculptor, painter and poet, architect and military engineer.

The boy was placed under the immediate care of one of the professors of the Liceo Fiorentino;[a] and the loss of Giuseppe was amply supplied to him. His intellect was now characterised with sobriety and steadiness; and it was no longer necessary (to speak in the language of Tasso), that the cup which contained the medicine of the mind should have its edges moistened with artificial sweetness, to induce the patient to drain its contents.[b]

One additional branch of instruction which / Cloudesley brought forward at this time, was the study of the English language. This was an acquisition that the protector of Julian thought necessary, in relation to the views which he entertained respecting the future destination of his ward. But he was additionally prompted to take up this matter on the present occasion, by the circumstance of having accidentally fallen in with a young Englishman of extraordinary endowments and an enthusiastical temper at Florence, of the name of Elliot.

He introduced this young man into his house. Julian had already made considerable progress in Latin, and had some smattering of Greek. Cloudesley led Elliot in the presence of the boy, into a sort of discussion as to the comparative excellencies of different languages, and the merits of the writers by whom they had been cultivated. Elliot was liberal and generous in his praise of all that was admirable in / the authors in the various tongues of which he spoke. But he claimed an unquestionable superiority for the writers of his native land. He said, that they only of all the moderns had been touched by the genius of freedom, that they dared to utter all that they thought, and that by necessary consequence they had penetrated into the secrets of nature, and laid open the recesses of mind. He talked of Bacon and Hobbes, of Shakespear and Milton, and of an incomparable genius that had lately honoured and adorned his country, the admirable Berkeley.[c] Elliot knew how to give to each of these his appropriate praise, and spoke of them all in turn with a fervour of soul, which it was next to impossible to witness unmoved. He said, that the nations of the continent of Europe had undoubtedly produced great men; but he would not allow that a rival to any one of these could be found throughout the world. Julian listened / with earnest attention to the music of Elliot's discourse. He was far from understanding the half of what he said; but he caught the enthusiasm of the speaker, and his little heart palpitated with emotion at the emotions which displayed themselves in the voice, the gestures, and the eye of Elliot. He recollected that English was the native tongue of his father; and he exclaimed with startling and singular vehemence, I will learn English.

In the various pursuits therefore of classical studies and of the English

---

[a] Florentine College.

[b] Torquato Tasso (1544–95), Italian poet.

[c] Francis Bacon, Baron Verulam of Verulam, Viscount St Albans (1561–1626), English philosopher and statesman; Thomas Hobbes (1588–1679), English philosopher; George Berkeley (1685–1753), Anglican bishop and subjectivist philosopher.

language, in a word, of every thing adapted to his years, the progress of Julian was at this time astonishingly rapid. In the course of the next six or seven years he shook off every thing that was childish and puerile, without substituting in its stead the slightest tincture of pedantry. The frankness and nobility of his spirit defended him from all danger on that side. The constitution / of his nature was incapable of combining itself with any alloy of the fop or the coxcomb. All his motions were free, animated and elastic. They sprung into being instant and as by inspiration, without waiting to demand the sanction of the deliberative faculty. They were born perfect, as Minerva is feigned to have sprung in complete panoply from the head of Jove.[a] The sentiments of his mind unfolded themselves without trench or wrinkle, in his honest countenance, and impassioned features. Into that starry region no disguise could ever intrude: and the clear and melodious tones of his voice were a transparent medium to the thoughts of his heart. Persuasion hung on all he said; and it was next to impossible that the most rugged nature and the most inexorable spirit should dispute his bidding. And this was the case, because all he did was in love, in warm affection, in a single desire for the happiness of those / about him. Everyone hastened to perform his behests, because the idea of empire and command never entered into his thoughts. He seemed as if he lived in a world made expressly for him; so precisely did all with whom he came into contact, appear to form their tone on his.

And, in the midst of all his studies and literary improvement, he in no wise neglected any of that bodily dexterity by which he had been early distinguished. His mastery in swimming, in handling the dart and the bow, in swiftness of foot, and in wrestling, kept pace with his other accomplishments. Nor was his corporal strength any way behind his other endowments. He could throw the discus higher and farther than any of his competitors. But his greatest excellence in this kind was in horsemanship. He sprung from the ground like a bird, as if his natural quality had been to mount into the / air. He vaulted into his seat, like an angel that had descended into it from the conveyance of a sunbeam. He had a favourite horse, familiar, as it were, with all the thoughts of his rider, and that shewed himself pleased and proud of the notice of the noble youth. He snorted, and bent his neck in the most graceful attitudes, and beat the ground with his hoof, and shewed himself impatient for the signal to leave the goal, and start into his utmost speed. Julian was master of his motions. He would stop, and wind,[b] and exhibit all his perfection of paces, with a whisper, or the lifting of a finger, from him whose approbation excited in the animal the supremest delight. – In a word, Julian won the favour of his elders by the clearness of his apprehension, and his progress in every thing that was taught

---

[a] Minerva, the Roman goddess of wisdom and patroness of the arts and trades, is fabled to have sprung fully armed from the brain of Jove, the Roman name for Jupiter.

[b] Sniff in order to scent.

him, and of his equals by his excellence in all kinds of sport and feats of /
dexterity, which could be equalled only by the modesty, the good humour, and
accommodating spirit with which he bore his honours, rendering others almost
as well satisfied with his superiority, as if the triumph had been their own. /

CHAPTER XIII

Cosmo (Cosimo) the Third, of the family of Medicis, had succeeded to the
authority of Grand Duke of Florence in 1670, which station he continued to
hold till 1723, the year of his death.[a] He was at that time eighty-one years of
age. He had been for many years exclusively under the direction of priests and
friars; and, during the whole of this period, the character of Tuscany had been
so altered, that it could scarcely in any way be recognised / for the same
principality that had shone with so peculiar lustre under the reign of his
predecessors. All public amusements, and that free and unrestrained intercourse of society, the parent of wit, gaiety, and the sports of poetry and
intellectual rivalry and contention, so eminently adapted to the Italian taste,
laboured under the most rigorous discountenance; and severe and frequently
capital punishments abounded in the administration of criminal justice.

Cosmo had two sons, Ferdinand and Giovanni, the elder born in the year
1663, the other eight years younger.[b] The character of Ferdinand was universally popular. He despised the narrow genius of his father's government, and
had a soul which seemed to be formed for great enterprises. He inherited from
his earlier ancestors the love of letters and the fine arts, and made it no secret
that, if ever he arrived at the supreme power, he would / reverse all the
principles of policy which then prevailed. Every generous spirit in Tuscany,
every lover of refinement or glory, looked forward with eager aspirations to the
period of his accession. But heaven had decreed that their hopes should be
frustrated. He had no sooner reached the forty-eighth year of his age, than he
was seized with a lingering disease, which baffled all the skill of the physicians.
He languished under this sickness for two years, and at the end of that period
expired, with a constitution entirely exhausted, and a frame reduced to a
skeleton.

Upon the death of Ferdinand the hopes of the citizens of Florence rested
upon his younger brother. Each of these princes had married; the elder to

---

[a] Como Medici III, Grand Duke of Tuscany (1642–1723).
[b] Ferdinand Medici (1663–1713); Giovanni Gastone Medici (1671–1737).

Violante, daughter of the elector of Bavaria, and sister to the dauphiness of France; and the younger to a daughter of the empress of Germany.[a] The latter of these marriages / proved unfortunate. The wife of Giovanni had no brilliant qualities, and, after a short time, separated herself from her husband, and retired to her native country of Bohemia. The princess Violante on the contrary won strongly the esteem and affection of the people of Tuscany. She had entered into all the views of her husband, and was a zealous patroness of letters and the arts. She was a woman of exemplary piety, and constant in the practice of every Christian virtue. Along with this, she was eminently distinguished by the grace and nobleness of her carriage, and her extraordinary endowments of intellect. She was a lover of accomplished society, and had a frankness and gaiety of disposition, which, as they never exceeded the bounds of true discretion, engaged every heart in her favour. In addition to this, she was thoroughly qualified for the direction of state affairs, and her advices were / always found to lead to the benefit of the principality. The great loved her for her courteousness, the sweetness of her manners, and the charms of her demeanour; and the people, because she was ever desirous of their ease and prosperity.

Giovanni, the surviving son of the grand duke, contracted a very sincere friendship for her, and, when he succeeded to the supreme authority upon the death of his father, in the year 1723, he consulted her on all occasions, and was governed in every thing by her advice. Though by no means her equal in the soundness of her understanding and the delicacy of her taste, he was of a cheerful and animated humour, was all mettle and fire, and passionately fond of assemblies, dancing, and elegant female society. The freaks in which he would otherwise probably have indulged, were restrained by the discretion of Violante; by her / suggestion the imposts[b] under which the public laboured were materially reduced; and she even superintended the administration of the finances. Giovanni devoted himself both from sentiment and conviction to the judgment of his sister-in-law. The consequence was that, immediately upon his accession, the city of Florence assumed an entirely new face. The palace of the grand duke was crowded with young persons of the most agreeable manners and the most lively wit. Banquets and public entertainments were the order of the day; and a thousand caprices, and innocent and agreeable frolics were incessantly started for the general amusement.

The *conversazioni*[c] that were held in the apartments of the princess, were not remarked only for the liveliness of youthful spirits, and the elevated manners and rank of those who frequented them. They also derived every grace / from the cultivation of the arts. Painters and musicians were secure of an enlightened encouragement from the delicacy of her taste. But poetry above all was that to

---

[a] Violante of Bavaria (d. 1731); Anna Maria of Saxe-Lauenburg (d. 1741).
[b] Taxes.
[c] (Italian) Social gatherings for discussion of the arts, literature, etc.

which she was enthusiastically attached. She studied the immortal productions of Dante, Petrarca and Ariosto;[a] and, by the mode in which she indicated their beauties to her favoured associates, inspired into others a true relish of their excellence, and made the great classics of the language an universal fashion, that every one was ashamed not to subscribe to.

In addition however to her avowed admiration of the great pillars of Italian literature, the princess Violante was forward to encourage every indication of talent among the present generation of Tuscans. Several authors who devoted themselves to the illustration of the history of Italy, or to the preparing new and improved editions of the writers of ancient / Greece and Rome, were distinguished by her patronage, and judiciously assisted by her in bringing the fruits of their investigations before the public. The most pleasing poets of the day basked in the sunshine of her favour. But there was one species of poetry, which particularly flourished at the present period. This was the effusions of persons who, a subject being given them by others, immediately poured out a copious stream of verses, figurative, impassioned and eloquent, before a numerous audience, assembled to witness their performances. The Italian language is particularly adapted to this species of exhibition. Pronounced with fervour and animation, it seems to be the very soul of music; and, by its structure and inflexions, appears to fall easily into almost any species of verse at the pleasure of the speaker. The character of the people of Italy is not less suited to the success of the experiment. Their / first appearance is that of being open, uncontroled in the expression of their emotions, and enthusiastic and voluble in giving utterance to their feelings.

The most eminent of these individuals was a person of the name of Bernardino Perfetti, a native of Siena.[b] His limbs were active, his carriage animated, and his voice melodious. His figure was beautiful: but his countenance was heaven. The bones stood out; the chin was pronounced and projecting; the cheekbones were high; the complexion was fair, even to transparency. There was no incumbrance of flesh, and no deficiency. His eyes were liquid and soft, full of tenderness, full of delicate and diversified meaning. There was an ingenuousness in his visage, impossible to be described, impossible to be resisted. It said, Here I am at your mercy; use me at your pleasure; but I know you will not hurt me. /

Bernardino was specially in favour with the princess; and it seldom failed that he was called on once or twice a week at her assemblies to give a specimen of his powers. The subjects of his verses, as I have said, were almost always furnished by the different persons who happened to be present. They were usually written on slips of paper, which were thrown into a box, and then

---

[a] See notes to pp. 81, 148.

[b] Bernardino Perfetti (1681–1747), improvisator and leading Italian scholar whom Godwin may have learned about through Percy and Mary Shelley.

drawn out fortuitously by a lady named to that office. This ceremony was first performed; and the artist was then summoned into the apartment. The subjects were sometimes classical, sometimes of a courtly stamp, having reference to some beneficial and gracious act of the government, and sometimes to topics of gallantry and the praises of the beauties of the court. However trite or hackneyed might be the materials of the composition, or the figures with which it was adorned, the sustained fervour and the / varied manner of the speaker effectually for the time concealed these defects.

But the most extraordinary part of Bernardino's performances was a comedy, with which his exhibitions were always concluded. The materials of these comedies were indeed in a great degree common-place: a peevish and avaricious father, a beautiful and simple-hearted daughter, a lover slenderly endowed with the goods of fortune, but graceful and irresistible in his addresses, a lacquey inexhaustible in tricks, disguises and imposition, and a soubrette who assisted the lacquey in all his arts.[a] But, simple as these materials were, they were inexhaustible in the hands of this consummate artist. The deceptions were so new, and the unsuspecting simplicity with which the father gave into them so ludicrous. The cautiousness of old age was multiplied to an extraordinary extent, yet was in all cases made a dupe of. The triumph of / the lovers was of the most exhilarating cast; yet they were again and again defeated, when they thought themselves most secure. Their disappointment and despair excited interest in the most callous spectator; and the earnestness of their affection was always in the end crowned with success. All this was represented by one performer, who by the changes of his position and his voice, the imbecility of the dotard,[b] the devotedness of the young female, the ardour of the lover, the assurance of the lacquey, and the ever ready glosses of the soubrette, made you always apprehend who were the parties brought forward, without its being necessary to have recourse to the bungling expedient of naming them. Bernardino sometimes assisted himself with a scarf, or the voluminous folds of a cloak, which he caught up, or cast aside at pleasure, but his great resource was in the endless variety that he gave to the lines and expression of his / countenance, sometimes discharging it of all appearance of understanding, and looking now with inexpressible innocence, demureness, slyness, penetration, consciousness, dexterity, and even wit. The attention of the audience was unremitted; but their applauses were frugal and well discriminated, the most frequent and gratifying being uncontroled bursts of genuine hilarity and laughter.

Cosmo the Third died in October 1723; and in the following spring the princess Violante took a journey to Rome. She proceeded *incognita*, under the assumed name of the contessa Pitigliano; but the disguise was only so far kept

---

[a] Lacquey or lackey, a footman, or valet; soubrette, a minor female role in comedy, often that of a pert lady's maid.

[b] A person who is weak-minded, especially through senility.

up, as to excuse her from certain formalities which she desired to dispense with. She experienced the utmost courtesy from Benedict the Thirteenth, who was newly advanced to the papal chair; and cardinal Lorenzo Corsini, afterwards pope, was specially directed to consult / her pleasure.[a] She brought Bernardino in her suite; she held her *conversazioni* precisely as she had done in Florence; and this accomplished artist was called on, in his mistress's apartments and elsewhere, to exhibit the wonders of his genius. His success was astonishing, insomuch that the princess demanded for him the honour of receiving the laurel in solemn pomp in the capitol; a grace, which had been solicited by many in successive centuries, but had been conferred on none, since it had been received by Petrarca in the year 1341.[b] /

CHAPTER XIV

The scenes I have mentioned occurred five years before the time when Julian took up his residence in Florence. But the princess Violante lived till the year 1731; and, even after her death, the tone which she had inspired into the best society there, for a long time survived the accomplished personage to whom it was indebted for its existence. Bernardino had in no wise decreased in powers or popularity, either when Julian arrived at Florence, being then ten / years of age, or for several winters following. The English boy had heard repeatedly of the fame of the exhibitions of the *improvvisatore*; and he intreated his protector to allow him the gratification of being present. The indulgence was attended with no difficulty. The mode was for the grand duke or any of the principal nobility to grant to Bernardino for the occasion the use of a hall in their palace, and all who were admitted to the entertainment paid at entering a piece of money at the door.

It was not till the beginning of the third year of Julian's residence at Florence, that he enjoyed the pleasure of which he had formed such sanguine expectations. On the death of the princess, an event equally unexpected and afflicting, all public entertainments had been suspended for several weeks. The occasion on which Julian first saw and heard Bernardino, was the first on which this extraordinary man stood forward / before a public assembly, since the death of his patroness. It was announced, that in this exhibition all his performances

---

[a] Benedict XIII, Pietro Francesco Orsini, pope from 1724–30; Lorenzo Corsini, Pope Clement XII, from 1730–40.

[b] Laurel, emblem of distinction in poetry; capitol, state building housing the legislature.

would be of a serious cast, to conclude with a monody on the death of the princess.

Julian was fresh from the perusal of Ariosto and the popular Italian poets. He had familiarised himself with their language; he was in the daily practice of conning their most admired passages. He was in fact, practically speaking, native to the dialect of the peninsula, and as if 'to the manner born.'[a] He had therefore no difficulties which lay in the way of his gratification. He instantly entered into the phraseology and sentiment of Bernardino. But how great was to him the contrast between the school-boy reading of the poets, and the formal glosses of his instructors to which he had been accustomed, and the vehement, and, as it / seemed the inspired delivery of the *improvvisatore*!

One of the subjects was the leaping of signor Costantino Boccali on horseback, from the bridge into the river of the Adige, at the command of his scornful mistress, as recorded by Bandello, in the Forty-seventh Novel of his First Book, which Bernardino was called on to describe in extemporary verse.[b] It was done to perfection. The disdain of the lady, and the generous devotedness of the lover were painted in the most glowing colours. You saw the desperate leap which the cavalier made; you saw the deep and rapid course of the river, swelled as it was with autumnal rains, and chilled with the bleak wind that swept over the Alps. The horse and his rider sank at once to the bottom, and then rose like a ball, Boccali still maintaining his seat with firmness. He directed / his steed towards the bank; but, more attentive to the observing his mistress than to his own safety, he approached where the cliff was perpendicular, and it was impossible to land. Turning the bridle to correct his error, and struggling with the swiftness of the stream, an unexpected start of the animal deprived him of the stirrups and his seat, while he had still hold of the reins. He threw away them and his cloak, and set himself to swim with all his force. The spectators on the bridge shivered and screamed at sight of the imminent peril to which he was exposed; and his mistress, hitherto so unfeeling, was drowned in tears, and expressed the bitterest agony. The sight of her sympathy gave him tenfold courage. Through tremendous dangers he reached a more accessible part of the shore, and stood on dry land. His horse, freed from the load that confined him, was equally successful. Dripping as he was, the / lover hastened to the feet of his mistress; and, moved by the sight of the daring and terrible act by which he had proved the sincerity of his passion, she at once dismissed the severity in which she had prided herself, and ever after considered the attachment of her cavalier as her chiefest glory.

---

[a] *Hamlet*, I. iv. 15.

[b] Bandello wrote four Books of stories. The forty-seventh 'novel' of Bandello's first Book (1554) is more properly designated a story, being only twelve pages long. Its full title is: 'A Castellan, Finding his Wife in Adultery With His Lord, Slayeth Him; by Reason Whereof He and Many Others Die Miserably'. The hubris following upon rash gratification of passionate impulse is a familiar theme in all Godwin's later novels.

Julian was entranced with the narrative of the *improvvisatore*. All the circumstances as they were described, were to his apprehension realities. He saw the bridge and the river, familiar objects as they had been to him for years past. He felt with intense earnestness for the perils which Boccali encountered, and entered deeply into the courage with which he breasted them. He could scarcely keep his seat for emotion. His youthful faculties were fully commensurate to take in the thing which the poet described. He was astonished at the completeness and the living colours in which / the whole was placed before him. He was filled with admiration and enthusiasm.

Bernardino at length proceeded to his monody for the princess Violante. He expatiated on her charms and her indescribable grace. He spoke of the sweetness of her smiles, and the melody of her voice. No taste, as her panegyrist affirmed, could be so true as hers; no sympathy so unbounded and entire. All that Rome or Greece ever knew of literature and the mimetic arts, was her own. As a stateswoman and a financier she was perfect; and no being in human form ever felt so entire a passion for the improvement and happiness of all within the reach of her influence. The poet then described the sudden revolution in the health of the princess, from a state of the most entire vigour and energy to the doors of the grave. She had been only a few days indisposed. The instant she was known to be in / danger, all Florence was in alarm. It seemed as if the life of the court and of all the inhabitants was suspended on her life. And, when Bernardino came to speak of the last hours of her existence, that night of terror, that night of disaster, when the news suddenly burst on those who filled the avenues of the palace with anxious expectation, Violante is dying, our mistress is no more – the audience was drowned in tears; their sobs were audible; and the speaker was compelled to pause in his discourse by the vehemence of his emotions.

The exhibition of this morning constituted an era in the life of Julian. The seats for the audience, filled with the first society in Florence, and the area prepared for the exhibitor, were alike a scene to him. The fervour of the speaker, and the sympathy of the hearers, acted with united influence on his soul. To add to the whole, there was a youth who sat / next him, two or three years older than himself, who engaged him in conversation, who told him what was to come next, explained the method and arrangement of the whole, and was 'as good as a chorus' to him.[a] This youth was nephew to the *improvvisatore*.

Julian was eager for a repetition of that which had afforded him so high a delight; and no difficulty was made in indulging his wish. His late associate presently found him out, and was eager to join him again. There was something in Julian that won upon the good will of almost every one with whom he was brought into contact. His eye was so open and frank, and the diversified lines of

---

[a] *Hamlet*, III. ii. 259. Ophelia's words to Hamlet are, 'You are a good chorus, my lord.'

his cheeks and lips promised so much discrimination and tact, combined with the utmost benignity and sweetness of disposition, that all anticipated that they should find gratification in being associated with such a companion. His manner was so animated, and / the activity of his limbs and spirits so great, as to rouse the partiality of the most careless observer.

Francesco Perfetti (that was the name of the stranger youth) revealed to him in this interview his kindred with the laureated exhibitor, and offered to present Julian to his uncle. With native modesty, but with unspeakable anticipation of the pleasure and distinction of such an interview, Julian accepted the proposal. As was usually his fortune with strangers, the *improvvisatore* conceived an immediate liking to the boy. Bernardino was himself of the most mercurial disposition, indulging in a thousand freaks, never, but when he was engaged in the rehearsing or utterance of his compositions, able to contain himself for any time in one posture, quick in impulse, joyous of temperament, and with as many whims as an ape. So long as he devoted himself to the embodying and / development of one thought, he was all in that thought, his powers of mind and body flowed in that single direction. Nothing could interrupt or disturb him: you would say that, if the roof that covered him fell on his head, he would not be aware of it. But, when he had finished the purpose to which he had vowed his efforts, it seemed as it he revenged himself for the periodical singleness and concentration of his mind, by a quick succession of the most extravagant humours and fantasies.

Julian had never in his life fallen in with a person of this cast; and he felt himself singularly gratified and deeply interested in watching all his motions. Bernardino on his part was flattered in observing the demonstrations of Julian's transport. He told a multitude of stories and anecdotes, interspersing them with the dialogue, the sarcasms, and lively remarks of the low Italians, and occasionally mimicking / the solemn discourse and pedantic expostulations of one of the professors of the *Liceo*.[a] He would then suddenly become grave and enthusiastic, would undertake the personation of Dante, Petrarca or Ariosto, and, habiting himself in their costume as it appears in their pictures and statues, and assuming in a certain degree their countenance and gesture (an art in which he particularly excelled), would pour out his thoughts in extempore verse, in imitation of the style of these various writers, which, in the first surprise of novelty, and aided by the graces of the speaker, appeared scarcely inferior to those of these great apostles of Italian literature. All this was done without seeming preparation, by a sort of instantaneous conversion of himself into the person he represented. You would have thought that by a kind of legerdemain, or the spell of a powerful incantation, the souls of these illustrious persons had descended / from the blessed abodes, to inspire with their conceptions the favoured individual who, with fervent and harmonious accents, engrossed the soul of the delighted hearer.

---

[a] (Italian) High school, or college.

Julian listened with never-ending amazement to the rhapsodies of this wonderful artist. His first feeling was unmingled delight; his next, admiration of the talent that could produce such stupendous effects. When these sensations were in some degree exhausted, his thoughts reverted to himself. He had always been regarded as something wonderful; all his efforts had been applauded; he had felt that he at all times accomplished with ease whatever he set himself to perform. But every thing that he had ever done seemed to shrink into nothing, in comparison with the achievements of Bernardino. This circumstance afforded him a salutary lesson of diffidence and modesty. He felt that, if nature had done much for him, there / was also much to be effected by application and diligence. He felt that, if his present acquisitions were by no means contemptible, there was still a wide field before him, the cultivation of which might occupy many industrious days, and be a theme for the meditation of many anxious nights. Instead of being depressed and disheartened by this discovery, he regarded it as a new spur to his ambition. He rejoiced to see the prospect widening and lengthening before him, and that there was much in the arts of civilisation, and within the scope of his faculties, worth living for. He felt impelled to gird up the loins of his mind, and was like a man revelling in the fulness of vigour and activity, when he prepares himself for the race.

It had hitherto been one of his favourite amusements to declaim from memory, and with all the energy of juvenile enthusiasm, long passages from Homer and Ariosto, in the solitude / of his chamber, or as he wandered in the fields or on the banks of the Arno.[a] The thought now first occurred to him with vividness, Might he not be a poet himself? In the rawness of his unfledged conceptions he found some parity between the venerable Grecian bard, and the modern Italian to whom he had just been introduced. Homer is said to have recited his verses before numerous audiences of assembled Greeks. What we now receive for the successive books of the Iliad and Odyssey, are understood to have been originally named his Rhapsodies.[b] Might they not sometimes have been the animated effusions of extempore verse? At least such was the appearance which they presented to his hearers. Julian sought for subjects on which he might exercise his unfledged muse. Nor did he search long. In the circle of his new sensations, in the various incidents that presented themselves in their freshest gloss / to his unworn observation; in the persons he saw, in the different topics that were the subject of his studies, he drew from time to time matters that inspired him with the deepest interest. They found their way to his tongue; they formed themselves into numbers; and he also was an improvisor.

---

[a] River Arno, major Italian river, rising on Mount Falterona and flowing west through Florence to the sea, which it enters seven miles after passing through Pisa.

[b] In Ancient Greece, a rhapsode was a professional reciter of poetry; some claim Homer was a rhapsode.

Yet Julian was not the fool of his own enthusiasm. He knew that he was neither a Homer nor a Bernardino. He was delighted with the music of his own verses as they first suggested themselves. But he was a youth of an enquiring spirit. He called them to mind afterwards; he looked at them sceptically; he tried them by the test of being committed to paper. He found them sometimes flat, sometimes childish: he suspected his muse of not being blessed with a sustained and a soaring wing, but rather of belonging to that species of birds, which rise from the ground, and make / their way for a little, but presently, from their own weight and want of inherent strength, are brought again to the earth, and betray their want of a genuine nobility. /

CHAPTER XV

Another circumstance occurred to Julian at this time, which was of more momentous and permanent import to him than his intercourse with Bernardino. Bernardino was between thirty and forty years of age, the laureated poet of the Vatican, protected by the grand duke and the princess, and welcomed by and courted in nearly all the great families of Florence. He had a character to support, which, if it did not advance, must decline; and he was therefore / compelled, however careless and airy he might seem, to ruminate, to read, to exercise his powers in solitary essays, and to prepare his mind for what were called his unpremeditated effusions. He could be little of a companion for the sportive, the thoughtless, and the joyous orphan protected by Cloudesley. But all that was wanting to that end in Bernardino, was accumulated in the nephew. Francesco was barely two years older than Julian. The latter had hitherto had many associates, but no friend.

Francesco instantly took a fancy to our youth, and in a short time they became sworn brothers. The points in which they differed brought them nearer to each other. Julian was serious, and English; Francesco was subtle, dextrous, restless and Italian. The one required to be amused; the other longed for a companion who would listen to him and admire. The one was / daring and undaunted; the other diffident and retiring. The inequality of their ages, however trifling, contributed to the result. Francesco was desirous to be the leader and to instruct; Julian willingly confessed his inferiority in many shewy and obtrusive accomplishments. Though now long practised to the Italian language, he felt that he was not, like the other, a native. Francesco was the better singer and instrumental performer.

Cloudesley was specially alive to the question of the persons with whom his youthful favourite should associate. But he knew that he could not be without a companion; and he did not wish him to be without. Many of the most valuable lessons and practices that a young person can acquire, are only to be learned in society with those of his own age. 'It is not good for man to be alone.'[a] And that man is substantially alone, though living in the midst / of crowds and tumults, who has not a companion circumstanced in various particulars like himself. These are the points in which human creatures touch one another, at which the virtues and the sympathies of mortals become inter-infused. The existence of a man may be continued for seventy years, and he may pass through an incalcul-able variety of fortunes, while yet there maybe many a nerve and vein of character that shall have lain dormant in him from the cradle to the grave, if he have never encountered an equal, one to whom he has stood forth as open and undisguised as to his own soul, between whom and himself every thought has been shaped into words, and they have mutually poured their sensations into each other's bosom, even as a mighty river carries along with it all the spars and corks, and feathers and straws, that float upon its stream. They must have been together in sadness and festivity, / alike when the mind subsides into despair, and when it is made frantic with unlooked for joy, in difficulties and in plenty, in sickness and in health. It is thus that man is made that frank creature, above all disguises, bold, confident, unfearing and unsuspicious, that beneficent nature intended him to be.

Cloudesley therefore was upon the whole not displeased with the intimacy that took place between Julian and Francesco. The latter was the nephew of the laureated poet of the Vatican, a man in whose praise every tongue was wanton, 'the observed of all observers,'[b] and whom no nobleman and magnifico of Florence could be contented without in some degree enlisting in his coteries. The lustre of the uncle reflected on the nephew; and no mean hopes might be entertained that he would one day tread in the steps, and perhaps equal the fame, of Bernardino. Cloudesley was minute in his enquiries / into the qualities and habits of Francesco, and judged him to be hitherto faultless.

Though Cloudesley was partial to Julian with all a father's fondness, yet the very affection he bore him, made him in one sense the more hawk's-eyed to discover in him any thing that might be better, any thing that, remaining as it was, might obstruct his progress in the affections of those with whom he grew acquainted, or impede the germinating of his prosperity and good-fortune. Julian was somewhat too modest. He occasionally distrusted his own powers, when it would have been more beneficial to him to rely upon them. He calculated too nicely upon the result of an adventure, when to plunge at once into the apparent danger, might have led to a sequel more auspicious. These faults would be corrected by coming in contact with the opposite extreme as it

---

[a] Gen. 2: 18.
[b] *Hamlet*, III. i. 163.

existed in Francesco; and in reality society, and the / impulse of a feeling entertained in common with others, is an eminent inspirer and cherisher of lofty courage.

Francesco was a youth, setting his foot on the threshold of life, and determined to make the most of the gratifications it afforded. He was a voluptuary in constitution and judgment. He remarked the boundless varieties of Italian society, and resolved to enter into them all. He took for his motto the precept of the apostle, however perversely expounded, 'Prove all things.'[a] In reality however the line of his life was modelled by no system. He observed every thing with a survey equally rapid and penetrating, and plunged into each as it happened to come before him. He made it a law to himself, to 'rejoice, as a young man, in his youth, and let his heart cheer him in the days of his youth, to walk in the ways of his heart, and in the sight of his eyes,' and made no account of / that after-reckoning and retribution, which the wise man denounces as inseparable from such a proceeding.[b] Fame seemed to be within his reach; he had the example of his uncle before him; and he felt in himself the powers that should enable him to gain possession of that arduous prize: but for that very reason he slighted it. He would not be the slave of renown. He would not, like a monk, inflict on himself penances, and be made subject to privations, that he might secure that, which many hold at no lower rate than the power to climb into the heaven of heavens.

Thus disposed, he early began to rally his new English friend upon his preposterous desire after excellence, and the severe labour and self-denial to which he was willing to devote himself, that by earnest and repeated efforts he might at length attain to be something. This sophistry was new to the ears of Julian. His / mind was fundamentally inquisitive. He resolved not to be the dupe of old saws and prejudices. He resolved to examine every thing, to become a citizen of the world, to see with his own eyes, to be as if he belonged to no one, as if he had by some accident been detached from the remotest orb in our system, to judge of all truth and all conduct without the alloy of any partial bias and favour.

Yet, notwithstanding these heroic resolutions, he found that he could not make himself in the experiment so rigorous and cynical a judge in all points, as his friend Francesco. He had still some leaning to the prejudices, in case they were prejudices, of virtue and honour, nay, even of fame. He loved the persons from whom he had experienced kindness, and those in whom from his own observation he knew to exist the noblest qualities. He was a believer in generosity, single-heartedness and patriotism. / Nothing could ever persuade him, that mankind was the same in all ages, and that the most magnificent

---

[a] 1 Thess. 1: 21–22. 'Prove [i.e. test] everything; hold fast what is good, abstain from every form of evil.'
[b] Eccles. 11: 9 (adapted).

character recorded by Plutarch was in the last resort no better than a savage cannibal or a Hottentot.[a] He endeavoured to analyse the sordid, the profligate, the debauched, and the corrupt personages of the worst times of modern Europe, and could scarcely persuade himself that they belonged to the same species of beings, as Aristides and Pericles and Fabricius and Cincinnatus and Cato.[b]

Yet he had a saving clause for his friend. He believed Francesco to be essentially better than he pretended to be. He thought he found in him an inverted ambition to pass himself for a being impudent, audacious, unprincipled and reckless, at the same time that the best qualities lurked unacknowledged at the bottom of his heart. He believed him to be in reality ashamed of his virtues, acting well, at the same time that / by way of thesis he pleaded the cause of every petty delinquency.

One of the arts of Francesco was to appear a different being in the presence of Cloudesley and Eudocia, from what he was when, withdrawn from all observation, he was alone with Julian in their solitary rambles. The English boy did not altogether approve of this. It was however necessary to his purposes. He resolved to enter on the career of life unshackled. He considered his parents, for as such he regarded them, as being, however good and pure in their intentions, yet narrow-minded and timid. It was his determination, not to be put in cotton and kept in a bandbox.[c] The scene of human life was, like the coat which the doating patriarch bestowed on his favourite son, of many colours, tinted with a thousand glorious and glossy and contrasted hues.[d] He did not intend to pass off the stage of mortal existence, without / having first made himself acquainted with the different ingredients of which that existence is composed. He was strongly confirmed in this resolution by the exhortations of Francesco. It was necessary therefore to his views, that their private and sequestered consultations should be of a different character from what passed between them in the presence of their elders.

Francesco introduced him to other lads about his own age. When they were collected together, there appeared to be a freedom and fire in these youths strongly prepossessing in their favour a novice observer, unpractised in the scenes into which they led him. They were all considerably accomplished in the

---

[a] One of mixed Bushman-Hamite descent in SW Africa.

[b] Aristides (550–468 BC), Athenian statesman and general surnamed 'the Just'; Pericles (c. 490–429 BC), leading Athenian statesman under whose patronage Greek sculpture and architecture reached a pinnacle; Gaius Lusinus Fabricius (d. c. 270 BC), Roman consul, hero of the war against Pyrrhus, and noted for his incorruptibility and honesty; Lucius Quinctius Cincinnatus (c. 519–438 BC), favourite hero of the old Roman republic who, when not called upon to conduct affairs of state, worked his small farm; Marcus Porcius Cato (234–149 BC), known as Cato the Elder, or the Censor, Roman statesman and writer whose name has become synonymous with the practice of self-denying habits, strict justice and bluntness of speech.

[c] Lightweight usually cylindrical box used for holding small articles.

[d] The reference is to Jacob's gift to his favourite son Joseph in Gen. 37: 3.

sports congenial to their age. The athletic exercises so well adapted to these milder climates they excelled in. They knew how to 'urge the flying ball,' and 'to cleave with pliant arm the glassy wave.'[a] These pursuits inspired them with hilarity / and high spirits. Their buoyant temper led them to the mountain's top. The clear and bell-like tones of their voice sent the animating soul, as if by a single touch, through a numerous groupe. Their eyes flashed fire. Their dark-brown cheeks glowed with health. They were swift-footed, like Achilles,[b] and seemed fitted to outstrip the winds. Cloudesley was occasionally a witness of their sports, and was delighted to find his darling ward no stranger to such a school.

They were all, as the Italian youth generally are, of a turn more or less musical. This quality in them furnished an agreeable resting-place or interlude, when their more turbulent and active spirits were somewhat worn away by the effect of their rustic exercises. One sang and then another, sometimes a shorter piece and sometimes a longer, the performer for the most part accompanying his voice with the / symphony of his instrument. Then they would join in a general chorus or full piece, making the very air ring with the melody of their voices. Every thing they did contributed to the common hilarity and high spirits; and much was calculated to fill the soul with tender and affectionate sentiments, and apparently to prepare the parties engaged for acts of kindness and humanity.

Julian was not without familiars and friends among the students of the *Liceo*. But these for the most part consisted of persons of a superior degree in the social scale; they were much under the eye of their superiors; they thought of their future destination on the theatre of life; and were like wild trees inoculated with the slips of ambition. They had a certain air of consciousness in their manner, thought much of themselves and how they were / regarded by others, and had, if not a pedantry, at least a certain loftiness and disdain, which seemed to hedge in and cripple their more attractive graces.

The companions of Francesco on the other hand were easy and unrestrained. They scarcely thought of character, but did in almost all cases whatever their minds suggested to them to do. They 'daft the world aside, and bid it pass.'[c] They were children of the sun by day, and minions of the moon by night. They perpetually trod as it were on the brink of what was indecorum or guilt, at the same time that they seemed scarcely in any instance to overstep the separating line. There was noise and frolic and wantonness, light laughter, 'the brood of folly without father bred,'[d] all the pleasures,

---

[a] Thomas Gray, *Ode on a Distant Prospect of Eton College* (1747), 30. 25–6.
[b] See note a p. 46.
[c] *Henry IV, Part I*, IV. i. 96–7. To daf or daff, to throw off or thrust something aside.
[d] Milton, *Il Penseroso* (1645), l. 2.

> That fancy can beget on youthful thoughts,
> When the fresh blood grows lively, and returns
> Brisk as the April buds in primrose-season.[a] /

Insensibly and by degrees the new set of companions with whom Julian associated himself, and Francesco in particular, began to desert that moderation which had hitherto stamped their proceedings. Innocence was no longer the clear characteristic of their conduct. They dabbled with the arguments of vice, and found out that such as trampled upon the censure of the world had much that might be said on their side of the question. Their proceeding had the marks of enterprise; their souls rose above the musty rules of priests and professors; and swelled with that defiance of the iron rod of tyranny, which Milton has ascribed to his devils.[b] Virtue on the other hand they designated as poor-spirited and timid. The virtuous youth, (thus they discoursed) who bowed their necks to the yoke of their spiritual and collegiate instructors, and 'kept themselves unspotted from the world,'[c] looked with a certain / longing upon the enjoyments of the presumptuous and daring,

> But let I dare not, wait upon I would,
> Like the poor cat in the adage.[d]

Julian was now in a critical situation. He had not the lessons of experience to guide him, and did not perceive his danger. Cloudesley, though with more knowledge of the world, had a confidence in his ward, that rendered him no less blind. Julian had to his eye an *aureola*, a circle of glory that encompassed his head, such as we see in the pictures of Jesus and his apostles, 'driving far off each thing of sin and guilt,' and rendering him inaccessible to contamination.[e] He had also great reliance upon Francesco, the nephew and chosen favourite of the laureat. In a word, as has been already said, Cloudesley was unvisited with any apprehensions, and delighted to find his darling no stranger to such a school. /

---

[a] Milton, *Masque*, ll. 669–71.
[b] In *Paradise Lost*.
[c] Jas. 1: 27 (adapted).
[d] *Macbeth*, i. vii. 44–5 (adapted).
[e] Milton, *Masque*, 453.

CHAPTER XVI

An event occurred at this time by no means conducive to the welfare of Julian. This was no other than the death of Eudocia, the female Greek, whom he had always looked up to as his mother. She was seized with a fever in the full prime of her age and constitution, and carried off in a few days. The effect of this event to both Cloudesley and Julian was of a memorable sort.

To Cloudesley it changed all his views, and / in some sense broke up his establishment. Eudocia was not his first love; and his passion for her had not been enthusiastic and overwhelming. But he entertained for her a most sincere attachment. He had found her attractive and amusing. She had those advantages which frequently fall to the lot of females of her nation. She was lively, sportive and acute; her eyes and her every feature beamed with intelligence. Her gaiety and perpetual good spirits happily qualified and relieved the saturnine and English character of her husband. She had proved to him an admirable partner in his domestic concerns; since, though full of sallies and vivacity, she readily entered into his views, and exhibited a religious deference to his will. She had therefore made his days glide serenely, and assisted him in all his purposes, being in the fullest sense a helpmate to him.

But what was most important, she had shared / with him, in his cares for the great object of his anxieties and love, the youthful Julian. She regarded the boy with the sincerest affection. In his early years her attentions had perhaps been even of more importance than those of Cloudesley. When the guardian of the child was compelled to be absent upon any of the various offices which fall to the share of the male superintendant of an establishment, she competently supplied his place. And her character as a Greek, and her long habits of intercourse with Colocotroni and his daughter, had given her a refinement to which her husband was a stranger. From her Julian had received his first lessons of tenderness and sensibility, so far as these can be learned from another. She had the enthusiasm and the fervent mind of a Greek. Cloudesley made it his purpose to cultivate the fortune and the integrity of his pupil; but Eudocia entered more into the detail of life, / and observed and in many cases guided a variety of those minuter matters, which escaped the observation of the coarser and more manlike senses of the English yeoman.

But, if Cloudesley were greatly affected by the loss of the partner of his life, Julian felt the event more deeply. He was conscious that he had lost something that was unique among the blessings of our sublunary existence, and that could never be replaced. Cloudesley might again enter into the married state, and be satisfied; but Julian could never have another mother. In this relation between human creatures there is a species of religion. As mortal beings collectively derive from the author of the universe all that they have, and all that they value, so the first object that the child contemplates is its mother; and she is its guardian while as yet it knows nothing of the supplies necessary for its support, and the dangers with which it is / surrounded. She first fashions its tongue to utter an articulate sound, and gives it its earliest lessons of working-day wisdom. Julian found therefore a portentous blank occasioned to him by the loss of Eudocia. The house in which he dwelt seemed deprived of its most precious ornament; her couch, her place at the table, the chair in which she had been accustomed to sit, were vacant: she no longer cultivated the flowers of the garden, and took care of the active and busy inhabitants of the poultry-yard. But, which was more than this, the attachment of the boy to Eudocia was of a very different sort from that which he entertained for Cloudesley. Cloudesley was his superintendent and director; he appeared to bring in the means by which the houshold was supported, and to regulate their employment. But to Eudocia appertained more of the functions of intimacy and / friendship. There was a character of sex in the intercourse of her and the boy. Maternity and companionship were blended. She was younger than her husband, and her deportment to Julian was at once sportive and tender. He was more at his ease with his mother, and poured out his youthful heart to her with greater unreserve. If she had lived longer, she would perhaps have been less to him. But, in the years through which he had hitherto passed, a woman was to him more than a man. If to the softer sex belong more fickleness and inconsistency, if they have less firmness of purpose and depth of combination than are to be found in us, this was to the present moment totally, or almost totally, unadverted to by Julian. – Add to these considerations, that we never know the value of a thing but by its loss, and that the benefit which has escaped from our grasp, is that to which our recollection / is linked; so that, while our misfortune is recent, we can scarcely think of, and scarcely esteem, any thing else.

Julian was eighteen years of age, at the period of the death of Eudocia. But he had been brought up in so much simplicity; there was such a primitive and unornamented integrity in the houshold intercourse of himself and his supposed parents; that within the walls of that home, he continued to be like a child. He had learned many things; he was dextrous and accomplished in all the exercises belonging to his years; he had made some proficiency in science and the arts, and still more in literature, ancient and modern. But he did not on that account take upon him by the domestic hearth to play the arrogant, the disdainful, and the rebellious. In the sports which were pursued by him among his equals in the open air, though even in them he was distinguished by good temper and humanity, / yet he could occasionally repress the presumptuous, and assert against the insolent the consideration that was his due. But, when he entered beneath the lintel of the house of his supposed father, he left at the door the petulance of the full-grown stripling, and was all tractableness and deference to the kind and affectionate woman he called his mother.

The boy evidently drooped for the loss of his only female friend. He was often found in tears. He had almost fainted at the funeral of Eudocia; and he frequently visited her grave. His sports and his serious occupations grew languid to him. He wandered in solitude, and was lost in reverie. He sighed often and heavily; appetite and sleep seemed almost to desert him. Ambition faded from his thoughts; and the brilliant colours with which youthful imagination embellishes the future, became to the eye of Julian dim, confused and undiscernible. His / cheek was flushed with an unhealthy hue; and the roundness and elasticity of his frame visibly wasted.

The alteration which took place in him excited the attention of all. Every one according to his mode sought to apply a remedy; but no person was so eager and irremovable in his efforts as Francesco. He would seat him by the side of Julian, with looks of the most earnest interest and friendship, without uttering a word. He would walk by his side in silence, determined not to intrude upon the sacredness of his grief. The melancholy which had apparently taken up its abode in the bosom of the youthful stranger, seemed doubly to endear him to the affections of Francesco.

On the other hand the attentions of the Italian boy were by no means thrown away upon Julian. Hitherto he had regarded Francesco principally as a source of amusement, and an / object of wonder, almost of envy. He had believed him too light of heart, too dissipated, too much the slave of rattle and high spirits, to be capable of postponing his own enjoyments, or of sacrificing his constitutional impulses to the sorrows and the misfortunes of others. The death of Eudocia shewed him in a new light. He now exhibited in himself the disinterested friend, who could resort spontaneously to the house of mourning, could devote his mind to the taking part in the sorrows of another, and occupy his faculties in contriving the means to alleviate the griefs of his associate. It is difficult to be expressed, how much the character of Francesco gained by his being placed in this situation. Julian had before sought his society from other considerations; he now plainly felt that he loved him. He viewed him as an amiable person, and not unqualified for the reciprocities and endearments of friendship. /

In the first instance Francesco, as I have said, seated himself by the side of Julian, and insensibly called him off from the abstraction and uncommunicativeness of his sorrows, by placing in his view the figure of another human being, who grieved because he was grieved. By degrees he induced him to leave the monotony of his silent home, and wrung from him his consent that they should wander side by side in some of the most gloomy and solitary walks in the purlieus[a]

---

[a] Outskirts.

of Florence. Two people can scarcely engage in strolling together apart from the world, and long shut themselves out from the society of articulate speech. They talked of all gloomy things, of the deceitfulness and instability of sublunary gratifications, and mutually interchanged their hoarded tales of adversity, calamity and woe. Sorrow in this sense serves as the alleviation of sorrow: we are led / to perceive that trouble in some sort is the lot of all, and no longer repiningly exclaim that we are singled out a mark for the arrows of misfortune.

In proportion as they were drawn off from the melancholy past, they began to turn their speech to anticipations of the future. As by the topics in which they had engaged their hearts were made tender, and their feelings blended into the same key, Julian began to think that he could never be so happy as in the society of Francesco. Friendship is the balm of life; and, as the poor youth had just lost his earliest and most faithful friend, he naturally conceived that his best chance for enjoyment hereafter was to substitute a new friendship that should have a greater promise of permanence. His mind was fresh from the histories of Achilles and Patroclus, Orestes and Pylades, / Damon and Pythias; and he persuaded himself that there could be no true felicity but in the ardours of a romantic friendship, where neither party should have the smallest reserve from the other, pleasure should only be pleasure in proportion as it was participated, and on both sides they should be prepared for the most unbounded sacrifices for each other's preservation and advantage.[a] Julian communicated these ideas to Francesco, by whom they were cordially encountered. The rapid and high-wrought tone of mind which was native to the Italian boy, and which had been rendered firmer and stronger by the habits of the *improvvisatore*, fitted him to receive the impression with undiminished force. By collision they raised the first sparks of friendship into a brilliant and mighty flame, and walked about amidst the groves and on the banks of the Arno, regarding / the rest of the world as if it were not, and swearing that they would build a temple of attachment and love, in comparison of which all the examples of antiquity should fade into nothing. /

---

[a] When in order to annoy Agamemnon Achilles refused to fight, his gentle and amiable friend Patroclus appeared in the armour of Achilles at the head of the Myrmidons and was slain by Hector; Orestes, son of Agamemnon and Clytemnestra, who killed his mother and her lover Aegisthus in revenge for their murder of his father; Pylades was a fast friend of Orestes who helped him in this act of vengeance, and afterwards married his sister, Electra; Damon and Pythias (more correctly Phintias, 4th century BC), two Pythagoreans of Syracuse, also remembered as models of faithful friendship: Pythias having been condemned to death by Dionysius of Syracuse for treason, Damon offered himself as a hostage for his friend, to which Dionysius consented, and when Pythias returned to save his friend's life, the tyrant was so impressed he both pardoned Pythias and requested admittance into the sacred fellowship of the friends.

CHAPTER XVII

Francesco however was of a gay and companionable frame of mind, in love with 'quips and jests and youthful jollity,' and, though he was at the moment perfectly sincere in his protestations, would scarcely have been satisfied to retire into an uninhabited island with his friend, there to dwell in two moss-grown cells by the side of a rippling brook for the rest of their lives.[a] It happened therefore, somewhat fortunately in respect of the depressed and dejected tone of / mind of Julian, that Bernardino had occasion to send his nephew to Verona, and Francesco solicited his friend to bear him company in the excursion. Julian at first refused the invitation. Though delighted with the society of the Italian boy, and desirous of all occasions of intercourse and intimacy, it seemed to him a violation of what he owed to the memory of Eudocia, that he should for the present yield to amusement, and enter into the distractions and animation of a traveller. Cloudesley however, who upon almost any other occasion would have felt an unwillingness to trust his ward so far out of his sight, forwardly seconded the proposal. He knew that the familiarity of the young with the young was the ordination of nature, and that nothing he could do to relieve the sorrows of Julian, could have half so favourable an effect as such an excursion. Besides that, Julian and himself had suffered under the same calamity, / and would be from time to time recurring to the thought of what they had lost. It would be better that the ideas of his ward should be turned into an entirely new channel.

The youths accordingly set out together, attended each of them by a servant. The season of the year was fine; and, conformably to the nature and constitution of human creatures, they felt their hearts expanded, and their finer spirits called into action, by the bare effect of the elastic air playing upon their lungs and the circulations of the animal frame. The objects of sight equally contributed to inspire sensations of gaiety. The deep blue of the concave heavens, and the beautiful and various scenery of this part of Italy, irresistibly imparted cheerfulness and serenity to the soul. Francesco was the first to betray the delicious feelings he experienced. He had nothing within him to check the pleasures that offered themselves. / His mind, so to speak, was like a sheet of white paper, prepared to receive the impression of the landscape, umbrageous[b]

---

[a] Milton, *L'Allegro* (1632), 26–7 (adapted).
[b] Providing shade.

or extensive, diversified with rivers or villages, with flowers and fruits, corn-fields and the vintage.[a] The birds warbled in every bush. Francesco sang snatches of tunes, or poured forth such rhapsodies as occurred to him of love or chivalry. Julian caught the animation of his friend. He could not play the cynic or the misanthrope to quarrel with or to check so innocent an opening of the heart; and, not doing this, he was insensibly carried away with the example.

They were two days on the road; and, when they arrived, Julian found that there were gratifications in store for him, such as he could not have experienced in any other journey. Verona had been his dwelling-place from the third year of his age to the tenth. He was now eighteen. He had no recollection of any thing prior to / the period in which he had been set down with his supposed father and mother in the environs of this noble city. It seemed to him as if all the senses of his frame, his eyes and his ears, had been originally given him in this glorious scene. Here he had first learned the use of his limbs, and the pleasures of which the morning of human life is susceptible. Here he had learned to shoot and to ride, to wrestle and to swim. Here he had first felt the emotion of love towards the creatures around him; at least here it had first become to him a reflex and a conscious act, something more than that mere instinct which man experiences in common with the brute. Here his mind had first been opened upon the stores of knowledge; here he had proceeded by just degrees from the alphabet to the grammar, from the saws[b] of the nurse to all that history and poetry have in store for the observing and contemplative of our species. He recollected / the kind and well adapted lessons of Giuseppe, that man of a sober and nicely regulated mind, whom he had so long lost sight of, but who could never cease to be dear to his recollections. The period of life from three years old to ten, if we are kindly treated, if we are not galled with the iron yoke of despotism, if we are made to feel that we have a will of our own, if we are not thwarted and thrust aside from our innocent desires by the caprice of persons older than ourselves, is in many respects the happiest epoch of human existence. Then is the sunshine of the bosom, the first vintage and harvest of our newly acquired senses, of perception and imagination, before dear-bought experience has convinced us of their futility and hollowness. It is the epoch in which, by the omnipotent charter of nature, we have no cares what we shall eat, or wherewithal we shall be clothed, but all is provided for us by a superintendence / that asks no aid from ourselves, and in which we have no participation of consciousness. It was this paradisaical period of existence that was once more set before the eyes of Julian, when he reached the territory of Verona.

---

[a] John Locke first used the image of the mind as being originally like a blank sheet of paper when attacking the theory of 'innate ideas' in his founding text of empirical philosophy, *An Essay Concerning Human Understanding* (1690); see Book 2, Ch. 12.
[b] Wise sayings, or proverbs.

He hastened from scene to scene, and thought he never could have his fill of these delicious reminiscences. He eagerly pointed to his friend the different spots where he had first hit the mark with his arrow, where he had first outstripped all his competitors in the race, where he had attained the mastery of that noble animal, the well-descended steed, and had found himself in full possession of the strength and manoeuvres of a swimmer. He shewed him where he had been accustomed to fly his kite, and to exercise his agility and skill in the pursuit of the ball. He sought for and he found his early preceptor Giuseppe, still a humble / retainer of the university. His sensations at this renewed encounter were full of pleasure; he pressed the hand of his quondam[a] instructor with all the ardour of affection; and felt convinced that there could not exist a being more single-minded and guileless.

There was one thought however that presented itself to chastise the gaiety and expansion of soul, which otherwise sprung up within him at revisiting Verona. That thought was Eudocia. He repaired to the *podere*, where Cloudesley had busied himself with the toils of the field, and Eudocia superintended the dairy, the milk-pans, and the various manufactures of cheeses, and of the cates[b] which had first afforded an exquisite repast to his youthful appetite. He saw her every where, her neatness, her activity, her never-ceasing vigilance; but, above all, her tender and considerate treatment, and her warm affection. He wiped from his eyes the last / streaming tears of the age of puberty. His very soul was sobered and afflicted by the mournful recollection.

One day, during the short period in which Julian and Francesco continued at Verona, they agreed to make a party on the water on the Lago di Garda. Francesco engaged a certain number of young men of the same stamp as himself, and Julian insisted upon including Giuseppe. They hired a sailing boat, which would conveniently accommodate twelve persons; and Julian and the rest of the young men were sufficiently skilful for the management of such a vessel. Giuseppe was the only one of the party, who was entirely out of his element on the occasion, being indeed a mere bookworm, unacquainted with the ways of the world, and especially with all juvenile and athletic exercises. After having sailed backward and forward on the lake, and amused themselves / with fishing, they drew up the boat on the peninsula of Sirmione, famous as the birth-place of the poet Catullus, where formerly there had been a town, and where there still existed a small castle, garrisoned by two or three invalid soldiers.[c] Here, in the midst of a shady grove, and in sight of the lake, they spread out their refreshments. An old woman, who had a hut near the spot, and who made it her business to serve the parties that resorted thither for their

---

[a] Former.

[b] Choice dishes.

[c] Sirmione, peninsular on the S shore of Lago di Garda, which lies between Brescia and Verona in N Italy; Catullus, Gaius Valerius (84?–54? BC), Roman lyric poet, noted for his love poems.

pleasure, dressed for them the fish they had taken, at a fire lighted in the open air for that purpose. They had brought with them flasks of wine, and various sorts of fruit, and began to wax merry over their entertainment. They sang songs; they had two or three musical instruments; and, some peasant-girls happening to stray near the spot where they had been feasting, they pressed them into the service, and engaged themselves in dancing. /

The Lago di Garda is proverbially of a treacherous character. In calm and serene weather it is as smooth as glass; nothing can be more beautiful than its fresh and lively surface, imparting gaiety and peace to every beholder, and faithfully giving back the image of every surrounding object, and of whatever floats on its waters, even to the smallest lineament. But it is also subject to storms. Virgil describes it, as notorious for the tumultuousness and terror of its waves, and the deafening roar which attends them, not inferior to that of the ocean when swelled into fury.[a] The morning and the middle part of the day had on this occasion been extremely fine; and the Lago had appeared even like a beautiful courtesan, decorated in all her jewels, alluring with a thousand blandishments, and holding out a promise of endless enjoyment. The party continued on the turf, thoughtless of the future, and imagining / that the present serenity of the waters and the sky would last for ever.

As the evening advanced however, a dark cloud appeared in the horizon, and a fresh puff of wind swept over the Lago. Those who were best acquainted with the treachery of the waters took the alarm, and hastily summoned their companions. All hands were busy in a moment; they packed up the furniture of their feast, and were speedily on board. They seated themselves on the benches, and spread their little sail. The Lago is twenty-five miles long, and seven at its greatest breadth. At first the party flattered themselves with a safe return, and believed that the breeze that had sprung up would only bring them the more quickly to the point from which they started. As they advanced, the blast became more shrill; and, whereas at first a small cloud, no bigger than a man's hand, shewed itself in the heavens, in / no long time dark vapours gathered from every side, the hemisphere became black, and the light of day seemed to be suddenly extinguished. The waters of the lake rolled tumultuously with an uneasy motion, as if anticipating the coming storm. At length a fierce west wind roared along the lake, and the waves swelled into mountains. Immediately after, an immense sheet of lightning pierced the thickness of the gloom, and a deafening peal of thunder reverberated with a thousand echoes among the nearer Alps. This was succeeded by heavy rain, and a fall of hail so hard and impetuous that it even rattled against the bottom of the boat, and fiercely annoyed the crew.

The fresh-water sailors of whom the party consisted, felt appalled at so

---

[a] In *The Georgics*, II. 160, Virgil pictures Lake Benacus as *fluctibus adsurgens fremetique marcino* ('rising with the swell and roar of ocean').

sudden an assault. Having spent the day in careless jollity and mirth, they were the less prepared for this reverse, and savoured it in all its bitterness. / The hand that managed the sail was an unskilful one; and, there being no concert between him and the man at the rudder, the boat was overset in a moment, and every soul it contained was thrown overboard.

Julian, as I have already mentioned, was a consummate swimmer. He was confounded for a few moments. But he speedily recovered his presence of mind; and then his first thought was of the poor Giuseppe, who was the most disqualified for such an encounter of the whole party, who could never swim in his life, and in reality had been pressed into the amusement against his will, by the well meant importunity of his former pupil. It fortunately happened that the boat had been driven near to the eastern bank of the lake, before the disaster happened. Julian and his preceptor had been next each other in the boat; and they were tumbled together into the lake. The ward of / Cloudesley had been aware of this; and, after having made one or two strokes as a swimmer, turned round that he might find his partner. Giuseppe was kept for a brief interval from sinking, by the buoyancy and force of the wave that caught him in his fall, and bore him considerably above the level of the boat. Julian by the most fortunate accident met him as the wave subsided, and threw his left arm round the object of his solicitude. He then strenuously, and with the utmost application of his skill, made for the shore. He seemed in a manner to have reached it; he felt the ground; when the retiring of the wave carried him back to no inconsiderable distance from the point he sought. He renewed his effort, and was again baffled; the third time he accomplished his purpose, and placed Giuseppe, nearly in a state of insensibility, on the dry land.

Presently Julian became collected, and as / fresh as ever. He saw his companions tumbling this way and that, and contending with the waves. In an instant Francesco came into his mind, the youth who had so assiduously watched over him in his grief, and between whom and himself there had passed a vow of everlasting friendship. He thought he saw him; he could not be mistaken. He called to him; he shouted. It seemed to him that he was heard; it seemed that he was not. He fixed his gaze intently on his object, as if his whole soul went out in that one effort. Francesco was fast approaching. Suddenly the body of the swimmer was wheeled round as by some external force. Julian could see that his friend was struggling in uncertain efforts, and no longer possessed the command of his course. The moment was critical. Julian instantly dashed into the water with a resolution that appeared more than human; in vain did the wave seem to exert an almighty force to / tear Francesco from his aid; he pushed on with undoubting mind and a swelling soul. Fortune favours the strenuous, and deserts the coward. However it was, the effort of Julian was crowned with success. He reached the very side of Francesco, as if some god had guided his exertions. The Italian was at his last gasp; his limbs were powerless; he could act no more. Julian saw that he was lost; he caught hold of

him by one hand. It was enough. The weight of the body of his friend was
nothing; the waters of the lake sustained him. Julian had no more to do than to
retain his hold, and exert his muscular powers to reach the land. Francesco
followed, as if it had been a thread merely that Julian drew along, and there had
been no weight attached to the other end. Francesco came ashore in a state of
insensibility. With great care, and by placing the body so as was best calculated
to free the / stomach from the load of water it had engulphed, Julian at length
brought him to himself. The remainder of the scene was frightful. Two of the
party were irretrievably lost. /

CHAPTER XVIII

Cloudesley, as has sufficiently been seen, had no other attachment on earth
than to his ward. The more he had confirmed himself now for a course of years
in resolute misanthropy, the more vehement was his partiality where his affections had become fixed. It was thus that he had loved the father of Julian; it was
thus that he loved the child. That child had been rendered dear to him by a
thousand circumstances. He was the sole relic of his illustrious benefactor. He /
was the instrument that had procured for him income and independence.
Cloudesley felt that he had committed a great crime towards the youth, a
defenceless orphan, a being that had every claim upon his worship and support. The contract between Cloudesley and myself by which Julian was de-
spoiled of his all, had been sealed before the child was born, when he was a
creature of the understanding only, respecting which something might be
affirmed or denied. The case was altered, when he had become an object of the
senses. The cherished idea of Cloudesley had ever been that he had himself
been the mark against which others had directed their villainy, having never
committed offence against any. This had been the source of his internal
bitterness. He could least of all therefore bear the idea that he also had
contaminated his soul with an act of baseness.

It was thus that he had been prepared to receive / Julian under his charge.
The child was no doubt a beautiful child, with every attribute that should
prepossess a well disposed mind. But to Cloudesley he was like a god, that had
descended to dwell under his roof. He always felt that his ward was not in his
·place, and that much of his original and native 'brightness was obscured.'[a] For

---

[a] Milton, *Paradise Lost*, I. 591–4 (adapted).

this reason he viewed every thing about him with prepossession, and a heart attuned to admire.

He regarded Julian as a prodigy of intellect. He had observed him from the first dawnings of his infant apprehension. He had remarked his searching and inquisitive mind, the clearness of his views, the decisiveness of his elections, the truth of his movements, of the eye, of the hand, of every corresponding gesture and limb. All that Julian learned had seemed to come to him as if by inspiration; and he had an intuitive faculty for mastering languages. His progress / in literature was inconceivably rapid; nothing was a toil to him. His memory was accurate; his questions apt; his observations full of acuteness. But he had also to an extraordinary degree the creative faculty. His sports for the most part had been studies. 'He cut his roots in characters, and sauced'[a] his play, as if Mercury, the author of all inventions, had dwelt within him. He savoured every thing with unerring truth; and, when he recited the verses of the English or Italian poets, they flowed with an eloquence that no other tongue could have given them, and found their way irresistibly to the heart. When too he essayed his own vein, he was, at least in Cloudesley's apprehension, in no way inferior to the masters who had pointed out his path to the Temple of the Muses. He considered him as born for all times, and never to be forgotten as long as the memory of man should endure. /

But what Cloudesley valued most in Julian, what led away his soul in captivity, was his heart. He had never known a father or a mother. Yet he had ever been filial to their counterfeit representatives. He had never failed in any attentions to them. He had never mutinied or murmured against their commands. He had regarded them with the most deferential duty. He had never given them a moment's pain, but had always been to them the source of inestimable gratification. Cloudesley remembered the exemplary behaviour of Julian, when he lay, as he believed, on his own death-bed, and his pious attendance on the illness of Cloudesley himself. He had on all occasions, and towards all with whom he had intercourse, shewn himself the soul of generosity. He had never betrayed any mean passions, selfishness or envy. He gave away all he had, as if he had been the inheritor of exhaustless wealth. / He forgave all that offended, as from a soul incapable of harbouring any of the malignant passions. He was ever ready with heart and hand to assist such as were in suffering or distress. He could not sleep, if he were away that any one he knew was unhappy.

Cloudesley remembered the several instances in which Julian had manifested these dispositions. He recollected how he had conducted himself at Verona, when Giuseppe had imputed to him a palpable falshood, and had treated him harshly in consequence. He called to mind the generous fervour with which,

---

[a] *Cymbeline*, IV. i. 49–50 (adapted).

when Cloudesley expressed a fierce indignation at this treatment, Julian had interceded in behalf of his preceptor. It was but a short time ago that Eudocia had died, and the exemplary youth had appeared as drooping, and ready to sink into the grave with sorrow for his supposed mother. /

But the two recent examples of the nobility of the nature of Julian, had by their lustre entirely eclipsed all the virtues and excellencies he had displayed in his former years.

First came his mourning for the death of Eudocia. How many a youth, at the presumptuous and arrogant age of eighteen, looks with disdain upon the care, the advices, the forewarnings of a being of the frailer sex, and will treat his own mother, however accomplished, however sagacious, however intellectual, with contumely! Proud with opinion of manly and superior wisdom, he thrusts aside the suggestions of female solicitude and tenderness, as unworthy of his notice. He forgets all the maternal yearnings of soul with which that mother watched over his helpless infancy, how she composed his limbs, and supplied his wants, and relieved his speechless griefs, and smoothed his pillow, and sat for weary days and nights beside / his cradle, and brought him safely through a thousand perils. But Julian forgot nothing. He recollected all the loving-kindness of Eudocia, her innumerable and indescribable exertions for his benefit. It was all to him as if it had been yesterday, so living, so perfect in his soul was the image of those scenes and those actions, over which long years of oblivion might be thought to have rolled.

Story has recorded a variety of instances, in which a friend could not survive the loss of a friend, and a lover has pined himself into mortal sickness and death for the expiring of his mistress. But what occurred in this instance in Julian was more memorable. The most fervent affection of which a human being is susceptible is for his like, his equal, one with whom he has walked in the paths of adolescence, while their youthful hearts have simultaneously poured out their feelings and conceptions into each / other's bosoms, and in the course of nature they may expect to sink into old age and the grave together. It is the order of human things that the old should yield to the empire of mortality before the young, the parent before the child. Our minds are constituted accordingly. We commit the mother that bore us to the silent earth, and return to the functions and duties of a mortal being towards his fellows. But Julian seemed to break through these adamantine boundaries. He mourned over the hearse of Eudocia, and refused to be comforted. He withdrew into solitary places and silence, and found his best consolation in his tears. It was only the persevering affection and the unwearied attentions of Francesco, that could restore him to himself. He undoubtedly exceeded all discreet and reasonable .measure in the excess of his grief. But, if in this he departed from the precepts of sobriety, his weakness was at least amiable; and / a generous observer would love him the more, for what the philosophy of the stoics might denominate his vice.

But what crowned the triumph of Julian in the heart of his imagined father was the scene that immediately followed. No sooner had Julian roused himself, and been prevailed on to engage in this little excursion to Verona, than his first act had been to plunge himself in the tempestuous waves, and risk his life for the recovery of those he loved. The presence of mind, the gallantry, the sound judgment, the entire contempt of self, which he had shewn in the misadventure of the boat, was above all praise. The first person he ventured his life to save, was the only one that perhaps in the course of his existence he had known to treat him with flagrant injustice. But Julian thought only of the danger, greater than that of any one else, to which this person was exposed, and / recollected that he was himself the immediate cause of that danger. Exhausted with his former exertions, with contending against the angry waters, and saving the life of Giuseppe, nothing could prevent him, when he saw that of Francesco, the brother of his soul, in peril, from dashing again into the foaming flood, and dragging to shore the senseless body of his friend.

It was the generous and disinterested behaviour of Julian eleven years before, that had decided Cloudesley to make a strenuous effort to restore him to his rank and his title, and no longer to suffer, if he could by any means put an end to it, the miserable delusion to go on, to which in one dishonourable moment he had subscribed. On that occasion he had written me a letter, which had wrung me to my inmost soul, and which, for many months after, had entailed on me paroxysms and anguish so great, / that the wonder was that any compound of mortal elements could outlive them. I resisted his expostulations and importunity; and on further consideration he determined at that time to proceed no further.

But now he resolved to put an end to the juggle that had been carried on. For this purpose the scheme he chalked out to himself was, instantly to set out for Ireland, and to present himself before me unexpected. He did not believe that I should be able to resist what he would have the power to urge upon me. A letter is a dead and powerless pleader. All that it says is already put down; and the man that answers it pronounces a decision where there is no one near to dispute or to remonstrate. A personal conference between the guilty individual and the confident of his guilt, is a very different thing. He has then before him an eye under which his eye shrinks, and a voice that / can speak in all tones from the most melting persuasion to the terrors of earthly thunder. The hearer knows not what shall be said next, nor of consequence how sudden may be the rebound, or how unavailing the resistance. A letter, once answered, leaves to the receiver an interval of days, perhaps months, during which he has nothing more to apprehend. But the man who addresses another in person, sees at once the adversary's weak side, observes where he shrinks back and distrusts his ability, discovers all this by the fearful eye, the faltering voice, and the trembling nerve, and pursues his advantage by adding blow upon blow, without giving him breathing time, or the intermission of a moment.

Cloudesley saw all this, and resolved to put all his strength into the enterprise, and stake his existence on the undertaking. He was like what is related of
the bee, when its anger is / stirred up within, that seizes desperately upon the
aggressor, fixes its sting deep in the living vein, and is entirely content to leave
its own life in the wound it inflicts. Even thus Cloudesley cared not for the issue
to himself. He had a purpose to execute, an object to effect, and his whole soul
was in that. He left Julian behind him at Florence. He resolved to be unshackled and at large in his motions, not to be reduced to consult the sentiments and
the preferences of his ward, or to be in any way restrained by considerations for
the safety of the youth he loved. /

CLOUDESLEY:

A TALE.

BY

THE AUTHOR OF "CALEB WILLIAMS."

IN THREE VOLUMES.

VOL. III.

LONDON:

HENRY COLBURN AND RICHARD BENTLEY,
NEW BURLINGTON STREET.
1830.

CHAPTER I

Eleven years had now elapsed since I first received the letter from Cloudesley, which threatened me with what I regarded as the consummation of mortal evils. That comsummation did not arrive. But in what respect was I the better? The expectation of what is tremendous is perhaps more dreadful than the event. He who is cast prostrate to the earth can fall no lower. If I had been driven from the society of my fellow men, if I had inhabited a wretched hovel on a barren heath, if I had / had nothing to subsist on but the roots that my own hand had cultivated, if I had known that, wherever my name was repeated among the inhabitants of the earth, I was regarded as a monster, betraying the most sacred trust, and perpetrating the most cold-hearted villainy, I should then have known the worst. There is a principle in human nature, by which the sufferer in almost all cases reconciles himself to what is inevitable, is complete, and cannot be reversed. He looks round, and considers rather what he has left, than what he has lost. He gathers up the fragments of the wreck; he arranges them along the walls of his cell; he says to himself, This is my dowry and inheritance for the remainder of my existence; he desperately adapts himself to the hardness of his fortune, and considers how he shall make the best of it.

But the man who, every morning that he wakes, wakes with a dull, aching pain, with a mighty depression of spirits, with an indescribable / load weighing at his heart, and who after a few moments recollects what all this means, and what he has to expect, he is truly a wretch. Expectation, fearful expectation, is to him the vulture of Prometheus, preying on his liver, which still grows again, as fast as it is devoured.[a] His wound is ever fresh; no time cures it; no balm has the virtue to skin it over. I knew not on what day the final mischief would arrive; but I had an assured conviction that arrive it must.

Yet my days and my hours were not all of sorrow. I had a wife, the most exemplary of her sex; I had children that improved every day in towardliness and beauty. I looked upon them, and was joyful: I looked a second time, and my agonies grew a thousand times the fiercer, because I had such relations and holds on my affection. Fool that I was! Why had I not had the courage to take the hard lot which I had brought upon myself, alone, and / without involving others in the miseries that awaited me? Villain and poltroon that I was![b] What

---

[a] See note to p. 8.
[b] Poltroon, a spiritless coward.

right had I to embark all these innocents among the storms that were engendered by my crime?

My wife had borne me a son and a daughter, before the time in which I received Cloudesley's letter; she brought me two more children, one of either sex, afterwards. They were as beautiful as the day, and not less affectionate and docile than they were beautiful. You have seen the youngest. What was there wanting, to make me the happiest of men? Yet I was miserable. I have lost the whole of this family, one by one, except this last.

My children were exactly similar in constitution the one to the other, cast, as I may say, in one mould. They came into the world with every promise of health, of vigour, and of living to the farthest period of human existence. They knew no sickness, were for ever joyous and / happy from morning till night. Their limbs were formed in the most exquisite proportion, and their cheeks were marked with the roses of health. Intelligence and sweetness rivalled each other in their infant countenances. They grew from month to month, and from year to year, 'in stature,' and, as it should seem, 'in favour with God and man.'[a] Every added season appeared to be productive of a new tendril, twining itself round the heart of their father and mother. Their first essays to walk, to hurry with doubtful, eager steps from the arms of parent to parent sitting at a little distance from each other, their unassured lispings of articulate sound, and attempts to give to each of us an appropriate, endearing name, were delicious beyond the power of words to describe. Their learning to read, and all the little lessons we excited them to commit to memory and repeat, were an inexhaustible source of entertainment to us. Their gambols on the turf, their races after / one another, their wrestling in sport, their struggles for mastery, their tumbling and rising, and the cheerful laughter that crowed in their little throats, and ran over from their eyes, we could sit for hours to observe. To these wild and lawless amusements, the jargon of the babe, succeeded, in due course of years, the song and the dance, the musical instrument and the pencil. In all they gave us satisfaction.

We were the most gratified of parents, till my eldest boy had nearly completed the eleventh year of his age. We then gradually perceived an alteration in his health. His cheeks burned with a low fever. His nights were marked with profuse perspiration. His flesh daily wasted away. His appetite decayed. He grew languid and averse to activity and exertion. Our anxiety respecting him became extreme, and we consulted a multitude of physicians. They knew not how to account for his disease, and called it atrophy.[b] We tried change of air, and / bathing in all its forms. Nothing was of the smallest service to him. The malady proceeded with gigantic strides; and in less than two months from the first attack, he was a corpse. It was almost impossible to conceive so perfect a

---

[a] Luke 2: 52.
[b] Wasting.

skeleton, as he was when his body was stretched on the bier. At first he appeared to suffer much from the inroads and tediousness of the disease, the lengthened days and sleepless nights. But he never murmured, and was always anxious to relieve the uneasiness of his parents. And, when he died, it was without a struggle. It was in a manner impossible to discern when the final change took place. He expired at a beautiful watering-place in the south of Ireland; and we deposited his remains in a vault, appertaining to the barons of Alton in our own parish.

It is scarcely in words to express the grief that Selina and myself felt for his loss. He was our first-born, the heir to all my titles and / estates, and the heir in reversion to the rank and property of the elder branch of my family in England. Such he would infallibly have proved if he had lived, unless a certain fatal reverse had occurred, of the possibility of which Selina had no suspicion, and which I could scarcely be said seriously to have expected. He was two years older than our next child, a daughter; and our hearts were bound up in the life of the boy.

But, beside the direct sorrow with which this event afflicted us, it altered all our views and feelings on the point of domestic comfort. Life and death are conceptions of a peculiar sort; we habitually combine the idea of death with that of an age in a certain degree advanced; this is what we call the course of nature; we know that every man's time must come, and that all must die. But, when we look on the roses and gaiety of youth, the mournful idea of mortality is altogether alien to our thoughts. / We have heard of it as a speculation and a tale;[a] but nothing but experience can bring it home to us. Infancy is indeed subject to peculiar perils; but my son had outlived the hazards of infancy. Parents who lose their children in infancy, for the most part endure their loss with philosophy. The children in so short a period had not had time to entangle them in a thousand webs, to become the heart of their hearts. But at eleven years of age the case is totally different. We have watched their stature, the unfolding of their limbs, the growing feeling and thought that speaks in their eye, their accumulating proficiency. I began to regard my boy almost as a companion; I asked his thoughts upon a variety of questions; I drew hints for deliberation from his innocent and guileless suggestions. I began to connect the thought of him with the idea of the world, to consider what would be the destination and fortune of his manhood, in what occupation or pursuit he would be likely / to prove most happy or most honoured. Every year he loved his parents better; every year we loved him more. All this was suddenly extinguished. In less than two months we saw him decline from the most enviable health; he became a corpse, and the earth hid him for ever from our sight.

---

[a] cf. *Macbeth*, V. v. 26–8 and Psalm 90: 9.

The loss of my son had introduced a new inmate under our roof. This was the grim spectre, Death. Hitherto our residence had been sacred; it seemed as if he dared not invade it. The 'customary suits of solemn black,'[a] usual in families, so that such as are easy and luxurious in their circumstances, are induced to lay up in readiness what may be called for at a short notice, were entirely unknown at Dunmaine. Death came to us a stranger-guest from a far country, never before seen within our walls. We did not place a chair at our social board for our ever to be regretted son; but, in spite of that omission, we felt that there was a vacant / place, and that place always seemed to be tenanted by the fearful enemy to our peace. He for ever brandished his dart, and we knew not whom he would strike next.

We watched with indescribable anxiety over our remaining children. We were like persons whose house had been robbed of its most valuable property with circumstances of peculiar atrocity, who find a voice in every wind, and who, if a stair does but creak, expect the next moment to see ruffians, armed with cutlasses and bludgeons, bursting their chamber-door, and standing by their bedside. Every wind that breathed, every shower that fell, might be the outpost of the foe descending from the mountains, and might bring pestilence and desolation on its wings. We never felt secure. We watched the flushed cheek, and the heavy eye; an interrupted perspiration filled us with alarm; and a cough shook us to our inmost soul. But all our terrors were nugatory. The / children that remained to us had every appearance of doing well, and living long; their high spirits, and from time to time even their boisterous mirth, seemed to mock at the timidity which haunted us in all our enjoyments. Thus we went on for the space of two years.

At length the enemy came. My pretty Teresa complained one evening that she felt herself quite out of order, and that she had a violent pain in her side. We put her to bed. She will be well to-morrow, I said. Remember, Selina, how often we have teazed ourselves with useless forebodings! – She was not well to-morrow. Another and another day came; but brought with it no amendment. Her symptoms had a frightful resemblance to those of her lamented brother. Selina attended her with the most unremitted perseverance. She did every thing she could devise to inspire the child with cheerfulness and hope.

But, when Selina withdrew from the couch of / the suffering and affectionate Teresa, and found herself alone with me, she no longer put a curb on her anguish. I see it all! she said. There is a black and noisome vapour that hangs over our house, which nothing can drive away or disperse. Exactly at this age our son sickened. Exactly at the same age all our children shall perish. To an unobserving and superficial spectator our two youngest still appear full of health and of promise. I see them even now the ghosts of themselves. To my

---

[a] *Hamlet*, I. i. 78.

maternal and prophetic soul they exhibit the parched and withering surface, that indicates the internal fire which consumes them. Death has surprised our castle, and has already planted his stations and his sentinels, securing to him the perpetual possession. An inexorable providence has given us children, that greatest of earthly blessings, only that they may insensibly mix with our blood, and identify themselves with every fibre of our frames, that they may become the / substance of our lives, and the air that we inhale; and that, when this incorporation has been completed, they may be taken from us, that the main pillars upon which our house reposed may be struck away, and the whole be made a heap of rubbish, and a monument of desolation.

Teresa expired, even as her brother had died, the same mere skeleton, the same shriveled assemblage of bones with a covering of skin. From the period of this melancholy event Selina never looked cheerful, or recovered her former self. Yet the uninterrupted constitution of things held on its course, alike indifferent to our hopes and alarms. We had now only two children remaining; but they, with the buoyant spirits of youth, soon forgot their former companions, and were a frolicsome and playful, as if those companions had not even already sat in the clouds, and beckoned to the others to come after them. Selina however, as I have said, was never consoled; and the burthen of her / complaint was, I see myself childless. I have lived in vain, – for it is the province, the glory, the function of woman on earth, in sorrow to bring forth children, and so to rear them that with credit and honour they may occupy their place in the rising generation, and equal at least – it is to be hoped more than equal – the parents that gave them birth. It is impossible that I can survive the pernicious blast that is sweeping away our house. – Thus was Selina like the patriarch's sultana-wife in the scriptures: 'In Rama was there a voice heard, lamentation and much weeping, Rachel that wept for her children, and refused to be comforted.'[a]

Almost exactly at the expected season our third child sickened. Selina was the victim of instant despair. The most pitiable of all spectacles, at least to a doating husband, is that of a beautiful woman, his wife, hanging over the sick bed of their child, knowing that all her / labour is vain, and the end inevitable, yet desperately bent upon the discharge of her duties to the minutest particular, administering the draught which is to bring no cure, preaching encouragement and hope to the child, that she knows to be treacherous and hollow, smoothing the pillow which is soon to be exchanged for the pillow of the tomb, and supporting the head which is shortly to wear the deathlike hue of the grave. If Selina could have given way to her feelings, that would have been a mitigation; if, after each separate function of her nurse-like occupation, she could have tossed about her arms in despair, if she could have relieved her agony with torrents of tears, if she could have pierced the very roof that covered her with

---

[a] Matt. 2: 18 (adapted).

cries and shrieks, her situation would have been less deplorable. But, no: she was compelled to restrain herself, not to betray by look, or gesture, or sound, what passed within her, to smooth her brow, to dress her countenance / with deceiving smiles, and to speak composure and consolation, while her heart was breaking.

The fate of our remaining daughter was no sooner decided and complete, than the dreadful and destructive effects of all that had passed became visible in Selina. The heart of her heart was gone. She said, she was fully aware that she had at least one remaining duty to perform on earth, attendance on the days, and an endeavour to sustain the failing strength, and mitigate the last struggles and suffering, of our surviving son. He was beyond doubt destined to follow the others, and to die as they had died. She frankly confessed, that the affections of a wife and a mother in the course of nature grew weaker to her husband, and fixed with the intensest interest upon her children. She in pathetic and ingenuous, heartfelt strains intreated me to forgive this. She was truly grieved, she said, that she should be disabled from performing to the end the duties of a mother, / from receiving the last breath of her now only child.

But there was no chance that this could be the case. My youngest son flourished in reckless infancy. Sometimes – but seldom – he recollected that he had had sisters and a brother; often he gazed with an affectionate and wistful eye upon the drooping form of his mother. But the spring of youth was upon him. He was heart-whole, and perfect in the healthful hue and circulations of a beginning existence. No dart of disease had ever yet grazed the smooth and wholesome surface of his frame. While on the other hand the life of his mother was rapidly undermined by mournful recollections of the past, and fearful anticipation of the future.

She could neither eat nor sleep. She was surrounded to her own perceptions by a heavy and dismal atmosphere, such as we may fancy hanging over a city, already in the arms of pestilence, / and the inhabitants of which are dying by fifties and hundreds in an hour. The sun brought no light to her; and the moon and the stars refused their office of communicating serenity to her soul, and revealing the images of other systems and inhabited worlds.

Before she was yet too weak for the task, she caused me to be called to her bedside, that she might impart to me her latest wishes. She said, My beloved Richard, we have yet one child left. Be tender of him; watch over him; be to him father and mother in one. Perhaps you may be more fortunate in your care of him than I could be. You are a man. You have sinews and a composure fit for the office. You can look on these things, and not be shaken. You have borne the bereavement of all that we had, while I could not. To your steady mind then, and to your masculine fortitude, I bequeath the care of our last and only hope. May your administration of this our revenue and estate be more successful than mine has been. / God bless my husband! and, God bless my child!

Thus did Selina in these last solemn moments misread my character. I shed no tears: but no tongue can tell what I suffered. I preserved a plausible and a manlike exterior. But it was not possible that my wife should suffer the thousandth part of the agonies that I did. She saw the course of events: but I only possessed the key that explained and opened the whole. To her it was only an unheard of oppression of adverse incidents: but I saw in it the hand of God. It was justice, that he who had robbed and maltreated his brother's orphan, should himself be made childless, that he who had stolen the inheritance of his brother, should be denied the fruit of his loins to inherit after him. All these innocents, my wife and her offspring, perished from the face of the earth; but I was the guilty cause. They died from me one by one; and I live to tell the story.

When my whole family had perished, and I / with my youngest son was left alone, it is not in words to express the anguish that overwhelmed me. I had found my misery, my solitary state, and the curse that followed me, insupportable; and I married. I sought, by surrounding myself with all the dearest objects of human affection, to obtain relief from the remorse and self-abhorrence, which in my sequestered state for ever preyed on my vitals. It was not likely that, having felt the consolations of a husband and a father, and been again deprived of them, I should suffer in patience the evils from which they had relieved me. I saw the hand of the governor of the universe in all. He was my enemy! Where would he stop in the just retribution inflicted for my crime? What sort of a monument of divine vengeance was I to become? I saw all the miseries that had hitherto overtaken me. But it was beyond the penetration of my prophetic spirit to discern what was to come. /

With an aching heart I had deposited the remains of my youngest daughter in the tomb of her sister and brother, and had turned back from the narrow house of death to dwell among the porticos and halls of my ancestors, when in the space of two little months the vault once more opened its jaws to receive the insensible corpse of their mother. I sent my only son under the care of his tutor to see the last offices performed, and he fainted on the steps that led down into the house of death. I sat at home alone in my chamber, chewing the cud of bitterness which I had myself been for years preparing for my own entertainment. I had yet a duty, the duty Selina had recommended to me on her death-bed; and I now resolved to live for that, and that alone. /

CHAPTER II

It was one evening in autumn that I sat alone, a few weeks after the funeral of her who had for fifteen years been the partner of my bosom. The day had been close and sultry, and the hour of silence and retreat had been ushered in with a few heavy drops of rain. I was fondly cherishing my melancholy thoughts with the memory of her I had so lately lost. I had scattered before me fragments of her hand-writing, some of her personal ornaments, her miniature, and a lock of her hair. I had busied myself as I could during the day, with meditations for the advantage of my only son; he had studied in one corner of my apartment; I had talked to / him of his dear mother (I could talk of nothing else,) and had made him observe her portrait with attention. I wept over the dark and uncertain fortune that was reserved for him in the journey of life; for I still believed he would live, and that, as Selina said, 'my administration of this our revenue and estate would be more successful than hers had been.' I kissed him, and dismissed him to his pillow. And, now that I was at length alone, I occupied myself with all that could set his mother most vividly before me.

The evening was already advanced to an hour at which, in my retreat in the county of Cork, it was very unusual for a visitor to announce himself. My valet approached me to say, that a stranger on horseback with one attendant had just arrived at the mansion, who refused to give in his name. He bade me say, continued the valet, that he came last from Florence, and added, that your lordship would / know from that circumstance who it was that desired to see you. He further remarked that his business was of the highest importance, and could not be postponed. – It is scarcely necessary to say that my visitor was Cloudesley. I detained him in the hall for a few minutes, while I hurried into concealment the precious relics before me. I then ordered him to be admitted, and paced with disturbed steps up and down the apartment till he made his appearance.

While he was abroad, Cloudesley had taken measures to be duly informed of whatever happened to me, and whatever changes had taken place in my situation. He had no relations in the place of his nativity; and the events which in early life had soured his temper towards his kind, had led him to resolve, when he left the shores of his native country, to break off as much as possible from every thing that should remind him of England. In the service of his / beloved master, and as his follower, he would unhesitatingly have gone thither; or, if there were any other country more hateful to him than England, to that he would have been drawn by so dear an inducement. But, when by subsequent events his system of life had been decided, his income was made to depend upon an accomplice at a distance, and the plans he brooded on for his master's child led him in the same direction, he felt, that it would be his wisdom to cultivate a connection in the province of his birth. He recollected a playmate of his youth who resided within a small distance of Milwood Park, and opened a correspondence with him. Cloudesley was not unendowed with the gifts of ingenuity and a sagacious mind, and he well knew how to write letters respecting what he saw in foreign countries, which were highly acceptable in so remote a place; and all he asked in return was accounts from time to time of the intimates of his youth, and particularly / of the Danvers family in its different branches. Thus he obtained from his correspondent the intelligence he wanted, without exciting the slightest suspicion that he had any motive for desiring it, beyond the curiosity that is incident to almost every human mind. It was thus that he was already informed of the deaths of my eldest son and eldest daughter. My recent calamities had not reached his ear, till subsequently to his arrival in Ireland.

How changed was our position! It was eighteen years since I had seen him. This lengthened period could not have been without leaving its traces and the marks of its varied fortune upon the persons of both. We had been young when we parted; we were now somewhat beyond the middle period of human life. When we parted, Cloudesley had already passed several months in the service of a liberal master. He had consequently contracted the alertness, the docile and obedient spirit, and / the complacent gesture and turn of countenance, incident to that walk of life. He had spent all the interval in a state of independence. His look therefore now betokened the erect and self-centred spirit of an English yeoman, with a slight surface of the manner, at once animated and officious, of that class of Italian gentry with whom he had been in frequent intercourse. Such was his appearance, as he stood unabashed in my presence.

But the alteration in me was much more memorable. He had known me in the most brilliant and faultless period of my life. I had already conquered the jealous and envious temper which had disfigured my youth. I loved my brother with a generous sincerity, and had formed myself upon his model. I had served with distinction in the imperial armies, under the command of the incomparable Eugene. I was no disadvantageous specimen of a younger branch of the English nobility. At the time / we parted, the demon of avarice, injustice and fraud had entered my bosom; but there had not been time for the effecting a radical change in my exterior and my general demeanour. But now he saw me after the thoughts of guilt, remorse and shame had been for eighteen years the inmates of my breast. Mine was the roving and suspicious eye; mine the worm of conscience veiled under a fair outside; mine the complexion of dun and tarnished red, the colour uniform through every region of the face, which told that no food had to me the effect of kindly nourishment, and that no beam of serenity and cheerfulness ever gladdened my soul by night or by day.

I said to him, with as firm and lofty an air as I could assume, as he entered, What make you here? [*sic*] This is a violation of the contract between us.

I have not come, retorted Cloudesley in a determined manner, from Florence to the / south of Ireland, without having first maturely considered my purpose. The lands and seas I have traversed are a pledge to you, that I will not return without a perfect success. I have been driven by an impulse that it was out of my power to control, by a voice from heaven; and I swear that I will not leave this house of my ward and his ancestors, till I have accomplished the purpose for which I came.

We meet as two guilty creatures. In the face of the world we might blush and hang down our heads, if mankind could read the secret of our souls: but to each other we are familiar, and have arrived beyond the reach of shame.

There was a day when we entered into a hellish contract, and mutually agreed on that which might worthily expel us from every 'good man's feast,' and shut us out of such societies 'where bells have knolled to church.'[a] My oblivion of the great bond by which communities / are held together, was short; I have expiated my sin in undying repentance; I have sought by every means in my power to atone for and repair my injustice. You have rioted in impunity for eighteen years; no moment of compunction has visited you; you have not thought for an instant of retracing your downward steps. This error, this guilt, this usurpation, this breach of every thing that is holy, must have an end; and I am come to put a close to all further delay and reprieve. Let your reparation be open and without reserve; it is your wisdom to make it so; for, in one way or the other, I come to tell you that this house and these revenues shall no longer be yours, and that the title you bear must be laid down for ever.

This is the essence of guilt. I drank the cup of bitterness to the very dregs. There is but one thing that can truly humble a man; and that is crime. I was born a nobleman; I / was bred a military commander, having numbers of human creatures implicitly under my control. In each of these characters with what disdain should I have looked down upon this man, this cockney, this serf, born to be sold with the land he tilled, had it not been for the guilt that broke down the energies of my soul! Homer says, that the day that takes from a man his personal liberty, takes away half his worth. How much more truly may it be affirmed, of the day that takes from a man his integrity and innocence! I was compelled to endure the presence of this Cloudesley, while he loaded me with all varieties of opprobrious appellation, and threatened me, as if he were the man of station, and I the slave. But why do I say, it was much for me to bear it

---

[a] *As You Like It*, II. vii. 114–5.

from him? Had I kept my integrity, I would not have borne it from a satrap or a prince.

> To the liege lord of my dear native land
> I owe a subject's homage:[a] /

but even from him I would not have borne, what I bore from Cloudesley. If I could not have defied him, it I could not have smote him with my sword, at least I would not have stood in his presence, I would not have breathed the same air, I would not have dwelt on the same soil. I would have endenisened myself in a country where I could make myself respected; I would have dwelt in a community where my treatment should be that which a gentleman expects from his inferiors, or from those who are essentially his equals.

But, as it was, I was compelled to endure every thing, to digest every thing. This fellow had me in his meshes; and it was necessary for me to keep terms with him. What he could do, I knew not; whether formally and by law he could eject me from all that I possessed, and all which, further than this, I expected. But he could at least beard me, not as now, man to man in my private apartment; but on the / theatre of the world. He could tell 'a shameful tale for public sport,'[b] could make me the subject of base discussion with every clown, could cause them to point the finger, and thrust out the lip, in scorn against me. No: this I would never encounter.

> 'Twas fixed, I'd die, rather than bear the insolence
> Of each dissembling wretch should tell my story.[c]

But why do I say, I would die? That is a miserable refuge in such a case as mine. I should leave my name to be torn in pieces. I should leave my dust to be trampled on. I should leave my bones to be burned in ignominy, and the ashes to be scattered to all the winds of heaven. As long as I was remembered, my appellation would be used as a by-word of horror.

And what gave this man the ascendancy over me? He was as great an offender as I. We had entered into a common league of infamy, to strip of his rights the infant that had none to / help him. But in infamy, it is wisely provided that he who stands highest in the ranks of society, has the heaviest load to sustain. Oh, what would I not give, to creep into enviable obscurity, to have no name by which I could be traced, no lineaments by which I could be recognised, to wash myself from the stains that darken my skin, and are mixed up with my blood, and to come forth a new man, sinless as the unborn infant! Fool that I was, I had thought myself secure. If I were a gainer by the forgery we had concocted, he also, in proportion to his station and his habits, was a gainer too.

---

[a] Quotation unidentified.
[b] Quotation unidentified.
[c] Quotation unidentified.

I thought I had held him in firmest bonds by a provision of five hundred pounds a year. I had not dreamed that he would ever disturb me in my ill-gotten possession, since, as I judged, he could not do so, but by an act that would turn him out a beggar. How short-sighted is guilt!

In fine, I was reduced to the soul-sickening / alternative, to expostulate with my tyrant, to endeavour by words to disarm his hostility, and prevail on him to treat me with lenity and forbearance. With a concentred mind, and a pacifying, intreating tone, which it cost me torments inexpressible to adopt, I said:

Cloudesley, it would be the height of felicity to me, if I could recall the past. Oh, that I could place myself now, as I stood when I closed my brother's eyes at the seat of the baron Stahlhoffen in Bavaria! No man knows the value of innocence and integrity, but he who has lost them. How fearful is the state of mortals, when a single blow that is made, the motion of a finger, the stroke of a pen, the articulation of a syllable, can change a man at once, from being a subject of universal commendation and envy, into the mark for all men's indignation and scorn, a being that the myrmidons of the law shall hunt, and who can only appease the vengeance of the community / against him by an ignominious death! Willingly would I resign all I have, and go out again naked and portionless into the world, if by so doing I could regain my innocence. But, no: that is impossible!

I must therefore retain the part I have chosen. I must preserve the advantage I have purchased. I have bought this world's honours and wealth for myself and the little son that is left me, at a fearful price; and shall I make a voluntary surrender of them? Give me back, give me back, the mighty store that I gave in exchange, peace of mind, and an unstained conscience, and I am content. But I cannot consent to part at once with what I gave, and what I got. I can now lift up my head in the face of the world, and appear without reproach. The legal evidences of my succession are entire and complete. It is not in your power to shake them. This is the pillar of all the honours my country yields me; and on this foundation will I rest. /

And why should you desire to disturb me? Your adopted son is happy at present. How can he be more so? You praise his docility, his acquirements, his generosity, the contentment and cheerfulness of his dispositions. Would he be happier, if he possessed those things to the inheritance of which he was born? Philosophers and moralists have agreed that a moderate condition in life is that which is most to be desired. You would strip me of all I possess. You would take from my child all that from the first dawning of his understanding he has been prompted to expect. You would brand upon my forehead and his the signature of dishonour. You would affix to the name of Herbert, and to the titles of Alton and Danvers, an everlasting disgrace. That disgrace would even contaminate the whole blood of the house, and rebound on your ward. And for what would you do this? To remove him from a situation with which he is satisfied, and place / him in one untried, for which no previous habits have prepared him, and in which he might find himself a stranger and a malcontent. You have at present what is to you and to him a competence. If you say, that you hold this by a precarious tenure, and that, when you die, he may be turned out an unprovided wanderer, I am contented to settle it upon the joint lives of both by the strictest bonds that can be devised. Accept these terms. Be satisfied with this, and whatever else I can do, short of upsetting all that is established, signing myself a villain, and bringing down the grey hairs of the earl Danvers, the head of our house, to the grave with anguish.

You possess a fearful power over me. Use it with moderation and temperance. Remember that I am a nobleman, the brother of him who rescued you from a jail, and whose name you reverence beyond every thing that ever bore the form of man. Can you bear to trample me in / the dust, to thrust me forth to universal scorn? This you believe to be in your power: but will you use your power to that end? No such evil can happen to your ward, if you yield to my expostulations. He may pass his days in usefulness and honour. He will regret nothing, for he knows not that he has lost anything. You were born the son of a cultivator of the earth, belonging to a cast of society essentially inferior to mine. In the order of things you could not approach to any one of the blood of the Altons and the Danverses, but to offer your services, and to receive our commands. A concurrence of circumstances has put it in your power to destroy me. But is it generous, is it noble, to use your power to that end? Remember too, that I could never have been placed in this precarious, ignoble situation without you. You stood in my presence in the crisis of my fate. There was that in your countenance and manner, which suggested unlawful / contemplations, or cherished and warmed them into life, if they existed in embryo already. Cloudesley, you are my evil genius; you were my tempter! Man! having made me what I am, and destroyed my soul, can you have the daring to make use of this predicament in which we stand, to thrust me down to the pit, and think that you shall enter the rank of the angels in heaven? I do not mean to offend you. But I must speak. This is not a time for half-measures and temporising. Begone! Return to Italy from whence you came. Thus far you have done prosperously. You have reaped the advantage of your part of the conspiracy into which we entered. Do not think, having steeped your soul in villainy, to come forth as if you were without spot! Be content!

My whole soul seemed to take possession of every lineament of my countenance, as I spoke. The fervour of passion penetrated and devoured me. My voice swelled, and seemed to my own / ears like the voice of thunder. Cloudesley trembled. For some moments he was speechless. It was easy to perceive that he repented the having placed himself in my presence, exposed himself to hear the bitterness of my reproaches, the confounding truths I set before him, the measure of retaliation to which I was driven. – By degrees he recovered his self-possession and firmness.

It is useless, he said, to consider how far I have myself wandered from the path of integrity and virtue. I am deeply conscious of the wrong I have committed, and for years have steeped the recollection in the hot and bitter tears of repentance. The past is beyond our power. It can no more be reversed, than the calamities and crimes that occurred myriads of years before we were called into existence. The future is the empire of the human will; and I am most anxious to atone for the errors of the past by the rectitude of what is to come. /

It belongs neither to you nor to me, to decide in what position the youth under my care, your nephew, will be most happy. According to the laws of all civilised communities he has rights, which we are not entitled to supersede. Let him be invested in those rights, and the principal part of our task, as it relates to him, will have been performed. He has perhaps no friend on the face of the globe but myself. At least, to me his person, his claims, his position in society, are confided. I live but for this object; I have no other passion. My days and nights, my thoughts waking and sleeping, my exertions, my journeys by sea and land, are devoted to this. I will never relax from this sacred undertaking; no motive, no temptation, no bribe, shall turn me aside; and I feel in my inmost heart that it shall be accomplished. He shall be publicly known and acknow-ledged as baron Alton and earl Danvers; he shall be the / lord of this domain, and of the still more splendid mansion in the isle of Axholme.

I shook my head expressively, in rejection of his proposals, and in disregard of his threats.

It is well, said he. What I desired was, that we should act together in the accomplishment of this holy purpose. Together we contrived, and together perpetrated, an unheard-of crime. It was my most earnest wish that we should have cooperated in the generous restoration of the youth we have injured. We have done that, which, if known, would blast our characters in the judgment of all honourable men, nay, of all men, whether virtuous or profligate. It is in our power, uncompelled, of our own free will, by our spontaneous act, to set right that in which we have offended, and to shew that there is in us a principle and spring of justice and truth. /

But, if I cannot have your assistance, that shall not turn me from my purpose. In what manner I shall proceed to effect it, as yet I know not. I will not act without mature deliberation, and without much advice. But I will not rest. My proceeding shall be as rapid, as my plan shall be well-digested and firm. Do not therefore for a moment imagine yourself secure. Your ruin shall come when you least expect. Like a thief in the night, it shall take you unawares and unprepared. And, as you refuse to accept, what is now offered you, honour in the event that is to be effected, be assured that I shall entertain no considera-tion for your feelings, and no forbearance as to the consequences that will follow to your fortune or your peace!

He said all this with a passion and an impetuosity that carried him out of himself. It was like a horse in the full career of his speed, who has the bridle thrown on his neck, and whom / neither rocks, nor declivities, nor barriers, nor seas can stop in his course. – Having spoken, he burst from my presence, and quitted the mansion and park where I resided.

I remained for some time motionless, stunned with the scene in which I had been a partaker. What a thing is guilt! I had been pressed down to the earth by the series of calamities that had occurred within my domestic circle. And here came the visit of a man, who was like a savage that had broken loose from the woods, or like Polyphemus, when Ulysses and his companions had unwarily entered his cave, who, having no consideration for the unparalleled sufferings his victims had for years endured, thought only of his own object, and the accomplishment of his unrelenting purpose.[a]

I sat still, and was helpless. I waited one day, and another day, expecting when my adversary would make his second appearance. I dared do nothing, fearful of the consequences / of irritating a person who had so much in his power.

If I had dared, I would have asked Cloudesley a thousand questions. I longed to lift the veil, but was terrified at the thought of the appalling, the heart-withering objects it might disclose. In what I had said I had taken it for granted that Julian knew nothing of his true birth and his claims. But was that the case? Had Cloudesley never in the fulness of his soul poured out its fraught into the bosom of the youth he adored? Had he made no other men the confidents of my perilous secret, thus multiplying on every side the persons who would have it in their power, if not to take from me every thing I possessed, at least to publish my shame to the whole world, and make my pretensions a subject of discourse to every one I saw? He had said, that he would not act without mature deliberation, or without much advice. Whom did he purpose to consult? / Would he prepare, or would he instruct another so as to cause him to prepare, a brief, containing all the particulars of my disgraceful tale? I would have given the world for an answer to the least of these questions. But I dared not breathe them to the air of my most secret apartment.

Was there a wretch existing on the face of the earth so very miserable, that he would have consented to change places with the possessor of the barony of Alton, and the near successor to the earls Danvers? Yet I resolved to persevere. I would not be the assassin of my own fame, or the destroyer of the dear boy on whom I doated, the only survivor of the circle that had surrounded me, but who on that account was a thousand times dearer to me than ever. /

---

[a] In Greek mythology, Polyphemus was a Cyclops ruling over Sicily who imprisoned Odysseus (or Ulysses) and his companions in his cave, eating half of them. Odysseus and the rest effected their escape by blinding Polyphemus.

CHAPTER III

It was not till after the lapse of many days, that I learned by mere accident that Cloudesley had suddenly, and apparently upon a minute's warning, quitted my neighbourhood, and set out on his return to Italy.

He had proceeded for the furthest west upon a sudden impulse, separated from his beloved charge by a distance of two thousand miles, and for an absence which must necessarily be of some months' continuance. Eudocia was recently dead, and Julian must be left to a considerable degree in the hands of strangers. He was just arrived at the critical age of eighteen. The disadvantages that attended Cloudesley's / enterprise under these circumstances were serious; but for this he did not perceive any remedy. It was, as he apprehended, his duty without loss of time to assert the cause of his ward, and endeavour to restore him to his rights. This was an affair that fastened itself like a polypus upon his heart; and he could have neither rest nor repose so long as he neglected any thing that might effect this sacred purpose.[a]

How different would be the situation of Julian, when this object was once accomplished! Now he dwelt in a foreign land, appeared to belong to no one, and passed for the son of an Englishman of very ordinary rank. If he could be placed by Cloudesley's means in the situation to which his birth entitled him, he would immediately be acknowledged as an integral member of the first ranks in the country of his ancestors; he would be a peer of Ireland, and in no distant succession to an earldom in the superior / country. The critical circumstances, which arose out of the period of life he had attained, cried in Cloudesley's ear with a voice that could in no sort be controled, for his instant advancement and restoration. Too long had he been deemed the descendant of ignoble blood; and 'the wanton heir of some inglorious' Italian count 'perhaps had scorned him in his youthful sports.'[b] It was time that he should mix on an equal footing with the junior scions of illustrious birth. Elevated and magnificent conceptions would thus be engendered in his bosom. Perhaps in the years of childhood and early instruction it was little injury that he should wander heedless and inconscious, unacknowledged by others, and unpenetrated himself with the knowledge of his true vocation. But this must not continue. He was arrived at the epoch when the habits of mortals strike the deepest root, and they must be great or little for the

---

[a] i.e. Polyp, small vascularized growth.
[b] Quotation unidentified.

remainder of his existence. It was / part of Cloudesley's plan to place his charge under the protection and auspices of the English earl, the head of his house, and that nobleman's period of life, and the late precarious state of his health, assured him that there was therefore no time to be lost.

Cloudesley accordingly looked about him to discover the safest protection under which he could leave his charge, during the season of that necessary absence on his part, which was dedicated to the promotion of Julian's most important interests.

The English yeoman had lately formed an intimacy with an Italian of an extraordinary character, whose name was Borromeo.[a] His first destination had been the sea, and he had made several voyages in the employment of the merchantmen of Livorno.[b] In one of these voyages he had been taken prisoner by the Algerines, and sold for a slave.[c] There was in him a remarkable independence and stubborness / of temper, very ill adapted to the condition into which he had fallen. He seemed on no occasion to 'set his life at a pin's fee.'[d] He always went straight to his purpose, indifferent to the consequences that might accrue to him from the disapprobation of others. He therefore acquired among his fellow-slaves the appellation of Ironsides.[e] Yet his bluntness, his soul that nothing could bend, or subject to the influence of inticement or menace, and his fearlessness of danger, had in a thousand instances proved his preservation. Those who had the power of life and death over him, for the most part suffered him to go his own way, convinced that they might as soon attempt to soften rocks, or arrest the gusts of heaven, as to produce any effect upon his impenetrable temper.

Yet this character on the part of Borromeo was not established, but through the means of various experiments of a truly Algerine fashion. He had gone through as many hardships as / Saint Paul relates of himself: 'in stripes above measure, in prisons more frequent, in deaths oft; many times had he been beaten with rods, and been tried with weariness and watching, with hunger and thirst, with cold and nakedness.'[f] He was like Anaxarchus in the Grecian story: if you pounded him 'in a mortar, you could but beat upon the case of the philosopher; you could not touch his soul.[g] Despotism and savage fury

---

[a] Possibly named after the famous and benevolent sixteenth century Italian cardinal and archbishop of Milan, St Carlo Borromeo (1538–84).

[b] Port in Tuscany, W. central Italy.

[c] Algerines, natives of Algeria.

[d] *Hamlet*, I. iv. 65.

[e] Ironsides, a person with great stamina or resistance. Capitalized, the term in the Civil War was applied to the cavalry regiment trained and commanded by Oliver Cromwell, and sometimes to Cromwell's whole army. Ironside was also the nickname given to King Edmund II of England (980?–1016).

[f] 2 Cor. 11: 23–7 (adapted).

[g] Anaxarchus (4th century BC), philosopher of Abdera, follower of Democritus and friend of Alexander. Nicocreon, who 'pounded' him as Godwin describes, also threatened to cut out his tongue for his insolent observations, whereupon Anaxarchus bit it off himself and spat it into the tyrant's face.

themselves were obliged to confess that they had met with somewhat above them. But, though the Algerine captains and pirates owned their impotence, and refrained from assailing, they did not love him. He scowled on them; and they scowled on him, in return. He had frequently changed masters. At length however they found that he was not altogether without his value. He did not desire to be idle. And, merely to satisfy the impulses of his own mind, he would, uncommanded and uncompelled, cultivate the fields of / his proprietor, or take care of his flocks and herds. – He spent twenty of the best years of his life in captivity. At length he was freed by the interposition of the monks of the order of mercy. The price of his redemption was small; for, though, left to himself, he was a serviceable slave, yet no Algerine proprietor felt comfortable in intercourse with a person thus rated at a price, yet no less independent and unalterable in his purposes than the master who owned him.

The training that Borromeo had thus received, was certainly of a singular sort. He had no doubt had a temper of no ordinary cast before he was made a slave, if he had not in reality brought it into the world with him. It must have been this that made him take slavery in the way he had done, differently perhaps from any other individual, either in ancient or modern times, that had ever been placed in that condition. /

Few things can be more dissimilar, than is frequently the outside of a man from what passes within him. The slave-drivers of the African coast could find in Borromeo no symptoms expressive of pain or injury; no muscle flinched, no feature altered, for all they could do to him. It was their observation, that you might as well fight with the intrenchant air, or lay your lashes on the sea, as expect by severities to produce an effect upon Borromeo. But, though his muscles did not alter, and he did not gratify the malice of his tyrants by uttering a groan or a sigh, it was all laid up in the innermost core of his heart, and generated in him a creed of a peculiar nature. He never lied: for, as he feared nothing, and encountered both menaces and inflictions with unalterable firmness, he had no motive to deceive. It was not out of consideration for others, but respect for himself, that he always bluntly uttered the truth. Meanness is the child of hope or fear, / of something that terrifies, or something that entices; but, as Borromeo had perceptibly neither hope nor fear, and conducted himself in a way independently of what man could do to him, it followed of necessity that he had no meanness. Utterly regardless of the treatment he might receive, he viewed his fellow-mortals with ineffable contempt. They were to him like so many powerless insects, that we do not even give ourselves the trouble to brush away, but suffer them to enact their pleasure without control and without observation. Yet this man was eminently a moral being. He had certain rules of right to which he rigorously adhered, not for the sake of the good to result to others, but, as certain theologians inculcate in their systems, from the simple love of justice, and without care for the consequences to result.

The exterior of Borromeo corresponded to the discipline of his mind; or, as certain painters express themselves, he had much character, / and little expression. In other words, he was strongly marked for those qualities which were peculiar to him, and scarcely dwelt in any other man; but these marks were trenched in his visage, while neither anger, nor complacency, nor any of those things we call emotions, produced any flexible and evanescent variation either of countenance or gesture. His complexion and the texture of his skin was like the hide of a beast dried in the sun; his eyebrows were thick and bushy; his eyes looked out dark and penetrating under the pent-house of his brow; and his voice was full and unmodulated, and upon all occasions produced a sensation something like fear in the sensorium of a stranger.

At the same time he was a man of excellent sense, of sound judgment, inflexible in his purposes, and confident in the rectitude of his projects, and the strength he possessed to effect them. In this respect however his efforts were / frequently abortive, because he thought much of the design he had fixed on, and little of the temper and prejudices of those whose concurrence it might demand.

This man, thus qualitied, was scarcely acceptable to any of his countrymen. They were animated, and full of gesticulation. He stood, or sate, like a block of marble. He scorned to inforce what he said by contortions of the body. He scarcely looked any one in the face; not that he feared to be detected in any thing, but that he did not think any thing in human shape entitled to that degree of deference and worship. He made no account of them. He had at no time had the national marks of an Italian; and his long residence among the pirates of Africa had rendered him still more unlike the bulk of his countrymen.

But there was that in him that excited the partiality of Cloudesley. Cloudesley was an / Englishman; and the English in general are undemonstrative, and have little gesticulation. Cloudesley was bred among the lower orders of his countrymen, a rustic. The Italians are by nature, as it were, courtiers, desirous of the good opinion of others, desirous to be serviceable, supple. Cloudesley was tired of this, as he called it, sycophantic outside, and welcomed with peculiar zest the rugged exterior of Borromeo. They agreed in their creed of misanthropy. Add to which, Borromeo was endowed with many excellent qualities. At first sight he offended almost every one that approached him. But that had a tendancy to wear off; and then, the more you knew him, the more you were sure to like him. His good qualities came out one by one, like stars at the setting in of the night. Though fearless, he was by no means without affections; and, where he took, he truly loved. It was difficult to touch and to awake / him; but, in proportion to the rareness of the first steps, his attachments were by so much the more rooted and unalterable.

There was another thing that brought Borromeo and Cloudesley together. The temper of Cloudesley, since he had become a misanthrope, was, as the name implies, rugged to the mass of mankind, though it was tender and affectionate to the few that he loved. He saw therefore a copy of himself in Borromeo, though with this, difference, that the oppression and loss of liberty that he had suffered had endured less than twenty months, but Borromeo's for twenty years. Add to which, Cloudesley had dwelt in habitual intercourse with some that he regarded with unfeigned affection; but Borromeo had scarcely ever had a friend. Sympathy is one of the principles most widely rooted in our nature: we rejoice to see ourselves reflected in another; and, perversely enough, we sometimes have a secret pleasure in seeing the sin which dwells in / ourselves, existing under a deformed and monstrous aspect in another. Thus the miser will love to associate with another miser, who, if we judge by the stature of his vice, we may call his elder brother. He sees in him his own quality, and thus his being becomes multiplied to his apprehension: but he also sees it in its full-grown ugliness; and this answers two purposes to him. First, he laughs at the man who proceeds to that extremity of folly; and next, he encourages and makes much of himself, exclaiming, I am not so bad as he neither. There intermingled a sentiment of this sort in the Englishman's attachment to the Italian.

When Cloudesley had determined on a journey to Ireland, he looked round him to choose in what custody he should leave his charge during his absence. Julian had been brought up with the greatest tenderness; his nominal parents had always considered him as a being of another order from themselves, and had treated / him accordingly; he had scarcely ever been contradicted; and there was a gentleness and rationality in his nature, that made it scarcely possible that contradiction could be necessary in bringing him up. He had arrived at that period of life, that removal from childhood towards maturity, which is beyond all others most critical for human beings. He had hitherto for the most part been led; he must now in many respects act according to his own discretion. Eudocia was unfortunately dead; otherwise Cloudesley would have left him under her inspection and vigilance with the most perfect security.

It cost his protector much reflection and many sleepless nights, to determine what he should do with this, in his estimation, most precious of all deposits. He knew of but one person thoroughly trust-worthy in the whole circle of his acquaintance: and this person was Borromeo. It is true, Julian and Borromeo were the very / antitheses of each other: the one all gentleness and loveliness; the other the most rugged and stern of human beings. If you could have put the portrait of the two upon one canvas, they would have exhibited the most memorable contrast that the pencil of any artist could have delineated. It would have been the blunt and oracular Silenus, with Bacchus, his pupil, fair as the morning, and blooming as a bank of new-blown roses, such as the luxuriance of the poets of antiquity has described them.[a]

---

[a] In Greek mythology, Silenus was a chief of the satyrs and foster-father to Dionysus, often depicted riding drunkenly on a donkey; Bacchus, a god of wine and giver of ecstacy in Roman mythology, identified with the Greek Dionysus.

Yet Cloudesley conceived that he had no choice: and all that, as he believed, remained to him, was carefully to prepare each party for this intimate connection. He said to Julian,

My son, a business of the last importance takes me to England (he did not mention Ireland). It is necessary for a few weeks that we should part. You cannot imagine how this separation weighs on my spirits. Yet I can scarcely tell why it should do so. You are so good, that I / am persuaded you might pass along the very brink of destruction without losing the presence of your mind, and through the midst of moral contagion without the danger that one particle of infection should fasten upon you, and corrupt the purity of your soul. But my solicitude demands to be assured even against impossibilities. And Eudocia, my wife, your mother, is dead: I am left without a confidential friend in the world.

You have seen Borromeo (Julian started). I know that you and he do not well suit each other. There are no two persons on earth more unlike. But there is no being on the face of the earth in whom I have entire confidence, except him. He has a thousand virtues. For my sake therefore, my dear Julian, be reconciled to him. Love him, because I love him. Give me this token of your filial piety and genuine regard. Consent for a few weeks to live under his roof. Bear with the ruggedness of his manners, and / lay yourself out to win his affections. It will, I doubt not, be a sacrifice to you; but are you not willing to make some sacrifice, in return for the immense stock of love I bear you, and all my anxieties and exertions for your benefit, from the first hour of your helpless infancy to the present day? I shall rest tranquil and at peace during the trying period of this distant removal, if I know that you are under the eye of my friend.'

To Borromeo Cloudesley held a language in like manner conciliatory and inviting. He said,

My friend, it is, I know, an arduous and unpleasing task that I desire to impose upon you. But you are my brother; and you will not refuse to me the office of a brother. You cannot imagine how dear this youth is to me. He is the one thing that ties me to earth: it is for him only that the future has any thing for me to hope or to fear. From the hour of his birth to the present moment we have scarcely been / separated; or, if separated, I have left him till now under the guardianship of the exemplary and affectionate Eudocia, that incomparable matron whom we have so recently lost. An irresistible necessity compels me to undertake this journey, and I must leave my boy behind. There is no one that I can trust but you; in you I have perfect confidence. The task however is new to you; you have no experience to guide you. Let me therefore prevail on you to listen to a few suggestions which I will take the liberty to offer. You are the best man in the world. Your manners are rough and unpolished; but those manners have only served to endear you to me the more. Remember however, that my poor boy has been used to the utmost tenderness. Both I and my wife have felt that our lives were bound up in the life of the child. And it never required any harshness to conduct him. He was so innocent, so complying and affectionate; that we could lead him / with a thread through the world. How human creatures ought to be conducted in the period of their nonage, I leave it to the wise men of this world to dispute. But Julian, having always been treated, till now that he has completed the eighteenth year of his age, with forbearance and tenderness, would feel the authority and constraint frequently exercised by those of mature age towards the young, a thousand times the more, because it would be new to him. It is but for a few weeks; and I earnestly hope that you will put a little force upon your temper for my sake for so short a time.

To all this tirade Borromeo replied: Look ye now, do not expect from me that I shall alter my character! I am far from desiring the office you impose upon me; I would not undertake it for any other man. As it is, I consent to take the lad under my protection; and I will do for him as well as I can. But I have my own ideas as to what right conduct requires of / me; and I never suffered any one to turn me aside from the proceeding which my judgment suggested. I then, whom never yet the whip and violence and slavery could force for a moment from the line of conduct I chose for myself, am not going to turn over a new leaf now. I do not know your son; I have at present a motive to study him, and consider what his welfare may require. I shall be governed in my actions by circumstances to which I am hitherto a stranger. I give you fair warning. If you take me with all my faults, my violence, and my obstinacy in pursuing what I think right, here I am at your service. If not, why, there is no harm done: I shall not be in the slightest degree offended, if, after this fair exposition of my mind, you should think proper to adopt a different course, and leave me to myself.

Such was the separation between Julian and his supposed father; and the heart of Cloudesley ached for what might happen in the period of / his absence. But the separation seemed to him indispensible; and the rigid integrity of Borromeo he regarded as his best security against any cardinal and deadly evil. He could not bear that his charge should be watched over, during this brief suspension of his own superintendence, by any eye less pure and circumspect than that of his friend.

Cloudesley and Julian were both at the same period removed to a new scene. Cloudesley departed upon an expedition of nearly seven hundred leagues. He had quitted the British isles twenty years before, and never revisited them during that period. Julian removed to the house of Borromeo five miles from Florence.

The change however to the feelings of Julian was incomparably the greater of the two. From infancy he had basked in the lap of undulgence, and experienced an almost uninterrupted succession of gay and cheerful sensations. The house of Borromeo was of that melancholy sort, / so difficult to imagine in the midst of the genial and splendid scenes of Italy. It was rambling, and squalid, and dark. The apartments were numerous; the furniture mean and slender. The windows were narrow, and imperfectly lighted the rooms and the staircase. The edifice itself formed two sides of a quadrangle; the other two being shut in with a bank of earth. The area of the court was paved with small flint-stones. The entrance was by a gate under an archway of stone, which had been constructed for the accommodation of carriages, but which was now rarely frequented. The whole had a striking air of desolation and neglect, and was calculated to communicate a feeling of sadness and discouragement to the heart of the stranger who entered under its battlements.

The only fixed inhabitants of this building were Borromeo and three or four servants. As he had passed his best days among the despots / and slaves of Algiers, he had scarcely the idea of any other intercourse in use between man and man, except that of absolute command on the one hand, and instant submission on the other. With Cloudesley indeed and two or three select companions he relaxed; he was narrative, and even after a coarse and boisterous manner facetious. But that was the exception; the other was the rule. He had no practice in the scenes of childhood and youth; he had had no experience of them since he was a child himself; and he had almost forgotten that that was ever the case. The sweet intercourse between human beings arrived at maturity on the one hand, and those who are still in their nonage on the other, the delicious emotions that arise between the parent and his offspring, and their mutual endearments, were things of which he had no conception. He required of young persons, if he ever came into communication with them to be wise, or, if they / had no stock of that commodity in their stores, to put off their follies, and take their rules of action from the wisdom of their elders.

What a situation was that of Julian under the roof of this Italian! he, the whole of whose life had been passed amidst smiles and sport, who had constantly associated with young persons as gay as himself, or, when he came into communication with his elders, who found them treating him with deference, and shewing by a thousand mute and inexplicable tokens, that they thought themselves honoured in providing for his pleasure! Such was the result of his peculiar situation, Cloudesley and Eudocia having the secret feeling that they were entertaining under their roof a being of a superior sphere, and who was destined one day to break out with a splendour that was truly his own.

Before Cloudesley set off for Ireland, he had deemed it necessary to make a disclosure of his most cherished secret to Borromeo. He had / never yet imparted it to a human creature. This was a painful alternative; but upon mature deliberation he judged it indispensible to adopt it. We are told that, a century or two ago, it was frequently the practice with persons of property to make their wills in due form, preparatory to their setting out upon a journey of a hundred or a hundred and fifty miles from their provincial residence for London. Cloudesley was going two thousand miles. He purposed to be absent only for a short time. But how many dangers might beset him by land and sea during his route! He was leaving Julian in a land of strangers. He deemed it therefore incumbent on him to communicate the knowledge of what he was to a second individual, that, in case of any accident to one, there might still be a survivor that possessed it. It had always been in the keeping of two; and, now that Eudocia was no more, Cloudesley thought proper to constitute Borromeo her successor. /

He had imagined that by so doing he should give to his friend an additional motive to the punctual discharge of his trust. But in this he found himself mistaken. Cloudesley believed that he had the fortune of his ward in his hands. He persuaded himself that he had only to put forth his full strength, in order to the entire removal of any resistance to the claims of the stripling. He was as sure as he was of his own existence, that justice would finally prevail, and that his charge would be restored to the rights of his ancestors. Not so Borromeo. He looked at the question with a mind unprepossessed; at the same time that he viewed all human affairs through the medium of his misanthropical creed. He saw the adversary in possession of the title and estate, abetted by his personal friends, and the friends of his family; while Julian was a stranger to the British dominions, and with very slender means at his command. He felt certain, that he would be regarded as an interloper / and am impostor, and that no other alternative remained to him, but either to live and die the reputed son of Cloudesley, or to spend his days with that most miserable of all characters, a discredited pretender.

Julian came under the roof of Borromeo with every disposition to conduct himself in the most inoffensive manner, and to accommodate his own humours to those of his host. He comforted himself that it was likely to be only for a very short time that this would be required of him; and he thought within his own heart that he owed a much greater sacrifice than this to the will of his only surviving parent.

But his was not the age of patience and long-suffering; and there are cases where it is much easier to make good resolutions, than to persevere in reducing them to practice. He found the house of Borromeo a much more intolerable residence than he had figured it to himself. His host was a man of the most saturnine habits, / perpetually in the frown. Borromeo however thought he did much for the accommodation of Julian; he gave him his choice what apartment in the house he would call his own; he ordered his cook to enquire of the youth what he would choose to have for his meals, and at what hours they should be served. This was a sacrifice that Borromeo would have made in such a case to no consideration, but his desire to fulfil the expectations of Cloudesley. His manners however were stiff and morose. And, what was worse, there was in his opinion an insurmountable barrier between a youth in his teens, and a man between forty and fifty. On the present occasion he did what he could. But the concessions he made were in his own apprehension unnatural and unjust. He believed that a young person should approach a man of sense and experience, as an individual deeply imbued with the religion of the ancients would have approached an oracle. He could form no conception / that it was any part of the business of one advanced in the vale of years to entertain the young, to lead them on by insensible endearments in the path of virtue, and to endeavour by means of kindness and affection to obtain their confidence. The divinity that represented moral truth, was in his apprehension stern; and the temple in which she was worshipped severe, and destitute of ornament. /

CHAPTER IV

In this situation Julian's natural resource was in Francesco. He resolved to shew himself conformable and docile in the house of Borromeo; but he conceived that he had a right to choose his own companions when he was out of that house. Francesco was a familiar with whom Cloudesley had been pleased that he should associate; and, now that Julian resided in the gloomy abode of his temporary protector, he felt that a cheerful circle of friends was more than ever necessary to him.

Francesco was a much worse man than Cloudesley had understood him to be. His situation in life was considerably changed, since the time / when Julian began to be acquainted with him. The princess Violante, sister by marriage to the grand duke, had died in 1731, when Julian was twelve years of age; and, after that event, Bernardino had by no means figured in so brilliant a way in the first circles of Florence, as he had done before. Bernardino survived his patroness seven years; and his death had been a circumstance changing the career of his nephew for the worse, and throwing him upon a new sphere of society.

Among the most intimate of the present associates of Francesco, was Federigo count of Camaldoli. He might seem to stand for an exception to the idea that Francesco was fallen upon a less reputable set of acquaintance. The person of Federigo was among the most faultless. He was somewhat above the middle stature. He had a broad and capacious forehead; his eyes and hair were black; his nose was formed with peculiar delicacy; and his limbs / seemed as if moulded by the Graces. There was a native nobility in his appearance, which struck every beholder. His carriage was easy and unaffected; and his presence of mind never deserted him. He stood as disengaged and unembarrassed when addressing himself to persons of the highest rank, as before the poorest clown. He seemed formed for woman's love. He shone particularly in the airy motions and elegant attitudes of a consummate dancer. And his horsemanship had never been equalled in that part of Italy. He managed the most fiery steed, and appeared to make of that noble animal his plaything, mounting and dismounting, and displaying every variety of attitude, so as to impress the spectator with a feeling, as if he and the quadruped he bestrode, had a magnetic sympathy, and were moved by an impulse that at the same instant acted on both. But that which distinguished him more than all the rest of his qualities, was courage. Danger was / a conception that had no power to disturb the clearness of his thoughts, at the same time that the activity of his spirit shot forth on all sides at once. He discovered by the quick glance of his eye every symptom of impending mischief; and the strength of his arm, and the play of his limbs were such as to subdue every thing that opposed him.

Julian was instantly captivated with the attractions of Federigo, and felt that he had never before seen so perfect an example of the idea we may suppose to have been conceived by the Creator of the world, when he resolved to produce that crown of all his productions, man. Federigo indeed had not studied, or perhaps had not been adapted by nature for, those extraordinary effusions of composition and poetry, which Julian had witnessed in Bernardino and Francesco. But to the dazzled eye of his new acquaintance he appeared to possess qualities of a loftier and freer nature, with which these / artificial and elaborate trainings could not assimilate. Your impression was, that he had started forth complete and entire into the world, even as Minerva sprang from the head of Jove.[a] No shackles could come near him; he had never bowed the neck to the direction of a master. Whatever he exhibited appeared to be the unfolding of something laid up in the germ of his existence; his perfections disclosing themselves in endless succession, even as one occasion or another called them into act.

Julian remarked with an inquisitive spirit the qualities of his two friends. He was yet on the threshold of manhood; and, at this period of human life, it may naturally be expected that we should revise our judgments, and regard the present day as furnishing a commentary on the day that preceded. One of the most extraordinary persons it had fallen to Julian's lot to encounter, while yet a boy, was Bernardino Perfetti, the laureated poet of the capitol. It / was unavoidable that he should feel his active attachments more strongly called forth by the nephew of Bernardino, a youth by only a few years older than himself, and who appeared likely to tread in the steps of the favourite of Violante. They walked together, and poured out the effusions of their juvenile imaginations, full, unadulterated, and genuine, into each other's ears. Julian resolved that he would be Pylades, and Francesco should be his Orestes,[b] that he would be Pirithous, and Francesco should be his Theseus.[c]

---

[a] See note to p. 150.

[b] See note a p. 169.

[c] In Greek mythology, Pirithous was a prince of the Lapiths (a people of Thessaly), famous for accomplishing many great deeds; Theseus, friend of Pirithous and a hero of Attica noted for slaying the Minotaur, for conquering the Amazons, and for searching out the Golden Fleece.

But, when Camaldoli became known to him, the boy then felt that he had gained a new standard of excellence, and was persuaded that this man rather than Francesco was the friend his soul was compelled to elect. In the qualities that seemed to him to constitute the nobility of man Camaldoli was infinitely the superior. Francesco was the creature of artificial society, formed to shine in a court, to present / himself before a crowded audience, to awaken their emotions, and extort their applause. But Camaldoli was the man of all ages and all times. He would have been distinguished among savages, among the feudal followers of Charlemagne, or among the crusaders, as well as in the wars of Camillus and Scipio, or in the heroic games of Olympia.[a] He needed no artificial state of society to be prepared for the reception and the display of his accomplishments. Francesco was like some metaphysical theorists, to whose discoveries, we are told, we cannot render an entire justice, till we have previously qualified ourselves by a noviciate of years. He was a plant that would not thrive but in a congenial climate. While, in whatever sphere Camaldoli had been dropped, in the east or the west, the north or the south, he would have been found at home. His qualities appealed to the unvitiated mind and the genuine tastes of natural man. /

But there was another point in which Camaldoli had still more evidently the advantage of Francesco. Julian regretted to find in the latter, features of character which he could well have wished him to be without. Francesco did not in all respects improve upon more intimate acquaintance. It has already been seen that he had within him a vein of licentiousness and profligacy. He had tried upon Julian the sophistries of vice; and, though the English youth did not for this abjure his society, yet certain it is that he approved, and that he liked him the less. But Camaldoli had a native nobleness of soul, from which no adversity and no trials could divide him. The first election of his heart was excellence, genuine moral excellence; and 'whatever there was that was honest, and just, and lovely, and pure,'[b] he no sooner saw these things, than he felt his soul irresistibly drawn out towards them. Under all these circumstances it was inevitable, that / Camaldoli should to a certain degree supplant Francesco in the affections of Julian.

Such were the two most considerable persons in whose society Julian now spent his days; and he thought himself the most fortunate of human beings, that his lot had fallen to him with these choice associates. There were other young persons, their comrades, whose various qualifications diversified the

---

[a] Charlemagne (742?–814 AD), King of the Franks 768–814, and as Charles I, Holy Roman Emperor 800–14; L. Furius Camillus (445–365 BC), celebrated Roman, called a second Romulus for saving Rome from the Gauls in 365; Publius Cornelius Scipio Africanus Major (237–183 BC), Roman general who commanded the invasion of Carthage in the Second Punic War, 218–202 BC; Olympia, a plain in the NW Peloponnese, in ancient times a sanctuary of Zeus, and the site of the original Olympic games.

[b] Phil. 4: 8 (adapted).

pleasures of which he partook. It is easy to imagine how these scenes contrasted themselves with the gloomy abode of Borromeo.

Count Camaldoli for the present resided in one of the most magnificent palaces that Florence had to boast. The furniture was splendid, the pictures, and the statues. His entertainments were characterised with every thing that could enchant the sense. Julian was engaged in a perpetual series of pleasures. He forgot the uncouth and repulsive authority of Borromeo; he even forgot for a time the merits / and claims of his reputed father. He forgot the road to the *podere* of him under whose eye and direction Cloudesley had placed him during his expedition; he absented himself for whole days, and at length did not make his appearance for several nights together.

In the midst of one of these estrangements Borromeo met him accidentally in the streets of Florence. Julian started at the sight: the recollection of all the offences he had committed against the duty he owed to his earliest friend rushed upon him at once.

Borromeo motioned to the young man to follow him, and led him to one of the most retired walks of a spacious inclosure in the midst of the city. They two were alone. Borromeo began in a severe style.

Young man, said he, I have undertaken a commission, and must execute it. You I hold for nothing. You have been brought up in habits of the most pernicious indulgence; and I am / not now to learn to what ends such habits, acquired on the threshold of life, ultimately lead. But I owe an account to your father; I have engaged in a business; and I must see that he is not baffled, and I am not dishonoured. Your conduct exceeds my expectation. I judged you a novice; and I find you a veteran.

I require, sir, that you should return with me to my home. I shall not suffer you henceforth out of my sight, or at least without a keeper. I require you instantly and without recall to break off from the worthless connections you have formed. You are a boy, and know nothing of human life and human character. But I have acquainted myself with the pursuits of these persons, and find that they are worthless men and villains, who have forfeited all claim to the good opinion of their kind, are thrust out from honourable society, have trampled on all laws human and divine, and will finally expiate their crimes by the axe or the / wheel. Have done with them therefore, now and for ever! If you resist my command, I shall apply to the authorities of Florence, and the prisons of the city shall be put in requisition to subdue your rebellion.

Julian was astounded by the fierceness and torrent of this invective. His presence of mind was annihilated; he submitted like a lamb to the beck of his present overseer, and, leaving the walls of Florence, repaired with Borromeo to the squalid and gloomy mansion which owned that person for its master. How could a youth of eighteen act otherwise?

The harshness of his guide was a little softened by the quiet and unresisting submission of Julian. The youth however was no sooner shut up in the solitude of his own apartment, than a different train of ideas rushed tumultuously upon him. He who had never been subjected to the arbitrariness of control, now received the mandate of a man, against whose manners his / very soul revolted. Should he yield to be a slave? Should he suffer himself to be locked up, as a novice-monk at the mandate of his reverence the abbot? Should he at once be cut off from the intercourse of those who were dearest to his heart? If he submitted, should he not make himself a party to the aspersions which Borromeo had heaped upon them? He knew them to be gay, to be innocent, to be meritorious. Borromeo had plainly done nothing more, than string together all the foulest names that the language of modern Europe would afford, and cast them, without distinction, and without the shadow of reason, upon Federigo, Francesco, and their associates. No; he was bound to shew by his conduct, how much he scorned, and how utterly he rejected such imputations. If Borromeo had observed any moderation in his despotism, if he had told Julian that he must not spend whole days with his friends, that he must not withdraw himself / whole nights, that would have been different, that might have been entitled to some consideration.

The crisis in which Julian was now placed came exactly at the period of life, when, according to an expressive phrase, the youth begins to feel himself entitled to write man. It is not superior wisdom, experience, or genius, that gives to one human creature a control over the liberty of another. It is corporal strength, and that only.[a] It is because the child or the boy is small in stature, and unconfirmed in muscles and limbs, that he is driven about like a beast. He feels that he has not the power to resist. Many of those persons who have been the ornaments of the species, never were children, had always reflection, and calculation, and sobriety, and foresight, and judgment. And yet they were tyrannised over by pedants and clowns, merely because they had no more than three or four feet of stature. Julian was / now the subject of the undefined developments of puberty, and believed that he was entitled to a certain consideration and deference in the intercourse of his elders. He no longer bowed his neck to the yoke. When this sensation and consciousness are wholly new, it is then that we are peculiarly jealous of our rights.

A further consideration, that no doubt had its share in determining him not to submit, was the unendurable tediousness of the solitary confinement to which he was condemned. He paced his chamber with impatient steps. He looked at the dreary walls and narrow windows of his apartment. He was like the fiery courser,[b]

---

[a] cf. *Political Justice* III. 6, 'Of Obedience': 'Government is nothing but regulated force; force is its appropriate claim upon your attention.'
[b] Swift horse.

> —— that pants in every vein,
> And, pawing, seems to beat the distant plain;
> Hills, vales and floods appear already cross'd,
> And, ere he starts, a thousand steps are lost.[a]

Julian however did not admit to his own thoughts, that so ignoble a consideration as impatience of quiet, and the passion to be occupied, / had any share in his determination. He dwelt only on the intolerableness of tyranny, and the justice he owed to the calumniated merits of those he loved.

He had soon fixed his resolution as to the course he would pursue. But he waited till four in the morning, before he took a step in the execution of his purposes. He supped with Borromeo, and asked him several questions respecting the course of the journey of his reputed father, and when they might look for his return. The Italian answered him as he could, taking care not to disclose the particulars he was enjoined to conceal. Julian, having formed his plan, and determined in what way the vehemence of his spirit should explode, was the better able to present an exterior of good humour and docility. Borromeo grew more and more pleased with himself, that he had proceeded to cut the Gordian knot at once, and to shew the youth, the charge of whom he had / undertaken, that implicit obedience only would satisfy him.[b] They wished each other a good repose, and parted for the night.

But no sooner did the clock announce to Julian the hour he had determined on, than he took his lamp, and desended the staircase. He repaired to the stable, where he found his steed in security; and he performed for himself the functions of a groom. He went forward at first with careful steps, so as to produce the least possible noise and chance of alarm. But he had no sooner reached the great road than he urged his horse to his speed. He had had the precaution to take with him a *valise* ,[c] furnished with a few changes of linen.

To his great surprise, when he arrived at the palace of Federigo, he found it with every appearance of being uninhabited. He knocked several times at the gate without obtaining an answer. At length an old man and his wife of very ordinary seeming shewed themselves, and / enquired his pleasure. He asked for the count. They said, they knew no such person; the last occupier of the house was gone, and they could not tell what was become of him; they were placed there by the proprietor, to take care of every thing till he should have a new tenant.

Julian was filled with the utmost perplexity at this intelligence. It had been his design to solicit Camaldoli to admit him as an inmate under his roof for the short time that was likely to elapse before the return of Cloudesley from his

---

[a] Pope, 'Windsor Forest' (1713), ll. 151–4.

[b] In Greek mythology, a complicated knot tied by King Gordius of Phrygia, which Alexander the Great proceeded to cut with a sword.

[c] (French) Suitcase, bag.

western expedition. He sought Francesco; but Francesco had lately had no residence but in the palace of the count.

What was Julian to do? He had left the abode of Borromeo, because to dwell there was intolerable to his thoughts. The matter was rendered worse to him by his late nocturnal elopement. He felt like a banished man, who never from the hour of his birth had been without a certain and a pleasant home, but who / was suddenly cast upon the great congregation of mankind without a protector or a friend. He passed along the peopled streets of Florence, and saw scarcely an acquaintance, and no one who cared for him, at least as he had been accustomed to be cared for.

His mind was in the most disconsolate state, when suddenly he espied Francesco. He was transported with the sight, and accosted him with the utmost eagerness. He told the little story of his woes, and the arbitrary and tyrannical treatment he had received from Borromeo.

Francesco in return informed him, that it was true that Camaldoli had suddenly disappeared from Florence, that he was gone to his residence among the Apennines,[a] but that he (Francesco) and several of his friends had promised to join him there, and he was sure that Camaldoli would be most happy to see Julian with the rest.

The youth needed little invitation, and asked / few questions. He had a natural love of romantic scenery, and promised himself much pleasure among the wild inequalities of the mountains. He had secretly repined, that his life was too common-place and too uniform. He was just at an age when the passion for novelty and adventure has the greatest dominion over the soul; and he was not wrong in imagining that this passion would find the aptest field in the expedition now proposed to him. Francesco and Julian were attached to each other, and therefore the former had, almost without reflection, given to his friend the invitation I have mentioned.

Some of the particulars I have described were not learned till afterwards. Borromeo heard in the morning to his extreme surprise, that Julian was no where to be found. Upon further examination it was discovered that his horse had also disappeared. Julian had retired to rest at the usual time; and, at the early hour at which / men in the rural parts of Italy rise, he was already gone. It was even found that he had not once undressed himself, or lain down in his bed.

Borromeo was roused from his usual self-confidence by an incident which he knew would be a source of the greatest distress to the English yeoman. He repaired to the palace of Camaldoli. He found only an old labourer and his wife left in charge of it. It was as if Camaldoli had suddenly sunk in the earth, and left no trace behind. Borromeo sought after Francesco, and the other persons

---

[a] Italian chain of mountains branching off from the Alps at Savona in NW Italy and extending 740 miles throughout the whole 'spine' of the nation's peninsular.

whose society Julian had been accustomed to frequent. Several of the young ones had withdrawn at the same period; those who remained could supply no information. He felt at a loss what was the next step he could take for the recovery of Julian: and he was not a little mortified at an event which made his preceding conduct so contemptible even in his own eyes. It was certainly no small thing, that a youth, in whom his friend / had centred all his wishes and desires, and to whose history, whatever might finally become of his pretensions, such extraordinary circumstances were annexed, should be thus calamitously lost. Borromeo had formed the worst opinion of the present associates of Julian. He even believed that the pretended count Camaldoli was no other than the famous St Elmo, a robber, who with his followers had for a considerable time infested the Apennines, and set at defiance the united efforts of the governments of Florence, Venice and Genoa. Borromeo was sure that Julian was wholly unsuspicious of the true character and pursuits of the persons with whom he had got connected. The Italian formed indeed a very unfavourable judgment of the education the youth had received, and the fond and tender indulgence with which he had always been treated. But he did not on that account doubt of the purity and innocence of his mind, and his high sense of honour, setting / him at an immeasurable distance from all ideas of duplicity, treachery, profligacy and violence. That such a youth, at the immature age of eighteen, should be irretrievably involved with a nest of freebooters and desperadoes, was an event the most wretched and pitiable that could be imagined.

Borromeo however judged it to be his duty, without the loss of a moment to communicate the melancholy intelligence to Cloudesley; and it was the letter he wrote on this occasion, that caused my adversary so suddenly to withdraw from Ireland, and, dismissing all other projects and imaginations, instantly to set out for Florence. /

CHAPTER V

Julian and Francesco set out together from Florence; and they soon plunged into the Apennines. Their route was devious; and they passed along in one direction and another, where there were no marks that any human foot had ever preceded them. Often they were obliged to force their way through thickets and briars; and often they were on the edge of the most dangerous precipices. The horses had great difficulty to make good their way. It seemed almost impossible that the travellers should tread their path back again: and, if his companion had suddenly disappeared, and Julian had been left alone, it would probably have been / days ere he could have escaped the intricacies of his journey, and found his way back to Florence. Yet Francesco appeared to encounter no difficulty, he never paused, or made shew as if he had any doubt whether the direction he pursued was the right one.

At length they reached a ravine, which seemed gradually to open on either side. Here Francesco suddenly stopped his horse, and said, 'This is our home:'[a] while Julian, like Gilblas when brought to the robbers' cave, looked on every side, and could discern no mark of a human habitation. They turned however a projection of the mountain, and in a moment saw three or four tents in the plain before them.

The conjectures of Borromeo were right. It was the redoubted St Elmo, under whose protection Julian had placed himself.

From an early period of modern Italy there had been bands of men voluntarily associated under some eminent military leader, who acknowledged / no country, and subjected themselves to the laws of no sovereign prince or state, but sold their services sometimes to one power and sometimes to another, just as any government might conceive itself to stand in need of their aid. They are known in history by the name of *condottieri*. In time of peace still many of these parties did not disband, but, retiring to their mountains and fastnesses, waited for their prey, and supplied themselves with the necessary means of subsistence, by lawless attacks upon single travellers, and such small parties as were not provided with the power to resist them, till they should once more be called into regular employment, and constitute a part of some public army. They invaded solitary houses and even small villages, and imposed an arbitrary contribution upon the inhabitants. Many of the princes of Italy secretly connived at these abuses, that they might have experienced and resolute soldiers ready / for their service, without being at the expence of maintaining them while they were not wanted.

It was by slow degrees that this sort of abuse subsided; and the kings of Naples in particular privately favoured the depredators long after the period of their most flourishing state, while the mountains of the Abruzzi,[b] and even the whole range of the Apennines, afforded them opportunities of refuge and concealment.

The consequence of all this was, that the profession of a highway-robber was considered in a very different light, from that in which it is regarded in more settled and tranquil dominions. These bands were sometimes established, and sometimes recruited, by men of rank and education, who, impatient of the tyranny of the governments under which they were bred, had engaged in conspiracies for the assertion of public liberty, and, these conspiracies being

---

[a] Alain-René Le Sage, *The Adventures of Gil Blas* (1715–35), Vols. 1 and 2 (1715), Vol. 3 (1724), Vol. 4 (1735).

[b] Region of central Italy in the loftiest portion of the Apennines.

defeated, fled from the menace of the cord and the wheel, and preferred even the most precarious / and violent occupations to the hazard of being brought to a public and ignominious end.

St Elmo was one of the characters that these times produced. He was a compound of the most irreconcilable qualities. He had been bred in the highest cast of society, and had nourished his youthful mind in dreams of liberty and patriotism. He had associated in the morning of his days with young men of his own age, and whose passions were like his, either from a similarity of nature, or being inspired with the same views by frequent communication, by the fire of his mind, and the fervour of his speech. Together they had ventured their all in what appeared to them the noblest of causes; together they had miscarried; and together retired to caves and dens of the earth, where, if they had lost every thing else, they believed that they should preserve their independence.

Such men as these could not be idle. In addition to which, it is obvious that they could / not subsist themselves, their followers and their horses, without attacking others less adventurous and desperate, and drawing the supplies of which they stood in need from those who were too weak to think of resisting, or who could not resist with success. They formed therefore to themselves an appropriate code of morality. They glossed over their actions, and endeavoured to turn what was arbitrary and lawless, into justice and merit. They took, as they affirmed, only from the rich their useless abundance. They took from others that for which they had no wholsome and virtuous destination, and 'shook the superflux from them, to shew the heavens more just.'[a] They gave out, that they abstracted from the rich, and imparted to the poor. They spared the means of the needy, and would allow no violence to be committed against the weaker sex; but they robbed the opulent man and the oppressor, and willingly made spoil of monasteries, of / pampered monks and luxurious prelates. They could not however proceed in this course without bloodshed; they filled all the regions they visited with terror, and compelled the more pacific states to arm against their depredations, while the halter and the wheel formed the threatened termination of their course, and their ranks were thinned by the sword of the military and the office of the executioner, the most gallant of their members being ever and anon cut off in the very commencement and flower of manhood.

The life of a bandit was disgusting to St Elmo; and he from time to time took freaks in his mind, and resolved to return for a period to the scenes of society to which he had been originally destined. He was a native of Corsica, and had fought at an early period against the usurpation of the Genoese.[b] He had been smitten with a fervent passion for the independence of his country. At length, after a series / of disasters, Corsica had fallen prostrate under the yoke of the

---

[a] *King Lear*, III, v, 35–6 (adapted).

[b] From 1729–69 a rebellion led by rural notables took place whereby the Genoese were eventually driven out.

conqueror. St Elmo was thrown into prison; and there was for some time every appearance that he would be publicly executed for the crime of what his adversaries called rebellion. He escaped however to the *terra firma* of Italy, and, with several other persons in similar circumstances, retired to the mountains, where they subsisted themselves by pillage. His meditations by day and his dreams by night had been of the liberation of his country; and, defeated in that object, he had run into the most desperate extreme. Henceforth he swore upon the altars of immutable justice an everlasting war against all governments, and an open defiance to all law. He regarded what is called civilised society as a conspiracy against the inherent rights of man, and determined to pay no attention to its regulations. He had lost his country, and was become a banished man. He had lost his estates, and was reduced / to beggary. In a word, he devoted the remainder of his life to the becoming a leader of banditti.

Though at all times liberal in the division of his spoils, he had been able to accumulate treasure, which he hid in the most inaccessible parts of the mountains. With this treasure he occasionally indulged himself in a relaxation and retreat such as this to Florence had been: and, as his person was little known there, he had fixed on that city, as a place where he could reside for a time with the greatest security. At length an incident had occurred, which had reasonably filled him with alarm, and determined him without the smallest delay to join his companions in the mountains.

St Elmo was greatly distressed at the arrival of Julian. He took Francesco aside, and asked how this had happened, and whether the youth was previously apprised of the pursuits and habits of himself and his associates. Francesco / confessed that that had not been the case, and that he had been informed of nothing more than that Francesco was going to join count Camaldoli at his residence among the mountains. He added the story of Julian's misunderstanding with Borromeo, and that he had found him apparently determined, not to return to the protection under which his father had placed him. St Elmo severely reproached Francesco for having led on the youth under false colours. It was a first principle with the chieftain to practise no deceit with his followers. He was well convinced that the profession of a bandit was a most unhappy vocation; and he therefore made it a point with those who were desirous to enlist in his troop, to set before them all its disadvantages, and to shew them that, in entering into such an engagement, they passed a bourne[a] from which there was no return to the pale of civilised society.[b]

What was he to do with Julian? He could / not drive him back from the refuge he had eagerly sought. Yet he was fully resolved not to assist in ruining the prospects of a youth, before whom a fair and honourable career was apparently spread. Julian was at an immature age; he was accomplished and

---

[a] Boundary.
[b] Pale, fence or enclosing barrier.

promising; he had friends that loved him; his days were without a sin, and without a blemish. It would be the basest of all acts, for St Elmo to cut him off, by any misbehaviour of his, from a course which would probably be innocent, and which might be glorious. Far was it from the disposition of this chieftain, because he was himself branded with disgrace, to desire to draw in another to similar ruin. He resolved therefore to afford a refuge to the youth for the few weeks that were in question, carefully to conceal from him the occupation and habits of his followers, and, the moment he should hear of Cloudesley's return, to dismiss him with a thousand good wishes and tender farewels, and then, and not / before, to inform him of the imminent danger to which he had been exposed. St Elmo in fact, though he did not confess it to himself, was influenced in this determination by the real affection he felt for the English youth, while he persuaded himself that he might innocently indulge in a few weeks longer of his society, which thus seemed to be thrown upon him without contrivance on his part, while the protection he afforded to Julian might probably be safer, than his situation would be, if St Elmo insisted upon his instant return to Florence. Add to the rest, that the robber-chieftain, a man originally of the most exemplary dispositions, was deeply disgusted with the profligate and desperate character of the majority of his companions, and eagerly embraced the relief that would accrue to him from a few weeks' cordial association with an innocent and well disposed human creature.

It was the practice of these banditti sometimes to sleep in tents, and sometimes in the open air / with no other cover than a clump of trees, while in the winter they sheltered themselves in certain ruins scattered here and there among the Apennines, with which they were well acquainted.

Julian looked earnestly at the prospect before him, and felt considerable surprise. As count Camaldoli had occupied a palace at Florence, he expected in his rural retreat to find him the tenant of a spacious and magnificent castle. He however observed curiously, and said nothing. As he was new in the world, and had had little experience to guide him, he was but slenderly qualified to draw inferences from external objects; and the judgment he had he was inclined to distrust. Camaldoli was a man such as he had never known before; and he might therefore well be supposed to have other rules of conduct, and other modes of proceeding than are ordinary to persons of the same class. He might wish by way of variety, / entirely to divest himself of the state and incumbrances of a nobleman; he might be attached to the pleasures of a pastoral life. The whole looked a party, in which those who partook of it, determined to enact the personage of gipsies. They might, like the exiled duke in Shakespear, conceive these woods

> More free from peril than the envious court;
> While this their life, exempt from public haunt,

> Found tongues in trees, books in the running brooks,
> Sermons in stones, and good in every thing.[a]

Julian honoured his illustrious friend (as such he considered him) the more, for the present apparent simplicity of his tastes, that he could put off the nobleman, and continue not the less in the best sense of the word a man.

In this retreat, said the host to his guest, I am no longer count Camaldoli; I am known to my friends here by the name of St Elmo.

St Elmo then proceeded to introduce Julian to five or six of his followers, who happened to / be about him. He had previously made a sign to them, that it was his pleasure, that they should receive the stranger with courtesy and kindness, without discovering to him any part of their mystery. Julian was struck with the appearance of these men, as they passed in review before him. There was a daring and a desperateness in their countenances, similiar to that which he had before had occasion to observe in the profligate companions of Francesco at Florence, but more conspicuous and prominent. They were all however subdued to the temper of St Elmo, and plainly regarded him with a sentiment of homage, as belonging to a different order of beings from themselves. In person they were alert, muscular and strong; their eye was quick; and they seemed prepared in a high degree to use their corporeal energies with determination and skill. Their talk was vulgar, and indicative of the coarseness of the subjects about which their thoughts were habitually engaged. / They however constrained themselves, and put on their best behaviour, that they might make a favourable impression upon the new comer. Julian in a short time began to look upon them with more favourable thoughts than had first suggested themselves. The friends of count Camaldoli must be persons of merit; and he soon taught himself to regard them with optics supplied to him by the apparent construction which was made of them by their leader.

But, though they were in a memorable degree subjected to the will of St Elmo, this did not prevent them from having opinions and judgments of their own. The lawless life which they led, as it taught them to disdain the fears by which the bulk of mankind are controled, so it gave them an impulse to be daring and independent even in their own private circle. They received Julian with attention and courtesy, for such was the pleasure of their commander; and / the ingenuousness of his youth and the suavity of his manners were of much service to him. At first they were willing to admit him as a probationer; but in a short time they murmured. Theirs was a profession full of hardship and danger; and it was not fit that any should share in their advantages, who did not take part in the industry and peril. Theirs was a hive of activity and vigilance; the honey was to be collected, when opportunity presented itself, and the sun shone; and no drone ought to be suffered in their community.

---

[a] *As You Like It*, II. i. 4, 15–7 (adapted).

By degrees Julian got the better of this prepossession against him. The life of these robbers was of a mingled nature: sometimes it was all effort and exertion and enterprise; at other times it was reckless and joyous, as if they were exposed to no vicissitudes, and knew no cares. They were Italians, and aspired to excel in song, and in various kinds of instrumental music; and, where their skill was small, they at / all events caroled their lays with indefatigable perseverance, and could distinguish what was admirable, when it offered itself to their observation. In this respect Julian entitled himself to their approbation, or, which was better, penetrated their souls with emotion, and thrilled their bosoms with pleasure. The glens, far remote from the ears of the suspicious and the hostile, had before from time to time resounded with the unskilful songs of the banditti, but now became the very haunt of the Muses. Julian was an enthusiast; and his music tamed the rugged souls of the banditti, and carried them out of themselves. St Elmo and Francesco were well qualified to second his efforts; others felt inspired with emulation by the example. The veteran banditti were not in all instances without their skill; but their dangerous mode of life, and the consciousness that they were armed against all the world, and the world against them, indisposed them to these / peaceful pursuits. The innocent spirit of Julian, his soul a stranger to fear and crime, broke through the shackles that had hitherto repressed their powers, and he in some degree converted these desolate scenes into a paradise.

He excelled not less in other matters of innocent emulation. He was unerring in the use of the bow. He was an accomplished swordsman. In these things he surpassed all his competitors; or, where he found an equal, they were not less astonished, that a youth so immature could do so much, and could match the most skilful of his elders. Still he bore his honours with unexampled meekness. His brow was always open; his intercourse always cordial. He was at all times prepared to assist and to sympathise. He had no enemies; and every day increased the number and the attachment of his friends.

The band of St Elmo amounted to nearly one hundred men. But they were never all assembled together. They were distributed in / the mountain-passes which led to Venice, to Ferrara, to Parma, to Genoa, wherever it was thought likely they should meet with a prey such as they desired. Some of their haunts extended as far as the Abruzzi and the neighbourhood of Naples. In those who immediately attended on the person of their leader there was a perpetual change, some being dispatched on a new expedition, and others returning from an expedition already finished, and expecting to receive further instructions. Prey was in all cases the object they pursued; bloodshed was in some the unavoidable result. They had places appointed for the deposit of the acquisitions they made; the bodies of those they slew, were sometimes left on the spot where they fell, and at others removed to but a small distance. None of the frightful results of the enterprises of the brigands ever met the eye of Julian. St Elmo was not accustomed to go on actual service, unless on a very extraordinary occasion: / he was the heart of this anomalous body, which for the most part acted by the instrumentality of the limbs only. He kept Julian perpetually about his person; or, if an undertaking which demanded his immediate interference once or twice occurred, he committed the young man to the charge of his old friend Francesco.

Julian was wholly unconscious of the complicated machinery of this union. There is nothing that renders a human creature so insensible to the perversities and crookedness of vice, as innocence and truth. It is common to recommend great cautiousness as to the books that shall be put into the hands of young persons. Nothing can be so senseless and futile as this. In almost all cases he that shall be corrupted by the details of what he reads, must bring a corrupt heart to the perusal. The old, and those who are used to the ways of vice, find guilt and the provocatives of guilt in every page. The young pass them by, unconscious / of their existence. In this, the noblest of all senses, it may be said in the language of holy writ, 'To the pure all things are pure.'[a] Even thus to Julian the mysterious slang of the banditti, their becks and signs by which they conveyed a world of meaning to each other, expressed nothing: he wanted the interpreter in his own breast, which should give sense to the dialect. The indications that presented themselves, which would have told the whole secret to a mind on the alert, to his unsuspicious soul passed away without exciting the smallest alarm. The man who is armed with innocence,

> May trace huge forests, and unharboured heaths,
> Infamous hills, and sandy, perilous wilds,
> Yea, there, where very desolation dwells,
> By grots and caverns, shagged with horrid shades,
> With unblenched majesty; –
> Be it not done in pride or in presumption.[b]

A circumstance which greatly contributed to baffle the penetration that Julian might otherwise / have exercised upon the incidents which passed before him, arose out of the position in which he had first known St Elmo, in the character of count Camaldoli, occupying one of the most sumptuous palaces in Florence. It therefore never occurred to him that his protector and friend could be scanted in the current means of expence. Several of the present companions of St Elmo might, for aught that Julian knew, be also possessed of a competent income. The whole scene struck him as a sort of masquerade, in which the customary dwellers in the opulent cities of Italy, had resolved, like the heroes of the Astraea,[c] to retire into the shades, and indulge themselves in such pleasures,

---

[a] Tit. 1: 15.

[b] Milton, *Masque*, ll. 423–30 (adapted and omitting ll. 425–7: 'Where through the sacred rays of chastity, / No savage fierce bandit, or mountaineer / will dare to soil her virgin purity').

[c] i.e. Golden Age, called the Age of Astraea by the ancient poets.

and engage in such pursuits, as were most congenial to a scenery of mountains, forests and cataracts.

Upon Cloudesley's arrival at Florence he wrote me a letter, detailing the above circumstances. He was moved beyond measure at the / evasion of Julian, to whom he was intimately and entirely devoted. Cloudesley had for years regarded it as the single object of his existence, to forward the prosperity and happiness of Julian. It was this motive alone that impelled him to undertake the journey from Italy to Ireland. And now, what were the consequences of this expedition! With me he had failed. And the young man, in whose life and honour his life was bound up, had in consequence of his absence withdrawn himself, no one knew whither. Nay, there was reason to fear that he had united himself with rogues and vagabonds, with cut-throats and assassins, men rejected and proscribed by all communities, whose language was blasphemy, whose lives were debauchery, and whose thoughts were outrage, violence and murder, an interminable war against all upon which the security and happiness of civilised man repose.

On the very instant that Cloudesley had / heard of a calamity thus surpassing all imagination, he had banished from his mind every other consideration. The errand which had brought him to the western extremity of the world, was as offal and dust in his sight. He had hastened night and day to reach the city in which he and the child had last parted. He was worn almost to the state in which a man has no command either of his mind or his limbs, by the labour he had performed. He allowed himself one day for repose, previously to the setting out again for the restoration of Julian, a task that he would never quit but with life; and a part of that day he devoted to the writing this letter. God knew what the issue of the undertaking might be! His thoughts were solemn; his anticipations of the blackest hue.

Cloudesley concluded his letter – it might be the last I should ever receive from him – with conjuring me to add this to all the other arguments / he had suggested, to induce me without the loss of an instant to enter upon the great business of repairing the most complicated wrong that had ever been perpetrated from the creation of the world, the most dastardly, the most in violation of the most sacred obligations that could be imposed upon man. Whatever might be the issue of the present critical situation, however tragical might be the result to which it should lead, I ought to consider myself as the sole cause of all the evil that ensued. If Julian should become a robber on the public highway, if the remainder of his life should be passed in the most flagitious excesses, and if he were finally to be led to expiate his offences by a death of the blackest disgrace, and his carcase hung up between earth and heaven to be torn piecemeal by the vultures and the ravens, I and I only was doubtless accountable for so frightful and tremendous a catastrophe. /

CHAPTER VI

The next letter I received was from Borromeo: Cloudesley was no more!

The style of this letter was characteristic. So far as the soul of the writer was concerned, it was cold, rigid and without any of those sentiments, and intimations of sentiment, by which human beings, accustomed to yield to their impulses, interchange their feelings. Borromeo was in all cases rugged, blunt and abrupt in his way of expressing himself. Towards me and my conduct he entertained the most rooted abhorrence. The only difference between him and Cloudesley on the subject, was that Cloudesley thought that I might be wrought upon / to an honourable proceeding, and Borromeo held that to be impossible. Borromeo scorned to adopt any language for the purpose of softening me: he even scorned to give words to the antipathy he entertained for me. But I shall not attempt to present to you the image of his style; I shall simply narrate the facts his letters purposed to communicate.

Cloudesley had resolved to leave no effort untried for the recovery of Julian. He was too well convinced that the young man was associated with a band of robbers. How then was he to proceed? There was little probability that either letter or message could be conveyed to him. Where was he to be found? Who could tell? Beside, that Cloudesley resolved that not a moment should be lost. Who could predict even the value of a moment in so terrific a crisis? Here was a character to be redeemed; the innocence of a being, in Cloudesley's estimation, the most lovely, and the most sacred, / to be preserved. Julian, thus his protector painted it to himself, was on the edge of a fearful precipice: the depth could never be fathomed; the calamitous results of the least false step could never be calculated. Julian, so his foster-parent was entirely convinced, was wholly unaware of the perilous condition in which he stood. He was hoodwinked. How anxious a caution was necessary, in removing the bandage that hid from him his real situation! If this were done by any of the unhappy beings into whose hands he had so calamitously fallen, the issue might be fatal. This was indeed a crisis, most worthy that an angel from the empyrean[a] should descend, to rescue the secure and undistrusting victim! Cloudesley was deeply persuaded that a more interesting juncture could not arise among the various fortunes of imperial man.

---

[a] Heavens or sky.

The thoughts of the yeoman in undertaking his expedition, were solemn; his anticipations / of the blackest hue. He knew that he must be deterred by nothing in the execution of what he proposed, that he must penetrate the very dens of the enchanter, and 'enter the lime-twigs of his spells.'[a] He judged it necessary therefore to be more explicit and minute in his explanations to Borromeo than he had hitherto been. The innermost determination of his soul was that Julian should never become that most contemptible of all spectacles, a pretender, a needy and disappointed adventurer. He was therefore never to be trusted with the secret of his own birth, till it was certain that that secret could be triumphantly divulged to the whole world.

The proceeding now taken with Borromeo, was adopted by Cloudesley under the apprehension that he might perish in his present undertaking. Upon that supposition it was necessary to take certain steps for the purpose of securing to his ward the means of an honourable / subsistence. From the hour of Julian's birth I had punctually disbursed the annual sum of five hundred pounds to his protector. Cloudesley was entirely convinced that it had never been my design, to suffer my brother's son to be pennyless and a beggar. But, if the yeoman perished, and the place of Julian's existence were unknown, that must inevitably happen. In the event of his own death, Cloudesley therefore resolved to constitute Borromeo the guardian of the child, with sufficient powers and instructions to enable him to discharge that office in its fullest extent. Borromeo was to be in that case the successor of Cloudesley, to become my correspondent, and the medium through which the subsistence of the youthful wanderer was to be provided for.

As the heart of Cloudesley was in the present crisis, he employed every species of precaution that might tend to secure the success of his undertaking. Having maturely reflected / on all the information he could collect from Borromeo, it occurred to him that there was a person now in Florence, who could furnish him with important lights for the regulation of his conduct. This was an individual of some consideration in the place, and of unimpeachable character, who had nevertheless been noted for his familiarity and amicable intercourse with count Camaldoli. To this individual Cloudesley immediately resorted. Personally they were strangers to each other. But the Englishman believed, that in the story he had to tell there was that which could not fail to awaken the sympathies of a man of integrity and virtue.

He related his case without any reserve, except the not disclosing the family and actual descent of his ward. In that point he intreated the Florentine to whom he addressed himself, to excuse him. It was a question of the greatest delicacy, and never to be brought forward unless on an occasion of the highest urgency. But / he assured Gallotti, that was the name of the Florentine, that the

---

[a] Milton, *Masque*, l. 645 (adapted).

youth in question belonged to one of the first families in England, and was eventual heir to a very extensive property. Cloudesley was just returned from the British dominions, where he had been to solicit the interests of his ward. In this interval of his absence the unhappy circumstance had occurred which he had now to deplore. The youth was of unexceptionable dispositions, of the highest promise, and had been educated in all the literature and accomplishments that Italy had to boast.

The person in whom Cloudesley reposed his confidence was every way worthy of so generous a distinction. He had known St Elmo in his youth; they had been bred at the same university; and they had at that time conceived the warmest attachment for each other. When their education was finished, their lots had been cast in different directions; but Gallotti had / never lost sight of his friend. They had had frequent communication by letters; St Elmo had darkly insinuated to his more fortunate ally his various impulses and ardent desires for the liberation of his native isle; and Gallotti had entered enthusiastically into the feelings of the Corsican patriot. He had proportionally sympathised in the utter overthrow of St Elmo's hopes which had speedily followed.

The generous mind of the Florentine instantly entered into the case which Cloudesley laid before him. He frankly said, that under no other circumstance would he betray the secrets of his friend. But the rescue of such a young man as was described to him from the companionship of a troop of banditti, was not a thing to be neglected for a moment. Gallotti proposed to write to St Elmo; but Cloudesley could not admit of so slow a proceeding. He therefore at once confessed that he had recently had a letter from his friend, and could exactly / describe the spot where the party was quartered. St Elmo, he was satisfied, would be as forward to restore Julian to his natural protector, as that protector himself could be to receive his ward.

In the midst of the wilds of the Apennines, to an unpractised eye one mountain and one defile is exactly like another; the traveller, when he leaves the beaten road, is immediately lost in a chaos of forest and underwood; he can scarcely find his way out again, and has no power of tracing the invisible courses and paths of the mountains. But it was not so with those who were familiar with the scene. They knew the particular projection of a rock and the tree of unusual appearance, which admonished them to turn, now to the right, and now to the left, so that they were nothing more at a loss, than a town-bred man among the streets of the city in which he was born.

Cloudesley set forth furnished with a letter from Gallotti to his friend, in which he briefly / explained the object that brought the Englishman into the Apennines, and emphatically urged upon St Elmo the indispensibleness of his concurring in so holy a purpose. This letter would beside serve Cloudesley as a sort of passport among the perils he might have to encounter. The superscription addressed to the commander would shew that the bearer was no accidental traveller; and several of St Elmo's troop were no strangers to the handwriting of

Gallotti. For the more security however Cloudesley hired two stout-bodied attendants, to whom he disclosed nothing more than that he had occasion to pass the Apennines into the Ecclesiastical State, and that, as the passes were beset with freebooters,[a] he sought their aid to protect him against the dangers of the road. He was also accompanied by his own servant.

They had not gone far before they entered that ridge of hills, extending for several hundred miles, from Genoa to the straits of Messina, / which is styled by Virgil *pater Apenninus,* either on account of the multitude of rivers which take their rise among its eminences, and water the plains of Italy, emptying themselves into the Tuscan sea to the east, and the Adriatic to the west, or for its importance, being vastly the most considerable of the mountains of that favoured climate.[b] Cloudesley however shortly after returned to the plain, and proceeded by the public road as far as Spoleto,[c] pursuant to the instructions he had received from Gallotti, before he finally entered the rocky defiles which were to lead to the place of his destination. He then passed along among the sinuosities of the mountains, till he reached the Lago Velino, out of which flows the river which bears the same name. On this spot is one of the finest waterfalls in the world. The site of the lake is greatly elevated above the neighbouring country, at the same time that its serene and placid surface is surrounded by peaks of mountains, / rugged and steep, the tops of which seem to pierce the sky. At no great distance from the lake, the river, sixty feet in breadth, tumbles from a height of one hundred yards into a sightless gulph of snow-white vapour, which rises for ever and for ever from a circle of black crags, and then, leaping downwards, forms five or six other cataracts, each from fifty to one hundred feet high. A thunder comes up from the abyss, rendering every other sound impossible to be heard, while the eternal clamour, modulated by the changeful motion of the waters, rises and falls intermittingly, and is never the same. The surrounding scenery is in its kind the loveliest and most magnificent that can be conceived. The river-bank is fringed with orange trees; and the glen is inclosed with pinnacles of pyramidical rock, clothed with all evergreen plants and trees, the vast pine, the everlasting ilex, and the arbutus with glittering leaves and crimson fruit.[d] /

The solitude thus produced, amidst the miracles of nature, and far remote from the vestiges of human industry and skill, produces an indescribable effect upon the spectator. It composes the soul to solemnity, and raises the thoughts to all that is majestic and invisible. The works and inventions of man shrink into their genuine nothingness. The traveller stands in the midst of all that is

---

[a] Those living by plunder.

[b] The Apennine range.

[c] Archiepiscopal city on a rocky hill 60 miles NE of Rome.

[d] Ilex, widely distributed tree or shrub genus, such as the holly and inkberry; arbutus, a genus of temperate ericaceous shrub, especially the strawberry tree of southern Europe, which has clusters of white or pinkish flowers, broad evergreen leaves, and strawberry-like berries.

illimitable, and all that is eternal, the same yesterday, to-day, and for ever. He is united to the great whole, the vast congregation of all that is beautiful or astonishing, of all that spreads itself and is alive, a scene to which speech and articulate sound appear to be a profanation. One hour of this elevation and delight seems to be equivalent to ages of the ordinary life of mortals.

Yet such was the state of Italy at this time, that no person, attached to the modes of civilised life, could enter the scene, without the imminent risk that he should not come out alive. / It was frequented only by the birds of the air, and the wild animals of the mountains. Lawless men, whose pursuits were murder and pillage, alone visited it. To all others it was forbidden ground, and they avoided it, as they would whatever is most pestilential and destructive. The unfortunate man, who lost his way, and was entangled among these wild and pathless solitudes, was overwhelmed with terror, and fled as for his life. Nothing he saw, was majestic and tranquilising to him. He heard the report of a musket in every echo, and beheld the countenance and the glittering steel of the assassin whichever way he turned.

Cloudesley however came hither with a firm and a determined spirit. He had an object in visiting the scene which gave discernment and sedateness to his mind. There was but one purpose for the present in his apprehension worth living for, the rescuing the youth to whose welfare all his powers had been devoted, from / his present state of peril, and restoring him to the pale of cultivated life. He recognised the spot at which he had arrived, and which Gallotti had accurately described, and knew that he had but one or two turns more to trace, and a small circuit to make, and he would reach the glen where he was assured that St Elmo and his companions were quartered.

He arrived at the place, and it was vacant: not a human creature to be seen. He examined it with a scrutinising eye, and found ashes, and brands partly burning and partly consumed, and two or three places where fire had been, and the earth was in consequence bare of herbage. There was also fragments of provisions, and other indications that a troop, that, as he was persuaded, which he sought, had recently quitted the vale. /

CHAPTER VII

Cloudesley continued a few minutes in rumination, considering which way he might direct his steps with the best chance of success. While he was in this uncertainty, he perceived a man on the edge of the valley, who seemed inclined to approach. Cloudesley beckoned to him. He obeyed the sign. As he advanced, it was impossible not to be startled at his appearance. He shewed like one rejected of human society, and prepared to bid defiance to all. He was grim-visaged and beetle-browed, and his savage eyes, looking out under his bushy eyebrows, were calculated to strike awe into every beholder. His hair was black, matted / and stiff. For the rest, he was apparently coarse, muscular and athletic. He had two pistols and a dagger visible in his girdle. These indications however alarmed not Cloudesley. His purpose in repairing to the spot on which he stood, banished all other emotions; and attended as he was by two powerful supporters, he could fear nothing from the single individual before him. He accosted the man.

My friend, I came here to seek a person named St Elmo. Is it in your power to direct me to him?

It is, replied the brigand. He left the ground on which we stand early this morning. I am one of his followers. Having performed some little matters necessary to be done, I am going to join him. Will you put yourself under my guidance?

Cloudesley accepted his proposal. The views of the one and the other were of an opposite nature. Cloudesley's errand was simple and / direct. He desired only in a peaceable manner to obtain from St Elmo the dismission of his ward. He believed the letter he bore from Gallotti would make this a matter of no difficulty. The only thing that perplexed him, was to find the chieftain, and deliver his credentials. If any thing further was necessary, he relied on the eloquence of his own feelings, and would not allow himself to doubt that, if he came into the presence of St Elmo, he should bend the man, though a robber, to his views, and obtain the object on which his heart was fixed. He resolved not to discover the design of his expedition to another, but to present it, untouched and unanticipated, to the leader of the band.

The ideas of the bravo to whom he had now joined himself, were of a different sort. He had that morning been dismissed with opprobrium from the band of St Elmo. The maxims of that chieftain were generous. As I before / mentioned, it was a canon laid down with his followers, that they spared the needy, and would allow no violence to be committed against the weaker sex, but robbed the rich man and the oppressor, and willingly made spoil of monasteries, of pampered monks and luxurious prelates. Corrado, such was the name of the bravo whom Cloudesley had fallen in with, had no relish for these restrictions. The habits of his life had been base, and he had stained his dagger with the blood of assassination. Yet he was a desperate fellow, never calculating the odds that were opposed to him, and scorning to turn aside for any danger. For these qualities he had been admitted into the troop, contrary to the judgment of its leader. He was however of the most malicious and vindic-tive dispositions; and, provided he could mortally injure the person who had offended him, cared little for any results to himself. Several times St Elmo / had been on the point of dismissing him from the company, but as often, at the intercession of others, had remitted his sentence.

Just now however a case of peculiar atrocity occurred. Corrado, and a few of those who most resembled him in character, had fallen in with a company of three of four ladies, who, wishing to proceed by the shortest way to the place of their destination, had ventured into the Apennines, and had thought themselves sufficiently protected by the escort of two fellows, who had promised mountains of valour, and sworn that they would not turn their backs upon fifty men that should attack them. The instant however that Corrado and the rest made their appearance with demonstrations of menace, these vaunting serjeants made the best of their way to escape, and left the ladies to shift as they could. The master of the mules, anxious for his cattle, remained; and he was instantly shot by one of the banditti. The ladies were obliged / to dismount, and were rifled; under the direction of Corrado their hands were tied behind them; and he seemed disposed to proceed to worse extremities, when by an extraordinary accident St Elmo with two followers came in sight from a neighbouring eminence. The ruffians were too busy to observe the interruption that was about to occur; and St Elmo, struck with what he saw, hastened with the utmost expedition to the spot. He immediately ordered the release of the captives, told them they were perfectly safe, enquired what had been taken from them, and caused it to be restored to the minutest particular, and finally ordered one of his companions, and one of those who had come with Corrado, to escort them, till they arrived within sight of the public road and the open country. This done, he applied himself to investigate the merits of the transaction he had just witnessed; and, finding that Corrado was the ringleader of the outrage, he instantly, and with / great indignation, ordered him to quit the company, and never come in his way again, under pain of being shot as a rebel to the society.

Corrado submitted, for he knew it was to no purpose to resist or dispute the orders of his chief. But his heart was bursting with resentment. He believed himself to be the most meritorious of the corps, the person in whom the true character of a bandit flourished in the greatest energy. He had a thousand times murmured, that the squeamish and mealy-mouthed maxims of St Elmo would be the ruin of the whole troop. But he had the mortification to see that, notwithstanding his disaffection, the chief daily became more and more rooted in the good will of his associates. Finally, Corrado cherished a hatred to the entire corps for the sake of St Elmo.

When he saw Cloudesley and his two followers, it suddenly occurred to him that they were emissaries of the goverment sent out in / search of the banditti. He knew that, if the Ecclesiastical State had taken up the affair, and had seriously resolved to put an end to these depredations, a considerable military force would be employed. But he apprehended that these might be scouts sent on before, to discover the position of the enemy. St Elmo, as he had said, had broken up his encampment early in the morning; and Corrado, uneasy in his new and forlorn situation, had hung upon their rear, not daring to join them, and unwilling to credit that he was for ever separated from his late companions. He surveyed with bitter sensations the field they had left, and felt something like the melancholy of a lover, who has taken an eternal farewel of the mistress of his affections. The sight of the persons who now entered the field where the tents had been, interrupted his mood. All at once he said to himself, If I am no longer admitted into their ranks, I can do something else. They shall / feel me! They shall know I am not to be insulted with impunity! If they will not rob with me, they shall find that they shall not rob without me! The first words that Cloudesley addressed to him, confirmed him in the impression he had entertained. Corrado entered into no explanations. He conceived that, if he had any terms to make with the government, he must address himself to persons higher in authority than any of those who stood before him. He knew that he should have merit enough, if he could hereafter allege that he had been the means of putting St Elmo and his followers into the power of their pursuers. And in the mean time, till the affair had assumed a more explicit form, he held himself in reserve, that he might act hereafter as circumstances should suggest.

It was not true that Corrado was apprised of the precise covert which St Elmo had fixed on for his next encampment. But he had been a / considerable time in the troop; and he was sufficiently acquainted with the spots in which it was found most convenient to them to take up their residence. As I have said, he hung upon their march, and had observed the direction they pursued. And now he led his new companions along the line of the Apennines, to what is called the Abruzzi. Cloudesley with his party had already passed one night among the mountains, taking refuge, as they could, during the season of darkness, under such shelter as the forest-trees of the declivities afforded. Night overtook them a second time, under the leading of Corrado, on the banks of the Salto.[a]

The next morning they had the lake of Celano[b] before them, not far from which they expected to find the encampment of St Elmo. The mountains, as they advanced, assumed a wilder character; the rocks were naked and overhanging; and the torrent, leaping from fragment to fragment, roared below. Trees, / growing on the edge of crags that seemed ready to tumble on your head, clung by their roots only to the surface from which they sprung, while the branches, and frequently the trunk itself, darkened the waters beneath, its position being horizontal, or the line it described often pointing downward, and much below the horizontal. Every thing talked of desolation and horror.

In the midst of this scene a party in ambush suddenly sprung forth from a position nearly in contact with the travellers. Corrado saw that they consisted

---

[a] River in the Abruzzi region, central Italy.

[b] Former lake, also known as the Lago Fucino, now reclaimed for agricultural use.

of the followers of St Elmo. The incident was hostile to the design he meditated. He judged it to be the purpose of the persons he had joined, to play the
scout, to observe the position and numbers of the enemy, and then to carry the
intelligence of what they saw to those who sent them. In proportion as they
approached nearer to the expected place of the encampment, it had been his
plan to conduct them along / one of the ridges of the mountain, with the line of
which he was perfectly acquainted, and to place them where they might
accurately observe all that he imagined them sent to discover, at the same time
that they should themselves be completely unseen. But his scheme was baffled.
He and those to whom he officiated as a guide, had not yet reached the point at
which he imagined caution would be necessary, and where he intended to lead
them by the higher road, before they fell in with this detachment of the
adversary.

Francesco had the command of the marauding party. They stopped for a
moment to reconnoitre. It was the system of the banditti, when they found
nothing pointedly of a hostile character in the travellers they lighted upon, to
summon them quietly to surrender such booty as might excite the cupidity of
the assailants, and then to dismiss them, unburthened of whatever they might
possess that was valuable, but in / other respects uninjured. Francesco cast an
eager and enquiring glance upon the strangers, and immediately detected the
person of Corrado. He guessed the rest. He believed that these were not
ordinary travellers, who had come by chance into the Apennines, but that their
purpose was expressly hostile. His party doubled the number of strangers. He
gave the word to fire. Corrado was killed on the spot; and Cloudesley fell
desperately wounded. Francesco was then satisfied with the effect produced,
and immediately drew off his party into the hollow of the mountain. Between
the moment that he gave the word to fire, and the destructive result, a second
glance had given him the image of Cloudesley, and he was smitten with the
deepest compunction as he viewed his fall.

Thus terminated the generous exploit of the English yeoman for the recovery
of his ward. Of the three survivors no one knew the purpose which had
brought him so far: that secret was / lodged in his own breast. The remaining
care therefore was cast on the servant that Cloudesley had brought along with
him. The men he hired for the occasion, willingly took their directions from
this servant. He determined to convey his master to Tagliacozzo,[a] the town
nearest to the scene where the fatal event had occurred, and from thence to
conduct him in a litter and by easy stages to Florence. A medical man who was
consulted at Tagliacozzo did not oppose this determination. Cloudesley survived, but was speechless. As soon as the servant was left alone with his master,
he thought it his duty to take into his own custody the money and valuables

---

[a] Town in S Central Italy.

which Cloudesley had about him. Respecting the body of Corrado he gave himself no concern.

Francesco did not communicate to his companions the secret of what had occurred. He told nothing more, than that, seeing their late expelled confederate at the head of a party of / four other persons, he had immediately concluded that these persons were sent out by the government, and that Corrado having made one with them, plainly indicated that he had joined them for purposes hostile to the band from which he had been expelled. The robbers, entertaining the same opinion, approved of the result. They therefore readily returned with their leader to the encampment, and foresaw no other consequence, than that it might be necessary for the whole body to change its quarters with all expedition, and to retire into some remote rendezvous to which there should be no danger of their being pursued.

Such was the sentiment of the rest. But Francesco no sooner saw that Cloudesley was of the party, than the whole truth flashed upon him at once. He judged that they in no way belonged to the police of the state, and that they had come with no hostile intention. He / was overwhelmed with sorrow at what had occurred. He believed that he had unwarily perpetrated that which had been furthest from his thoughts, and had probably caused the death of the father of the youth who was dear to him beyond any other person in the world.

When they arrived at the encampment, Francesco took the commander aside, and informed him of the fatal event. St Elmo felt to his inmost soul the tragic circumstance that had occurred. He had received Julian into his bosom, that he might preserve him from injury, and restore him safe and unhurt to his natural protector. How terrible the event, that by so doing he had been the means of robbing him of that protector for ever! He felt it with all the anguish that marks the perpetration of a crime, as if he had himself guided the bullet to the bosom of Cloudesley, as if he had himself annihilated all future peace in the mind of the / darling youth, and turned him out, friendless and alone, upon the wild and tempestuous ocean of human society.

It might not however be all over. The end of the scene had not arrived. Francesco told St Elmo that he had seen Cloudesley fall, and that, having turned for the last time to observe the result of the fatal mistake he had committed, he had perceived the survivors gathering anxiously about the body of the Englishman, and raising it gently from the earth, while that of Corrado was wholly neglected. Cloudesley therefore was not dead. He might survive. He might not be mortally wounded. This was all St Elmo had to trust to.

A consultation immediately took place between Francesco and the commander, in what way the intelligence was to be communicated to Julian. The innocent boy had never known the pursuits and occupation of the band among whom he was harboured. St Elmo was now / more anxious than ever, that he never should know it. If Julian had been informed of the whole truth of his situation and what had passed, he might with some justice regard himself and his conduct as the cause of the death of his father. From that worst of all pangs St Elmo determined to save him. It was settled therefore between the two, that Francesco should relate, that, amidst his wanderings that morning in the mountains, he had overheard a firing of musquetry, that, being near one of the highest peaks of the Apennine ridge, he had taken advantage of the circumstance to endeavour to discover from whence the alarm proceeded, that he had seen a gang of robbers setting upon a party of peaceful travellers, and that Francesco and his companions, having shewn themselves, and set up a tremendous shout, had terrified the banditti into flight. Francesco added that, having hastened with all speed to the field of action, he / had discovered, to his infinite dismay, that the banditti had killed one of the travellers and wounded another, and that the wounded man was Cloudesley, whose person he instantly recognised. The survivors of the travellers who were unwounded, amounted to three, who insisted that the care of their disabled companion should be left to them, that they had quitted the mountains by the shortest way, and that their design appeared to be to convey the wounded man by easy stages to Florence.

Julian felt at once, that the only consideration that could have brought Cloudesley so far into the south, must have been that he was himself the object of his father's search. He was saved, by the affectionate precaution of St Elmo, from that acutest aggravation of the event, that Cloudesley had sought the youth with a knowledge that he had taken refuge among a party of banditti. But, this impression being taken away, there was anguish enough. / Why had Julian left Florence in the absence of his father? Why had he withdrawn himself from the superintendence of him under whose care Cloudesley had placed him? Ought he not to have submitted to every thing and endured every thing, rather than disobey in the minutest particular the injunctions of him to whom he was indebted for all that he enjoyed, and, as he believed, for life itself?

For a few moments Julian was transfixed with horror. But that speedily passed away. When a creature of manly mind is placed in a situation where he has an urgent duty to perform, that circumstance never fails to rush on his spirit, to dispel every cloud from the intellect, and incapacitating agitation from the heart, and to carry him forward with irresistible impulse, to the place where he ought to be, to the act he is bound to engage in. Julian caught the hand of St Elmo, and wrung it in the vehemence of his anguish. /

I cannot speak, said he. I must be gone. My soul is at the foot of the bier, which sustains the author of my being.

St Elmo entered into the feelings of the afflicted youth. He would not detain him for a moment. He mounted him on a swift steed, and sent Francesco and two others to conduct him, till he came within sight of the steeples of Tagliacozzo. That done, Julian wished to be left to himself; and there were obvious reasons why neither St Elmo nor Francesco desired that he should be attended by any of the party with which he had been associated in the Apennines.

Julian reached Tagliacozzo. Cloudesley and his attendants had already left the place. He followed them without delay by the road of Otricoli;[a] and he had not proceeded many miles, before he perceived, at some distance before him, descending from a higher to a lower part of the road, what appeared to be the object / he sought. He urged his horse to redoubled speed. As soon as he was within hearing, he called to them to stop. The servant of Cloudesley, even at that distance, from his figure, and a certain individuality of gesture, knew him.

The vehicle stopped. The servant went up to his master, and, speaking softly in his ear, said, Here is my young master! here is your son!

Cloudesley lay on his bier, seemingly insensible. His eyes were shut. He opened them. At that moment Julian leaped from his steed, and stood by the side of his protector, enquiring silently, but with quick and impatient glances, what was the state of the sufferer.' As soon as Cloudesley saw him, a divine smile came over his countenance, which seemed to say, It is enough; I have gained my end; if I must die even now, I die content. His lips moved; but they uttered no sound. He stretched out / his hand; Julian caught it with fervour; the sentiments were innumerable and of the most affecting sort, that that pressure conveyed from each to each. The agitation was too much for the wounded man; Cloudesley fainted. That circumstance allowed Julian without restraint the full scope to his feelings. He was almost choaked. He threw himself on the support of the man who stood next him. His whole frame was convulsed; a vehement gush of tears came to his relief, and saved him from falling to the earth. In a very short time he recovered; but the syncope of Cloudesley continued. Julian took hold of his hands; they were cold: he felt for the pulses; they were suspended: the action of the heart for a brief period had ceased. He is dead! he is dead! exclaimed Julian, in all the bitterness of despair.

After a considerable interval these symptoms disappeared; and the patient shewed the cardinal, the almost indefeasible, indications of a / living being; he breathed, and his pulses were perceptible. But he was greatly weakened by the shock he had sustained. For an hour it was judged indispensible that Julian should be kept from his sight. By the end of that period Cloudesley regained his powers of observation. His eye wandered, uneasily and dissatisfied, from one to another of the groupe around him. It was evident that he missed something; and his manner seemed to say, that the disappointment was most grievous to him. Julian approached. By this time his emotions were schooled; and he felt that it was necessary to shew himself quiet. He controled every gesture; he regulated every feature. But the depth of his sympathy was but the more visible under that state of constraint to the indifferent spectator.

They proceeded by slow journeys to Florence. Cloudesley reached that place, and the house in which he had for eight years resided, / alive. His wound was as severe and dangerous as it could be, not to have occasioned immediate

---

[a] Town about 25 miles NW of Rome.

death. Julian never quitted his person. The servant asked the young man whether he should send for Borromeo; to which Julian replied, By all means. Cloudesley was gratified by the sight of his friend. He sufficiently expressed by his countenance, that he knew every one about him. He kissed the hand first of Julian, and then of Borromeo, and placed them the one in the other. He had intervals of serenity, but at other times was a victim to the sharpest agonies. He survived the night of the day on which he arrived; but, about five o'clock in the morning of the following day, he expired.

Julian was with great difficulty torn away from the body of his protector, his father. He was told by a sedate and sober person (the assistant of the surgeon who had visited Cloudesley and examined the dressing of his wound, and who had left this person in office, that nothing / might be neglected, and that he might have instant notice of any change where his skill should be requisite), – that there were certain functions indispensibly to be performed to one recently deceased: and the youth, whose apprehension was at all times too luminous and clear not immediately to give way to what was justly proposed, suffered himself to be led into another apartment. Most glad he would have been to have performed the meanest and most sordid offices for one he so entirely and everlastingly loved; but he felt that he could not then exercise the steadiness and composure which such offices demanded. He would have been liable from moment to moment to that animal shock, which, without waiting for our consent, and without previous notice, thrills through the nerves, and electrifies the brain, and convulses every muscle in the human frame. – When he got to the door, he burst away from those who led him, and threw himself on / the bed, and kissed the cheeks and the lips of his only friend with surpassing emotion; and then raised himself, and quitted the room with desperate composure. /

CHAPTER VIII

Borromeo now assumed the command as to every thing that was necessary. Julian felt that the direction could not be placed in more competent hands, and, wrapping himself up in the compass of his own sensations, surrendered all his faculties to the agony of grief. His thoughts were disordered and wild; he fell in a short time into complete delirium. He 'saw more devils than vast hell can hold;'[a]

---

[a] *A Midsummer-Night's Dream*, V. i. 9 (adapted).

he knew not where he was, nor what he was. He would not eat; he would not speak. Sometimes he comforted himself with the agitation of a madman, and uttered his voice in piercing shrieks; at others, he would subside into a state without / motion, without perception, and, as it seemed, without life. Whoever spoke to him, he heeded it not; whatever noise, whatever crash occurred near him, he perceived it not. But there was apparently a perpetual working of the inner senses, too feeble to produce any action of the limbs or features, too incoherent and unpronounced to be a subject of after-recollection. When he awoke out of one of these paroxysms, he appeared like a man recovered from an ecstacy; he stared about him for a time, and knew nothing. He did not shed a tear, though his countenance was the picture of despair. He slept neither night nor day.

Borromeo had the precaution to forbear him in these moods. He left him in the care of the servant of the deceased. He was of opinion that nature knew her own time, and that both appetite and sleep, particularly to a person at that time of life, would return, when the frame could no longer subsist without sleep and food. / He took upon him the superintendence of the affairs of the deceased. Julian was at an age, when in no civilised country a young man is held competent to this; beside that Cloudesley had given his special instructions to the Italian. He had even left a paper in the possession of Borromeo, which might be considered in the nature of a will, though with special orders that it should never be exhibited, but in a case of so peculiar urgency as Cloudesley did not conceive could ever occur. The English yeoman however had deeply meditated on the position of his ward; it was the theme of all his contemplations. No man then in existence but Cloudesley and myself were fully in the secret of the legitimate descent of the Alton and Danvers estates; me he regarded as the unalterable adversary of what the equity of nations has established on the subject; he was therefore the only person authorised and disposed to assert the birthrights of Julian. Life, the life of an individual, / is necessarily precarious; and Cloudesley would have thought himself guilty of a crime of the deepest dye, if he suffered the future condition of his ward to depend upon how long he should himself live, and in what manner he should die. He had therefore provided, as far as human prudence could suggest, against every contingency.

Under these circumstances Borromeo thought himself entitled to administer. The funeral of Cloudesley, according to the custom of Italy, had occurred the day after his decease, at a time when Julian was incapable of attending to any thing, and when in reality he knew nothing of what was passing. It took place in the vicinity of the dwelling of Borromeo. After the lapse of six or eight days the Italian informed Julian, that it was proper that the house in which Cloudesley had dwelt should be shut up, and the property disposed of, and added that it was the direction of the deceased, that the young / man should be removed, and take up his residence under the roof of Borromeo. Julian submitted: he suffered himself like a lamb to be led to the house, from which several weeks before he had fled with unconquerable repugnance. – The directions of Cloudesley had been framed on the eve of his expedition to Ireland, and had not been altered since.

Julian sat in the apartment that had formerly been assigned him, like a wild beast in his lair. He spoke to no one; he observed nothing. The valet of Cloudesley, to whose attendance he had in former times been familiar, waited on him. He seemed like one planet-struck; some mighty revolution had gone on within him, which made him altogether different from the being he had been. Nothing interested him; nothing excited him. He read nothing, and dedicated himself to no occupation. By night he would occasionally wander in the garden, or, beyond it, on the neighbouring hills. At these / times the valet always followed and watched him.

Borromeo was awed by these extraordinary and unlooked-for appearances. He thought it little less than miraculous, that a young man's wits should be frail, and scattered, and, in a manner, perished and vanishing away, depending on an old man's life. He waited for the period of calmness and illumination, that he might communicate to the youth all that he was authorised to tell him of his situation and expectations. But, though Julian scarcely noticed any thing that occurred, it was impossible not to perceive that an involuntary shuddering came over him whenever Borromeo appeared in his presence; and this was even more observable, the more he approached to a state of comparative calmness, and seemed to pay some imperfect attention to things around him. Grief has moods of its own. In this respect it is of the nature of music. It feeds on its own thoughts, / and its own tones. And, if something of a totally opposite nature presents itself, the shock of an earthquake would scarcely produce a more unendurable situation. When a fancied wise man and a monitor approaches him who is absorbed in grief and will not be comforted, and this person is expected to tell the mourner of the uselessness of his sorrows, and to undertake to rouse the man of reason and firmness within him, the mourner would, if it were possible, 'take the wings of the morning, and dwell in the uttermost parts of the sea,'[a] rather than encounter the words that should be spoken.

Julian sometimes imagined Cloudesley to be still living, and to be present with him in his chamber. In these cases he would occasionally assume the attitude of one earnestly listening, careful that not a sound that was uttered should escape him. He would then answer, but in a low voice, and with words scarcely articulate, so that only a few syllables could be collected. / This was in the nature of what we call a trance. He would often dream of the deceased, and say something of his dreams in the morning to the servant. My father, he would say,

---

[a] Psalm 139: 9.

as long as the day-light lasts, is dead; but, in the watches of the night, he comes to me, and speaks, and acts, and I am satisfied that we were all under a delusion when we thought we saw him expire: it is no such thing. By degrees the tragical truth came upon Julian, and came with so much the more bitterness, because for a short while he had deceived himself. Yet these dreams returned so perpetually, that the poor youth seemed to have two lives, one of sweet and soothing and consolatory imaginations, and one of desolate and withering reality.

As he grew more collected, he began to enquire of the servant, where the body of Cloudesley had been committed to the earth. It was in a church-yard, or more properly a field of tombs and graves, adjoining to a neighbouring / friary. The grave itself was near the wall of the cemetery, and a large yew-tree over-shadowed it with its branches. A bank of green-sward extended from the wall to the foot of the tree. Julian at his own desire was led to the spot; and, when he had found it, he requested to be left alone. The servant accordingly withdrew, and, as he had been directed, hid himself behind a monument on the further side of the inclosure. The young man threw himself on his knees on the earth, kissed the turf that covered the dead body of his protector, and wrung his hands with anguish. He supported himself on the bank of green-sward that was at hand. Two hours elapsed, ere he quitted the spot, and returned by the way he came. When he had retreated half the length of the burial-ground, he rushed back again, and in all his gestures expressed the extremity of his anguish. At length he passed the wicket of the cemetery, and came home. /

The first thing that Julian asked for, was to be led to the grave of the deceased. Having thus far his thoughts opened to what was real and external, he began in a certain degree to observe other things. Having once been led to the grave of Cloudesley, he afterwards repaired to it again and again without a guide. He observed the road that led to it, and the objects with which it was surrounded. Thus began to be reawakened in him the organs of the bodily senses. Till this time he had been like a man swallowed in a profound and a long sleep. 'Whether he were in the body, or out of the body, he could not tell,'[a] But, when his eyes were unsealed, what a blank did the world appear to him! He saw nothing that he valued, and no one that he loved. As has been said of those in whom suspended animation has been restored; the first sensation is an aching void, and the patient longs to be delivered back / to the insensibility from which he has been so painfully ravished.

Julian shewed himself utterly averse to oral communication; and he scarcely read. More or less however, almost every day, he committed his thoughts to paper. Some of these memorandums he destroyed; some he threw aside, and thought of no more; and others he folded away, and locked in his escritoire. A

---

[a] 2 Cor. 12: 2.

few were taken up by the servant, and given to Borromeo. One of them was this.

'Where art thou, my protector, my father? Dost thou exist in some distant sphere? Or, dost thou still watch over, and guard, though unseen, the child thou so entirely lovedst? Oh, that I could see thee, speak to thee! Sometimes I hear the sound of thy voice, its sweet and soothing tones, as I walk in the garden in the dusk of the evening. Sometimes in my bed, even when awake, thou seemest to draw back / my curtain, and look upon me with pity and love! –

'Never was father so entitled to the affection of a son. From my earliest recollection I have seen that I was all thy care. Thou removedst from Austria to Verona, and from Verona to Florence, that my opportunities of improvement and means of happiness might be more ample. Thou seemedst to think of nothing else: it is as if the hairs of my head were numbered by thee.[a] With what eyes of love didst thou observe me! With what care didst thou watch by my bed of sickness! How did thy heart exult in my imputed good qualities and improvement! How did thy eyes glisten at the sound of my praise; praise, that I was principally incited to earn, because it afforded so pure a gratification to thee! –

'Thou wert every thing to me; and now – I am nothing! Who cares for me? In whose eyes do I discover tenderness and the affection / of a parent? I have neither father, nor mother, nor uncle, nor aunt, nor brother, nor sister, nor cousin. I, who am so full even to bursting, of all human kindnesses, have no one on whom to bestow them. The eyes of all I meet are hard, and glittering, and indifferent, the eyes of the stranger. They look on me, and pass by on the other side. If I die, there is no one to miss me, to consecrate my ashes with one solitary tear. 'From Cain, the first male-child, to him that did but yesterday suspire,' there never was one so alone in the world![b] The full meaning of the word – banishment, – that name that I had been taught to consider as the inseparable concomitant of crime, – has all been accumulated on my devoted head.'

I am induced to interrupt the narrative of lord Danvers in this place, for the purpose of observing that, great as the merits of Cloudesley appeared in the eyes of his ward, they were in reality greater than he apprehended. There is / perhaps no example in the records of mankind of one who did all that he did. Julian thought of him as his father; he was not his father. For a son peradventure some fathers would even dare to die. But there was no kindred between Julian and his protector. Whatever might have been the faults of Cloudesley's past life, from the hour he was left alone with his ward in his hands, his thoughts and deeds were without a blemish. For one short interval his good

---

[a] cf. Matt. 10: 30.
[b] *King John*, III. iv. 79–80. Suspire, sigh, or utter with a sigh.

genius deserted him, and he constented to an act of baseness in lending himself to assist the uncle in stripping his infant nephew of his birthright and his name. But all that followed, was a life of expiation for that act. His thoughts by day and by night, from the infancy of Julian to the death of his protector, were how to premote the interests and the welfare of his pupil. He cast to earth 'all trivial, fond records;'[a] he cleansed his bosom of all those passions, which till then perhaps had twined their tendrils / round his heart, and lived for one thing alone. He saw in the child that was for ever before him, and was his only delight, the monument of his for-ever-repented and execrated delinquency, and never thought he could make atonement enough. It was his consolation, to heap endless benefits on his head, to raise him, as far as his efforts and industry could bring the thing to effect, into a model of all that is excellent in man, to traverse sea and land for his advantage, and, if it were possible for human perseverance to accomplish it, finally to place him in the stall of all his honoured ancestors, and to homage to him there. The guilt of Cloudesley in becoming the accessory of the uncle's usurpation, hung over him like a cloud of portentous blackness. For a time it was opake and impenetrable; it shut out from him the light of the sun, and made day and night alike to him. In proportion as he effected any good for the forlorn youth, the darkness became / less, and a twilight of the soul cheered him. But he waited with unappeasable earnestness, till the whole mischief that had been done should be removed, and Julian, his sun, should shine out in all his glory. If his offence were great, never was penitence so exemplary. All the voluntary expiations recorded in the lying legends of saints, shrink into nothing in the comparison. It is not improbable, that, as he lay on his death-bed, it was his greatest consolation, that at least he died for Julian. And, as it has become my province to record this memorable history, I could not restrain myself from these slight observations on the singular merits of the man.

First of penitents, and most devoted of guardians, hail, and farewel! /

CHAPTER IX

The lapse of days and weeks by no means contributed to reconcile Julian to his situation. He had before conceived a distaste to the manners and the house of Borromeo. Now, that his heart was made tender and sensitive by the grief that

---

[a] *Hamlet*, I. v. 99.

preyed on his vitals, the matter was rendered worse. The countenance of Borromeo was austere and repulsive; his speech was sharp and sailor-like, little accommodated to the ear of one brought up in all the elegance of refinement, less so of one whose organs were rendered delicate and morbid by the visitations of grief. The house of Borromeo was plain, and blank-looking, and gloomy. And to all these / disadvantages Julian now, his guardian and his father being no more, saw no termination.

Meanwhile it is to be mentioned, that the character of Borromeo underwent a singular modification on this occasion. Before, he had looked upon Julian with a certain superciliousness and disdain. He had viewed him as a spoiled child, a creature unduly pampered and indulged, and therefore worthless and unprepared for the ordinary difficulties of human life. In this character he owed him a sort of spite, and thought, agreeably to his notions of right and justice, that it was incumbent on him to restore the true state of the balance, and to bring forward some of those ruggednesses, harsh tones and unpalatable contradictions, which had been so improperly withheld from the youth in the course of his boyhood.

Now the case was altered. Here was Julian, undrilled to the hardships of existence, his path thus far carefully smoothed before him and every / pebble removed that might gall the soles of his feet, now suddenly thrust out upon the world without guide, overseer, or ruler. Hitherto every question of experience, before it arose, was studied for him by another; and care, anxiety or foresight on his part was rendered superfluous. Now, he was like a youth, shipwrecked on a foreign shore, surrounded with strange faces, and persons utterly indifferent whether the first step he took might not lead to irretrievable destruction. And all this was the work of a moment.

This situation awed Borromeo. It changed in a memorable degree the tone of his mind. The ruggedness of his nature, which had been accustomed to regard no man's feelings, now gave place to a timidity altogether new. But his proceeding was in the utmost degree injudicious. He wished to tame his manner, and modulate his voice; but he could not. He wished to express sympathy; but he wanted / the organ. He could not find words to convey the feelings of his mind. He looked with a certain fear and anxiety upon the orphan youth; but his stubborn features refused to transmit the sentiments that lived in his bosom.

Under these circumstances he suddenly became, so far as related to the intercourse of Julian, diffident and silent. When he desired to speak, he hesitated, and could not determine in what manner to begin. There was a sacredness in filial sorrow, that he knew not how to break in upon. The orphan state of Julian was a sort of hallowed ground, not thoughtlessly to be invaded by the feet of the profane. – This fashion of proceeding however on the part of Borromeo was not likely to last long. His habitual manners would soon have resumed their ascendancy. And indeed it was but justice, that the young man should be informed respecting his real situation, and what provision he was to look forward to for his future existence. /

But the reserve of the Italian continued long enough to be productive of the most memorable effects. At a more advanced period of life, it is not to be supposed but that the young man himself would have called upon his new guardian, to give an account of his stewardship, and inform him of the circumstances in which Cloudesley had died. Julian was as ignorant on this topic as a new-born babe. His supposed father had peculiar reasons for not being communicative. And, in case of any thing sudden happening to himself, he had, as has been seen, left the whole question in the hands of Borromeo.

Borromeo had altered his manners to the orphan youth. But Julian did not possess the clue which should aid him to expound this alteration. The taciturnity of the Italian now, was scarcely more satisfactory to the youth, than his rigid and unpalatable admonitions had been formerly. The state of Julian's mind very ill fitted him for the task of breaking the ice, / and soliciting a communication. Grief for the loss of his parent and protector was his predominant feeling. A youth of eighteen, even if not otherwise disabled, was scarcely qualified to call to account a man of Borromeo's stern and arbitrary habits. Beside which, Julian had encouraged himself to cherish an antipathy to the individual, in whose dwelling he was now an inmate. His impulse, at least for the present, was to have no more communication with the Italian than decency required; and indeed their intercourse scarcely amounted to that.

The mind of the youth was at first solely occupied with the thought of what he had lost, and the tragical circumstances with which that loss had been attended. By and by, like a man escaped from a shipwreck, or from a habitation consumed by devouring flames, he began to look round upon what had been saved from the wide-spreading ruin. He was but just in the dawning of human life, and in the course of / nature might expect to live through many future years. Taken under this aspect, the house of Borromeo, and the society of its master were loathsome to his thoughts. Julian was by nature of an affectionate disposition, that sought with unappeasable appetite the gratification, to love and be loved. He was habitually of an aspiring mind, and, most of all, of a spirit free and uncontroled. The house of Borromeo therefore appeared to him a prison, and the most gloomy of prisons. All that lived in it were the phantoms of men, and not men, mocking him with the semblance of humanity, and by that means perpetually bringing to his mind what goodly realities might elsewhere be found. He recollected the severe non-intercourse inhibitions which had formerly been promulgated by Borromeo; and, though they were not repeated now, he believed they had lost none of their force and vitality. He saw that, whenever he went out, though in his present state of / mind that seldom occurred, his steps were carefully watched. All that he loved best in the world of living men, was to be found in the labyrinths of the Apennines.

The intellectual powers of Julian had been cultivated, and his wants supplied, but he scarcely knew any thing of the machinery of human existence, and how the things necessary to mortal life were produced and distributed. He was aware that his supposed father occupied a certain number of acres of land, arable, or devoted to the breeding of animals for food; and he supposed that an interest in this land and stock devolved to himself, as the sole surviving representative of the deceased. These points at some time or other must be brought into discussion, and submitted to a certain order; and the explanation must in the first instance be had with Borromeo. But Julian, with the weight of sorrow under which he at present laboured, and the painful impression / that he had not a human creature near him to whom he could open his heart, and with whom he could consult, felt the deepest aversion to enter upon these cold and mechanical topics with a stranger, and most of all with the person under whose roof he resided. As he had never known what want was, and every thing he needed had been at all times supplied to him before he asked it, he did not see the question in the same urgent light, as it would have appeared in to any one of more varied experience. It was to him as if the birds of the air had brought him food, as they did to Elijah in the desert: when he was hungry, a table had always been spread to allay his appetite, and so of the rest.[a] He did not therefore form to himself the conception, that any exertion or foresight would be required on his part, to prevent these vulgar inconveniences.

For a certain space of time Julian lived only in the recollection of the past; and sorrow may / be said to have served him for meat and for drink. He observed none of the things that were around him; and it was the same thing to him whether he was in a hovel or a palace. But the violence of grief has its limits. No man can be for ever shut up in the things that are not; and especially no one in this early period of human life.

Julian had now many times visited the grave of his protector, where he had indulged the agony of his mood in solitude, and had then quietly returned to his apartment in the house of Borromeo. The first, the second, and the third time he had been watched; but his proceedings then became known; and it was thought unnecessary to dog him any longer. His visits to the shrine of Cloudesley were always by night, sometimes earlier, sometimes very late. In the solitary grange where Borromeo lived, it was not judged requisite to be very accurate / about bolts and bars; and Julian let himself out and in as he pleased.

At length the night came, when he passed the threshold, and returned no more. Nothing was thought of his absence, till the next morning. It was supposed that he had re-entered the house quietly, making no noise that he might not disturb the sleepers. In the morning however his bed and his chamber were found untenanted. The horse that St Elmo had lent to him, was also missing from the stables. Borromeo became alarmed; he caused Julian to

---

[a] cf. 1 Kings 17: 6.

be sought and enquired for in all directions; but in vain. He had already written to me an account of Cloudesley's death, and of Julian's being once more domesticated under his roof. He now wrote to me again, to inform me of the young man's disappearance. /

CHAPTER X

It was almost immediately after the time that Cloudesley departed for the continent, that the late lord Danvers died.

You will easily imagine what were my sensations upon this accession of new property and new honours. My heart has long been dead within me. The worm of remorse has been for years gnawing on my vitals. I have never known a tranquil moment, since I contrived the disinheritance of my brother's orphan son. And see, how the Governor of the Universe has avenged my crime! One by one, my wife and all my children have died – all, save this one, whose existence seems suspended by a hair. / And he also will die! – It may be so! But, if care, if devotion, if the skill of physicians, if the most accurate watchfulness for his diet, his exercise, the air he breathes, the tranquillity of his spirit, can save him, he shall be saved. Every thing about him shall talk of cheerfulness, of hilarity, of happiness. For myself I am nothing – I have long since dismissed the hope of peace, of serenity, of comfort. Heaven has decreed to make me a monument of its vengeance against broken vows and violated equity. But my son! – He shall outlive the blasted existence of his father; he shall never know adversity and sorrow. He shall be placed high among the nobles of the land; and the whole realm of which he is a member shall pay homage to his accomplishments and his virtues! – This is all that stands between me and despair.

What; have I paid the price, and shall I not obtain that which I have purchased for myself, I supposed, by the perdition of my soul? What / agonies have I suffered for ever and for ever! Oh, if any one could count up the tortures of the guilt of a treacherous uncle – no; no fortitude of man or devil would be equal to the sustaining them. I leave it to other men to pronounce, whether it is the wisdom of heaven, or the malignity of hell, which takes care that he should not open the book, and read the miseries of the guilty, that otherwise would crush him like the descent of a mountain on his head, but that one by one he learns to endure. I have drained the nauseous, intolerable cup of conscious crime day after day, and hour after hour; but it has still in it one drop of mitigation, the love I bear my son, and the anxious wish I entertain, that he may flourish for long years in spotless glory, as the lord of an ample estate, and an earl of the realm of England.

There is one aggravation of my sufferings, one fang that barbs the arrow that for ever rankles in my bosom, to which no words can / do justice: and this is the discordance of the world within, and the world without me. I do justice to my own demerits. But all that approach me applaud my worth, and pay homage to the good, the philanthropical, the excellent baron Alton, and earl Danvers. All but this I could endure. I feel that it would often be a relief to me, if they were to hoot at and to curse me. But the smooth, the smiling, the complacent countenances I am destined to encounter, this is the most cruel mockery. If I may employ the illustration without profaneness, it is like the Hail, king of the Jews! addressed by the lictors of Pilate to the Redeemer of Mankind.[a] For, all the time, I feel within my utter desolation, and that I envy the condition of the most forlorn and destitute beggar who knows that he has not deserved the hardships which are heaped upon him.

Something too much of this. – Yet, oh, Meadows, you can little think what a relief it is to / me to speak of myself without reserve! I am placed every day upon a stage. I appear for ever in an assumed character. No actor who comes forward for the amusement of a gaping crowd, is so unfortunate as I am. He struts his hour,[b] and then retires to his own fire-side, or sits with his brother-actors in the apartment of an obscure tavern, and unbends. He makes his jest, and tells his tale unreproved, and appears in a light the most contrasted with the mummery which he exhibits for a short interval to those who know him not as he is. But I must never forget my part. The eyes of mankind are for ever upon me. Willingly would I call upon the mountains to fall upon, and the hills to cover me from the prying observation of the indifferent spectators, who would 'pluck out the heart of my mystery, and sound me from my lowest note to the top of my compass.'[c]

Bear with me. For nearly twenty years I / have not shewn myself to any human creature in the undress of the soul. Even to Cloudesley, to whom alone I appeared as I was, I had still a cause to plead, and an object to effect, which could best be secured by arguments artificially arranged. With you it is otherwise. You are not my adversary; and I flatter myself never will be. It is for this reason that I have found a gratification in telling you my story with minuteness, and amplifying the parts that appeared to be of importance.

Nothing could be more galling to me at the moment, than the triumphal reception I experienced on my accession to my English honours. Look at this house, the seat of my ancestors! It was founded by men of one of the most illustrious and princely races that ever adorned with their magnificence the

---

[a] cf. Matt. 27: 29.
[b] *Macbeth*, V. iii. 24–5 (adapted).
[c] *Hamlet*, III. ii. 389–91.

annals of this island, the Mowbrays, dukes of Norfolk, one of whom threw down his gauntlet, and defied to mortal combat Henry duke of Hereford, afterwards / king Henry the Fourth, while Richard the Second, the reigning sovereign, sat umpire of the field.[a] When I approached to take possession of the inheritance of my ancestors, the applauses with which I was received, and the rejoicings that welcomed me, were of the most extravagant mirth and hilarity.

I landed at Chester, and proceeded across the country. When I arrived at Doncaster, I was met by a chosen deputation of my tenants. Still as I advanced upon the road, the number of my train perpetually increased. The hills were covered with spectators. A procession of the rustic inhabitants in their holiday clothes, to the amount of some hundreds, presently appeared, with drums, and trumpets, and a band of music. Temporary arches were erected for me and my attendants to pass under. Flags appeared waving in the air, with various inscriptions, and the arms of the different noble houses from which I am descended, painted / upon them. The whole mansion of Milwood Park, together with the houses of the adjoining village, was illuminated; and a number of fireworks, together with the broaching of many hogsheads[b] of ale, closed the honours of the day.

What was this to me, whose face was bleached with guilt and sorrow, and trenched with the furrows of care and disappointment; whose eyes were dim, whose heart was dead, and who had no longer a hope in the world, save in this child, that I have reason to fear will speedily be ravished from me? How gladly would I have escaped from this gaudy scene, and these joys, which were no joys to me! But I had strung my mind to the business in which I was compelled to engage. The most considerable of my tenants were formally introduced to me, and congratulated me upon that translation from the subordinate to the superior country, which aggravated all my woes. I was like a / soldier who has received his death's wound in the field of battle, whose limbs are shattered, and his bosom trenched, while every step in the progress of the vehicle that removes him, tears him to pieces with insufferable agonies.

It is now many months since I received from Borromeo the intelligence of my nephew's disappearance. He has been heard of no more. It is as if some gulph had suddenly opened in the surface of the earth, and had received him into her bowels. I have waited week after week, and month after month, with the hope that some intelligence would transpire respecting him. Borromeo has been unwearied in his researches. In vain.

I can bear this no longer. I never contemplated such a result of my misdeeds. I aspired to the goal of my childish envy, to be an elder brother, to be the heir, to be a lord. Fortune threw in my way the power of gratifying this the earliest

---

[a] Thomas Mowbray, 1st Duke of Norfolk, was ordered to fight Hereford on 16 September, 1398 by Richard, who stopped the duel to avoid bloodshed.
[b] Large cask used for storing, shipping and dispensing alcoholic beverages.

passion of my soul. Fortune, not / withstanding a thousand probabilities which had immediately preceded to the contrary, delivered into my arms the new-born heir, having neither father nor mother, and born on a foreign soil. Fortune thus, the basest of all seducers, resuscitated within me the evil passion, which had slept for years before, like the thing that had never been. I was tempted; and, which has fastened upon my soul the corroding canker of repentance never to be extirpated, I fell.

But, in the midst of the most devilish and villainous thoughts that ever harboured in my bosom, I deemed that I had fully provided for the happiness of this unfortunate outcast, – this outcast, for whom, even in my most ambitious and profligate aspirings, my very soul yearned. I allotted an ample, and not for one instant interrupted income, to provide for him. I knew, I thought I knew, to the very bottom the character of Cloudesley; – a selfish man, at open / war with his fellow-mortals, but in whom that alloy was counteracted by a thousand virtues. I was not deceived in him. In a moment pregnant with fate and crime to us both, he sold himself to the baseness of my heart. But from that day forward, his conduct has ever been exemplary and spotless.

Well then; I provided for the happiness of this infant outcast. I did not allow him to be recorded in the calendar of the peerage; I did not suffer him to inherit the possessions and the expectations of his father, a species of inheritance which has involved so many souls in the snares of perdition, even as it has involved mine. What is high birth, to him to whom high birth has never been the theme of his contemplation? What is a throne, to him who has never dreamed of a throne? Man is the offspring of nature, and of nature's God. He has appetites and feelings. He must be fed, and be clothed, and wants a roof to cover him. He is / endowed with the faculty of propagating his species, and of consequence is accessible to all the joys, the nameless refinements and susceptibilities of love. God has bestowed on him the powers of understanding and imagination. He is capable of becoming wise, and learned, and inventive, of lofty conceptions, of great undertakings, of enthusiasm admirable and divine. Of a truth, he is 'fearfully and wonderfully made,'[a] and is the crown and consummation of the Creator's works. All this I thoroughly know, and most readily confess.

But how are the faculties of man to be best developed, and his happiness secured? The state of a king is not favourable to this, nor the state of the noble and rich men of the earth. All this is artificial life, the inventions of vanity and grasping ambition, by which we have spoiled the man of nature, and of pure, simple and undistorted impulses. From my soul I believe, that the plan of life I had marked out for my / brother's son, was calculated to make him more truly great and happier, than that which the institutions of the British isles had prepared for him.

---

[a] Psalm 139: 14.

But all my projects are defeated. He is gone, no one knows whither. The provision I have made for him is suspended. Who now undertakes to supply to him what nature's wants require? Slender as are these demands, the absence of that which shall satisfy them, is one of the most dangerous invitations to depravity and crime. He that is without that supply may perish in the extremity of misery, or may be engaged in community with the worst of characters, or in the perpetration of those acts which civilised man most unrelentingly avenges.

Where is this unhappy youth? He was brought up, thanks to the affection and virtue of Cloudesley, in the midst of every wholesome advantage and indulgence. His education has / unfitted him to struggle with want; and his ingenuous habits have placed him at a distance from all suspiciousness, and rendered him eminently the prepared victim of delusion, sophistry and falshood.

I can bear these thoughts no longer. I have waited till patience is at an end. I have played my part scurvily, viley in human life; I know that. But I cannot endure that this poor youth, flesh of my flesh, and blood of my blood, should owe his destruction to me. I have drank deeply of the bitterness of self-reproach, compunction and misery; but this last thought is mortal to me. My soul is distracted; sleep is departed from me. If at any time I close my eyes, I see him naked, emaciated, tearing his very flesh in the sharp pangs of hunger. At another time I see him environed with a ferocious set of banditti and bravoes, whose diabolical qualities are visible to all other men, but hidden from him. I picture him to myself the victim of the / evil society with which he is united, convicted under the forms of justice of their crimes, and led forth to an ignominious and tormenting death. If I could fix on any one of these mischiefs, and say it is under this that he suffers, it would be something. It is their variety, and the exhaustlessness of their stores, that consumes me.

I perhaps do not thoroughly understand what I have been; but I know what I am. In the dire moment of my master-crime, I was peradventure a worse man than I am willing to acknowledge. When I brought my mind to contrive the fearful tissue of fraud and imposition by which my brother's son was disinherited, the basest parts of my nature were wrought to a tremendous height; scarcely any thing could have stopped me; I might perhaps (I tremble to think it) have been driven on to murder. My hands are unstained with blood: but I did all that my evil purposes demanded; if they had / required more, peradventure I should have done more.

But that is over now. I was then in the lustihood of life; I 'walked in the ways of my heart, and in the sight of my eyes.'[a] But I am now past the middle term of human existence, and descending in the vale of years. The glories of this world are used and at an end with me. What dazzled me once, dazzles me no more.

---

[a] Eccles. 11: 9 (adapted).

Splendour and rank and riches have faded away in my eyes. They 'play round the head, but come not to the heart,'[a] They are like the furniture of former generations, when set in a modern drawing-room, or like a galasuit,[b] when the lace is tarnished, and the cloth is worn threadbare. I hasten towards that bourne, which all men are destined to arrive at; and the scene of this world is fast closing upon me for ever.

Nor is it merely that I have outlived that dangerous period of human existence, that is so / eminently exposed to the inroads of 'the lust of the flesh, the lust of the eye, and the pride of life;'[c] but, independently of this, I have seen experimentally the emptiness of those things the very thought of which once subdued me to its sway. I have ascended the chair of the noble, and been the lord of thousands: and what has this done for me? Since the death of my elder brother, since the temptations of crime have mastered and possessed me, I have never known a moment's peace. I once lived to honour; I loved and was loved by the heroic Arthur; I was the soldier of glory. I was happy in the happiness and fame of my senior, and had no conception so mean as of a gratification, the first fruits of which were not his. As such I appeared and was acknowledged during the campaigns of Eugene, and in the autumn of 1718 when we resided at Vienna. I was the model and example of all that was becoming and praise-worthy in a younger brother. /

Twenty years have now passed since that period. I tried the experiment of a single life; it was too sad and too wretched to be endured. I married. Fortune was with me in the character of my wife, and the endowments of my children. Yet I was not happy. Happy did I say? The brilliant round that sends out the sunshine of the soul, was, as in a phantasmagoria, carried off to an immeasur-able distance, and brought to the vanishing point. Meanwhile the air that I breathed was that of fog and of mist, the foe to respiration, which, while it seemed destined to maintain the health of existence, served only the more effectually to destroy it. But what I had in the married life, is gone. The pleasure, or, to speak more accurately, the diminution of suffering, which I derived from my wife and my children, has served only as a new medium of misery. One by one I have lost them, with the bitter conviction that a just providence has cut them off in the morning of life, a judgment and / an expiation for my fault. Oh, how protracted and interminable has been the period of the rack on which my heartstrings have been stretched to the bursting! /

---

[a] cf. Pope, *An Essay on Man*, IV, l. 254: 'Plays round the head, but comes not to the heart.'
[b] Fine or showy dress worn at a gala.
[c] 1 John 2: 16.

CHAPTER XI

Such was the narrative of lord Danvers. I do not pretend to have put it down in his exact words. That every one will readily acknowledge to have been impossible. I feel that I have sometimes taken the liberty to interweave with it circumstances, that were not fully known to me till afterwards. It was scarcely in my power to do otherwise. I have given lord Danvers's narrative in the first person: without doing so I should scarcely have been able to introduce the language in which he described his feelings of compunction and remorse; and in this it has been my desire to be faithful and minute. After this it would have had a wretched / effect, if I had been scrupulous to separate what I learned from his lordship's lips, from the things respecting which my information was subsequently more complete; and thus to have formed two narratives, coincident in point of time, and separated only in the sources from which I received them. I have not therefore attempted to observe so barren a punctilio.[a] Let the reader be satisfied that the story is substantially true. I have not consciously narrated one circumstance, or given words to one thought, that does not truly make a part of this memorable story.

Having finished his history, his lordship proceeded to give me his instructions as to the task in which he desired me to engage. I was to proceed to Italy, to endeavour to find the young man in his hiding-place, to omit no enquiry or research, to spare no expence, and, if possible, not to return without having effected the object of my journey. Lord Danvers had / the goodness to say, that he found, from my story, and my letters from Russia which had been communicated to him, that I was in no common degree qualified for the commission in which he wished to employ me. To assure himself of this, had been the object of the questions with which he had tried me, as to my feelings respecting the incidents that had occurred during my abode in Russia, and the principles that had influenced my conduct there. I had had experience of a sailor's life, of the life of a college, and the life of a court. I had seen men and manners in no contemptible variety. I had had the opportunity of studying the characters of men, and the passions of the human heart, in manifold stations of society. And I had come out from the trial with dispositions uncontaminated and untainted.

The business in which I was to be employed was to find the nephew of lord

---

[a] Strict attention to minute points of etiquette.

Danvers, the true heir to the title, and to save him. It had / happened, by a strange concurrence of circumstances, that the youth for whom his lordship had always intended to set apart an income of five hundred *per annum,* was not only ignorant of his true parentage, but regarded himself as a portionless individual, cast upon the wide ocean of human society. Lord Danvers was in agonies, lest the nephew to whom he had done so much deliberate wrong, should suffer more than was necessary to his uncle's interests, and be irretrievably ruined, notwithstanding all the efforts that should be made to prevent it.

Lord Danvers continued: It is a delicate office, Meadows, in which I am about to employ you, and will need all the perspicacity and discernment for which I give you credit, exactly to fulfil it. Your business will be to save this youth, to extricate him from the imminent perils which it is too probable at this moment beset him, and to place him in that situation for which his education conspicuously qualifies / him, for which Cloudesley wished to prepare him, and in the attainment of which he has all my good wishes. May he be virtuous, and may he be happy! This issue is absolutely necessary to me, to prevent my being utterly and miserably destroyed by remorse for that which shall be the consequence of my crime. – This I may call your first point.

But you must stop there. I am firmly resolved not to surrender the prize, which, at so great a sacrifice, and by such dreadful sufferings, I have obtained. In this respect I have nothing to recommend to you, but that you should tread in the steps of the foster-father of Julian. It was the determination of Cloudesley, that the youth should never be an adventurer. This was his resolve, because he considered an adventurer as an unfortunate and contemptible character. But I have reasons of a very different importance, why I should require this conduct of you. I know, that the eminence on / which I am placed is impregnable, and that all the batteries by which it can be assailed will only accomplish the disgrace of the aggressor. But I have hitherto been so far fortunate. My rank and my possessions have not only been indisputable, but undisputed. I cannot brook the idea, that an upstart youth should come over to England, should go about among my relations and tenants, and proclaim that he is the true heir, and that I am an impostor. The very whisper of such a tale would destroy me. I had rather suffer a thousand deaths than be in such a situation. Beware, Meadows! I have placed myself at your mercy. I ask you to free me from a cruel remorse. But in attempting to confer on me that benefit, think what the result will be, if you are guilty of any indiscretion! Now the pretender is in the southern extremity of Italy; I need never see him; his name may never be pronounced in my hearing. But one false step on your part may bring him to England, / nay, to the county in which I dwell. He may haunt my park, may beset my doors, may climb my windows, and I may never dare to quit my threshold under the penalty of having this intruder, whom I have been hitherto so blessed as never to have encountered, to cross my steps, to beset my path, and to blast my eyesight. Rather than this, I confess to you, I should be well content that any thing however fatal should overtake him, that he should be a bandit, or an assassin, and that, after having gone through a course of atrocities, he should be swept from the earth by an ignominious death.

And remember, Meadows, that you will stand in a very different situation with this youth, from that which was occupied by Cloudesley. I have heard that he is a person of considerable abilities, of clear apprehension, and most likely, in a case where his own interests are so deeply concerned, of an inquisitive / mind. He will see in you a new character, a stranger, interesting himself in his affairs. How many questions will suggest themselves to an enquirer, for which you may not be prepared, and which you will not know how to answer! You will need the subtlety of Ulysses to guard your secret. You must be resolute of purpose, prepared at every avenue, with a voice that shall never falter, and with features that shall never betray what passes in your breast. With Cloudesley Julian had nothing to excite his enquiry: he had dwelt, as he believed, in the society of his father and his mother; and he was satisfied. With Cloudesley he lived in a certain awe; the English yeoman exercised over him the authority of a parent, and could effectually check his curiosity, if it proceeded to certain points, respecting which his protector did not choose to indulge him. But with you, if you meet, his curiosity will be excited, and he will not scruple to press you with the freedom / of an equal, and the rights of a person who, he may consider, as calling on you for that respecting which you can inform him, and which may be of the highest importance to his well being. He does not want audacity and enterprise; and he may urge you with the authority of one who is entitled to be satisfied, and with the importunity that shall invoke every generous feeling in the human bosom! Remember! Be prepared! I have voluntarily made you the depository of a secret, a thousand times more precious to me than life. Do not cause me to repent the confidence I have placed in you!

I cheerfully promised to lord Danvers every thing he required. I felt deeply interested in the story he had so unreservedly detailed to me. And, learning it as I did from the lips of a man, bearing an ancient title, and commanding ample possessions, a man highly educated, of a cultivated mind, who had figured honourably in the field, and who had stood in the presence / of princes, it struck me very differently from what it would have done, if I had met with it in a book, and read it as a memoir of incidents that had passed in a former generation. There was much that was commanding in the presence of lord Danvers, and impressive in his voice and his gestures. He had told me, as I firmly believed, the whole truth, without the reserve of a single particle, and had spoken of his misgivings and compunctions in a manner which, in spite of myself, made his feelings mine. There is something which can scarcely be resisted in the whole effect of a man, who tells you all, and speaks to you as ingenuously as he is bound to speak in the presence of his Creator. When he thus surrenders himself into your hands, it is scarcely possible that you should not give him in return your sympathy and your aid.

I felt besides that the commission in which he proposed to employ me, was a beneficent one. / Tried before the rigorous tribunal of everlasting justice, lord Danvers ought utterly to have resigned the title he had usurped, and the possessions that were none of his. I might have told him this. I might have reasoned, like Paul before Felix, 'of righteousness, temperance, and judgment to come;' and perhaps my hearer would have 'trembled.'[a] I could not do this. I, a stranger, a plebeian, and a beggar, who had just set my foot upon my native soil after many years' absence, and who was sent for by the proprietor of the magnificent mansion at Milwood Park, and the actual possessor of the fee simple of nearly the whole isle of Axholme! I had no power to inforce justice upon him; and what likelihood was there that I could prevail on him to make a voluntary cession? It is one of the oldest maxims of moral prudence, Do not, by aspiring to what is impracticable, lose the opportunity of doing the good you can effect! /

Under the circumstances, I resolved to put myself implicitly into the hands of lord Danvers. It was much to me, in this vacation from all the business of human life, to be honourably employed. I should visit foreign countries. I had seen Archangel and Petersburgh, the frozen regions of the north; I should now see Italy, and perhaps France. I should have a motive of high energy, impelling me to travel, to search and enquire. The rising sun of every day would bring hope with its beams. I should enquire; I should be led from point to point; I should approach to the goal. Difficulties would only increase my zeal, and urge me to proceed, and to conquer them. I resolved to set out, in the spirit that lord Danvers recommended to me, bent not to return without having effected the object of my journey.

I proceeded immediately to London, and from London by sea to Leghorn. I had scarcely / landed, when I met in the streets Stephanoff, the young man, who had so generously saved me from the rage of Biren, and shipped me for Amsterdam. We immediately knew each other. Little more than a year had passed, since we sat together at a desk in the bureau of the duke of Courland. After mutual salutations, I eagerly enquired of him respecting the health and welfare of my beloved. Naturally speaking, it was scarcely probable that Isabella and myself should ever meet again. She was bound to Russia, and had no means of quitting that country. I could not dare, at least during the reign of Biren, to set my foot on that shore; and I had no establishment to offer her, that could make it prudent or becoming for her to expatriate herself. But I was not capable of reasonings of this sort. Love makes no account of ordinary obstacles; 'the light wings of the God will overperch'[a] barriers insuperable to / other powers; and, like the attendant spirit in Comus,

---

[a] Acts: 24: 25.
[b] *Romeo and Juliet*, II. ii. 66 (adapted).

> He can fly, or he can run
> Quickly to the green earth's end,
> Where the bowed welkin slow doth bend,
> And from thence can soar as soon
> To the corners of the moon.[a]

In a word, I would not suffer myself to be persuaded that Isabella Scherbatoff and I were not destined for each other. I would serve seven years for the maiden; and they would 'seem but a few days for the love that I bore to her.'[b]

How much then was I chagrined, how overwhelmed with astonishment and horror, when Stephanoff told me that she was already married! Poor girl! she was dragged like a victim to the altar upon which she had been sacrificed. Biren had been worked into a fury of rage against me; and by dint of terror he had gained over madame Scherbatoff to his side. She had felt a timidity for her offspring, against which she was proof in the days of her youth, / and when the case was her own. I was in a far country, interdicted in Russia, and unable to return under the severest penalties. How absurd was it, thus she reasoned with the maiden, for the sake of a passion that was for ever cut off, that she should devote herself to perpetual celibacy! Isabella was pressed by the instances of her mother, and overawed by the authority of the all-powerful favourite of the empress! her brother was at a distance, and she had none to help her; and therefore, after much reluctance, and many evasions, she submitted to what she deemed inevitable. Once only had I addressed her in the language of an impassioned lover; and there was now no probability that she would ever again behold me.

It was well for me that the question that brought me to Italy was of a nature that would brook no delay: otherwise the shock I sustained from the unexpected intelligence of Stephanoff would have deprived me of all power of standing / up under it. But occupation, pressing occupation that will not be said nay, is a sovereign remedy for grief. I was under the most sacred engagments to lord Danvers; he had given me his instructions; he had furnished me with the means of executing his commission; the object I pursued was of the most essential importance to his peace; and any neglect on my part might involve the irretrievable destruction of a gallant and meritorious youth, who had been born to the most brilliant prospects. I resolved at once that I would fulfil my trust to the minutest letter, and that no unmanly indulgence of disappointment and despair should interfere with this duty. And, when I was once engaged, one opening, one glimpse of success, one anxiety, succeeded to another, so as to engross all the powers of my soul. The more obstacles I had encountered, the more I felt impelled to proceed, and the more impossible it

---

[a] Milton, *Masque*, 1013–7.
[b] Gen. 29: 20 (adapted).

seemed to me to draw back. One thought engrossed me, / to rescue Julian from the perils that might enchain him; and, by dint of the earnestness with which I devoted myself to this end, I conceived of nothing else by day, I dreamed of nothing else by night. /

CHAPTER XII

Lord Danvers had given me an Italian servant from his houshold, to serve me as an interpreter in my expedition. Mine was to be the intellect to conduct the affair; his was the mouth by which my communications were to be carried on. He was kept in the dark as to the purpose of my voyage; I intrusted him from moment to moment with the questions to be asked; and he knew about as much of their use, as a boy at grammar-school knows of the use of his declensions and conjugations, before he has been set a single sentence, to render the meaning of the original into his vernacular tongue.

Even during my voyage I applied myself to / the study of the Italian language. We had three passengers from that country, one of whom had been in the practice of giving lessons in his native tongue. The first book I applied myself to, independently of the Dialogues annexed to the Grammar, was the Adventures of Telemachus, which had been published thirty or forty years before, and the translation of which into Italian is the easiest book that can be put into the hands of a learner.[a] Having so interesting and express an object in making the acquisition, and with the advantage of conversation to assist my study, I was a scholar not altogether contemptible, when I first set foot upon the Tuscan shore.

I repaired to Borromeo, and was anxious to learn from him any particulars that might direct me in my search. As he was already in the secret of Julian's birth, I was the less disposed to conceal from him that I was commissioned by lord Danvers to discover the hiding-place of the / unhappy truant. I confessed to nothing more, than that the youth was in some way allied to my employer, who was anxious that he should come to no harm, and should be respectably provided for. I took care so to express myself, as might best support the inference that I had never heard so much as a rumour of Julian's being the true heir, and the so called lord Danvers an usurper. Borromeo had always felt that there was something romantic, and even improbable in Cloudesley's story, and

---

[a] François de Salignac de la Mothe Fénelon (1651–1715), *Les aventures de Télémaque* (1699).

was firmly persuaded at least that the pretensions of Julian would never be established. I found therefore the less difficulty in avoiding to betray all I knew; and we conversed as if by compact on the notion that lord Danvers had no mystery to observe with the youth, and that the ground of his solicitude respecting his future destination was compassion only. Borromeo entered with me into the history of the young man's connections with St Elmo and Francesco, assured me / that they were at the head of a company of banditti, and added that he had no doubt that Julian, at his late disappearance, had gone once more to unite himself to this wretched association.

A revolution had lately taken place in the government of Naples. This kingdom, which had been administered by Spanish and Austrian viceroys for centuries, was at length conquered by Philip of Bourbon king of Spain, in favour of his son, Don Carlos, in 1734. At the period of his accession Don Carlos was only eighteen years of age; but he immediately fixed his residence in the capital of his dominions, and in no long time began to distinguish himself by many judicious regulations in behalf of the happiness and good government of his people.[a] Among other things he expressed a determination to root out the gangs of banditti throughout his dominions, to put an end to the licentiousness with which they were accustomed to / invade solitary houses and even small villages, to free the high roads from their molestations, and to diffuse a general face of civilisation and security.

These ideas however were gradual in their progression. It was not till the third year of his reign, that they were brought into very active operation. Their effects began to be seen in the neighbourhood of the metropolis, and diffused themselves step by step, till they reached Otranto and the straits of Messina. Their next remove was to Sicily; and the nobleman, who presided as the representative of majesty at Palermo, was instructed to promulgate the edicts, and adopt the measures in his government, which were found to be attended with so auspicious effects in Don Carlos's dominions on the continent of Italy.

It was during the energy of these operations that I first arrived in Tuscany. Not one company of these endemial[b] brigands was any longer / to be heard of from Florence to the extreme point of Reggio.[c] For the moment however the natural effect was produced, that Sicily was in a more disturbed state than it had known for a series of years. The bodies of men who had been used to subsist themselves by their perpetual depredations, being driven from their haunts in Italia proper, as many of them as had not fallen by the sword of executive justice, or been won over by the judicious offers of indemnity held out by Don Carlos, had betaken themselves across the straits to the island-fastnesses, with which they had not failed before to be occasionally acquainted.

---

[a] Philip V (1683–1746) King of Spain from 1700; Don Carlos (1716–88) King of Spain from 1759.
[b] Endemic: i.e. having the status of social pests.
[c] Reggio di Calabria, port at the 'toe' of Italy, on the Strait of Messina separating Italy from Sicily.

It seemed for a time as if the viceroy of Sicily had been disposed to run exactly counter to the policy of the cabinet of Naples: he laid the instructions of his sovereign on the shelf; and, whether from a principle of insubordination or indolence, or that some of the leaders of the brigands secretly enjoyed his protection, he took no proceedings / that should be calculated to reduce Sicily into the same state of order, which already began to be established in the kingdom of Naples.

I did not cross the straits, till I had made to a certain degree a diligent search through the provinces on the continent. I was willing 'to leave no rubs nor botches in my work.'[a] Like those whose object is the conquest of wild beasts, I was disposed to hunt my prey into a corner from which there should be no escape. I thought it not impossible that St Elmo, who was of a higher and nobler character than his associates, might in this extremity separate himself from his companions, and lurk somewhere concealed in the wild and savage scenes which occasionally interpose themselves in the Neapolitan provinces.

Nor was my time unadvisedly spent during this period of the wariness of my progress. I got all the information I could, from officers of justice, from the confessions of criminals, and / even occasionally from communication with those to whom the government had extended its pardon, as to the gangs of banditti, their modes of proceeding, and their policy. I found the persons I conversed with for the most part sufficiently communicative. The Italians are for the generality of an impassioned disposition; and, if once you have satisfied them that you have no sinister view in your enquiries, and still more if you appear to afford your sympathy to the vicissitudes of their story, they willingly communicate to you the adventures of which the narrator is for the most part his own hero. I found they all of them knew something of St Elmo; many of them had heard of Francesco; but none knew any thing of Julian, the son of the English Cloudesley. They concurred in assuring me that St Elmo had passed over into Sicily.

I also now bent my course to that island. But even here the proceedings for the suppression of / the banditti had begun; and they did not now, as had been the case a short time before, prowl in the neighbourhood of the high roads, and advance to within a short distance of the considerable towns. Some scattered detachments, the forlorn hope of the mystery, had been taken by surprise, and thrown into prison. In one and another instance I had approached the site of the most noted recesses where they had been accustomed to harbour. I did this in all cases with a thousand precautions, fearful lest, while employed in tracing the object of my search, I should myself fall into the mercy of the robbers. I joined the military parties which were sent out to remove the disturbers of Sicily; but, when we had penetrated into the retreats where we chiefly hoped to

---

[a] *Macbeth*, III. i. 134 (adapted).

find the outlaws, we for the most part discovered in them vestiges of fires that had recently gone out, and some culinary utensils no longer capable of service, but no living inhabitant. A considerable time was / spent by me in this business; as I sometimes proceeded in company with persons officially instructed by the government, and at others, as the object of my pursuit was very different from theirs, detached myself from the rest, that I might mix with the country-people, and engage in enquiries which would be sure to be very cautiously answered to persons who apparently came armed with civil or military authority.

It was in one of these rambles, and when I had scrutinized nearly every part of the island, that I met with an adventure, which seemed to change the whole prospect of the affair, and to render all further search hopeless. I was wandering near mount Enna,[a] now called Castro Giovanni, where Pluto is said to have found Proserpine, surrounded by her train of females, and gathering flowers at the foot of the hill, and, seizing her by force, to have carried her off to the shades below. I pleased myself with the luxuriant imagery with which Ovid has painted / the scene,[b] and, transported into the times when this beautiful island was peopled with demigods and gods, forgot for the moment the errand which had brought me so far, and the clash of swords and discharge of musquetry that had lately disfigured the country. I approached the very cavern, through which, a passage being opened to the subterranean realms that are never visited by the beams of the sun, the god is said to have plunged with his chariot, carrying off in truimph the prize he had seized. The lake, formerly called Pergusa, now the Lake of Goridan, adjoins to the mountain; and hard by is the cavern which has been shewn as that through which Pluto opened his way to the infernal regions.

I was busily employed in exploring the scenery, and had with me no one but the servant that lord Danvers had given to attend me, when, turning an angle in the direction I was pursuing, two armed men rushed out upon / us from a thicket, and, presenting their guns, ordered us to dismount, while two others came out of the wood behind, so as to cut off the possibility of retreat. They took from us our horses, and called upon me to deliver my money, and whatever else that was valuable I might have about me.

This incident did not much disconcert me. I persuaded myself that I was not in great danger for my life; and I thought that the banditti into whose hands I had fallen might belong to the followers of St Elmo, and that therefore it was not impossible that, though with some personal risk, I might obtain from them the intelligence of which I was in pursuit.

This however would require no little management on my part. The gentlemen who belong to the profession in which they were engaged, are not in the habit of giving information, though they are exceedingly willing to receive such

---

[a] Mount Etna.

[b] Ovid, *Metamorphoses*, Book 5, Fable 6, 'The Rape of Proserpine'.

as may be of any assistance in directing / them to their objects. They have many good qualities, and are punctilious upon their principles of honour; they are never known to make a promise that they do not perform; and, wherever they profess to borrow money, they repay it to the uttermost penny. But they are humorous in temper, and instant in executing whatever their minds prompt them to do. It is dangerous for a man who is placed at their mercy, to appear inquisitive, or desirous to search into their haunts or intentions. And, as society sets no value on their lives, but is bent to destroy them whenever there is opportunity, so they make no account of the lives of others. The stiletto is their ever ready weapon; and whoever gives them umbrage, is likely without the smallest previous notice to receive it in his heart.

I found that they had mistaken me for one of the nobles of the country, who had invidiously distinguished himself by his zeal for their / suppression, and who they were informed was to pass that way upon the present occasion. They had resolved therefore to seize upon, and to destroy him, or make him pay a very exorbitant price for his ransom. He in reality did pass the defile about an hour before; and it was only by a singular accident that he missed falling into their hands. They were of necessity soon convinced that I was not the prize they sought: but they began to negociate with me as to the sum I should pay for the recovery of my freedom.

A regular branch of the revenue of these freebooters consists in the ransom they can exact from the captives that fall into their hands. The mode is, that they cause the prisoner to write a letter to his banker, to his steward or tenants, if a nobleman, or to his townsmen, if a medical character, a priest, or a tradesman, calling on them to send a specified sum by the bearer, and assuring them that his life depends / upon their compliance. The banditti then fix upon some peasant in the neighbourhood for their messenger, dispatch him from a point at a certain distance from their rendezvous, and fix an hour for his return, at which he will be met by one or more of the party. If he discharges his mission faithfully, he is sure of a reward; and the rustics have an undoubting persuasion that, if they are guilty of foul play to the robbers, their lives will in one way or another pay the forfeit.

The negociation respecting my ransom led to a certain degree of intercourse and conversation with the robbers, that they were not inclined to look on with suspicion, since the object it had in view was of their own proposing. I studiously prolonged it, regarding it as a means that might lead to the accomplishment of my commission. I told them that I was an Englishman, wandering through Sicily from motives of curiosity; and they, satisfied of the truth of my / tale, looked upon me with the less umbrage. They asked me when I had left England, how long I had remained in the kingdom of Naples, and at what time I had passed over into Sicily. They convinced themselves that I was not an agent of the government. They told me however, that it was in vain to pretend that I was not able to pay a ransom for my liberty, that I had fallen into their hands with two horses and a servant, and that a foreigner thus visiting their country, always brought with him a credit upon a banker, and letters of introduction to some of the principal nobility of the state he visited.

At length we came to terms. I wrote a letter to Gergenti, the last considerable place I had visited, and, having reduced my ransom to the lowest price that I could, stated to a man of business with whom I had had some intercourse there, the circumstance that had befallen me, and represented the imminent peril to which I should be exposed, if the sum I had stipulated / for should not be forwarded to me by the bearer. We waited two days in expectation of the answer.

During this period I was marched from place to place by the persons who had me in custody, more, as far as I could judge, from the restlessness of their disposition, than from any settled purpose they had in view. One and another of their fraternity joined us on the first day and the second. During the season of repose to which they were accustomed in the middle of the day, I kept myself awake, but affected to sleep, that I might collect what I could from their casual communications; and, as a stranger from a distant country, they were less suspicious and on the reserve with me, not apprehending that any thing that fell from them in my hearing would turn to their injury. Twice I heard from them the name of St Elmo, and once that of Francesco Perfetti.

Encouraged by these notices, I began to think / I could not do more wisely, than to explain to the chief individual of those I saw, the object that had brought me into Sicily. I mentioned that I had heard from his lips, if I were not mistaken, the name of St Elmo, and therefore with his permission I would disclose to him at once the errand which had brought me from England. There was a youth about twenty years of age, born of English parents, who had been seen several times in company with St Elmo. His name was Julian Cloudesley; his residence for years past had been Florence and its neighbourhood; and he had recently had the misfortune to lose his father there by a casualty, from whom he had scarcely been separated from the hour of his birth. This youth, upon the death of his father, had immediately withdrawn from Florence; no intelligence could in any way be gathered as to what was become of him; and his relatives in England had become in the highest degree anxious as to his / welfare and his fate. I was nearly connected with some of those relatives; and, seeing their uneasiness, and there being nothing in the way to prevent my undertaking the journey, I had offered myself to go over to Italy, to endeavour to find the young man, and to fix him in some situation, where his connections should be unimpeachable, and he should be enabled to pass his days in reputation and honour. I intreated the person to whom I addressed myself to tell me ingenuously whether he knew any thing of this youth, and, as I had taken so long a journey purely for his benefit, not to allow me to return home without having accomplished my commission, if it were in his power to prevent it.

The bandit listened attentively to all the circumstances I detailed to him, and in reply said, he would deal frankly with me, and tell me all he knew. It was contrary to their system of action to make revelations. They were at war with the governments of the countries in which / they dwelt; and of consequence they carried on their proceedings in secrecy. The places where they continued for any time, and took up their abode, were by every imaginable precaution rendered undiscernible to the rest of the world; their numbers and their names were as little as might be divulged. It was by some strange want of precaution and vigilance on his part, that I had heard from his lips the name of St Elmo, but, relying on the veracity of my tale, and that nothing he said would be turned to the disadvantage of himself and his associates, he would unreservedly tell me all he knew, that could be of any service to the business in which I was engaged.

He confessed, that St Elmo was the principal leader of the body of men of which he was a member, and that St Elmo was at this moment in Sicily. He added, that he had himself seen the youth of whom I was in quest, and that he had for a short time taken up his residence / among them. Julian had been extremely attached to St Elmo, and St Elmo had conceived a sincere affection for Julian. But the youth was no longer among them. St Elmo, he supposed, had taken pity upon his tender years and his innocence; and, as their captain was of the most generous and noble dispositions, he had prevailed upon the youth to quit their society, and enter himself into some less perilous course of life. At all events Julian had not been seen among them for some time, and had never crossed the straits of Messina. Whither he had directed his steps, my friendly bandit could not inform me. St Elmo had formerly figured in the most elevated circles of society, and could certainly, if he pleased, furnish the person whom he thus liberally dismissed, with introductions into the world that would be of eminent service to him.

What the bandit thus related to me, was well as far as it went, but was by no means completely / to my satisfaction. I had not come from the isle of Axholme to Sicily, to be then contented to return with my commission imperfectly performed. The whole story of this unfortunate orphan had awakened the deepest interest in my mind. Lord Danvers, from views of inordinate ambition, had been contented to turn him adrift in the world, unknown and an outcast, under the imperfect and inadequate protection of Cloudesley. But I had no sympathy for the ambitious aims of this treacherous uncle. I had accepted a commission, and would perform it to the letter; I had only become acquainted with the pretensions of Julian by a confidence voluntarily reposed in me; and I did not think I had a right to turn this communication to the ruin of my employer. But I could not help cherishing a secret hope that Julian would one day be established in the full possession of his patrimony. I resolved therefore, that, if possible, I would not return / to England, without having seen him, become acquainted with his connections and his situation, ascertained where he was at all times to be found, and arranged in what manner the proposed income of five hundred pounds a year should be applied to his benefit. In fact, the commission with which lord Danvers had invested me, went to all these points.

I was therefore extremely earnest with the bandit to whom I had proposed my questions, to lead me to St Elmo himself. I observed to him, that the commission I had undertaken included my becoming acquainted with the abode of Julian, and having an interview with him. Though my kind informer was unable to assist me in effecting these points, St Elmo could no doubt furnish me with the information I desired. I represented to the individual to whom I addressed myself, of how much importance it appeared to the persons I had left in England, that the adventure I had undertaken should be / fully achieved; and I adjured him, in addition to the kindness I had already received from him, to grant me this favour also, which I had no doubt would enable me to perfect all I desired.

Popoli (that was the name borne by the person with whom I had this explanation) now suddenly changed his tone and manner to me. He drew himself up into an erect attitude so as somewhat to startle me; his brow loured, and his eyes flashed fire. He told me, I was forgetting where I was, and with whom I talked. I was a prisoner, and my life lay at their mercy. He bade me be pleased to remember, that they acknowledged themselves subject to no laws, and there was nothing but arbitrary will, that stood between them and the death of any individual who fell into their power. It was one of the primary laws of their profession, that they were to dictate to all persons with whom they came into contact, but to be dictated to by / none. He had already gone unwarrantable lengths in consideration of the object I professed to have in view; and he advised me as a friend, not to think to take an undue advantage of his indulgence. As long as I was in their custody, I was to go with them wherever they went, and to see such persons as they had occasion to see; but I was not to move to the right or the left except as I received orders, and was not to ask to have communication with any one, but to communicate only with those whose charge it was to dispose of me.

Having thus far addressed me in a peremptory style, and perceiving that the tone of menace and command he assumed had produced the desired effect upon me, he as suddenly reverted to his former manner, and addressed me in a spirit of courtesy and obligingness. It was like a summer cloud, hurried along by the west wind, which unexpectedly darkens the sun, and blackens the face of days, and then rapidly / passes away, while the orb which lightens the world, again pours out a flood of glory, and seems to laugh at the mood of the meteor, which for a moment appeared to usurp the meridian.

He said he felt a friendly disposition towards me, and was willing to confer on me any benefit which it was proper for him to grant. He had a consideration for me as a stranger and a foreigner, whose claims in no way interfered with theirs. I was not like the clergy, or the great lords of the soil, who pampered themselves with every imaginable indulgence, while they left the industrious and unpresuming *villaneria*[a] to starve. I had not come among them with purposes of hostility, or with views of merchandise and lucre, but simply from a benevolent intention, and a laudable desire of assisting a youth who might stand in need of my aid. He was willing therefore no longer to detain me, nor insist upon any ransom for my liberty. / From this moment I was free, with my servant and my horses, to go wherever I pleased.

I was greatly disappointed with this result of my negociation. Liberty is no doubt one of the choicest gifts that can fall to the lot of man: but it was not in pursuit of liberty that I had left England, and made this long journey to the south of the Mediterranean sea. Having gained intelligence thus recent respecting the society that Julian had frequented, and the places he had visited, it was insupportably grievous to me to be thus cut short in my pursuit. Which way was I to direct my steps? The clue that had led me thus far was cut off, and I had nothing now left to guide my search. I had proposed to myself the discovery of St Elmo and Francesco. I might now almost say that I had found them: but Julian was not with them. I did not venture to renew my request of an interview with St Elmo; but I intreated Popoli to indulge me so far as to convey a letter to his / hands. The bandit consented, answering me however in vague terms, that what I should think proper to write should be delivered to their leader, whenever an opportunity should occur for that purpose.

In this letter I earnestly pressed the bandit chief to aid me in the purpose that had brought me to Sicily. I said, that I was under engagement to the persons who interested themselves in the fate of Julian Cloudesley in England, to find him out, to see him, and provide for his welfare. More good, I assured St Elmo, was meant to him, than the young man was aware of; and the concurrence of the person to whom I addressed myself might be of the last importance to his fate. I added, that I had heard much of the generous and noble dispositions of St Elmo; and I would not allow myself to doubt, that his humanity would induce him to furnish me with the information that might enable me to find the person of whom I was / in search. I concluded, that I would wait one month, if it were necessary, at Messina; but that I fervently hoped he would put an end to my suspense, long before the expiration of that period.

I confided this letter to the person who had now for some days had me in his keeping, and then set out with a heavy heart and disappointed feelings for the north-eastern extremity of the island. It was a tedious interval I passed in expectation of the desired intelligence. I enquired day after day at the post-office for the answer. Nothing came. – Twelve months were elapsed, from the period when I set out from Milwood Park. Another twelve months had been

---

[a] (Italian) Peasants.

consumed in the transactions, from Cloudesley's last visit to England, to my first interview with lord Danvers. Julian was now in the twenty-first year of his age. /

CHAPTER XIII

It was in the fifth week of my forced stay at Messina, that, stepping into a coffee-house to beguile the weary hours, I overheard a conversation in an adjoining box which immediately arrested my attention. The principal speaker was a young officer, who had just arrived from Taranto in Apulia.[a] He said, the greatest novelty of the place at the time he left it, was an *improvvisatore,* not more than twenty years of age, who greatly surpassed every thing he had before heard of the kind. He was countenanced by the duke of Taranto and the archbishop. Nobody seemed to know where he came from. One of the compositions that the officer had / heard from his lips was a poem in which he represented himself as an orphan, who had just lost his only parent, shot by a company of banditti in the mountains, and who was left without a friend. He complained of a cruel guardian, that had treated him with intolerable austerity. He related that, flying from this guardian, he had taken refuge in the woods, had fallen in with banditti, and even made one among them. He was at that time wholly unconscious in what manner his father had come to his untimely end, and had by the most unexpected accident discovered, that the individual with whom he had entered into terms of the closest friendship, had fired the musket that rendered him fatherless. He described in the most expressive language the horror with which he was seized, the instantaneousness with which he quitted his new associates, and the detestation he conceived of their pursuits, and in a most eloquent peroration threw himself / upon the compassion and pity of his auditors. The whole company was in tears; and nothing was to be heard for some time after he had concluded, but sobs and groans from every one present. In a short while however they recovered from this transport; and the clapping and applause that followed lasted a considerable time.

My whole soul was engrossed with the tale of the officer; but I was scarcely able to arrive at any satisfactory conclusion from what I heard. On the one hand I recollected Julian's having early associated himself with *improvvisatori,* and the perfection he was said to have reached in their art. On the other hand I

---

[a] Taranto, the old name for Ionio, one of the five provinces comprising Apulia, in SE Italy.

could hardly persuade myself that he would have chosen in his own person to become the hero of his tale: there was an indelicacy in the idea to which I could not reconcile myself. But then there were so many circumstances that favoured the conclusion – his age, his unquestionable talents / the coincidence of the stories in such a variety of particulars. I took an opportunity of questioning the officer as to the voice, the features, and the air of the speaker: but I had never seen Julian; and therefore the answers I received could lead me but a little way. What I heard now sufficiently agreed with what I had learned no long time before from the lips of lord Danvers. At all events I felt impelled to set out immediately for Taranto.

I arrived. I found the young man of whom the officer had spoken at Messina. I encountered him just as he had finished one of these exhibitions; and I never saw a more interesting countenance. He was in the first bloom of youth, when ingenuousness is marked in every lineament; and had that very moment closed the scene, in which he had presented himself as an extempore poet to an admiring audience. His hair hung in beautiful disorder; his eyes sparkled; his whole frame trembled with emotion; / he was out of breath. I perused his features with the keenest attention; I said to myself, Is this the youth who is rightful heir to an English earldom, but who is made an outcast and a vagabond, a being without a name, by a cold-blooded usurper?

I found in him no trace of the features of earl Danvers, or of lord Bardsley, the uncle and cousin of Julian. His face was perfectly beautiful, but of the true Italian cast. He answered all my questions with perfect unreserve. He said, he was of Siena, and had been first excited to embrace the profession of an *improvvisatore* by witnessing the performance of the celebrated Perfetti. On these occasions he had seen both Francesco and Julian.

I asked him, how he came by the story, the particulars of which had so much roused my attention at Messina? He replied, that he had heard it as a tale, he believed founded in fact, but knew nothing of the parties. He did not / in the smallest degree connect it with the person of the young Cloudesley. It struck him as remarkably well adapted for a poetical narrative to be recited in public; and he adopted it accordingly. The mode in the sort of exhibitions with which he was concerned, is for the company indiscriminately to suggest subjects for the poet; and he contrived that this should be drawn out of the box, and put into his hand as if by accident. As the manners of this person were the very mirror of frankness, we talked of several subjects, beside that on which I first accosted him; and, among other things, I said I had come from England, on purpose to endeavour to be of service to the young Cloudesley.

The next morning, to my exceeding surprise, I had no sooner opened the door of my lodging, than my acquaintance of yesterday presented himself before me. He had a printed paper in his hand. It contained a list of certain banditti, / who had been captured by a party of the military, and brought prisoners into Palermo. They amounted to twenty persons. At the head of the list was the name of St Elmo. Among those that followed was Francesco Perfetti, and the object of all my solicitude, the unfortunate Julian. My visitor observed, that, after what had fallen from me yesterday on the subject, he could do no less, however unwelcome the intelligence might be, than bring me the earliest information. He observed, that the affair did not admit of the delay of a moment, and that the resolution that had been avowed by the king of the two Sicilies, to reform the police of his dominions, and to introduce the most perfect security every where, rendered the case of these prisoners a matter in the highest degree critical.

I confess it did not strike me in that light. I was perfectly convinced that Julian was not a robber; he had never joined in any of their depredations, / though he might have lived among them. I could not bring myself to believe that any criminal proceeding could touch the life of this interesting youth. – The affair however assumed a very different aspect from any thing I had anticipated. /

CHAPTER XIV

The chief minister of the new king of Naples was the marchese Tanucci.[a] He was a man of great talents, and of a mind in a high degree liberal and enlightened. He was the person who set on foot the unrolling of the manuscripts at Herculaneum on a magnificent scale. The ruins of this city had been first discovered in 1713; but the discovery excited little attention till more than twenty years after. He conducted with great ability the project for relieving the kingdom of Naples from the usurpations of the papal see, and, among other things, abolished the degrading tribute of an ambling nag and a hundred dollars, annually paid by the former / to the latter as a token of subjection. One of the projects he had most at heart was that of establishing a complete security in private life, so that neither the traveller on the road, nor the cottage of the meanest peasant, should be liable to attack from the free-booter. Too long had this licentiousness been the dishonour of the beautiful regions of Italy; and Tanucci resolved to effect its extirpation. For this purpose he held it necessary to afford some examples of an unsparing severity. – These circumstances I did not fully consider till afterwards.

The whole adventure of Julian in this memorable scene of his life was

---

[a] Bernard Tanucci (1698–1783), Neapolitan minister.

extraordinary. He had been for a considerable time sunk in the very depths of sorrow for the untimely fate of his supposed father. He had never entertained the remotest suspicion of how that event had been produced. When he returned from the absolute abstraction in which he had for a period been involved, he was smitten with despair. / He saw nothing about him, but Borromeo, and the menials of Borromeo. He seemed to himself inclosed in a wilderness of rocks, exhibiting an imperfect resemblance of the human figure, but without having among them a human soul. They were like the limnings of the poet:

> Sometimes we see a cloud that's dragonish;
> A vapour, – sometime like a bear or lion,
> A towered citadel, a pendant rock,
> A forked mountain, or blue promontory,
> With trees upon it, that nod unto the world,
> And mock our eyes with air.[a]

Unlike however in this: that the indifferent and uninteresting forms that Julian saw, experienced no change, but seemed to remain, the same yesterday, to-day, and for ever. It was a bitter aggravation of his lot, that he was not in solitude, in some wild scene of desolation, where he might even forget the face of man. Death is that which closes the scene of human things, and feelingly convinces us that what we have seen and doated on, we shall see no more. / Cloudesley and Eudocia being lost for ever, the mind of Julian vehemently reverted to the friend he had left in the Apennines. He was a being in whom Julian could yet find sympathy. He did not desire any thing that should rouse his mind. If he could be introduced into any new society, though endowed with every quality and every grace that could elevate human nature, though it were the society of angels, this introduction would be distressing to him. But with St Elmo, or even with Francesco, he would experience no shock. They would leave him quietly to his moods.

He accordingly sought them; and though they were removed to a considerable distance from the scene they occupied at the time he withdrew himself, yet, by instinct, or by the overruling influence of his destiny, he found them. They were surprised, and even shocked at his appearance among them, after the melancholy event which had separated them, as it / seemed, for ever. Sympathy however, and a deep feeling for the extraordinary situation in which he was placed, sealed the door of their lips. They could not say to him, Behold in us the murderers of your father! The tenderness that was thus excited in the generous bosom of St Elmo modified all his gestures, and every inflection of his richly toned melodious voice.

The attachment for this robber-leader, which had before been lighted up in

---

[a] *Antony and Cleopatra*, IV. xii. 2–7.

the breast of Julian, was thus inexpressibly increased. He wondered at the demeanour of St Elmo towards him; and the friendly yearnings of his heart to his protector rose to a degree which has rarely been paralleled. He felt the sentiment that has been described as existing between Theseus and Pirithous, Achilles and Patroclus, or Damon and Pythias in ancient times.[a] He would have encountered any peril, and even had laid down his life, for his friend. A tie of this sort seemed necessary to his existence. He / required something to look up to, something to cherish with even a filial affection, something to regard with mysterious reverence, and to contemplate as too high to be comprehended, and considered as governed by impulses of the most exalted kind, which he was unable to unravel. It may seem strange that Julian found all this in a man living in the rambling and disorderly kind of life in which St Elmo lived. But St Elmo had originally been a noble and a patriot; and it was only when he was defeated in his patriotic views, and driven into exile, that he had betaken himself to his present courses.

> His form had yet not lost
> All her original brightness, nor appeared
> Less than arch-angel ruined, and the excess
> Of glory obscured.[b]

And, when we add to this general character the indescribable softness and mildness with which he treated Julian, from the consideration of his peculiar situation, as unconsciously / dwelling among the destroyers of his father, we shall be less at a loss to explain the singular devotion with which the English youth was impressed towards his Italian protector.

At length Julian discovered the real pursuits of the band to which he had joined himself. But it was too late. The society into which he was thrown, had strangely discomposed all his systems of reasoning. Independence of thinking is one of the latest improvements of the human mind, and is rarely attained at so early a period of life as that which Julian had reached. In the classes of Florence he had studied the ethics of Aristotle and the visionary refinements of Plato. In his supposed father and mother he had seen models of that irreproachable conduct, which renders the human form in some sort a habitation for the divinity. But, in the connection in which he was now placed, he began to question whether the saws of morality which he had hitherto listened to, were any thing more / than the prejudices of weak minds, and the interested growth of artificial society. Not that he extended the indulgence he accorded to the breach of these laws, any further than to the single person of St Elmo. The rest of the band he saw in their true colours. He found them humorous, passionate, and intemperate, uncontroled in temper, sudden and fierce in displeasure, and ever prone on the slightest occasion to have recourse to the stiletto.

---

[a] See notes to pp. 46, 169, 208.
[b] *Paradise Lost*, I. 591–4.

When Julian made the discovery I have mentioned, St Elmo thought that a fitting time to urge him to return into the established walks of political community. He explained to the youth the circumstances which had had the power to induce him to adopt this mode of existence. Painful necessity had driven him from his country, and even from the boundaries of civilised life. But Julian had the career of honourable ambition before him. He was blessed with eminent talents; he had had every advantage of education; / his habits were honourable; his character was unassailed with blemish or aspersion. The walks of social institution were his to choose as he pleased. He might earn fame in any one of them. He would make to himself friends among the most virtuous members of the community; the laws of society would protect him; the orders of society would emulate each other in crowning and rewarding his labours. St Elmo called upon Julian to contrast this destination with the billet he had himself drawn in the lottery of life. He was compelled to hide his head where he could, to be a fugitive, to wander from place to place; and at last probably his fate would be, to be dragged before the tribunal of offended laws, and to expiate his disdain of the land-marks of the civilised world by an ignominious death.

Julian turned a deaf ear to this expostulation. The wayward boy in his moods found a gratification in entering into a contumacious opposition / to all that was soundest in argument, and most potent in remonstrance. Grief made him indifferent to the prejudices of his kind. He said to St Elmo, I am more unhappily circumstanced, than you were at the moment when the heroic exertions of your patriotism were utterly defeated. You still had approvers and friends. It was with you as has been said of the Roman Cato: 'The Gods, the invisible governors of the world, took part with your enemies, but your own heart and your conscience told you that you were right.'[a] There were still men, and the best of men, who approved of your conduct, who sympathised with your adversity, and cherished you in their heart of hearts. But what am I? I am alone in the world, without a friend, without one person to countenance my honest undertakings, and cheer my endeavours with a smile. Never was solitude like my solitude! – Thus soured with his fortune Julian found a perverse pleasure in attaching / himself to St Elmo the rather because he was an outlaw.

The robber-chief considered it as the most judicious mode of proceeding for the present, to humour the youthful mourner, rather than to engage in diametrical opposition to his visionary conceptions. He satisfied himself that the time would shortly come, when reason would resume its empire in the mind of Julian, and he would be accessible to the authority of sober advice. For the present they entered into a mutual arrangement; Julian was to remain with the

---

[a] cf. Lucan (39–65 AD), *De Bello Civili*, I. 128: *victrix causa deis placuit* ('if the victor had the gods on his side, the vanquished had Cato').

company of St Elmo, but to take no part in such of their active proceedings as were infractions of the system of political communities. In reality, however the mind of the youth had become destitute of its wholesome balance, it was yet in no sort depraved, and therefore he felt a genuine repugnance to engaging in the deeds of a free-booter.

It was not long after the contract had thus / been made between St Elmo and Julian, that the marchese Tanucci avowed his project for suppressing the infractions of the banditti throughout his master's dominions. This afforded a new opportunity to the robber-chief to press upon his young friend the necessity of separating himself from a set of men against whom the government of the country had declared open war. But Julian would not hear of it. What, should he quit his friend in the hour of danger? He would then indeed deserve to be branded to the universal world. – On the other hand St Elmo thought, that, if things came to extremity, it would in no case be possible, that an ingenuous youth, whose hands had never been stained with blood, and who had not been implicated in the slightest act of violence, should be involved in the fate of himself and his followers.

It turned out however very contrary to what he had anticipated. It was not long after this discussion between the young man and his protector, / that a scene occurred of the most disastrous nature. St Elmo and about fifty of his followers were surrounded by a party of the military in one of the mountain-passes. The surprise had been conducted with consummate skill. The robber-chieftain sent out his scouts on every side; but he found that he was entirely hemmed in. He had no choice, but to allow himself to be starved into surrender, or to determine by a desperate effort to cut his way through the enemy, and over their bleeding carcases to make good his retreat to some of the other fastnesses with which the island abounded. If he succeeded in this, he had conceived the plan of withdrawing entirely from Sicily, and offering the services of himself and those he should carry with him, to the bey of Tunis.

The conflict which took place was furious and bloody in the highest degree. The banditti performed prodigies of valour. St Elmo, and even Francesco, shewed themselves more than / men. On this occasion Julian refused to remain idle. He would never engage in those acts which constituted the occupation of the banditti; but could not stand by, and see the life of the man he so profoundly loved exposed to the most desperate hazards. He resolved at least to share in the resistance, and partake the peril. He seized a musket and a sword. He did not manifest this resolution till the last moment. St Elmo was yet anxious that he should remove from the scene of battle; strenuously and energetically he opposed the generous devotion of Julian; but it was too late. The crisis in which he stood hurried him along. The military possessed every advantage of position. They fought from a descent, and were covered by the precipices on either side as with a wall. Thirty of the banditti were killed, and fifteen of the soldiers of the king. Twenty of the free-booters, assailed as they momentarily were by fresh adversaries, some of them wounded, / others completely exhausted and powerless, were made prisoners. Among these were St Elmo, Francesco and Julian.

I no sooner heard of this event, than I set out with all expedition for Messina, and thence to Palermo. Every where as I passed along, I found the business regarded in a very serious light, the general opinion being, that the Sicilian government would make use of this occasion, to exhibit a terrible example, and shew their unalterable resolution that no more of these marauders should be permitted to exist. I arrived at Palermo. I found that the prisoners were confined in separate cells, and that no one was permitted to have access to them.

The condition in which he was now placed could not fail to have a memorable effect on the mind of Julian. Shut up in a solitary dungeon, without exercise or amusement, he had nothing upon which to occupy his thoughts but the image of his own situation. He had hitherto lived, / particularly during the last twelve months, in a dream. He grieved most bitterly, most persistingly, for the death of Cloudesley. He had been instigated by his grief to seek the society of the companions he had left in the Apennines. He did not desire any new connections; he would have shrunk from the encounter of new faces.

All this was well. But the case was different, when he understood from the language and manner of those who had him in custody, the only persons he saw, that he would probably barely be taken out of prison to be led to the scaffold. This was a kind of shock, greatly calculated to awaken a man out of a dream. Julian was young, and had seen little of the diversified scenes of human life. Existence is a thing that is regarded in a very different light by the young and the old. The springs of human nature are of a limited sort, and lie in a narrow compass; and, when we grow old, our / desires are declining, our faculties have lost their sharpness, and we are reasonably contented 'to close our eyes, and shut out daylight.'[a] But to the young it is a very different thing, particularly perhaps at twenty years of age. We are just come into the possession of all our faculties, and begin fully to be aware of our own independence. Every thing is new to us; and the larger half at least of what is new, is also agreeable. Pleasure spreads before us all its allurements. Knowledge unrols its ample page. We have every thing to learn, and every thing to enjoy. Ambition proffers its variegated visions; and we are at a loss on which side to fix our choice. It is easy to dally with death. The young man is like the coquette of the other sex: she had little objection to trifling with a displeasing and superannuated lover, so long as she is satisfied she is not within his clutches.

But all these considerations sunk into nothing when contrasted with the horrible death that / was prepared for him. Julian had hitherto been a stranger

---

[a] Quotation unidentified.

to adversity and pain. The path of his juvenile years had been smoothed to him
by the exemplary cares of Cloudesley and Eudocia. To his own apprehension
he was the favourite of fortune. All that he had read of tragic and disastrous in
the annals of mankind, seemed like a drama, prepared to make him wise by the
sorrows of others, without costing him a particle of the bitter price of experience. All that he had encountered of displeasing, was when he was the inmate
of Borromeo; and this, though felt by him as intolerable, he was aware had
been planned in a spirit of kindness. How terrible therefore was the reverse
that had now fallen upon him! That he, who had never contemplated the
slightest mischief to a human creature, whose life had been all kindness, and
beneficence, and good humour, should suddenly be treated as the vilest of
criminals, shut up in a dungeon, and destined to the scaffold, was a / thought
that overturned all his previous conceptions of human society and life. It filled
him with wildness and horror; it drove him to frenzy; from time to time he was
ready to burst into paroxysm, and dash out his desperate brains against the bars
of his prison. To exchange the most beautiful scene that paradise ever exhibited, for utter desolation and tremendous hurricane, that should tear up
rocks from their foundations, and overwhelm the produce of the earth with
rushing and uncontrolable waves, would feebly express the revolution that took
place in his mind. – He repented that he had ever again sought the society of
these alluring but pernicious friends. /

CHAPTER XV

I entered the city of Palermo under the impression of various sensations. It
stands in a rich and romantic country, and has a commanding view of the
Mediterranean sea. It is regarded as the capital of the island; and Don Carlos
was crowned here in the year 1735. Nine years before, a great part of the town
had been destroyed by an earthquake: many of the streets had been rebuilt: and
many still remained in the mournful and dilapidated state to which that
calamity had reduced them. The castle, which is also the prison, has a commanding and a solemn aspect, and frowns in the midst of the strangely mingled
scene of prosperity and / devastation which the city exhibits. I took a cursory
survey of the whole; but my attention was riveted on the castle, whose walls
inclosed the lately blooming and animated youth whom I had come thus far to
seek.

I was presently informed that, under the direction of the metropolitan
government, the prisoners were divided into two bodies of ten each, which

were destined to perish, the one a little earlier, the other a little later, as a striking example of the wholesome severity his Sicilian majesty purposed to exercise in repressing the disturbers of the public security. Ten of them, with St Elmo at their head, had already taken their trial, and were condemned to death. The space of three days was allowed between the pronouncing of the sentence and the actual execution. The execution of this portion of the prisoners was to take place the morning after my arrival. Julian was not among them.

I resolved to make one in the crowd of the / spectators of this melancholy scene. The prisoners were divided into two classes, accordingly as they were found to belong to the order of plebeians, and of gentry. Of the ten I saw executed, three belonged to the first, and seven to the second. The procession was attended with all imaginable solemnity, and a vast concourse of people. Such a sight had not been beheld in Palermo for a considerable number of years. It was accompanied with the beating of drums, the display of flags, and the presence of a considerable portion of the magistrates. The condemned were preceded by halberts,[a] and passed between two files of soldiers. They were abundantly attended by priests, the most considerable of whom were styled their godfathers, and were responsible for having done every thing in their power for the welfare of the souls of the sufferers. During the period between the sentence and the execution, these priests had never, day or night, been absent from / their penitents. The condemned were inclosed for the whole of this time in a small chapel within the walls of the prison, and carefully supplied with every accommodation and indulgence they could desire.

The three plebeian criminals were conveyed to the place of execution on mules, without saddle or bridle; and precautions had been taken that they should be supported in their position if necessary, that no accident might occur to them in their march. They were clothed in a loose garment of white crape. The other seven proceeded on horses, with saddles, bridles and spurs, as evidences of their superior rank. They were dressed in black.

The whole of these unhappy men were among the finest specimens of the human form. The plebeians indeed were cast in a somewhat coarser mould: but they were athletic, powerful and well proportioned. Their hair was thick; and their gloomy brows seemed to threaten, in / the midst of their present adversity. The gentlemen were of another sort. Their lofty looks appeared to disdain humiliation. Each of them, one perhaps excepted, sat his horse, and grasped his bridle, with an air of dignity. The expression of their features was concentrated, firm, and of a determined character. For the most part they looked little about them, and would not condescend to notice the parade with which they were environed. Now and then however, they cast a contemptuous glance around, and incontinently retired again into themselves. This was not the ordinary

---

[a] i.e. Halberds, a combination of spear and battle-axe, five to seven feet long: here the term refers to the soldiers armed with the weapons.

demeanour of banditti, but of banditti, formed and disciplined by, and who had made themselves up on the model of, St Elmo.

Last of all, came St Elmo himself. It was as Bacchus might have appeared, after being surprised in his sleep, and made captive by the Tyrrhene pirates – not Bacchus, as he is vulgarly / represented, the jolly god, with limbs plump and somewhat unwieldy, with laughing eyes, and intoxicated with wine – but Bacchus, as he might have been carved by the hand of Phidias, who mocked at the Tyrrhene sailors, – the conqueror of Asia. The limbs of St Elmo were framed to excel in the art of dancing. His countenance bore the true impress of nobility. He had long strung up his resolution to encounter the fate which had now overtaken him. He had finally quarreled with his kind, in the issue and miscarriage of the great effort he had made in behalf of his country. Yet he had a principle of elasticity moulded up in his natural constitution, that would not let him sink. He was essentially gay; and gay he could not help being in his unbendings, though with a baffled and disappointed spirit. It was this quality in him, perhaps as much as any, that astonished the observation, and fixed the attachment of Julian. / His soul was above his fate; and fate itself, however rigorous, could not pull him down from the sphere to which he was native.

The three plebeians were hanged upon a gibbet; and one executioner, agreeably to the Spanish mode, mounted himself upon the shoulders of each, the instant he was suspended, that the senses of the sufferer might the sooner be extinguished.

The seven of nobler rank were placed in chairs drawn up in a line, side by side, with a pillar at the back of each, through which the cord attached to the neck of the criminal was passed, and, at a signal, by the turning of a bar, the faculty of breathing and the principle of life were brought to an end. This operation was effected on all simultaneously, and death almost instantly followed.

Nothing could be more awful than the scene I thus witnessed. In no case could the line separating the living man from the dead one, / be more definitely marked. The seven persons who had thus mounted the scaffold, were all in the full vigour and energy of life. The cast of countenance in each, as they stood before me ranged on the platform, one by one as they ascended, grave, yet undaunted, was of that sort which is least liable ever to be forgotten. The man that beheld them thus, could scarcely forbear saying to himself, Lo, this is the machine that illustrates and ennobles the earth in which we dwell! Of what marvellously beneficial purposes, placed under proper direction and influences, is it capable! Of all the various acts of the human community, this is the most audacious – I had nearly said, the most impious – that in cold blood we take the being whom we have subdued, and, making a shew of him to the gaping crowd, in an instant convert this machine, whose price is above rubies, into a moveless clod – extinguish his conceptions and his hopes, all that which made / him 'in form and moving express and admirable, and in apprehension like a God.'[a]

If such was the impression that might have been made upon the ordinary spectator, with what additional force did it come to me, recollecting, as I did, the situation of the reputed son of Cloudesley! I had come from England to Italy to save him. He was the victim of the nefarious ambition of his nearest relative. He ought to have been numbered among the nobles of the first country in the world. He would have had, if his lot had not been intercepted, scores of retainers, of followers, of admirers, of persons who would have made it their pride to patronise, to shield, to protect him. Now he stood alone in the world. He was like the barren fig-tree, which the saviour of mankind is said to have cursed.[b]

What probability was there that any power on earth could save him! The authority that governed Sicily was proceeding with a / ponderous and a heartless march. By the direction of Tanucci his prisoners were divided into two decads, the one to die shortly after the other. I had seen the end of the first. Three days elapsed between their sentence and its execution. Seven more were to pass before the trial of the remaining ten. And the third day after was to witness the falling of the curtain and the close of the drama. /

CHAPTER XVI

The British nation had at this time two representatives in the dominions of the king of Sicily, Mr Chamberlain, the consul at Messina, and Mr Allen, the consul-general residing in the metropolitan city of Naples. Chamberlain was the nearest; but Allen was the superior and more influential. Add to which, the good that was to be done must be done at the court of the monarch. I hastened to Naples.

In going thither I must necessarily pass the straits, the Scylla and Charybdis, of which the ancients had so terrible an idea.[c] I trembled lest, at a moment

---

[a] *Hamlet*, II. ii. 24–7 (adapted).

[b] Luke 13: 6–9.

[c] Scylla and Charybdis, situated at the narrow Strait of Messina between Sicily and the Italian mainland. In Greek mythology Scylla was originally a beautiful nymph whom Circe transformed into a hideous sea monster with twelve feet and six heads, each with three rows of teeth. She dwelt on the rock of Scylla on the Italian side of the Straits, terrorising passing ships by seizing one of their crew with each of her heads as they passed; Charybdis was also a ship-devouring monster, but in the form of a whirlpool situated at and identified with the Sicilian headland, opposite Scylla in the Messina Straits. Horace says an author trying to avoid Scylla drifts into Charybdis, i.e. seeking to avoid one fault, he falls into another.

when time was every thing, any accident should happen to the skiff that / conveyed me. Every one that embarks on the waves of the sea exposes himself, and whatever he is engaged in, to peril. I crossed in safety. I reached Naples. I easily obtained an audience from Mr Allen.

I stated to him the purpose for which I applied. He was aware, I said, of the resolution of the Neapolitan government to exterminate the different troops of banditti within their territories. I had just come from Palermo, from witnessing the execution of the gallant and high-minded St Elmo, and nine of his followers. Ten more were reserved for a similar fate. Their trial was to commence within a week, and the execution to follow immediately. There was no doubt of the issue. One of these ten was an alien, born of an English father and a Greek mother. He was just twenty years of age. He was innocent and irreproachable. A series of accidents had thrown him into the society of this troop; but he had never participated / in any of their acts of violence and plunder.

And what am I to do in the case? said Allen. By your own account he is arraigned on a criminal charge. The power of a foreign minister or consul extends only to the protecting the subjects of his prince from the invasion of their property, or the undue infringement of their personal freedom. If a man is charged with a criminal act in the country he visits, he must take his trial by the laws and in the courts of that country. In entering on the territory he renders himself liable to be arraigned for any thing he does there, that may be conceived a subject for accusation in a court of justice. A foreign consul or minister cannot interfere with that.

But, I rejoined, this unhappy youth, is innocent. If there were any chance that justice would be done, I should feel secure. But it is plain that this is an indiscriminate and bloody / proceeding, where the merits of no man's acts are scrutinised. The government is resolved to have a certain number of victims. Men are brought up by the tale,[a] without consideration of their qualities and deserts. Permit me then to say, that this is a case beyond all others, where you are called on to interfere. It will be a blot to the crown of England, for a British minister to stand by, and see manifest and unquestionable innocence oppressed and done to death in the person of one of the subjects of his master.

The consul-general was impressed with the force of my reasoning. He was still more impressed with the fervour and intensity of my manner. He however answered me thus.

You are wrong, said he. I have no authority in this matter. But what I can, I will cheerfully do for you. I will obtain for you an audience of the marchese Tanucci, the prime minister. If by your representations you can / shake his purposes, it is well. That is all you have for it.

I was greatly chagrined at the issue of my conference with Mr Allen. I had

---

[a] i.e. Influenced by gossip and hearsay.

been anxious to effect my purpose by the clear and irresistible interposition of the name of his Britannic majesty. I augured ill of any grace I could hope to obtain from the hands, already imbrued with blood, of the marchese. It was however incumbent on me to omit no means that offered themselves.

I found the marchese a man in the prime of life, about forty years of age. He had a countenance placid, serene and contemplative. He had an air of much learning and study; for he had been bred in the university of Pisa, in which, immediately after having kept his terms and taken his degree, he was nominated a professor, and from that situation had been removed by Don Carlos to be employed in affairs of state. There was a latent air of superciliousness / in his manner, which however did not prevent him from exhibiting an exterior of much courtesy. His voice was silvery, and his carriage uncommonly affable and gracious.

I pressed the minister with the same considerations that I had already presented to the consul. I urged upon him the singular honour he would acquire by making a distinction among his victims. In the midst of justice, yet remember mercy. When ten men are tried together, it is impossible that the merits of each case should be thorough sifted. The person in whose behalf I presumed to address him, a stranger, a foreigner, a Briton, was much the youngest of the whole company. He had been mixed with them, without in any instance partaking of their practices. I could assure his excellency, by my soul, and in the presence of the all-seeing God, that his innocence was without a slur.

I produced no effect upon the impenetrable / marchese. He heard me with his mild and insinuating demeanour; but not a muscle of his countenance changed, quivered, or gave the slightest token of alteration, as I spoke.

I am grieved, said the minister, that I must refuse so powerful an appeal. But this is a complicated business. It is not merely an affair of banditti, with all the enormities that belong to that horrible trade. It comes nearly, if not altogether, within the guilt of treason. Here is a pitched battle. Forty or fifty lives were lost, fifteen of them soldiers of the king, my master. No, sir, this is a case, where there can be no interruption of the strict line of the law. If the person in whose favour you interest yourself, have any exculpatory circumstances to allege, he must produce them before the judges, and they will receive every consideration – and 'God grant him a good deliverance!'[a]

I did not allow myself to be silenced by these representations. I said, It is to your excellency / that I must look for the redress on which my heart is fixed. This youth never was a bandit or an outlaw. He was in the society of the men you have resolved to exterminate, without ever partaking in their counsels or their acts. The soldiery advanced against the party, and he was present. There was no parley, no offer of indemnity, no attempt to discriminate between the

---

[a] In the ritual observed at criminal trials, a form of proclamation on trial by jury used from 1660 onwards.

innocent and the guilty. The military were drawn up; their muskets were presented; those against whom they were directed were compelled to defend themselves. They were driven together in a narrow compass, and this individual had no power to detach himself from the rest. Is there any law that compels an innocent man to stand still to be shot at, without endeavouring, by resistance, and an effort to annoy the assailants, to preserve himself from destruction?

To all these allegations the marchese replied by asking me, how long the young man had / been in company with these brigands? He proceeded: The case against him seems to be complete by your own shewing. He that is found making one in company with a band of robbers, is in all sound construction a robber. He did not come that hour, or that morning, into their society; he was with them; he acted with them; and with them took arms against public authority. He must abide the consequences of this proceeding.

At the moment he spoke, the dispatch for the public accuser at Palermo lay on the minister's desk; and I had good reason to believe that its instructions were, to make no distinction between the case of one prisoner and another. – An express messenger came in, whose office it was to receive and convey it.

I was worked up to a sort of desperation by all I heard and saw. The celebrated philosopher, Locke, says, in explaining the nature of property, that, when the labour of an individual / becomes indissolubly mixed with that which was otherwise indifferently subject to the use of any, the substance or thing so circumstanced becomes the property of that man.[a] It was exactly thus with me. The riveted attention I had given to the narrative of lord Danvers, and the sacred engagement I had entered into to exert myself to the utmost for the rescue of his nephew, were the first steps in the series. Every mile I had travelled in my journey, every knot I had sailed, bound my undertaking upon me with additional strictness. Every approach I had made, my capture by the banditti, my journey from Messina to Taranto, and from Taranto to Palermo, the melancholy spectacle I had there witnessed, and my present visit to Naples and to the prime minister, rendered it impossible for me to desist. I had bodied out the person of the unfortunate Julian by the incessant efforts of my imagination. I seemed to myself as familiar with his features, as with my own figure in the glass. / I saw him in my dreams; I saw him in the twilight; I saw him wherever the shadow of a mountain or the depth of a glen produced a singular obscurity. I would perhaps sooner have consented to die myself, than that he should die.

I stood rooted to the floor, and could not quit the cabinet of the minister.

---

[a] John Locke (1632–1704), English philosopher, whose *Essay Concerning Human Understanding* (1690) and *Two Treatises of Government* (1690) established him as the founding father of liberal thought. The argument concerning labour and property is to be found in the second *Treatise of Government* ('An Essay Concerning the True Original Extent and End of Civil Government') in Chap. V, 'Of Property'.

Millions of thoughts chased one another with unprecedented rapidity in my mind; I was alive in every fibre of my frame. It was upon my tongue to say, 'The youth for whom I plead, is in reality one of the first persons on the roll of the peerage of Britain.' I should have made no account of my obligation to the individual who had sent me hither. What was that obligation, in comparison of a life to be saved, the life of an innocent person, of an unoffending youth, a stripling, robbed of his property, of his name, one of the first names in the records of his country, turned adrift in / the world in the high way to destruction. And see, what was the end of all this! – Should I be made the tool of the vilest conspiracy, the blackest and most audacious inspiration of fraud, ever heard of? There is no faith to be held with such men. Vows, to which one has become pledged under durance or misconception, are to be slighted and made nothing of, when the first and most cardinal duties of a human creature come in competition with them.

But, though I was worked up into fervour, even ecstasy, for the accomplishment of my purpose, yet I was not altogether mad. I should have been instantly asked, 'How am I to know this? Why am I to believe you? Here is the calendar of the offenders: his name is Julian Cloudesley. Is that the name of one of the first families in Britain?' I should have been driven with contumely and scorn from the presence of the marchese.

I went forth into the street under the influence / of the highest exaltation of mind. I said to myself, No, I have not done. 'I will do such things, – what they are, yet I know not.'[a] A thousand projects, senseless, impossible, passed through my thoughts. I was in a state of the wildest commotion, that ever befel any one who was not chained down, and bound with cords in a receptacle for lunatics. /

CHAPTER XVII

I turned the corner of the street. A carriage, drawn by four horses, approached me. By some impulse for which I cannot account, my attention was arrested by it. I was not calm – I was inexpressibly otherwise – but the reeling and restlessness of my motions were stilled. The carriage did not pass me, but took its direction up another street, at right angles with the one in which I was proceeding. I hastened to follow it. By the impetuosity that urged me, I

---

[a] *King Lear*, II. iv. 283–4.

overtook it, before it turned into the gateway of the hotel usually frequented by travellers from England. I saw the arms on the pannel of the vehicle: they were those of the Danvers' / family. I entered the court-yard of the hotel: the door of the carriage opened. The first person that descended was the gentleman of lord Danvers. The second was lord Danvers himself. They were in deep mourning.

There was considerable difficulty in getting him out of the carriage. His person was in an extraordinary degree emaciated. Whether it were the effect of the journey, or of previous ill health, I could not tell; but he appeared more feeble than many men at fourscore and ten. For the present at least he could not make a step, but as he was supported by two persons. If I had seen him in an accidental rencounter, I probably should not have known him, though it was not twelve months since I left him in England. But the English carriage, the family arms, the person of his gentleman, were all so many circumstances, assuring me that I could not be wrong.

It was sufficiently evident, when I left England, / to every dispassionate observer, that lord Bardsley had received the arrow of death in his vitals. But his father would not see it. The boy lingered on for successive months. With what intense anxiety did lord Danvers watch over him! He resolved the child should not die. This was now every thing, the single passion of his soul. In him the father saw something to love, something to hope for. This youth had met with nothing that should persuade him to quarrel with life. He had the smoothest and the fairest prospects before him. There were no dark shades, no brown horrors, to obscure in him the sunshine of the soul. His sea was without a storm. His bark was prepared to make a prosperous voyage, with Fortune on the prow, and guileless Innocence at the helm. Alas, the worm of disease was at hand to blast all these prospects!

As his distemper advanced, the father watched him with unutterable intensity. He leaned / over his couch; he remarked every smallest variation of his features and his colour, his panting bosom, his hectic cough; he felt the dryness of his hands, the increasing velocity of his pulse; he wiped away the cold damp that rose on his forehead; he spoke to him with a tenderness impossible to imagine, a voice in which passion was rigidly controled, but which had in it all the hints and under-indications of passion. When the physicians visited their patient, lord Danvers watched with palpitating eagerness the expression of their countenances: when they left the chamber, he hastened after them to hear his doom. From pity, and because it appeared to them that the father would never lift his head again when the son's fate was sealed, they softened every report they made, and cased with wool the strong blow that was to fell him to the earth. – Lord Bardsley died.

'When the servants of king David said to / their master, The child is dead! David arose, and washed,'[a] and shewed himself prepared for all that was

---

[a] 2 Sam. 12: 19–20 (adapted).

required of him. So did lord Danvers. He appeared like a man at whose feet a thunderbolt had fallen. He was appalled; but the powers of a human creature were left him. The colour disappeared from his face; life vanished from his eye; his limbs were stiffened with horror. But there was something for him to do; and he did it. He gave directions for the funeral: he even visited the corpse, and saw it, as it lay in the case prepared for it.

He told O'Reily that he should instantly set off for the continent, and ordered every thing to be got ready accordingly. He visited the grave of his son, the morning after the funeral.

Never was so perfect a revolution worked in mortal man, as on this occasion took place in lord Danvers. He had perpetrated an atrocious crime. He saw it in all its enormity. A more elaborate falshood never had been / palmed on the world. The ghosts of his brother and his brother's wife nightly haunted his couch. He bore up against this. He did not flinch by the breadth of a hair. He said to himself, as he had said to me, 'I have achieved the unhallowed deed; and I will clutch the reward.'[a] He looked to his son, the beautiful, the intellectual, the ingenuous. He said, Bardsley, for thee I have done all this! I am blasted by heaven's lightning, prostrate, never to rise. But I will place thee on a pinnacle; the world shall wonder at thee; thy glory shall be unrivalled. None of the shafts of dishonour, with which I am pierced in every articulation, shall reach up to thee.

Lord Danvers, to his own vivacious imagination, was prostrate on the earth. But the body itself of his son lay there in genuine reality. 'The worm was spread under him, and the worms covered him.'[b] This brought a new train of reflections to the mind of his father. – / What then am I? I have done the blackest deed: and in recompence my soul and all my thoughts are turned to the colour of hell. I am verily a man, to be crowned with honour, to be clothed in purple, to be covered with jewels, to sit in the seat of a senator, to be numbered with the houshold of a king! But I am this no longer than I please!

It was this train of thoughts that carried him abroad. He resolved to humble himself. It was in abasement only that he could find consolation. Not that he could look shame in the face. But he resolved, like Lear in the play, to 'put off his lendings,'[c] He would make the atonement that was yet in his power. He had been greatly terrified with the disappearance of Julian after Cloudesley's death, with the length of time that had elapsed, that he had become a vagabond, without means, the means which had always been intended for him, and which till then he had enjoyed. What was there of / tragic and disastrous that might not have befallen him!

Lord Danvers made me a sign to follow him to his apartment in the hotel.

---

[a] Quotation unidentified.
[b] Isa. 14: 11 (adapted).
[c] *King Lear*, III. iv. 108 (adapted).

We were left alone. He said, God be praised, I have found you! I judged from your latest letters that you must be either here or in Sicily. But where, where is my brother's son? Has your search been crowned with success? Has he been discovered? /

CHAPTER XVIII

I was inexpressibly rejoiced at the arrival of my employer. It was at the very moment that the fate of Julian seemed irretrievable. Never did the descent of a God in a tragic fable, come at a time when its advent was so indispensible. I related to his lordship all the particulars. I told him that his nephew had seven days to live.

The stranger newly arrived in Italy, listened with breathless attention to my narrative. He thanked me a thousand times for my diligence, my unwearied constancy. He followed with an earnest spirit all the changes I related. When it was certain that his nephew / had been once more a companion for banditti, he gasped for breath. The edict issued for the destruction of these pernicious bodies of men terrified him. He followed me to Enna, to Palermo, to Messina, to Taranto, and to Palermo again. I described to him the execution of St Elmo, and the unhappy issue of my audience of the marchese Tanucci, from which I had just come when I caught sight of his carriage in the street. He threw himself back in his chair; he struck his forehead with vehemence; he cast his eyes to heaven with a look of inexpressible horror. – How narrowly, said he, have I escaped being the murderer of this orphan boy! Gracious heaven, what would then have become of me!

He started from his chair, and drew himself up to his greatest height. – Let us away to the marchese Tanucci!

We went first to the consul-general, Mr Allen. He and lord Danvers were known to / each other. They had met occasionally in parties in London. Besides, his lordship had papers and documents about him, abundantly sufficient to shew who he was.

Mr Allen instantly dispatched his servant with a billet to the marchese, requesting an audience on business of the greatest importance. The consul and lord Danvers went together; and I was admitted to accompany them.

Mr Allen introduced the distinguished stranger. Lord Danvers, without preface or circumlocution, told his story, made a full and unreserved confession of his shame. He stated to the marchese in the presence of the consul the rank to which he had succeeded, the extent of his estates. He had come to Italy for the express purpose of resigning these, so long unjustly withheld, to the so called Julian Cloudesley, a prisoner under sentence of death in the castle of Palermo. The marchese and the consul were equally astonished at the disclosure. The minister / looked alternately at lord Danvers, at the consul, and at me. At the conclusion – The young man, said he, shall assuredly be set at liberty without delay. I will go instantly to the king, and return with the necessary papers.

This was of course a business to be transacted without *éclat*. Lord Danvers was desirous to hide himself from all the world.

Julian was set at liberty in a few days. Mr Allen sent his confidential secretary to conduct him to Naples; I accompanied the secretary. It was agreed that, previously to his arrival in that city, nothing should be unfolded to him. The secretary merely carried with him the proper warrant, directed to the governor of the castle, requiring him to discharge his prisoner from confinement, and send him to Naples. An officer of the royal army with a guard went with us, commissioned to see that what was directed was properly performed. As soon as we arrived at Naples, orders were given that the / young man should be delivered into the care of Mr Allen.

The consul told him the story of his birth, of his outcast state, of the usurpation of his uncle. He observed, that Julian was fully aware what justice had been done him in his infancy and his education, by his adoptive father. After the death of Cloudesley, and the young man's absconding from the protection under which he was left, his uncle had become in a high degree anxious for his fate, and had sent this gentleman (pointing to me) from England to Italy, to deliver him from the perils in which he might be involved. Not contented with this, the uncle had also taken this route himself, and had resolved to resign his title and all he possessed to the true heir.

The whole story appeared an universe of wonders to the poor Julian. Had it come under other circumstances, or from a less authority, he would have received the whole with incredulity, as an attempt to delude him into an imaginary / affluence. But the gravity of the speaker, the official situation he held, and his own sudden and unexplained deliverance from prison at Palermo, where he had received notice that he was in a few days to be tried for his life, commanded his attention, and proved that there was substance in the tale. He listened first with astonishment, then with a fixed and scrutinising look, as one engaged in weighing the probability and the evidences, and lastly with manly gravity, like a person accustomed to consider the scenes and vicissitudes of this sublunary state, and who could not be surprised into an unbecoming demeanour. He at no time appeared less than as the noblest of God's creatures, without levity, without intoxication, without idle elation of the senses or the heart.

When Mr Allen had concluded, I presented myself to him. I said, I should be glad to be allowed to relate to him at full my part in the affair. But we must no longer take up the time / of the consul; and with his permission I would conduct him to apartments that had been already prepared for him.

I there related minutely to Julian the state of mind in which I had left lord Danvers (so I will continue to call him), when twelve months before I had set out from Milwood Park for Italy, and the various adventures I had met with since. I had resolved that no difficulties should have power to make me desist from my search. I described to him the qualities of the young lord Bardsley, the infirmity under which he laboured, and his death. I told him how all the wishes and sentiments of the father had been centred in the life of the son; and, that being terminated, that lord Danvers had determined to resign his ill-gotten possessions, and quit the scene of the world for ever.

My narrative prepossessed the young man in my favour. He conceived the same predilection for me, that lord Danvers had done before. He / requested me to become his friend. He said, he had to enter the world like 'man new-made,'[a] with scarcely any connection that could be of service to him in the scene for which he seemed to be destined. It was his desire, that the same person whom his uncle had chosen to be his preserver and saviour, should accompany him and be his Mentor in his life to come. His whole behaviour and language won my admiration; and I felt at once that I could not have a destination more gratifying, than to spend my life in daily attendance on the son of Arthur and Irene.

It is fitting that I should mention that Francesco Perfetti and the other eight free-booters suffered the sentence of the law without interruption at Palermo.

In a short time I received a summons from lord Danvers, which I hastened to obey. I found him weaker than when I had first beheld him at Naples, exhausted with his interviews / with Mr Allen and Tanucci, and still more with the workings of a defeated, a prosprate, and a contrite spirit. I had not seen him subsequently to these interviews, having been engaged in the journey to Palermo, and in bringing Julian from that city to Naples. To confess the truth, I did not greatly desire to see lord Danvers. It is possible to have a deep sympathy with a criminal: but for that purpose it is necessary either to have known him long previously, and to have watched the better man in him, or, by actual observation or narrative, to have become familiar with his sufferings and struggles. I had not known lord Danvers long. He had worthy and honourable qualities: witness his unreserved conquest of the envy towards his elder brother which had beset him in early life, and the perpetual compunction and anguish of soul which had been the followers of his crime. A coarse and a brutal nature would have known little of this. But I was engaged / under other auspices. The noble youth, who was enriched with such extraordinary endowments, who had suffered the injustice and obscurity of so many years, and who had just been

---

[a] *Measure for Measure*, II. ii. 79.

discharged from so tremendous a condition, was master of all my affections. The comparison between him and his uncle was too much to the disadvantage of the latter.

Lord Danvers questioned me eagerly as to all that had passed with his nephew, and insisted to be informed of the minutest particulars.

It is well, said he. My task is finished. My enormities, I hope, are repaired. All I have further to ask is, that I may never see my successor. Think not that I entertain ill will towards him. On the contrary I recollect him with warm affection. I have followed him in imagination through all the perils of infancy and the hazards of youth. If it had not been / so, think you that the never-dying worm would so fearfully have gnawed at my heart, blanched my cheeks, and reduced this human figure of mine to an assemblage of skin only and bones? I offer him my sincerest congratulations. But I cannot see him. The moment he came into my presence I should expire in unimaginable agonies. Crime is of an insinuating nature; it steals upon us unperceived; the steps of its march are as the breadth of a hair. But, if my brother's son stood in my presence, my fate would be like that which the poets feign of the mother of Bacchus, who desired to see her lover, the king of Gods and men, in his proper form, and, the instant he appeared, was consumed to ashes by his effulgence.[a]

While lord Danvers was thus unbosoming himself, Mr Allen was announced. Yes, said the noble penitent, I will receive him. Divorced as I am irrevocably from human society, this sacrifice / is necessary. – Lord Danvers repeated to the consul a part of what he had been saying to me. He went on.

My minutes in this world are numbered. I have but one essential business left to perform; but that shall be discharged to the minutest letter. I have made my will. It is all in my own hand-writing. But I have studied whatever was necessary to give it validity; and it is sufficient. My servants have attested it, without knowing what it contained. In it I have inserted all that can be required for the restoration of my nephew, and have indicated the sources of such evidence as may satisfy the most incredulous. I believe this is in itself full and complete. But still I will leave nothing undone. Mr Murray, the celebrated pleader*, the most refined and accomplished individual of his times that adorns his profession, is at this / moment in Naples. Let him be consulted. Whatever he draws up, I will sign. Whatever he directs, I will do.

Lord Danvers outlived these communications by a few weeks. He was extenuated to a degree that can scarcely be credited. The death of his son, his journey to Italy, the acute apprehension of some dreadful event to befal his

* Afterwards Lord Mansfield.[b]

. [a] The mother of Bacchus was Semele, lover of Zeus.

[b] William Murray, first Earl of Mansfield (1705–93), lawyer and distinguished politician noted for his eloquent speeches both in court and in parliament. He supported the Catholic Relief Bill of 1778 and was rewarded by having his house sacked and burned by the mob during the Gordon Riots of 1780.

nephew, and the eternal shame and horror of his guilt, were enough to have killed the strongest man that ever lived. He died by degrees: it was scarcely possible to say when he expired. Though the whole election of my soul was elsewhere, I regarded it as my indispensible duty to attend him till the instant of his dissolution. When he was laid in the grave, and the oblivion he desired covered the spot where his body was laid, no stone told even his name to the passer by. But I visited the place, the last thing I did before I left Naples; and I regarded this grassy hillock as to me the most impressive legend of / the fatal end of imposture, usurpation and fraud, that ever was recorded.

There is little further that remains, to complete this narrative. Our first business when we arrived in England, that of Julian and myself, was to establish the legitimacy of the youthful heir. The marchese Tanucci easily admitted the truth of the proposition upon the simple protestation of the then holder of the title, and actual possessor of the estates. But it required another sort of evidence in the English courts. There was no opposing party; and that circum-stance greatly facilitated our proceedings. But the house of lords is the highest judicatory in England; and its steps on a subject of this nature are ordinarily conducted by the most skilful lawyers. Lord Danvers had by his indications rendered the greatest service to our cause. He had furnished us with a clue by which we were enabled to bring over from abroad witnesses, who established the pregnancy of Irene, and / that she was delivered of a living child. Some of these witnesses further proved that Eudocia had not become a mother during her residence in Austria. The age of the claimant to the inheritance, exactly tallied with the date of the death of Irene. Mr Murray, to whom Julian had been introduced in Naples, conducted the cause; and the rightful succession of the new earl Danvers was established to the conviction of all.

The education of Julian's early years was of the greatest service to his maturer life. He had been bred in obscurity; but he had experienced every advantage that instruction in almost all branches of improvement could bestow. An obscure station, when it does not bring along with it the withholding the seeds of knowledge, and the absence of those main benefits for ripening human faculties, emulation and applause, is the station most favourable to the growth of meditation, a deep-rooted enthusiasm, sobriety and virtue. The very errors into which / Julian had been seduced, were of eminent service to him; they intimately convinced him of the extent and the insinuating nature of human frailty, and impressed upon him the great apostolic lesson, 'Let him that thinketh he standeth, take heed lest he fall.'[a] The melancholy fate of Cloudesley and St Elmo were never absent from his recollection. The more he analysed the character of Cloudesley, the more he admired it. He willingly dismissed from his thoughts the one great blemish of his life, the momentary concurrence with

---

[a] 1 Cor. 10: 12.

Richard Herbert, falsely called earl Danvers, in his act of atrocious and cold-blooded fraud. Cloudesley had been to Julian a more than father; and the never-ceasing penitence of his error that lived within him, rendered him more exemplary and unalterable, than 'a just man who needed no repentance,'[a] could ever have been. Side by side in the cabinet of his memory with the image of Cloudesley stood that of St Elmo. Of all the persons Julian had / ever known, St Elmo was the most accomplished, was the man of the most generous and exalted sentiments. The first essay and enterprise of his early life, gloriously conceived, and profoundly meditated, but defeated by such unfavourable events as human sagacity cannot turn aside, had beggared him of his fortune, rendered him 'a man forbid,'[b] and thrust him out of the pale of civilised community. When Julian thought of his high qualities, he was lost in admiration. When he recollected the memorably base and ignominious termination of his life – no, he could never recollect it, and possess his soul in patience. In certain bitter moods, which on such occasions came over him, he was ready finally to abjure all human society, and fly to the desolate places of the earth.

> It led his wild desires to woods and caves,
> And taught that all but savages were slaves.[c]

How ridiculous, so he believed, are the refinements / of human policy, when such a man, endowed with every quality to render the most extensive and lasting benefit to his kind, instead of being studied, and carefully led back to his true position, and cherished, and honoured, is cut short in the midst of his career, and exhibited to the world as a being unworthy to exist!

CONCLUSION

One scene I have yet to describe. I have omitted it in the place to which it belonged; but in some respects it will come in better here.

In the course of our journey from Naples to England we made a short halt at Florence, that Julian might indulge himself in taking leave of several friends with whom he had been on terms of more or less intimacy during his residence of eight years in that city. In the scale of friendship there are many degrees, and, though there / were not a few persons in Florence, who remembered him with kindness, and the recollection of whom was soothing to his feelings, it may easily be imagined that there was not one that rivalled St Elmo in his affections,

[a] cf. Luke 15: 7 (adapted).
[b] *Macbeth*, I. iii. 21.
[c] cf. John Dryden, *Absalom and Achitophel* (1681), ll. 55–6: 'They led their wild desires to woods and caves, / And thought that all but savages were slaves.'

or with whom he could have felt easy in proposing to them, Receive me as an inmate of your establishment, and provide me with whatever I may want, during the absence of Cloudesley, my father, in this western expedition. Add to which, what he believed himself to stand in need of, was a host that should conceal him from the search of Borromeo, or refuse him to his requisition.

All the acquaintances that Julian visited at Florence, were delighted to see him again. Such had been the gentleness of his dispositions, and the cordiality of his manners, that every one he had ever known loved him, and emulously pursued him with their good wishes. When they heard of his unexpected good-fortune, and that he was now hastening to London, to claim / an earldom of the kingdom of Great Britain, with ample possessions that fell to him under the crown of that country, and that no doubt was entertained of the success of his suit, they seemed transported with the intelligence, almost in a manner as if the success had been their own. The Italian character in general is full of animation, and the natives enter into the interests and welfare of the stranger before them with a fervour that forbids all doubt of its sincerity, and that is truly surprising. And the extraordinary qualities of Julian called forth this peculiarity in all its brilliancy and beauty.

By the desire of Julian I had written a letter to Borromeo from Naples, to inform him of what had recently passed, of the imminent danger in which the young man had stood of being executed as a criminal, of his deliverance, of the arrival of the lately called lord Danvers at Naples, of his confession of the rights of Julian by birth, and the frauds that had been practised / against him, of the unquestionable claim of the youth as a peer of Great Britain and Ireland, and the death of the usurping uncle. Julian having taken leave of all his other friends, resolved to visit the grange-house of Borromeo, to make the *amende*[a] to his rugged, but well-meaning host, and to confess the impropriety of the conduct he had adopted. He sent a servant before him to announce the visit he purposed to pay about the hour of noon.

But Borromeo would not yield to this arrangement. As has before been related of him, he had a warm heart under a rugged and repulsive outside. He came to meet us, and we encountered him at about the half-way from Florence. Julian and the Italian farmer alighted, and drew aside into an alcove, that accidentally presented itself on the spot where they met. I was eager to witness their conference.

It was a striking spectacle to view the workings / of Borromeo's mind, as they expressed themselves in his countenance, or, perhaps more strictly speaking, in the action of his body and limbs. He drew Julian towards him with all the energy of affection; he then motioned him to retreat, that he might more carefully peruse the nobility of his air, and the beauty of his physiognomy. He

---

[a] To make amends.

laughed, like one transported with the victory that had been gained, and the high fortune that had succeeded to and dispersed the adversity under which the gallant youth had suffered. To his laughter succeeded a gush of tears; but they were tears of joy, the melting of the heart. He embraced him with the utmost fervour. Julian saw that Borromeo was bursting with emotion, and, in a style of the truest delicacy, gave way for his feelings to ease themselves in words.

My darling child, said Borromeo, this is a memorable day to me; the first day of my life, / of a new and better life. The scales are fallen from my eyes; God has 'taken from me the heart of stone, and given me a heart of flesh.'[a]

The world is not what I took it to be. It contains something more than the relative position of the bondsman and his lord. It contains warm hearts and entire affection. It is a beautiful world; but an entire eclipse hid it from my sight. What a dreary scene has it hitherto been to me! I have acted alternately the part of the master and the slave. Both are equally hard, unfeeling and unhappy.

The true key of the universe is love. That levels all inequalities, 'makes low the mountain, and exalts the valley,'[b] and brings human beings of every age and every station into a state of brotherhood. 'The lion and the lamb lie down together; the leopard dwells with the kid; and a little child shall lead them.'[c]

What unprejudiced man can look abroad in the world, and not see this? The splendid sun, / the cerulean sky, the majestic trees, the green earth, the thousand colours that enamel the mead, the silver stream, in beauty composed and serene, living in the endless flow of its waters, all talk of what softens the heart, and inspires affection and kindness to our dispositions and feelings. Has not God made man the crown of his works, and stamped all his limbs with majesty and grace? And shall we treat with harshness and indignity what God has chosen for his living temple?

No: the man that is austere to his brother-mortal is the true, the practical atheist. I have been this; I have spread blight all around me; I have frowned upon all; I have killed Cloudesley; I have almost killed thee, the dearest object of his affections.

Yes, the true system for governing the world, for fashioning the tender spirits of youth, for smoothing the pillow of age, is love. Nothing else could have made a Cloudesley; nothing / else could have made a Julian. I and lord Danvers have been the delinquents; he for base and selfish ends; I from an erroneous judgment.

The one thing that most exalts and illustrates man is disinterested affection. We are never so truly what we are capable of being, as when we are ready to sacrifice ourselves for others, and immolate our self-love on the altar of

---

[a] Ezek. 36: 26 (adapted).
[b] Isa. 40: 4 (adapted).
[c] Isa. 11: 6 (adapted).

beneficence. There is no joy like the joy of a generous sentiment, to go about doing good, to make it our meat and our drink to promote the happiness of others, and diffuse confidence and love to every one within the reach of our influence.

Thus, to the astonishment of us all, spoke the sour and stern misanthrope, the rigid Borromeo, converted from all he had been by the spectacle before his eyes, by the ascendancy of virtue, the success of gentleness, and the sight of the youth who bore his honours so meekly, / on whose brow majesty sat enshrined, whose eyes swam in affection, whose limbs were fashioned by generosity and liberty, and all whose motions were inspired by the clearness of his understanding and the soundness of his heart. /

For Product Safety Concerns and Information please contact our EU
representative GPSR@taylorandfrancis.com
Taylor & Francis Verlag GmbH, Kaufingerstraße 24, 80331 München, Germany

www.ingramcontent.com/pod-product-compliance
Lightning Source LLC
Chambersburg PA
CBHW070527310726
48976CB00002BA/554